THE COAL KING'S SLAVES

A Coal Miner's Story

A Historical Novel
by
William G. Williams

BURD STREET PRESS
SHIPPENSBURG, PENNSYLVANIA

This book is a work of historical fiction. Names, characters, places, and some incidents are products of the author's imagination but are based on actual events.

This Burd Street Press publication
was printed by
Beidel Printing House, Inc.
63 West Burd Street
Shippensburg, PA 17257-0708 USA

The acid-free paper used in this book meets the guidelines for permanence and durability of the Committee on Production Guidelines for Book Longevity of the Council on Library Resources.

For a complete list of available publications
please write
Burd Street Press
Division of White Mane Publishing Company, Inc.
P.O. Box 708
Shippensburg, PA 17257-0708 USA

Library of Congress Cataloging-in-Publication Data

Williams, William G.
    The coal king's slaves : a coal miner's story : a historical novel / by William G. Williams.
        p. cm.
    ISBN 1-57249-319-4 (alk. paper)
    1. Coal miners--Fiction. 2. Coal mines and mining--Fiction. 3. Fathers and sons--Fiction. 4. Pennsylvania--Fiction. 5. Brothers--Fiction. I. Title.

PS3573.I456217 C63 2002
813'.54--dc21

                                                                2002074736

Dedicated to Glyn Williams and Glyn Treharne;
To my father, grandfathers and uncles;
To friends;
And to all others who have labored underground.

Forty years I worked with pick and drill,
Down in the mines against my will,
The Coal King's slave, but now it's passed;
Thanks be to God I am free at last.

(Tombstone of an anthracite miner in a Hazleton, Pennsylvania, cemetery.)

Foreword

In America, and throughout the British Isles, as well as many other places in the world, men and often boys, and sometimes women and girls, have labored beneath the earth to mine coal. Their work too often became a sacrifice for the bare necessities of life—food, shelter, clothing—for themselves and their families. They faced horrific dangers every day from the poisonous gases which secretly stole the breath from their bodies to explosions and roof falls which crushed out their lives, from the lack of air caused by high water or blocked passages to the killer dust which surrounded them constantly. But they also faced the ever-present greed of mankind, particularly by some mine owners and managers who treated them worse than the mules used to haul coal from the pits.

This is the story of one man and his family, created to represent the hundreds of thousands like them who worked for a better life but often found that path blocked by greed, by intolerance, by ethnic hatred and by indifference. Though this family, the company they worked for, and those in their immediate surroundings are fictional their story is set in the context of historical events and historical characters.

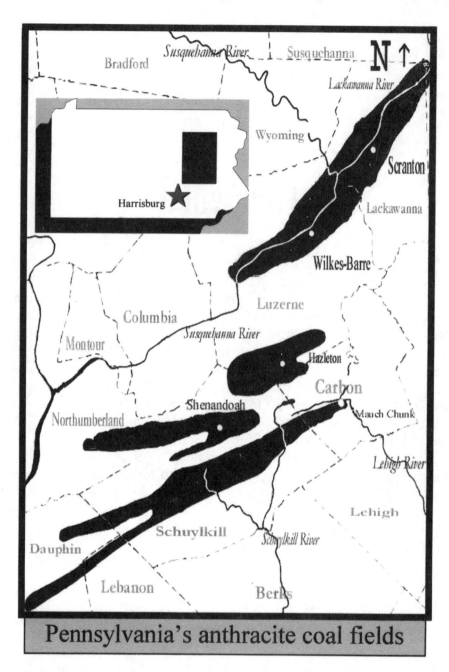

Pennsylvania's anthracite coal fields

Inset map shows the anthracite region (black box) of eastern Pennsylvania which begins just northeast of the state capital at Harrisburg. In the larger map, the four main coal fields in that region are shown in black. The city of Scranton is at upper right. Cities and towns appear in boldface type and counties in lightface.

Map courtesy of Jonathan G. Williams

Chapter One

Boulder-size lumps of coal thumped as they dumped into the car. The huge shovel scraped as small pieces were scooped up. Those sounds were the only proof needed that young Jamie Kerrigan was doing his job. The seasoned miner knew he didn't have to see the boy, just hear the noises to know he was doing what the miner paid him to do. In fact, the only way he could see Jamie was to turn his eyes toward the noises so the flame, which seemed to leap from his cap, shone a few feet in that direction.

"Nearing lunch time then, Mr. Jones?"

"It seems you ask me that every hour, Jamie."

"No sir, no sir, just when my belly starts yelling."

"Aye, and mine too."

Jones reached into the inside pocket of his vest for a small bundle. He held it at eye level to catch the light and carefully unwrapped the bit of wool which protected his pocket watch from dust and damage.

"Just noon now, boy. We've only been at it five hours. Another thirty minutes and we'll stop for a bite. Then this day will be almost half over."

"Yes, Mr. Jones."

The thudding and scraping continued.

"Cheese and bread again today, is it, Jamie?"

"Yes sir, and cold tea to wash it down. Mama says we have nothing else just now. Waiting for my next pay, she is, to buy a bit of beef."

"I know it's difficult for your mama, Jamie. What's it been now, since your father died in the explosion, six months?"

"Yes, Mr. Jones, six months in another fortnight. But it seems like just last week."

More thuds and scrapes as Jamie worked to load the mine car with good hard anthracite, but silence beyond that for minutes.

"Well, Mrs. Jones put enough beef in my pail for the two of us to enjoy a feast."

"I can't be taking your food, Mr. Jones. Mama says we owe you a great deal for taking me on as your laborer when Dada di...when Dada passed away. Without this job we'd be on the starving list, I fear."

"You earn your money, Jamie. For a fifteen-year-old lad, you do a man's work. When your brothers get to your age I'm sure they'll find something better than being breaker boys."

"Aye, they look forward to that day, but few miners are willing to take on a young boy as a laborer, particularly an Irish Catholic boy."

The miner's pick sang out as Jones, lying on his side, began to under-cut the coal face just above him. But between swings he answered.

"No need" — clink — "to bring" — clink — "that up" — clink — "with me." He paused to listen for telltale signs that the coal was cracking. "I pay no heed to a man's religion nor to his nationality. I need only someone to load that car." He began swinging the pick again, satisfied that nothing in the seam before him had begun to crack.

"But, from what I've heard, you pay me as fair a wage as any laborer in this pit. And Mama and I appreciate that, Mr. Jones."

The talking ended and the two worked on in their respective dark-ened worlds, lit only by the flame flickering above each one's head, unable to see beyond the few feet of their own illumination, using touch as much as sight to move the coal.

Jones had no time for the rowdy Irish, like those more than a decade ago accused of violence in the coal fields to the south in Schuylkill and Carbon Counties. But neither did he cotton to his own kind, some Welsh Congregationalists who hated Irish Catholics solely because they were Irish Catholics. And not just his denomination but some other Protestants as well who held the Irish down by denying them better jobs in or out of the mines. He hoped that someday young Jamie would be able to move up from laborer to contract miner, like him and so many others from Wales, Scotland and England. But he knew the boy's chances were slim. It was so unfair. Although he missed his homeland, Jones knew that he and Gwyneth had made the right move by immigrating to America and to northeastern Pennsylvania where the world's largest stock of hard coal provided so much employment. Jamie's grandparents, the boy had told him, starved to death during the potato famine and his parents, then both in their teens, almost met the same fate in a long, cruel voyage from Ireland to this new world.

He thought of his own son, Dylan, the youngest of three, just two years older than Jamie and working as a laborer with another contract miner in a room not two hundred feet away. Ah, Dylan, full of life, a joy to be with, a smiler, a joker, an energetic lad, a son to be proud of. But Glyn Jones knew that his son would progress faster and higher in the mining industry — or in any job — than Mrs. Kerrigan's Jamie. And there was not a damn thing he could do about it other, of course, than what he was doing, providing the lad with a job and paying him the going rate for a grown man who labored.

Jones picked away at the coal, undercutting two or three inches with each heavy stroke. Loose coal and rock pushed into his side and the top of his arm, causing him to wince when he swung and the loose stuff moved, digging through his shirt and scratching into his skin. The floor was wet too. Always water. Every mine he had ever worked, in Wales and now around Hyde Park and Scranton, was wet—a half inch at least always on the ground. But without the constant working of pumps he knew he'd be up to his waist, maybe higher, in the seeping damp.

And sweat permeated the rest of his clothing. His heavy work pants were filthy and wet. His boots, worn but still wearable, were drenched with part sweat, part mine water. Sweat was a normal byproduct of hard work but this mine, the fire boss always said, was a constant fifty-five degrees, no matter the outside temperature. Summer or winter, rain or heat, dry or damp—fifty-five. Jones never seemed to sweat outside his home chopping wood in fifty-five degrees. Why here? The worst feeling, he thought, was to come out of work, soaking wet, into a freezing winter wind and face the mile walk home. More than once, he smiled as he thought back, he walked into the lattice-framed back porch of the house, stepped out of his work pants and literally stood them up in the corner. And there they would stay until Gwyneth picked them up gingerly, carried them into the warm kitchen and lowered them into a bucket of hot, sudsy water. "Now, watch them slowly drown," she would chuckle.

His daydreaming quickly ended as the telltale creaking began.

"Caution now, lad, she's coming down."

"Aye, Mr. Jones, ready here, sir."

Jamie winced as he heard the coal cracking, not yet used to the thought that coal holding up the roof, at least part of it, was about to fall at their feet. He always wondered why it didn't bring the rock overhead down too.

"Part of a miner's knowledge, Mr. Jones?"

"What is, Jamie?"

"Knowing how far to cut and how much will fall from the seam without us being buried."

"Yes, part of the knowledge. You'll learn to hear the mine's sounds and its warnings."

"Like the rats running, Mr. Jones?"

"Aye, lad, when the rats run, we run too. They hear better than we do. They know when the roof is coming down. They may steal our food but they're our warning bell too. Stand fast now."

The coal cracked again, then fell away from the roof. Black chunks ranging from eight to twelve inches in diameter, a few larger, fell from the three-foot seam above where Jones's pick had undercut the coal. The man and the boy stepped back the length of a shovel to avoid having their shins torn by the ragged edges of the coal and they turned their heads to keep the whirling dust out of their eyes and nose and mouth. All was pitch-black for a minute. Jamie struggled to see, to make sure that only the coal and not the rock above it had fallen. But even the flame on his hat could not penetrate the thick dust.

"A good fall," he heard Mr. Jones say. "Load up, Jamie, and then it's time to eat."

Jamie's black and calloused hands reached down for a chunk, pulled it up to his waist, then to his chest, and dumped it into the mine car. In the few short months he had been Jones's laborer, the muscles in his arms and legs had developed noticeably from lifting ten or twelve tons of coal each shift, two tons for each car. He had learned to avoid rock, for which the company would not pay Jones or any other miner, and he shoveled only the larger scraps, not the dust or dirt which settled on the floor.

"Coal, good anthracite, that's what we get paid for, not rock and dirt, or bony as we call them, lad," Mr. Jones had told him all through the first week they worked together. "The weighmaster will dock us for bony."

"Aye, Mr. Jones, coal only, and big pieces at that."

The cut anthracite on the floor was enough to finish off the car, the third for the day, and Jamie began pushing it out on the temporary track through the room to the gangway. He knew that a boy about his age, whom everyone called Sliver because he was so thin, was coming. Jamie could hear the jangling cars moving along the gangway track and Sliver's whip cracking. He could see the faint glow of a candle attached to a cup atop the mule's head but he could not see the animal, nor the boy, nor the cars, just the glimmer of light far up the tunnel. He knew it was Sliver because he could hear the profanity: "Move yer feet, damn mule. Dumb-ass animule, move, ah ain't makin' a penny when ya drag yer carcass. Move, mule, or ah'll drop ya down a shaft ta hell." Jamie had come to learn it was all talk, from Sliver and the other drivers too. They really loved their mules, fed them well, kept their underground stalls clean, made sure they had water, but mules had a stubborn streak and when they didn't want to move they didn't. Some miners felt it was fear of the dark, not the heavy loads they pulled, that made the mules obstinate. Some drivers found they had to walk ahead of their mule to make him move, until the mule learned that he couldn't veer off the path in the narrow tunnels.

"Got one for you, Sliver," Jamie yelled as the train neared the entrance to his room.

"Aye, more work for me, Irish. Ah should make ya push it out yerself."

Nineteenth-century miner bores a hole for blasting while his laborer, apparently a teenager, loads chunks of coal.

MG369, Pennsylvania Historical and Museum Commission,
Bureau of Historic Sites and Museums, Anthracite Museum Complex

Jamie always wondered about Sliver's nationality. He spoke somewhat like an Englishman, but with strange expressions and a mixture of slang and pronunciation that sounded a bit American Southern, a bit Slavic and perhaps Scottish. Jamie didn't ask.

Sliver unhooked an empty from his train and moved the mule ahead ten feet while Jamie pushed the loaded car around the bend onto the main track. Then he moved the empty into the small tunnel leading into the working room while Sliver rehooked the train, flashed his whip in the air and screamed, "Move, Pete, ya dumb-ass mule, still got pretner a mile to pit bottom. Move, ya big-eared son-of-a-bitch."

Jamie smiled as he shoved the empty up the short run to the coal face where Mr. Jones was waiting. He wondered if Sliver cursed the mule as he was pushing loaded cars onto the cage that would haul them to the surface. Probably never stops, he thought.

"Time for your food, lad," Jones announced as he saw the boy's light hovering slightly above the rear of the car.

"Aye, thank you, Mr. Jones."

"Didn't lose any of that load now, did you?"

"No, Mr. Jones, not a piece."

The miner had explained to him on his first day as laborer that the company weighman topside credited the miner with the weight of the load, minus any bony in the car. And if any coal fell off in the tunnel or gangway or on the cage hoisting it up then the miner lost that bit in his pay too.

"Packing it tight, Jamie. That's good. Can't let them cheat us, and they'll do that if they can. Now then, enough about work. Sit, boy, here's a bit of beef," Jones said, pointing his eyes and his light toward his outstretched hand so that Jamie could see the food. "Sorry about the dirt, lad, just chew the beef and spit out whatever tastes like coal."

Both settled down on chunks of rock to avoid the watery floor and leaned against the ribs of the ever-growing room. They ate in silence, beef and bread, washing it down with cold tea.

In the quiet of their room, they could hear sounds traveling through the gangway and filtering up their tunnel. First just a noise, then louder, shouting, a sound of alarm. Jones was on his feet before Jamie knew he had moved, instinctively knowing the sounds were uncommon.

"Roof fall," yelled someone from the gangway. "Need help! Yancy's room! Quick! Need help!"

Someone was running through the gangway, expertly avoiding the overhanging rocks and threading a path between the rails and over the uneven ground. Jones grabbed his pick and headed for the gangway. "Bring your shovel, Jamie, hurry!" Jones said no more, his heart pounding into his lungs, his feet racing through the darkened cavern, his head tilted to escape the low overhead.

He would hurry for any emergency, for any man, but this call was different. This was more personal. Dylan was Yancy's laborer. Dylan was in that room. Dylan could be under tons of rock and coal.

Jamie was rushing to keep up. Other men were coming from their rooms into the gangway and rushing toward Andrew Yancy's room.

"Hurry, for God's sake, hurry," someone running behind Jamie was yelling. He tried to pick up the pace but, with his limited experience underground, he kept tripping over the ties under the rails and catching himself by putting his left hand up against the rough wall. He could feel the blood running from small cuts inflicted by the jagged rock. Mr. Jones was no longer in sight, only the flickering of several lights ahead. "Keep up, boy, keep up," the man behind yelled as he bumped Jamie's side and ran past.

"Yancy," Jones yelled as he turned up the tunnel to the coal face.

"Here, here," a voice shouted from the darkness and a light turned toward him. "That you, Glyn?"

"Aye, you alright, mon? Where's Dylan?"

"Dada, Dada, help me, Dada!"

"His hand is caught! I can't dig it out," Yancy yelled. "Piece of the roof came down, there where the timber buckled," he said, pointing his light up.

"Couple of you men please get some support under that," Jones shouted to no one in particular, though he knew several had run into the room behind him. He glanced up too, his light shining into a void where several huge pieces of the roof had dropped. He knew that another fall could bury Dylan, bury them all in fact. Immediately, axes were swinging into the oak logs lying nearby which Yancy and Dylan had been storing to shore up the roof. The miners knew how to cut quickly, move the uprights into place and shove a thick notched timber in above them, then sledge everything in tight.

"Carefully, boys, carefully. Don't bring any more down on us," Jones said just loud enough to be heard. He studied the roof quickly, thinking to himself that the timbering Yancy had supervised did not look adequate. It was a fault of many miners, knowing that they got nothing from the company for so-called dead work—timbering, laying track, those sorts of odd jobs necessary for safety and to move coal. But it was not the time to lay blame.

He knelt down, next to his son, confident now that the roof was safe, at least for awhile. His light shone into the frightened, contorted face of his youngest son, tears streaking through the black dirt on Dylan's cheeks. Then he moved his head to focus the flame on Dylan's left arm, most of it covered with small debris. From the wrist the boy's hand disappeared in a pool of red and black goo under a rock more than two feet thick.

"Dada, it hurts, Dada, oh gawd, it hurts!"

"Steady, Dylan, we'll get you out," Jones said, stroking his son's face with his left hand while his right hand searched the edges of the rock for a sign of soft material underneath. He was hoping to find gob, the dirt and small bits of coal that laborers shovelled to one side while loading a car. There was none. The rock seemed to be sitting on a hard surface, either part of the roof fall or the solid bottom of the room. On the far side, the huge rock was hard fast against the rib of the room, a fraction of an inch from one of the timbers still supporting part of the roof. Jones's first thought had been to try with tamping bars to roll the rock off Dylan's hand, but any movement away from the boy could put pressure on the supporting timber.

"Maybe crack it in pieces with our picks," Yancy suggested in a nervous voice.

"Any swinging up high in here could bring more of that roof down," Jones replied, knowing full well that his twenty-seven years' experience underground far outweighed the time that Yancy, only in his mid-twenties, had as a miner. "Best we try to dig under the rock, let it stay where it fell. Short pick strokes, mind you, and we need to watch Dylan's arm—not too close."

Two other miners moved in quickly, one on either side of the pinned arm, down on their knees. Then Jones lay down perpendicular to Dylan, braced up on his elbows, covering the boy's face with his body and putting his arms to either side of Dylan's pinned arm. If a digger missed, Jones's arm would feel the sharp point of a pick.

The first strike proved what he had feared, that the floor under Dylan's arm was solid and that cutting under the arm and hand would be slow, tedious work. "Hard surface, Glyn," whispered one of the two diggers, his head just inches away from Jones.

"Aye, cautious it is, boys."

"It's your arms I'm worried about, Glyn," said the other miner. "I need some power in the stroke to dig in. One miss and you'll..."

"Go to it, mon. I have great faith in your ability. But be quick too," Jones whispered, turning his head to glance at the roof.

The measured strokes went on for what seemed, to everyone, an eternity. Chips flew into the faces of the two diggers and into Jones and his son. Three other miners continued to cut timbers, with their axes carefully kept away from the damaged roof, and two more pushed the huge logs into standing positions and lifted the cross pieces into the axed notches.

"Jamie, go ring for the cage. We need it at pit bottom when we get Dylan loose," Jones shouted to a cluster of men and boys near the entrance of the room.

"I think someone already went, Glyn," a voice shouted back.

"Go anyhow, Jamie. Quick, boy, just to make sure."

"Aye, Mr. Jones, on my way."

"One of you others, get some rags, clean as you can find, maybe your underwear, and a piece of rope, a foot or more, or a belt," Jones sang out to the men still lingering in the room waiting for their chance to help.

The minutes flew by. The picks kept up their clatter against the hard floor, making holes in the rock close to Jones's arms. Dylan was silent and his breathing had become labored, his father noticed, whether from shock or loss of blood he knew not. He worried that the digging was taking too long but he did not know how to speed it up without endangering the boy or the fragile roof above.

"Yancy, take a look at his face. How does he look?"

"Oh my, his eyes are closed, but he's breathing, Glyn."

"Unconscious, is he?"

"Dylan, lad, can you hear me? It's Yancy."

There was no response.

"Aye, Glyn, unconscious it is."

"We've got to keep working to..." Jones's words were cut short when he and those near him heard a slight cracking noise. "Shush," he shouted to the men clustered nearby. "Listen."

"Glyn, Glyn, rats running over my feet," shouted Yancy. "Oh, my gawd!"

Another crack, this time louder. The diggers held their picks, looked up at the threatening roof over their heads and looked at Glyn.

"She's gonna come, Glyn!"

"I know, damn, I know! You boys back there, clear out to the gang-way, check the roof as you go, make sure nothing else is moving."

Jones was on his knees, his face and his light pointing up. He knew if the roof came again the whole room could be covered. Ten men, including his son, could be crushed.

"Stop the digging and get out, right now!" The two diggers hesitated, one shouting: "What do you plan on doing, Glyn?"

"Give me an axe," he yelled, pointing his light at the men notching the timbers. "Then all of you move back of me." The five miners moved past, the first handing Glyn his axe. "Out, out to the gangway!"

Then he motioned Yancy over to Dylan's feet: "Get ready to pick him up when I give the word."

"What are you going to do, Glyn?" Yancy shouted, but got no response.

Jones could feel the tears rolling down his blackened cheeks, but he knew the three men around him would not see them.

"We've got to get Dylan and all of us out of here now. That roof could drop any minute. I'm going...," he stammered, the sound stuck in his throat. "Have to do this, Dylan, forgive me, son," Jones screamed, his heart pound-ing, the tears gushing down onto the boy's forehead. With his face pointed at the boy's wrist where it disappeared under the rock, the flame on his cap wavering as his body shook in torment, Jones lifted the heavy axe and brought it down with all his might. It chopped through in one stroke, throwing bone and skin and blood into his face. Dylan's body flew up, a high-pitched scream rolled out of the boy, his eyes flashed wildly, his left arm—freed from the rock—snapped onto his chest. His head rolled to one side, the eyes closed again and the body relaxed and flopped back to the floor.

"My gawd!" Yancy screamed. "My gawd! Oh my gawd!"

"Pick him up, Yancy! Hurry, pick him up! Get his legs, Yancy, pick him up!"

Kneeling between Dylan's feet, Yancy froze, unable to fathom the hor-ror of what he had just witnessed.

"Grab his arms," Jones yelled at the two diggers. Both men moved quickly. One gulped, vomited to one side and took the arm which had been severed at the wrist. The second jumped to the other side, grabbed Dylan under his right arm and back and began to pull. Jones pushed Yancy away, put his hands under his boy's knees and began to lift.

Another crack from the roof, this one much louder, this one telling the miners they had perhaps only seconds. The two diggers had Dylan up and Jones was lifting his legs for the race to the gangway. Crack again! Dust began to fall, then small pieces. Jones could hear the timbers groaning. It wouldn't take long. He glanced back as he lifted his boy's limp legs. Yancy was still on his knees, still frozen, a look of terror in his eyes. With his left arm hooked under Dylan's legs, Jones reached down, grabbed Yancy by the back of his coat and pulled as they stumbled out of the room. The shaken miner, snapped from his inability to move, tripped and fell, his hands automatically reaching out to stop the fall. On his knees, he scrambled further, then rose and pushed against Jones as they fell into the gangway.

The lot of them were barely around the corner when the horrid sound of the roof falling smashed against their ears. Dust rolled in heavy waves from the room, covering all, dousing their lamps, pitching them into total darkness. Fear struck deeply. The older miners had been through these trying times before, had always escaped, but also knew the sickening sights when they had to dig out men and boys crushed under tons of rock and coal. Flattened bodies, flushed of all body fluids, unrecognizable even to close friends. Scrape up what was left, put it in a filthy coal bag, truck it to the surface, give it to the survivors.

The four men tried to lay Dylan down easily, but the rush to safety toppled all. They weren't down more than a few seconds, coughing and spitting out the black dirt that had invaded their mouths, their noses, their ears. There was nothing clean enough to wipe the dust from filmy eyes, but the miners ordered out of the breast earlier by Jones were on the run back to their comrades when they heard the roof cave in. First they relit the head lamps from their own flames, then each picked out one of the four rescuers and did what miners had always done to clean dirt from eyes. They held the eyelids open and wiped the eyeballs with their tongues, spitting out what the stickiness of the tongue had wiped away.

"Rope, piece of rope, quick," Jones yelled, "and a cloth!"

One of the men who had been outside the breast handed him a belt.

"Around Dylan's arm, above the elbow, tighten it, cut the blood," Jones shouted. The man pulled the belt around the unconscious boy's arm, slipped a simple knot and pulled tight. "Loosen it every few minutes..."

"I know, Glyn, I know, done this before," the man said softly.

"Here, bandage," another yelled, holding a large piece of grayish, wet cloth in his outstretched hand. "Leg offa my long johns, cleana part."

Jones glanced up, realizing that friends—not just fellow miners—surrounded him. They were all in danger but they all offered help. He smiled weakly. The pantleg came from an Italian laborer whom everyone called Joe because they couldn't pronounce his name.

"Thanks, Joe," Jones smiled again as he reached out, took the material and carefully wrapped it around the bloody raw stump of his son's arm. The smile disappeared instantly as he worked, knowing not whether his son would live, knowing not whether more of the roof would come down on all of them.

"We got an empty car, Glyn. You get in. We'll hand Dylan in to you. You cradle him while we push to the pit bottom. Cage will be waiting," another miner yelled to him.

"Aye, and move quick, boys! I don't want any of you hurt this day," Jones yelled back as he jumped into the empty car and sat down hard on the wooden bottom. Four men lifted the limp form of Dylan over the top and into the arms of his father. The man who had put the belt on Dylan's arm climbed in too, gently cradling the oozing wound as he sat next to Jones. Three men began pushing the car down the gangway while others ran ahead to make sure there were no obstructions on the track and to get the ventilation door opened quickly as they approached.

Yancy was the last to leave, giving others the chance to escape ahead of him. He felt ashamed that the roof in his room had collapsed on Glyn's son, the laborer, rather than on him, the miner. He wondered if the timbers he had notched and put up, with Dylan's help, were strong enough for the job, or if the roof would have come down regardless of who braced it. A guilty feeling washed through his heart as he stumbled along behind the gang of men and the car. Men from rooms further down the gangway had already moved past his room after the alarm was sounded. But Yancy heard no other rumblings, no other signs of rats moving swiftly. It seemed to be an isolated fall; at least he hoped so. Yet, an isolated fall could indicate that his knowledge of timbering was lacking, that this accident was strictly his fault. He ran on, trying to clear his mind of the guilt that was engulfing him, trying to think only of getting young Dylan to a doctor who could stop the bleeding, treat the shock and save a life.

The mile to pit bottom seemed to be taking more time than Jones normally spent walking from there to his room, but with men pushing the car at a fast trot he knew they were moving much quicker. He watched as the man tending the belt periodically loosened it, waited and then tightened it again. He trusted him; he had to. But he didn't know him well, only that he was a Scotsman named McSweeney, and that he had immigrated to Scranton several years ago. Most of the men on the shift simply called him Mac. Jones knew his first name was Brandon and that's how he preferred to address him. But knowing him and knowing how much he knew about controlling the flow of blood from a severed arm were simply two different matters. He watched intently as the car rolled through the dark tunnel. He could hear Dylan breathing, but only sparingly. He knew he was still unconscious, perhaps from loss of blood, perhaps from shock. But there was nothing more he, nor McSweeney, nor any of those rushing that car along could do.

"It's in God's hands, Brandon."

"Aye, mon, not ours, but we do what we can. We will get your son out of this hole and he will recover."

Jones knew it was only a gesture of goodwill on McSweeney's part, not any wisdom he had on the survival rate of injured mine workers, but he appreciated the comforting words.

"Thank you, my friend, for what you — and the others — are doing."

"You'd do the same, and more, for any of us," McSweeney answered.

Jones nodded, then lowered his head to look into Dylan's scratched and bloodied face. He wasn't much of a praying man, but pray he did at this hour, that God would let his son live and that Dylan would forgive his father for the brutal effort to get him out of the collapsing room. His mind wandered back to the boy's childhood, to happier days when Dylan was still too young to become possessed by the deadly arms of the mine, to a time when Gwyneth told him of the doctor's warning to have no more babies and the realization that this little chap would be their third and last child. But he thought then of Evan, now twenty-two and a miner like himself, and of Rhys, at twenty still a laborer but waiting for the chance to move up to a miner's job. He worried for them too but, at this moment, he was glad that they worked the night shift and would be home with Gwyneth and would have heard the breaker whistle announce there had been an accident. He knew all three would be on top after word reached the house that Dylan had been injured. He knew his two oldest would comfort their mother in this hour of need. And that knowledge comforted Glyn Jones in his hour of need too.

The cage was waiting when they arrived minutes later at pit bottom, and so was Charles Booth, the outside foreman for the Hyborne Coal Company.

"Get them out of the car. Rest of you men get back to work," Booth yelled over the confusion. "Damn accidents! Why did it take a dozen men to bring one boy out? How do you expect to make a living if you're not working?"

"Be fair, Mr. Booth, they were helping my son," Jones said politely over the top of the car.

"Help indeed!" Booth yelled into the car. "Put the boy down on the cage floor. We are not taking an empty car to the surface. Back to work, the lot of you. You too, McSweeney."

"He's keeping my son from bleeding to death, Mr. Booth," Jones pleaded, a hint of anger rising in his voice. He was trying to control his temper but he knew that Booth, an Englishman with little mining experience but lots of power above ground, could fire him and Evan and Rhys and, yes, even Dylan, by simply saying they were troublemakers. Jones had heard of mine bosses cursing injured men because production had stopped to help them. And he had heard of a mine boss down in Carbon County who made two other men lay aside the body of a comrade killed by a rock fall until they finished cleaning up the debris.

"Yah, let him go up," a strong voice sounded from back in the shadows of the gangway. Jones recognized it as Otto Bremmer's, the inside foreman, the man whose job it was to control matters underground. "Let McSweeney go up too. Da boy is in bad shape."

"And these others?" Booth demanded.

"I been checking. Only da roof in Yancy's room came down. Everything else looks alright. Dey can go back to vork. I take Yancy back to see vat has to be done," the brawny German foreman shouted. "Now get dat cage moving quick like."

Booth obviously feared his underground counterpart. Inside foremen were always ex-miners who knew the ropes and, if they treated miners with respect, they maintained good relationships. Bremmer commanded respect because he was big and tough, because he knew the ins and outs of mining and the dangers underground, but mostly because he treated the men fairly. However, he didn't push too hard against a man like Booth, a man who had the superintendent's ear. He did not resist Booth's order that the empty car be kept below for the loading of coal because he knew Dylan had to be lifted out of it, whether it was down here in the dark or four hundred feet above on the surface. He knew Booth had to give an order, any order, to maintain his dominance over Jones and McSweeney and every other miner in this company.

When Booth rang the surface to signal that the cage should be lifted he rang the bells to signify that both levels of the cage would be loaded. He got on the top level with Jones, his son Dylan and McSweeney and closed the door. The cage moved up eight feet and stopped while two men shoved a loaded coal car on the lower level. Then another signal and the trip to daylight finally began.

The veins in Jones's neck were bulging with anger. Making a critically injured boy wait just so another load of coal could go up; the thought alone forced his teeth to clench tightly. But he held his tongue. He knew that the owner, J. Wellington Hyborne, would be told little about the accident, if told at all. And, if told, immediately would blame Yancy. Like most owners in the anthracite counties of northeastern Pennsylvania, Mr. Hyborne took no responsibility for safety in his mine, that being, he said, the job of the contract miner, men like Jones and Yancy and a hundred others. Nor would he provide any compensation to Dylan. Jones knew that he himself would be held responsible for maiming his own son, regardless of the need for all of them to escape the weakened roof. And Jones plus all of the men who had helped Dylan would suffer financially because they would be paid nothing for the time spent in rescuing the boy. The company, he knew full well, paid neither for rescue operations nor the removal of bodies, unless of course it was a dead mule. The only report would probably go to Superintendent Joseph Lordman and he, like the owner, would assume no personal responsibility for the whole affair. The thought of how these men worshipped greed and power and arrogance fried in Jones's brain throughout the ride to the top. The foremen and the superintendent owed their very existence to Mr. Hyborne; he could blackball them in the mining industry if they crossed him. And Mr. Hyborne, whom Jones had never met, felt little for either his supervisors or his company employees, much less the contract miners who were paid not for their work but only for the tonnage of good hard anthracite they sent to the surface. It was, Jones decided, as though Hyborne not only owned his labor but also controlled his very soul.

There was no choice. It was work for the owner or starve. And owners knew it. They also knew that the more a man needed work to survive the easier he was to manipulate. They kept importing labor from Europe, not from England or Wales or Scotland or Germany; those skilled miners had come years ago. Now they were posting advertisements in Ireland, where two generations ago the potato famine had put thousands of Irish families in dire straits for years to come, where young men were looking for ways to escape the poverty of landlessness. The owners too were seeking men from the Slavic countries where labor was cheap and plentiful, promising them work in the rich coal veins of America. And yet there was a plentiful labor supply already in the steep hills and valleys of Pennsylvania's anthracite region, from just north of the capital in Harrisburg to Scranton, one hundred miles away. The plan was to flood the region with workers so that owners could control jobs and wages and family life — and earn huge profits for themselves and their investors. The owner felt superior and he believed it was because of where he stood in the social life of the community, not his family's money. The workers knew superiority was measured by the money, not the man behind it.

Sunlight, brighter as the cage neared the top, shook Jones out of his thoughts. Dylan had not stirred and Brandon McSweeney was paying close attention to the task of controlling bleeding from the stump. The cage stopped abruptly, as usual, and Jones stared through the latticework door.

There were two men with a dirty plank, the normal device used to carry an injured miner to a doctor or a dead one to his home. Behind them he could see Evan and Rhys standing on each side of Gwyneth, steadying her. She had lost her own father in a mine explosion back in Wales when she was still in her teens. At least she knew, or had been told, that Dylan was alive, though injured. Jones did not know how much else she knew.

When the door was opened, the two men rushed aboard and helped lay Dylan on their plank. Jones folded the boy's right arm onto his chest. McSweeney held the left arm up at an angle, the blood-drenched rag dripping onto the floor.

Gwyneth gasped as she caught sight of her son. Her two older sons, supporting her elbows, felt a momentary buckling as the plank was carried from the cage. They lifted and held her. The tears ran freely but she did not cry out. A strong woman she, Jones thought as he watched his wife. She did not stop those carrying her son but fell in alongside her husband as the procession moved through the colliery yard and through the gate.

"Doc Lewis is waiting in his office, Dada," Evan said softly. Jones nodded. No one asked how Dylan was or what had happened. He was not aware that no one had told his family that Dylan had lost his left hand nor did he want to mention it, not then, not there.

Outside the gate, neighbors waited with a small wagon. Dylan's silent body was loaded on with McSweeney still holding the arm. Jones helped his wife climb in and he crawled up beside her. The driver moved off at a slow pace, careful not to bump his cargo over the rock-strewn ground. Evan and Rhys jogged alongside the wagon as it moved ever so carefully to the doctor's office six blocks away. Jones felt that if Dylan had survived this long he had a good chance at living through his ordeal. In his lifetime in mining he had seen men in much worse shape come through, crippled perhaps but alive nonetheless. It was a part of their existence, this ongoing parade of tragedies, this surrender of body to the viper of working underground and of soul to those who controlled their very destiny.

Chapter Two

"Seeing Dylan lying up there brings doubts, girl."

"Of what, pray tell?"

"Did I do the right thing?"

"And if you hadn't used that axe, Glyn, our son would be lying in a cold grave rather than a warm bed. Don't be daft. You had to do it," Gwyneth said hurriedly, her voice touching on the edge of anger. Her husband's head was in his hands and she could see and hear that he was hurting. She mellowed, "You are a loving father. You did the right thing. You saved your son's life."

"And made him a cripple, Gwyn."

"Aye, and kept him alive. Better one hand than none, better life than none."

She stepped over to the wooden chair where he sat slowly puffing on his pipe and draped her hands over his gray head. Her hands slid down over his neck and she pulled his head gently into her stomach. "I carried that boy here for nine months and gave him life. And you, in one brave act, made sure that neither those nine months nor the past seventeen years were wasted."

"He doesn't talk any about it, does he, girl?"

"It has been only a fortnight, Glyn, give him time. He still has a lot of mending, both in his body and in his spirit."

"Doc Lewis? He was here today then?"

"Yes, and he still praises how you and Mr. McSweeney tended to Dylan. Another hour in that pit and the boy could have died, he said. Without the bandage and controlling the bleeding, he could have died. Oh, Glyn, it came so close to that." A tear rolled down past her nose and onto her lips.

"We could have lost him without Doc Lewis too, without the wisdom he gained during the war. He said it was a clean cut. He had no more to cut. It was..."

"Oh, Glyn, please, no details. I don't know how you had the strength to use that axe; I couldn't have. But you did. I just have a difficult time thinking about it."

Jones thought silently for a moment, about the times Doc Lewis had told him of the many amputations he performed on Union soldiers, even some Confederates. But medicine had grown in the two decades since the war ended, Lewis had said in one of their discussions years before Dylan's accident. "We know about sterilization now, about keeping wounds clean," the doctor had said.

At the age of sixty-three, Doc Lewis only operated when he had to. He normally left that delicate work to the younger men, those with recent training and steadier hands. But when an emergency arose in the mines, he was the first called. That's why he maintained his home and office in Hyde Park, near several large mines. He had to be there to help. He wished he could have been there when his own father perished for lack of medical treatment following a mine explosion. But Lewis was just a boy, only ten when his father died of burns hours after he was brought to the surface. Doctors in Wales then knew little about saving those burned or mangled or crushed in the unforgiving task of digging coal. As was the custom back then, fifty-three years ago, and now in 1890, the injured miner or his lifeless body was normally delivered to his house, left on the porch or carried in and laid on the kitchen table. It was up to the wife and her children to provide healing powers or to prepare the body for burial. Doc Lewis winced whenever he recalled his father being carried in by two other miners, the blackened body naked save for charred and still smoking work boots, the oozing flesh, the terror in his father's eyes, the seared throat unable to utter a sound. He died a horrible death in less than an hour but the boy, and his siblings, and especially his mother felt he knew he was at home, that he was dying in his house with his family there to comfort the last agonizing moments.

"If we had the drugs then that we have now we could have at least taken his pain away," the doctor had told Jones in one of those long-ago talks.

Jones knew that when he and McSweeney carried Dylan into the office, Doc Lewis was ready. Someone from the mine had raced to the office and then to the Jones house. Lewis knew that Dylan's left hand had been cut off to get him out of the collapsing room. He did not know who had cut it.

"It's a clean cut. I need to tie off the veins, clean the wound. But I've given Dylan something to keep him sleeping. It's touch and go, Glyn. He's young, strong. His body can take a great deal. But he's been through a shocking experience. I am confident he will survive."

"I'm so thankful for your ability, Doctor Lewis. My boy is precious to me, to his mother, to his older brothers."

"To us all, Glyn, to us all. But the key to his future will lie in his ability to get along without one hand. That will be the difficulty. Aye, that will be the challenge."

"We will be with him, Doctor. We will support him."

"Yes, that's what it will take, Glyn, but not too much, mind you. He has to learn to get along on his own. Neither you nor Gwyneth will be there his whole life."

"Right you are, Doctor, supportive love it is."

Glyn had missed no work since the accident, knowing that every dollar was needed now, to pay for Dylan's medical treatment, low as Doc Lewis charged, and to make up for Dylan's lost wages. There would be no pay for the boy now that the company could no longer use him. And there was no other help; no one could afford to give assistance. Normally, the miners would pass the hat to collect funds for a widow so that she would not be forced out of her home. But an accident victim? There were too many. And there never was enough money to even feed a family properly. Pity from friends, yes; help to care for the recuperating worker, yes; perhaps a bit of extra food for one or two meals, yes. But an ongoing fund? Perish the thought. No one, at least among the mining families, could afford that.

The Hyborne Coal Company was not concerned about injured or dead miners. Finding replacements was no problem. In fact, many of the coal barons continuously advertised in eastern European newspapers for workers. They didn't pay for their passage or offer them a definite job. They just advertised that jobs were plentiful in the anthracite coal fields of eastern Pennsylvania and that the pay was more than what these men could earn in Europe.

One day when Jones was at his coal face alone, having sent Jamie out looking for Sliver and an empty car to load, the inside foreman stopped for his weekly check of the room. Otto Bremmer had been a miner, in Germany and then in Scranton. He had been promoted because the company needed experienced miners who seemed inclined to resist efforts to support fledgling unions.

"I vork for Otto, not for udder men," Bremmer had told Jones when he learned of the promotion. It was a stance with which Jones did not agree but neither did he argue the point. Bremmer had a right to do what he felt was best for him and for his family, the Welshman figured. He liked the big German, knew he was fair to the men while working hard for the company, and knew, most importantly, that he could be trusted. He was not the unforgiving vulture that his outside counterpart, Charles Booth, had become.

"You ever met da superintendent?" Bremmer asked as the two men sat on chunks of coal awaiting Jamie's return.

"I've seen him, up top, on occasion, walking about, looking busy with...," Jones paused, not knowing if he had crossed the line in conversing with a company boss. He looked at Bremmer, not with fear but with that sudden feeling that perhaps he had overstepped the boundary of mutual respect.

The German laughed. "Yah, dat's Joseph Lordman alright. It's okay, Glyn. I not turn you in for being critical of da super. I don't like da guy either." Bremmer laughed again, then looked over his shoulder, leaned forward and whispered: "I like my job. It's good for da missus and da little ones. But I be fair. And I know you are fair too. Ve can talk, Glyn, no problem."

Jones smiled, relaxed, and then laughed too.

"You know," Bremmer whispered again, "your boy's name vas not even mentioned ven Booth and me had to tell Lordman vat happened dat day. He vant to know only vhy production slowed down according to da reports given to his office. Booth say, 'a laborer got hurt. Too many men stopped vork to get him back to da surface. I told dem to get back to vork or dey vould be out of a job.' Booth is a big talker but he valks around all day up top and don't give a damn vhat happens below. 'Dat's your job, Bremmer,' he told me.

"Yah, dat is my job. I told Lordman a labor boy named Dylan Jones vas caught in a fall and dat his father, Glyn, had to amputate his hand to get him out."

"'Velshmen, I suppose?' Lordman asked me. I nodded yes. 'Damn Velsh. Troublemakers, as bad as the Irish. Isn't dat correct, Booth?'

"And Booth, his head shaking in agreement all da time, says: 'Yes sir, Mr. Lordman, troublemakers, da lot of dem. Slowing down production to get one silly boy out.'"

Bremmer turned again, looked into the darkened passage leading to the gangway and leaned closer to Jones.

"'Cut his hand off, you say, his own son? Vhat an animal!' Dat was Lordman's opinion. I did not answer him. Den Booth, he laugh and say: 'Dere only arms and legs, Mr. Lordman, not men, just arms and legs. Dey don't have to think, just move der arms and legs, and move da coal out.'"

"I've heard that before and it angers me that someone can refer to human beings as arms and legs," Jones responded, his voice rising. "We have brains and hearts and feelings, just like them."

"You know dat, Glyn, and I know it. But ve dealing here vit people vho have never vorked down in da mine, only top side of da colliery. I vork all over da anthracite field in Pennsylvania—in Lackavanna and Luzerne, down in Carbon and Schuylkill. Da only counties I have not vorked are Vyoming and Northumberland. But it's da same all over. Da owner can replace a miner at no cost but he has to buy a new mule."

Bremmer stood up, walked out to the gangway and listened. There were no sounds of a mule or cars moving on the track, just the clink, clink of picks in nearby rooms.

"Damn Sliver, vere does he go with dose empties?" Bremmer exploded as he walked back to Jones at the working face.

"Yes, Otto, I've got coal here to load and no cars. I worked at a mine down near Wilkes-Barre where the inside foreman didn't like the Welsh or the Scots. He gave the extra empties to his English miners. Blacklisted us, he did. Can't make a living like that. Needed to control us, to keep us in check, he told one of my English friends."

"You are not suggesting dat I am holding back cars?"

"You would not do that, Otto. I know you too well."

"I am glad to hear dat. It sounded like you vere suggesting dat..."

"No, of course not, my friend. But others do it, you know."

"Yah, dat's true. Dey do. But da owner still controls you, doesn't he? All dat dead vork—laying track, timbering, moving rock, removing vater— none of dat gets you any pay. Only the coal you send up. Dat is the only measure."

"It's unfair to the miner, and to his laborer," Jones said. "But some-body has to timber and put down the track. There's a lot to do just to get at the coal. I protect myself and Jamie by doing a good job at supporting the roof."

"But you get paid by da ton, by da cars you mark and send up. Dat's da measure of your vork, Glyn."

"Someday it will change, Otto, someday someone will make them change the system."

"Da union? Da last one fell apart."

"More will come. Men cannot be treated as arms and legs."

"Vell, perhaps you are right. But for now, da owners should be rein-vesting der profits in safety, in der mines, not spending it elsewhere. Dey need to stop accidents like your son's."

"You sound like a miner."

"I am a miner, just in a different part of mining vork. But you and I, ve can still talk as friends, Glyn."

Bremmer stuck out a huge, grimy hand. Jones squeezed it tightly and shook it.

"I go see vere your damn car is."

Ten minutes passed before Jones heard the squeak of a car's wheels coming up to the face.

"Found a car, have you, Jamie?"

"I'm very sorry, Mr. Jones. Sliver's mule wouldn't move. She just sat down in her harness on the track and wouldn't move. He cursed her and kicked her and beat her with his whip. He even tried talking gently and kissing her nose, he did, sir. She wouldn't move. Then Mr. Bremmer came along. He grabbed that old mule's ears and whispered something. She was up in no time. I have no idea what he said."

"Mr. Bremmer became a mule driver when he was ten. Perhaps he knows what the mules like to hear," Jones chuckled.

"Oh, Mr. Jones, mules don't understand English."

"Aye, but Mr. Bremmer is German. Perhaps it's something in his native tongue."

"Oh, Mr. Jones, you're having a way with me," Jamie laughed as he picked up a chunk of anthracite and began loading the car.

Jones stood for a minute watching the boy work. He was full of movement, never stopping to rest. He had become a valued worker in the months since his father's death, but at first Jones wasn't sure. He knew little of Jamie, had never seen him work. And he knew that a laborer was key to getting the maximum amount of coal into a car and the car out to the gangway for pickup.

It was Jones's choice who would be his laborer; neither the mine owner nor his managers had any say in that. Jones was not sure he could get someone as good as the man he had, a man who had put in his time and was eligible for a room of his own. It was Bremmer who had suggested the boy.

"His father vas killed. His modder has younger children, so Jamie is now da bread vinner. He's goot boy."

Bremmer secretly told Jones how Jamie had been forced by his family's dire financial straits into working at the age of six. The father, a hell-raising Irishman, had incurred the wrath of his inside foreman at a Schuylkill County colliery when he publicly supported the Workingmen's Benevolent Association, an organization formed in 1868 but still fighting to gain membership in the 1880s.

"He vas blacklisted and could only get temporary vork, so he moved his family to live vith a cousin in Luzerne County. He got in as a laborer but da family needed more money, just to eat. He got Jamie hired as a breaker boy. Da boy vorked seven in da morning til six-tirty at night, six days a veek. He got forty-five cents a day."

Jones winced when he heard that. He remembered his own start as a breaker boy in Wales, but he was eight years old. He recalled his father saying that orphans were often taken from the public workhouses and apprenticed to mine owners for up to ten years, although Jones did not know any in the breaker in his village. Years before he was born, his father had said, some children forced into labor underground worked twelve to eighteen hours a day, often in spaces no more than two feet high.

The breaker in which he toiled he remembered as being very tall, perhaps one hundred feet, built that high, of course, so that cars from the pit hoisted up the long inclined track could dump their two-ton loads noisily at the top. The coal, still unpure with some slate and rock mixed in, would slide and roll down the metal chutes to be sorted by dozens of boys whose feet and legs slowed the flow and whose hands reached in to pick out the bony.

Every fourth worker at the colliery was a boy. The youngest were in the breaker. Older ones were apprentices in the machine shop or worked below ground as mule drivers or as door boys, whose lonely job was to open huge wooden ventilation doors thus allowing trams of coal cars to pass through. The oldest, of course, were doing what was considered a man's job—laborer to a full-fledged contract miner.

He recalled vividly his first few days in that dust-filled breaker, the continuous hammering of coal being dumped in and tumbling through to the crushers and then to the screens where it sorted itself into different sizes. Gloves were not allowed, even if a family could afford them. "Can't tell coal from rock with mitts on. Gotta have bare skin to feel the difference," the breaker boss had scolded one boy who had wrapped rags around each hand. Jones, the boy, soon had what everyone called "redtop"—fingers left bloody by the sharp edges of the moving coal and rock. Within a week, like other newcomers, he had developed welcomed calluses. Jones, the man, had vivid memories of sitting with dozens of other boys on the narrow boards which crossed the sloping floor of the building, crouched over for hours with nothing to support his aching back, with noise from the rushing coal so loud that conversation was impossible. And those who did try to shout something to a neighbor when the foreman was nearby soon felt a switch striking their back and a screamed order to "work, not talk."

Row after row of boys controlled the amount of rock and slate; what one boy up high on a chute missed, boys below him in other rows but on the same chute had to catch. Each wore a rag across his face in an effort to keep the thick dust out of his nose and mouth, but nothing could keep the minute particles out of eyes and any attempt to wipe one's eyes just resulted in pain. The dirt and what little light filtered in through the many breaker windows made it difficult to even see the rock rolling over their lacerated boots. The windows had long since blackened with the rising dust and summer's humidity, and no one ever attempted to wash them.

Two overseers—the one at right armed with a stick for striking those not working hard enough—watch young boys picking slate and other debris from coal in the Ewen Breaker at the Pennsylvania Coal Mine near South Pittston, Pennsylvania, in January 1911. The dust in such buildings virtually blotted out other people in the same room and penetrated the boys' lungs.

Lewis W. Hine Photo, National Archives and Records Administration

With about forty boys there were several men who worked in the breaker because they were either too old or too badly injured to work underground but still needed a payday to put food on their table. He recalled a one-legged ex-miner who hobbled up through the massive building each morning on a crutch cut from a tree branch. Once he got down on the narrow board the man would tie the crutch to the stump of his leg so that he, like others, had two limbs in the chute to slow the movement. It was this man who taught the boys to chew tobacco while working; he told them it would keep them from choking on the dust. The problem, Jones found, was that he seldom could afford even a small plug of tobacco, so like many others he just plopped a small piece of coal in his mouth. The sucking action brough saliva and saliva brought some relief. The only drawback was that he often found when he picked out bony that boys above him in other tiers often slathered the rock stream with huge gobs of spit or tobacco juice. His mother had raised him to be clean and relatively neat but he found, as a breaker boy, that a mother's wishes could not always be obeyed.

Jones, as he thought about his boyhood, remembered vividly how the breaker building shook as heavy chains moving the chutes clanked and the monstrous crushers ground huge chunks of coal into various sizes. He wondered, as a boy, what held the framework together and whether, some-day, he and his mates would be dashed to the lowest level and crushed as the entire building gave in to the shaking and crashed to the ground. He remembered the heat of a few summers, though normal summers in Wales were pleasant enough, with humidity adding to the wretchedness of the work. And he particularly remembered the frightful winters when icy blasts ripped through the breaker's many broken window panes and chilled him to the bone. One winter was exceptionally severe with snow falling for days, covering everything in a blanket of white. It was so deep that one of his breaker mates had to be carried into the building by his father because the boy was too small to walk through the drifts.

Four boys pose after finishing their shift at a coal breaker in this January 16, 1911, photo taken near Pittston, Pennsylvania. They could not wash their dirty faces nor change their filthy clothing until they got home.

Lewis W. Hine Photo, National Archives and Records Administration

Jamie had been lucky, Jones figured, to have survived so many young years in the breaker. Too many like him had been killed, or maimed for life, or died of diseases perhaps aggravated by the conditions under which they worked. And he knew it was not always a matter of parental abuse that put children in such situations. It was most often a matter of survival for the whole family, a matter of getting enough food to prevent starvation or sufficient clothes to keep from freezing or four walls and a roof to guarantee at least a night of rest. But when he was a boy there was no formal schooling except for those wealthy enough or fortunate enough to find a benefactor who would provide an education. It was quite normal for children to work. Now, as the nineteenth century entered its last decade, education had become more important, boys now could get up to five years of public schooling, girls as much as seven. Now, boys were generally at least ten before classes ended and a lifetime of work began in the mines and girls usually twelve before they closed the books and went to the mills or stayed at home to help mother cook and clean and launder and raise vegetables.

Just five years ago, in 1885, the Pennsylvania Legislature passed a law outlawing mine employment of boys under fourteen underground or under twelve on the surface. But the law was universally ignored by parents who simply lied about a boy's age. They cared but they had little choice and, besides, everyone did it. The mining companies didn't care because they paid the boys so little and needed so many of them for the expanding industry. The legislators, at least most of them, had no feelings either way; after all, they had performed their duty, they had passed the law. For everyone, it was an economic necessity: families ate regularly; miners merely felt that their sons were learning the trade; mine owners grew fat with riches; managers prospered and thus moved up the social scale; lawmakers who did not press authorities to enforce the law raked in monetary gifts from grateful coal barons. Meanwhile, the children suffered.

Jones recalled one tiny boy he had seen trudging to work many years before the Pennsylvania law was passed. "He was so small," he had told Gwyneth, "that his lunch bucket was too heavy to carry. The poor thing dragged it along as he climbed the hill to the breaker." Gwyneth cried that day and made him promise that their own sons, then ranging from two to seven, would get as much schooling as possible before they went to the colliery. He agreed. He wished they would never have to go underground, but he knew that was not very realistic. As they grew and, one by one, began work Jones gained confidence in their ability underground, in their consciousness of pit safety, in their common sense not to take chances. Dylan's accident had shaken that confidence but he knew from what

Yancy and Dylan had told him that they had followed procedure, that the quick fall of the roof was a freak, something unavoidable, like a sudden rainstorm. Still, he was apprehensive about his sons' being miners, but that apprehension had developed before Dylan was injured. It had now been ten months since Jones received a letter from his mother telling of a frightful explosion at a colliery back home.

"Last Thursday, February 6, at 8:45 a.m.," she wrote, "an explosion and fire killed 176 at Llanerch Colliery near Pontypool. Your cousin, Tudor, was fortunately on the night shift and had finished his work. He was at home and has told your father that the explosion sounded like a cannon shot coming up through the shaft. By the time Tudor got back up the hill to the mine the black smoke coming out was so thick that he could not see the winding house or the pithead."

Jones was accustomed to reading about horrific accidents, in the British Isles, in Pennsylvania, in West Virginia, in Colorado, anywhere that mines—coal or otherwise—were in abundance. What bothered him in his mother's letter was the family-oriented news. A miner from nearby Pontnewynydd and three of his sons were killed in the blast, she wrote, while in another family the father, two sons and two grandsons all perished. A miner named Brimble, she said, was too ill to go to work that day but his three sons went and died.

And what angered him was that the same mine had experienced a minor explosion in October 1889 which triggered a suggestion from a mine inspector that closed safety lamps be used. The managing director of the mine, she wrote, replied that "at present we think the colliery is thoroughly well-ventilated and safe to work with naked lights."

A case, Jones had thought as he read the letter, of company concern for costs overriding human safety. Such considerations were not confined to Wales or any other country. They occurred throughout the world as mining firms, pressed to find profit for greedy owners—absentees or not—sought the cheapest way to disturb Mother Earth.

Now he found himself with doubts. As he listened to Jamie dumping coal into the car, Jones frequently glanced up at the roof, his light glistening on the barren, damp rock. Since Dylan's accident he seemed less inclined to trust the roof to sound; now he had to look too. He had always tested the roof with the butt end of a drill before beginning a shift, and still did. But from that point, he trusted his hearing to tell him if the roof was working, if slight noises indicated movement above, or if the timbers began to sound stressed. And, of course, he listened for rats. When they began squealing and running he knew it was time for him to run too. All that changed with the roof fall in Yancy's room, not because Jones had never witnessed a fall before but, he reasoned, because this fall changed Dylan's life forever.

Now, he found himself looking at the rock above, measuring with his eye any perceived movement. In the gangway he would look more closely at the hardwood that reinforced the sides of the tunnel. He would check the props and the wooden collar they held above in the fifteen-foot tunnel leading from the gangway to the room he was working. He would often stop and glance up at the supports as his cutting advanced into the coal. He knew he had become even more cautious than ever before, but his concern was that caution would not rush headlong into fear.

He seemed more aware now that hundreds of feet of rock and dirt separated him from the surface. He thought more of that distance than the thousand feet he had worked under back home in Wales. All miners he had talked to over the years expressed the fear of being trapped underground, slowly dying of the crushing weight bearing down upon their bodies, or the outbreak of fire and unable to move, or the slow lingering death of oxygen deprivation. Much better, they would say, to go quickly in an explosion. Miners learned to listen to a roof talking, warning them to be on guard, warning that something would happen, but never telling them exactly when. He had learned early on that timbering did not hold up a roof alone, that the timbers helped stabilize only. No, the most valid reason for timbering was to give a signal of disaster about to happen. When a roof began to work, the pressure from above would cause the wooden supports to bulge, then spread, then creak, then crack, then collapse. He wanted to be sure that his eyes were alert in case, with age, his ears were not.

Jamie noticed the attention his boss had been giving to the timbering too, but he was hesitant to ask, at least directly.

"What will happen in the future, Mr. Jones, when they run out of forests to cut for our timbers?"

Jones stopped, surprised somewhat by this question from a laborer who seldom spoke of such things, particularly when busy loading.

"Aye, well, lad," he stammered, stumped for an answer. "Never gave it much thought, really. All I know is what I read in the journals. Pennsylvania probably uses millions of cubic feet of trees every year just for timbering, and it all eventually rots underground, doesn't it? Aye, when you think of the shafts, and the tunnels, the gangways and air passageways, and cross headings, and rooms, my goodness, it would add up. But then, trees keep growing in the forests. I can't ever imagine that we would run out of wood; run out of coal first is more like it."

"I will no longer be working when that day comes."

"Nor I, Jamie, nor I. That day too will be a long way off. But look at the forests, just around this county, full they are of chestnut and beech and maple, white and red oak, birch, cherry, locust, red gum, the hardwoods we need. And ample they are of hemlock, spruce and other softwoods. No, the coal will go first, I'm afraid, but not in our lifetimes."

He had never given it much thought before, although he had read about the various types of wood needed for different uses at a colliery. But he didn't think about the quantity until he pictured the gangway in this mine, almost a mile long and the parallel air passageway, the same length, plus all the connecting cross headings. The gangway alone had timbers a foot thick and six feet high every three feet on both sides, with a log of equal thickness collared across the top. By itself, that one tunnel had consumed a goodly portion of some forest.

"Why not iron supports, Mr. Jones?"

"Iron would buckle quickly under pressure, maybe too quickly to give a warning. Timbers groan and moan and give you a chance to move away."

"Yancy's roof came down quite...," Jamie began but stopped abruptly. "Er, sorry, Mr. Jones."

The miner took a deep breath, knowing the boy could neither see nor hear that. "That's alright, Jamie. It happened quickly. Is that what you were going to say?"

"Yes sir."

"Yes, nothing is perfect in this world. That roof came down with too little warning. We cannot always depend on the timbers; as they rot they lose some of the ability to make sounds. And we cannot always depend on the rats; they may not be nearby when we're working. No, it's our ears and our eyes that we must trust, listening and looking for the slightest sign that it's time to leave. Less talk now, is it, lad. Time to work."

"And listen, Mr. Jones?"

"Aye, carefully, Jamie."

Young Kerrigan's question forced Jones to think about other parts of the mine and other workers whose degree of safety concerns were of vital interest to him and Jamie as well as to themselves. He pictured the ride down that morning, watching the sunlight dissolve into a small square and then a pinhead as the roofless cage plummeted four hundred feet to pit bottom. After his first few trips down a shaft as a boy — when sheer terror set the mood — he had never thought much about the daily experience, although some of that early on was boyhood bravado, not wanting the men or older boys to find fear in his face. Years of riding up and down six days a week had pushed the event into the back of his mind with each trip, thinking instead of something he had read in the community reading room or a conversation with Gwyneth or a soccer contest with the boys, or simply just a blank period of almost sleeping on his feet.

But the shaft was not a place where safety was compromised, or was it? He had never heard or read of a cage hoisting wire breaking and the cage carrying a dozen miners to a shattering death. Did someone inspect those thick and greasy wires? Could the man in the winding house be trusted to drop the cage at the proper speed (it always seemed to be one speed: fast)?

As he thought, he could picture the sides of the shaft in this mine, so at times he must have subconsciously watched as they descended. The superstructure above the hole housed two cages, two gates and wooden walls which prevented anyone from toppling down the hole when a cage was below, and the winding wheel machinery. The shaft, dug by hand, was about ten feet wide, enough to accommodate a coal car, and about twenty-four feet long, allowing the use of two winding cables and two cages, plus an unobstructed section through which air was sucked down into the depths and water was pumped up. The first twenty feet of the shaft were cribbed with timbers, cut log-cabin style and stacked along the sides to prevent soil near the surface from caving in. Then, for fifty feet below that the sides were lined with rough stone, cut to fit and cemented in to hold the weight of the timbers above. The foundation for the stone was bedrock of the area, blasted and chipped to form a shelf for the massive load above. From there to the bottom, the sides of the shaft were uneven but chiseled closely enough to allow movement of the cages without the possibility of striking the sides.

"Hell of a job to dig," a man who attended Jones's church had said to him months ago. "Pardon my French, but it was a hell of a job."

"Helped dig it, did you, Sam?"

"Aye, Glyn, years ago, before you came to Scranton. Dug many a shaft since too. Takes a good engineer to tell us just where to dig so's we hit the seam at the lowest part of the valley. Put the pumps there, you know, to drain the works."

"I'm quite familiar with that, Sam."

"Oh, by damn, sorry, Glyn. Forgot I'm talking to a real miner. Talk to so many jokers around here who think they know mining. Have to explain everything to them, you know."

"No apology needed. In fact, I've never seen a shaft dug from the beginning. I am interested to hear about it, particularly from a shaftman."

Sam's eyes lit up; he smiled: "Aye, well then, after we dig off the top soil and get down through the soft stuff, the shale and whatever else, then we bring in the drills and powder. After dropping more than a ladder length, we rig an iron bucket on a winch. Ride down in the bucket in the morning, haul muck and rock up all day, then we ride back up at the end."

"I've seen one of those buckets," Jones interrupted. "I thought when I was young that riding in a cage was a bit scary, but I don't think I'd want to swing down a hole in an iron bucket."

"Oh, great fun, mon, especially when you get down a few hundred feet and it crashes against the side a few times. Damn near tips you out, it does."

Jones knew shaftmen were proud of their ability to dig a huge hole, large enough sometimes for three or four cages, down hundreds of feet, and hit the exact spot. He had seen a shaft more than a thousand feet deep while it was still being dug in Wales—that is he had seen it from the edge of the top. The winch was whirling like the wind, hauling the bucket from the black depths, but looking over the edge Jones could see nothing. Suddenly, as it flew up through the last hundred feet he saw the bucket with three men hanging on to the mammoth handle to which was attached the thick wire cable. The bucket was spinning slowly as it approached the top, first clockwise and then, as the cable tightened, counterclockwise. He wondered how the shaftmen could even stand upright after that dizzying flight, but they did. They climbed out of the bucket, stepped onto the platform and briskly walked away.

Jones knew full well the time it took to get a new mine into operation, before it produced even a pound of coal. He knew that owners and their financial backers had to invest a great deal of money—he didn't know how much but estimated in the tens of thousands of dollars—to dig the shaft, build the hoisting and pumping apparatus and tunnel out the gangway along the seam, perhaps for an entire mile and usually uphill slightly so that heavy coal cars could be run down to shaft bottom and water would flow by gravity to the pumps. Then came a parallel tunnel, the airway, to allow for the circulation of life-giving air to the workmen. It wasn't until they began to drive the cross headings that any coal was produced. But the workers still had to be paid; timber and rails had to be purchased. Opening a mine was an expensive proposition. Once the coal began to flow, the owners' pockets bulged with the riches of black gold and the living got easier. For the workers, there was just the same pay for each ton of coal and the danger, always the danger, of dying.

He knew there were several methods of mining, but Jones's life experience was only with one—the pillar and breast, or pillar and room as some called it. He had explained it to his sons when they were quite young: "Think of a house with rooms and walls. Well, that's how we cut the coal. The space in which we work is the room, or breast, and the walls are the pillars, except that they are thicker than the walls of our house. In fact, the pillars are usually as wide as the breast. That means we are removing only half the coal, leaving the other half to support the roof. Depending on the condition of the roof we may open the room to twenty-four feet in width, perhaps as much as thirty-six feet. The inner end of the room, where we are cutting the coal, is the working face and the sides are called ribs."

"Like my ribs, Dada?" shouted Dylan, then five.

"Oh, don't be so daft," his ten-year-old brother, Evan, shouted back.

"Aye, a childish question from a baby," eight-year-old Rhys chimed in.

Dylan's eyes welled up but he said no more.

"Boys, boys, gentle on your brother. He's learning too, you know. Yes, Dylan, like your ribs, holding you altogether they are, is it?"

"Yes, Dada," Dylan smiled back.

"Aye, lad, just like the coal."

He explained to his sons how several rooms are worked simultaneously by teams of miners and laborers and how the rooms are connected by crossheadings so that air can be circulated throughout the workings. He drew a diagram to show how temporary tracks are lain into each room for a buggy road so that mine cars can be run right up to the diggings.

"When do you rob the pillars, Dada?" asked Evan, who had started as a breaker boy two years ago and already knew a lot of mining terms but was eager to know more.

Jones chuckled: "Oh, heard that, have you? Well, in some mines, after all the coal that can be mined safely is gone, they begin pulling down the pillars to get the rest, starting at the far end and working back toward the shaft. Dangerous work, that is. When the pillars go, the roof does too."

"And the ground falls too, doesn't it?"

"Yes, there can be subsidence on the surface, Evan, and we've had problems like that here in Scranton when mine owners and managers order work be done right under buildings or streets. Aye, dangerous work, lads, and not always the smart thing to do, regardless of profit."

"Profit is bad then, Dada?" Evan asked.

Jones pondered, cleared his throat, patted Dylan's blond hair, then answered, "Profit is necessary to keep the mines open and everyone working, Evan, but in the wrong hands profit can be a dangerous weapon."

He could tell from the looks in their eyes that the boys did not understand his answer, but they didn't question him further nor did he feel a need to give a better explanation, at least not now. That time would come, for all three, but not now.

Chapter Three

Gwyneth tiptoed into the room carrying a tray with a cup of steaming tea and a slice of freshly baked bread smeared with strawberry jam. It was Dylan's favorite breakfast. She lowered the tray to the wooden chair that served as a small table, not wanting to awaken her son too suddenly but knowing that she would have to rouse him while the tea was hot.

"I'm awake, Mama," a voice whispered from beneath the thin blanket.

"Ah, what a boy you are, pretending to be sleeping," Gwyneth said softly, still afraid three months after Dylan's accident to startle him. "Strawberry jam it is this morning, my sweet. Made from those berries your father picked just yesterday."

Dylan slowly rolled over, looked at his mother, then at the tray. He was hungry, no doubt, but he wondered how that could be so when all he did was rest in bed. Three months upstairs, getting up only to use the chamber pot and perhaps stare out the window onto the street. And of course eat. His father had been bringing home books on loan from the community reading room, but Dylan found it difficult to turn the pages and hold the book in his lap while sitting up in bed. The stump of his left arm, still heavily bandaged, was too tender to use in any way. But he managed. And the reading made him sleepy so that he took naps in late morning and afternoon. His mother came up to check on him as often as her chores allowed, and she would sit and talk to keep him company. Dylan knew that such frequent visits were wearing her down because she worked so late into the night to keep up with the demands of her house. Often, when he heard her footsteps on the creaking staircase, he would lay down his book, turn his head on the pillow and feign sleep. He would hear the door open and know she was staring at him. Then the door would close gently and the steps would creak again.

"What time is it then, Mama?"

"Half past seven."

"Dark out, it looks," Dylan said, though the shade was still drawn.

"Yes, well, raining it was earlier, and thus cloudy."

"Papa has left for work?"

"Yes, an hour ago, and your brothers too, back on day shift now, you know."

"Yes, Rhys told me last week they'd be changing. So now, alone up here all day," Dylan sighed. He thought his statement would carry the message that he wanted his mother to visit more often, so he added, "But that is fine, Mama. More time to read, I guess."

"Aye, I've noticed the books flowing through, I have. Your father has been carefully checking the shelves at the reading room for books you would enjoy, although the selection there is sparse. Ah, but here, I've almost forgotten. Doctor Lewis stopped in a few minutes ago after visiting Mrs. Evans across the street — she's expecting her first baby, you know; false alarm, he said — anyway, he thinks you're strong enough to come downstairs now. Change of scenery, my boy. And for October, the weather has been mild. The rain has stopped; perhaps you'd like to sit out back. Your father has nailed together a chair from some old boards that you can sit on."

Dylan smiled, thinking too of a needed change, "Yes, Mama, a change of scenery..."

"What is it, boy?" she asked as the smile suddenly drooped from his face.

"Sitting outside, well, someone may see me and, well, what if they want to talk about this?" he asked, shoving his damaged arm into the air. "I don't know, Mama, perhaps I should stay up here a bit longer."

Gwyneth didn't want to push. She remembered how Doctor Lewis had explained to her and Glyn the aftereffects of a disabling injury, healing of the spirit as well as the body, he had said. "Go slowly, at Dylan's pace, not yours. He will know his limitations."

"Ah, well, whenever you're ready, Dylan."

"I don't know if I'll ever be ready for anything," he lashed out, his voice rising with a touch of anger. "What good am I like this? I'm a cripple for life. What can I do? How can I earn my keep? Who's paying for me even now?"

Mother and son went silent. Gwyneth reached across the bed and took his right hand in hers. Tears rolled down Dylan's face as he stared at the dark window. He tried to hide them with the stump of his arm. His mother's eyes glistened as she fought to hold back the sadness which was building inside her.

"It will be all right, my boy," she said, stroking his head with her other hand.

"No, Mama, it won't. I am not a child. I know what it costs for us to live. I know it took all four pays to keep us in this large house. Now there are only three," he said, sobbing uncontrollably. "Why didn't he just let me die down there? That would have been one less mouth to feed."

"Dylan!" she shouted with authority. "I never want to hear that again! Your father did what he had to because he loves you very much! And I love you. We all do. I know how much you're hurting but that will gradually disappear and you will find your talent elsewhere. The Bible has given you a strong faith; now is the time to use it. You need help and we are all willing to give that help. But in time others will need help too and you will be there, you will be strong, you will be a provider."

He was stunned by his mother's tone. He had never heard her speak so sharply. But her words flew right to his heart. And although he was not quite ready to accept the truth he knew that somehow he would have to find his way again. He felt like a child.

"I am sorry, Mama, it's just so difficult to accept this," he said, poking his bandaged arm into the air again.

"We all know that, Dylan, but everyone suffers greatly at some point in their life, some many, many times. When your father and I were growing up in Wales we heard stories from our grandparents and our parents about hardship they had witnessed in their lives. My grandmother in her childhood heard old women talk about their work in the mines. Late in the 1700s and early in this century, women and their daughters in Britain were the ones who carried the coal out. These women would walk down a slope carrying huge baskets. At pit bottom the miners would roll in huge chunks of coal. Sometimes it took two of the men, mind you, to hoist the basket onto the carrier's head. Then it was a long trek back up the slope to unload her burden. She might carry two tons of coal each day, six days a week. My grandmother knew of one woman in her village who was destitute because her husband had been killed underground. She and her daughters carried coal for years, ten hours a day, weeping from pain as they struggled up the steep slope. Money was so scarce that the three used only one candle to light their way, the mother clenching that in her teeth as she steadied the load on her head with both hands and the daughters trudging behind in the darkness."

Dylan studied his mother's eyes. He could see her pain in recalling the stories.

"For almost half of the nineteenth century, women were still hauling coal from the mines but by then wicker baskets with leather straps were being used. They knelt down, put the strap around their forehead and, with a miner's help, stood with the basket on their back. Some could carry as much as two hundred pounds of coal each trip. And tubs were used too.

Women and children—sometimes old or injured men—were put into harness with a leather belt around the waist. Hooked to the belt in front was a chain which went between the legs and was fastened to the tub. These haulers would crawl through the tunnels on hands and knees, dragging the heavy tubs to the surface."

"That's not still going on, Mama, is it?"

"No, women's work underground, at least over there, was stopped by law in 1842. That was good, but it also meant that many families and particularly widows faced starvation if they couldn't find some other type of work."

Dylan winced. He could picture in his mind a woman, or a child, or an old man, crawling through water and muck, over sharp, cutting slivers of coal, in the pitch blackness, perhaps victim to biting, hungry rats. He knew his mother had never worked in a mine but he also knew that her daily life was not that of women from higher stations. He had seen her, day after day, working in the kitchen at half past five in the morning as he and his father and brothers got dressed for work. He never really knew what time she got up, or what woke her on such a steady schedule. He just knew she was there, boiling tea regardless of the season, spreading bread with homemade butter or jam for summer breakfast and oatmeal soaked in steaming water in the winter. Before they left, she had packed four lunch boxes, each containing a tin of tea, a piece of bread, a bit of cheese and, when the family could afford it, a cut of beef left over from Sunday dinner.

In the early dawn, after the men had begun their mile walk to the mine, Gwyneth, like other housewives in the families of industrial workmen, began her household chores. First, she would walk a half-block to the neighborhood spigot and wait her turn with two dozen other women to draw clear water into a wooden bucket. That was to wash breakfast dishes and to scrub both the kitchen floor and dirty smudges she found on other floors in the house. The trip to the spigot was repeated many times each day, particularly on Monday when everybody washed clothes. Those buckets of water not only had to be carried home but also had to be heated in a large pot in the kitchen fireplace.

Each day in the women's week had something special. Tuesday was for ironing, Wednesday for baking, Thursday sewing, Friday cleaning house and Saturday shopping for food. Sunday was an exception. Sunday for a woman meant church, family time and, if needed, rest, provided she got three meals out for her household.

Families who were desperate even resorted to searching the nearby culm banks for bits of coal, a task usually carried out by mothers and their youngest children. Technically, it was stealing—even though most coal companies never picked any saleable coal from the culm—and trespassers could be arrested by private company police. Glyn had told her never to go to the culm banks to pick coal, not just because of the police and the fact that it was company property but because of the danger. He told her about a woman down in Schuylkill County who was walking atop a bank of very fine dust that gave way. "She sunk in like it was quicksand and suffocated," he had said. Gwyneth felt fortunate they never had to resort to picking coal, but she knew that so many others often had no choice, particularly in the cold of winter.

She had, however, experienced the need for extra income when the boys were still small and satisfied it by taking in laundry, ironing and sewing from those in the community who could afford those luxuries. She also started a garden back then, a practice she continued, finding work in the soil raising vegetables, a welcome break from work inside and a good way to save money. The savings were particularly noticeable when the family lived further to the southwest, down in Luzerne County, before Dylan was born. She found it much cheaper to grow food and raise chickens than to spend every pay of Glyn's on overpriced food in the company store, the "pluck me store" as the miners' families called them. But now, in Scranton, there was no company store, no need with all the private grocers and butchers in business. The Hyborne Coal Company had long ago closed its store when the superintendent found he could no longer pressure workers, particularly "those independent, hard-nosed, nasty contract miners and their ugly wives" from shopping there.

She recalled a visit to their former home from the man who ran the company store for the mine where Glyn used to work. He came on a Saturday night. "What a pleasant home and what a fine housekeeper you are, Mrs. Jones," the man said as soon as Glyn ushered him into the front room. "Beautiful curtains on the window, Mrs. Jones. I don't recall any like that at our store, but they are quite nice. Did you buy them elsewhere?"

Gwyneth looked at Glyn, not sure what to say but knowing full well the reason for the question. Glyn's face had no answer for her.

"Why, ah, no, Mr. Miller, I, ah, bought them at, ah, Mr. Reese's shop, down the way," she stammered.

"Ah, yes, Mr. Reese, the newcomer. Haven't met him, yet. But he does seem to be taking a few of our customers."

"Well, Mr. Miller, his price for the curtains was a bit lower than the company's..."

"Ah, yes, Mrs. Jones, but Mr. Reese has done nothing for the community, has he? Whereas our company provides a living wage for almost two hundred families at the colliery. It would be a shame for any one of our employees to lose his job and not be able to afford Mr. Reese's curtains, wouldn't it?"

Glyn stepped between his wife and Miller. "Just a woman's curiosity over a new shop, it is, Mr. Miller. On Monday, my wife will be at your store."

"Ah, I would certainly enjoy seeing you again, Mrs. Jones," Miller said as he opened the door and stepped out. "Good evening, Mr. Jones."

As the door closed, Gwyneth put her hands on her hips, her face flushed with anger. "Well, I'll not enjoy seeing his stingy face again. Him and his company's high prices, indeed!"

"Yes, my love, I agree, but all he has to do is put my name on a scrap of paper and send it to the superintendent. I'd be out of a job and we'd be out of a house. Someday, we'll be away from the company store and the company house, but for now we'll just play their greedy game."

By the time they moved to Scranton, the Jones family had two sons working and bringing home a weekly pay. They were able to buy a five-room privately owned house. The Hyborne Coal Company no longer owned houses for miners. What they did own had been sold, at a good profit, to recently arrived Slavic families who loaded the houses up with family and boarders—in some cases, twenty people in four rooms, including the kitchen—so they could afford the monthly payments. The buildings were similar to company houses throughout the coal fields—paper-thin walls which leaked freezing winter winds and summer rains, roofs patched and repatched to keep dripping to a minimum, paneless windows covered with heavy paper soaked in grease. Glyn had worked with one of the Slavic miners who told him, in very broken English, that he and his wife and three children lived in a small downstairs room of their house, next to the kitchen, while they rented the two upstairs bedrooms to fourteen other mine workers, some single and some married men who had left their families back in the old country until they could afford to send money for boat passage. "Seven work day, seven work night, share beds, two sleep floor," the Slavic miner explained when Glyn asked how fourteen men could sleep in two beds.

Glyn had told Gwyneth that on payday the man's wife stood at the front door with her apron spread and each man, before entering, had to drop in sufficient coins to pay for a week's lodging in advance and the preparation of his meals and work lunch. "Aye, and we do that as well," Gwyneth had responded.

"Yes, but you're getting coins from a husband and three sons, she from her husband and fourteen other men. Wouldn't you be rich now, girl," Glyn laughed.

It had been traditional among the Welsh, and other nationalities too, for the woman of the house to collect all of the coins and paper money the men living in her house received on payday, and, like the Slavic housewife, most simply spread their aprons as the husband, sons, other male relatives and boarders entered. While non-family members paid just for their room and board, husbands and sons dumped every penny into the outstretched cloth, although there was an unwritten agreement that husbands could deduct "traveling money," the price of a pint of beer on the way home from work. Sons were a different matter. Regardless of age, as long as a working son lived with his parents, his mother collected every bit of his pay and then gave him a small portion as spending money. The rest went into a coffee can, or an urn, or any receptacle deemed the family treasury, for rent or house payments, for food, for clothing, for fuel, for any expense that kept the family fed, housed and clothed.

Gwyneth hadn't asked but when Glyn told her the story of the Slavic family and their fourteen boarders she wondered how the woman managed to carry all of the water, probably from a well, to her house so that fifteen men could bathe every day or night after work. At her house, when Glyn, Evan, Rhys and Dylan took their turns in the round, wooden tub in the kitchen each night it was she who scrubbed their backs with a large brush. She didn't ask Glyn if he knew how many backs the Slavic woman scrubbed and she wasn't sure she really wanted to know.

The worst part of being a mining wife, she decided, was the soaking every night of clothing that was full of coal dirt, sweat, mine water, oil, grease and often an odor of urine. She didn't call it "washing" because none of the long johns, trousers, shirts, coats or socks ever got clean; they just got stiffer as the week went by. On wash day, each worker's extra set of work clothes was boiled. That got the dirt, sweat, mine water, oil and odor of urine out, although everything still felt greasy. Ah, but at least then it was soft greasy.

Except for Sundays (and sometimes even then), Gwyneth was exhausted at the end of each day. That was a feeling every housewife she knew had at the end of the day, and those who had an injured husband or a sick child had the extra burden of being nurse through the day, and often the night too. She felt fortunate in having a husband and three strong sons who were relatively free of illness and, until now, without any disabilities. They brought coal in for the fireplace and helped with the garden. And they always insisted she not lift anything heavy. Most women she knew in the coal community did not fare that well. But she always faced that possibility — as all women did — that a shrill blast of the breaker whistle at odd times in the shift could mean that her miners were dead, or dying, or badly mangled, or horribly burned. The breaker whistle was the one sound that frightened all women. When it went off during a shift, everyone rushed to the pit head, sometimes waiting long, agonizing hours in the cold or the heat, the rain or the snow, until the cage came to the top and its awful cargo was unloaded. It was the woman's responsibility to get her miner home and onto the kitchen table—either to treat his injuries until a doctor arrived or wash his body for burial. Gwyneth had been through that once, with her mother in Wales, when her father was killed by gas which had fizzed into his work space when a worker's pick went through a thin wall into a long-abandoned section of the mine. Now she had gone through it again with Dylan; at least this time there was life at the end of the day.

Gwyneth began to nod off as she sat on the bed holding Dylan's hand. Her fleeting thoughts of days gone by stopped abruptly when she caught herself falling. Dylan had drifted off too but his mother's sudden movement shook him awake.

"You didn't answer my question, Mama."

"I've forgotten it, Dylan."

"I asked: who is paying for me now?"

Gwyneth hesitated. She had known for days that she would have to tell Dylan before the boarders arrived, but she was not sure what his reaction would be. Now, she had to explain.

"Well, your father and I discussed the lack of your pay. We could manage," she said, though not convincingly.

"It's been three months, Mama, three months without my pay! But I'm still eating and taking up space," Dylan shouted. Years of living under strict but fair rules laid down by his father prevented a further outbreak. "I am sorry, again, I am sorry, Mama. It's just that I…"

"Dylan, my sweet, I understand. You are entitled to speak out."

"There's also the matter of payments for medical care. Doctor Lewis cannot treat me free of any charge."

"He's been very fair with us," Gwyneth said softly. She knew she could not delay. He was pressing for answers. "We are paying what we can and we will pay all that we owe."

"I need to find work! I must do something," Dylan said softly, though his teeth were clenched and his jaw was set. All three of Gwyneth's sons did that when they were trying to control their anger.

"We have worked something out," Gwyneth began, taking a deep breath. "A man and his son, both miners, are arriving from Wales in December. Pastor Evans announced after service more than a month ago that he had received a letter from a minister in Wales saying that the two were seeking a temporary home in Scranton until they could afford a house and bring the rest of the family over."

Dylan could see what was coming. "You're not taking in boarders!"

Gwyneth sighed, knowing full well that the plan would not be accepted easily.

"It's only temporary, Dylan, and will provide enough to tide us over."

"That's too much work for you, Mama! Two boarders to clean up after, two more lunches to pack, more meals to prepare, washing. It's too much for you," Dylan protested.

"It's already been settled. They'll be here by Christmas."

"But we have only three bedrooms," he protested again. "And this one," he said, looking around the room, "cannot squeeze a double bed. It's large enough only for this single bed, the chair and that small chest."

"It has been worked out, Dylan. You'll stay here. Evan and Rhys will stay in their room across the hall. The new men will share the other room."

"But what of you and Dada? Where will you sleep if you give up that room?"

"We will put up a temporary partition in the front room. It is quite large and we seldom use it, except when company arrives. When it's just family we all sit in the kitchen anyway," Gwyneth smiled, relieved that the plan at least was now out in the open.

"I don't like it, Mama; it's unfair to you. I need to find work. There must be a better way," Dylan stammered, searching for an answer that both he and his mother knew didn't exist.

"Shhh, it will be okay, Dylan, just temporary it is. And we'll be helping two new arrivals just like your father and I were helped by strangers when we arrived twenty years ago with little Evan in my arms and Rhys just kicking to be born. We owe someone a return on that favor."

The logic of returning a favor struck home with Dylan. He had heard the story many times of how his parents and his oldest brother were met at the train station in Scranton after the all-day ride from the New York docks by a delegation from a Welsh Congregational church near Wilkes-Barre. Like the newcomers coming to live with them, the arrangement had been made by a minister.

"We came for a better life for our family to this wonderful country," Gwyneth whispered. "And during the last twenty years we have made progress, steady progress. Now we have the opportunity to help someone else fulfill their dream."

Dylan still didn't like the idea of his mother taking on more work because of his disability, but he couldn't argue with the thoughts she had expressed. The solution, he knew, would come from his ability to care for himself.

"After breakfast, I think I'll go outside and sit in the chair Papa made," he said.

Gwyneth smiled. She could see a crack in her son's resistance to the outside world and knew, because she understood Dylan, he was coming out of his shell.

The low-slung chair had been placed on the wooden walkway that led ten feet from the kitchen door to the shed Glyn had built for storage and as a summer kitchen so that Gwyneth could escape the heat of cooking in the hot summer days. Dylan sat cautiously, making sure to lower himself on his right hand, careful not to touch the bandaged stump. He knew instantly that his father had spent many hours fashioning the wooden chair, cutting and carving, shaping and filing to fit the human form. It looked like it was built from scraps salvaged from the carpenter's shop on Luzerne Street, but his father's skill could turn any scraps — whether wood, or metal, or coal for that matter — into something useful or beautiful, or both.

When he touched bottom, Dylan felt the hardness of the wood, a far cry from the softness of his feather-filled mattress. Strangely, it was a pleasant feeling, a change from the mushiness of a bed lain in for months. It was strong, solid, a manly piece of furniture, he thought. For a moment Dylan even smiled with a sweeping sense of control, a wave of being alive again, a surge of victory over whatever had kept him confined to his room day after day. The smile jumped into a yelp, however, as he momentarily forgot his injury and subconsciously plopped both limbs down onto the broad boards which swept forward as armrests.

"Oh, gawd," he shouted when the stump hit the wood, then looked around quickly to see if his mother, or anyone else, had heard him. There was no response; he was alone with his pain and his feelings. He stared up into the ashen sky; its low clouds seemed to be rushing down on him, like the roof of a mine. Instinctively he pulled the handless limb to his chest as if to protect it from further injury. He thought he could feel his left hand again, a thought so strong that he looked down at the bandage to make sure, and wondered how long it would take before he would be whole in spirit again. Try as he might, Dylan could not shake the ill will he had developed against his father. He would have preferred death under the rock to life as a cripple. No one loves cripples; no one employs cripples. They were, he was convinced, like the lepers of old he had read about in the Bible, barely able to sustain themselves, useless to anyone else, unloved by family, by former friends, by total strangers.

"He has made me a leper," Dylan whispered softly to the menacing black sky. "My own father! Why did he do that?"

Something inside fought the notion. Something reminded him that his father was a good man, a man who always saved a bit of his workday lunch to give to orphans and children from starving families who begged food from workers leaving the colliery yard; a man who showed respect for the rights and the beliefs of all those around him; a man who avoided heavy drinking and gambling so that all the fruits of his labor could be put on his family's table. The forces within him struggled with the arguments from both sides, and deep down Dylan felt he had reached a conclusion: that his father was a decent man who made one terrible decision, to chop off his son's hand. This father who could build a large serviceable chair with scraps could not repair the damage to a boy's small hand.

Dylan put his right hand down on the armrest, pushed himself up and stood looking down between the houses on his street. Just six blocks away loomed the tall, soot-black breaker at Hyborne Coal Company's largest works, the Hyde Park colliery, and Dylan knew that somewhere hundreds of feet under that ground lay a piece of him that would forever bar him from living a normal life. And for that he blamed just one person.

He wanted to walk back Washburn Street, step through the gate at the colliery and show anyone and everyone what mining and a miner had done to him, but at the same time he did not want to leave the backyard of his home. Instead, he stared at the breaker and thought about the boys slaving away in that dust-clogged building. He was eight before he started work there but he had known boys as young as six, toiling twelve hours a day, six days a week, dressed in ragged clothes pinned together by mothers to keep their urchins from being naked. Barefoot some were, their families unable to afford more than one pair of shoes per child and those being saved for special occasions, church every Sunday to be sure but other events too, happy times like family get-togethers and weddings, and sad hours like funerals.

He vividly remembered his first days in the breaker in 1881 — a little chap, the breaker boss had called him, barely weighing sixty pounds — dressed mostly in hand-me-downs from Rhys which earlier had been hand-me-downs from Evan. The trousers were patched in the seat and both knees and the cuffs were worn to a frazzle; the tattered coat, whose sleeves had to be rolled up, was held together in front with a thin rope his mother had run through the button holes; his dai cap, buttoned down in front, came from a clothing bin at church; the dark shirt had belonged to Evan but somehow managed to bypass Rhys; and for the winters a threadbare cardigan and stringy scarf. But he had boots, new boots in fact, with rags stuffed in the toes because they were bought big so they'd last a few years as his feet grew. He recalled his mother taking down the boots from a shelf in the kitchen, the smell of new leather oozing from the paper they had been wrapped in, and then saying: "Your father told me: 'If I have to send my son to work in the breaker, by heaven, he will not go barefoot. He will have new boots.'" The hobnail boots were Dylan's prize possession. He hoped they would be shiny forever but by the end of his first shift, with his boots

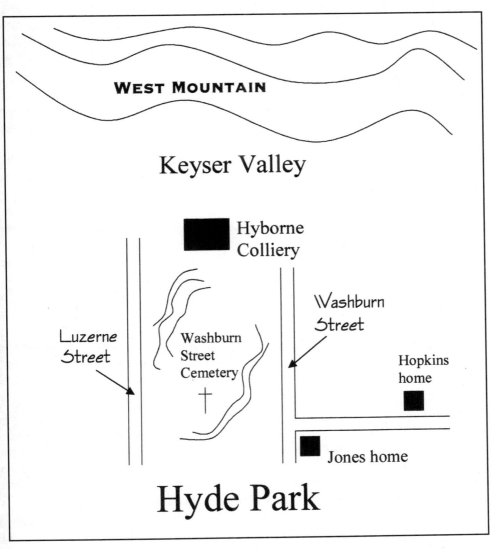

Hyde Park neighborhood of Scranton with the Hyborne
mine, the cemetery and the Jones and Hopkins homes.

Map courtesy of Jonathan G. Williams

stuck in the chute, sliding coal and slate had chewed into the leather and muddied them beyond recognition. That night, racked with pain from sitting on the wooden bench for almost twelve hours, his fingers bloodied and raw from the sharp-edged rocks, he cried. "A hard day, was it, my son?" his father had asked, the pipe withdrawn from his mouth and the Bible he had been reading put into his lap. Dylan, not wanting to admit his exhaustion, replied, "No, Dada, but my new boots, look, ruined they are." The pipe went back into his father's mouth and the Bible was raised back to reading level. "No, not ruined, boy, just the sign of a working man bringing home a wage for his dear old mother," his father smiled. Dylan, through his tears of pain, smiled too.

He recalled the quick explanation of his new job from the breaker boss, a former miner whose left foot had been amputated after he was pinned against the side of a gangway by a runaway string of coal cars. Hopping on his peg leg and his booted right foot, old Griff Reese had bounced up through the dusty breaker on boards which crossed the chutes, kicking a boy here and there with the wooden peg when they didn't move from his path. Dylan followed, watching Reese scamper while trying to keep his balance on the boards. "Be damn careful you don't fall into the chutes; you'd end up under a pile of coal," Reese shouted above the roar. A boy sitting nearby who chuckled loudly at Reese's warning got a wrap on the back of his hands from the broomstick Reese carried. "Work, boy, no laughing or talking. Pay attention to that run." At the top of the large room, Reese stopped next to a track which ran in through an opening. "Look here, Jones, those cars coming up the incline from the pit are dumped here into the iron chutes," he said, pointing through a grimy window and then to the chutes at their feet. Dylan could see the cars were attached to a large chain between the rails which slowly hauled them up a wooden bridge some seventy feet above ground level. Once inside the breaker and on a downward slant, each car's front-end gate was opened and two men with shovels helped gravity slide their black loads into the chutes. Thick clouds of dust arose as each car was emptied and then began its return trip to pit bottom.

Dylan watched as the coal slipped between huge iron teeth on a revolving cylinder which chewed the rock into smaller chunks. The noise of the grinder was almost deafening and Dylan found he could not hear what Reese was saying, only knowing that the boss was pointing down at the teeth and shaking his head. As they stepped down along the wall from bench to bench, Dylan could see the coal moving across metal grates and falling through holes of various widths which were roughly the sizes of the coal he knew was sold in the public market—rice, pea, stone and egg. Below him on the sloped floor the coal slid down other metal chutes. Above the chutes sat breaker boys on the benches, their feet slowing the coal to

**Breaker boys separate slate from coal under the
supervision of two men in a noisy, dirty breaker building.**

MG369, Pennsylvania Historical and Museum Commission,
Bureau of Historic Sites and Museums, Anthracite Museum Complex

give them time to pick out the worthless slate and toss it into a refuse chute. There were five boys for each chute, one below the other, so that by the time the coal reached the last boy at the bottom it, hopefully, had been picked clean. Dylan followed Reese down over the steplike seats to an empty spot. The boss motioned him down on the seat, then yelled in his ear: "Pick out the slate and don't miss any. We quit for lunch at one o'clock. No talking, boy."

Lunchtime meant leaving the breaker to play or fight on the culm bank outside and to eat a clean lunch of bread and cheese and cold tea with filthy hands. At that first lunch he had asked another lad what happened to the boy whose seat he now occupied. "Went down to another job, I suppose?"

"Went up to heaven," came the answer.

"Died?"

"Aye, I saw old Griff point you to the grinder and shake his head. Yesterday, that boy went running up to the top when the whistle blew for lunch. Chasing a boy who spit on him, he was. The grinder hadn't been turned off yet. He slipped. I heard him scream, even above the other noise. It chewed him up in pieces."

Dylan gulped, feeling his lunch come back up his throat. He gagged, turned his head and vomited. Then he spit out, took a gulp of tea to calm his stomach and stared at the boy. "I heard nothing about that."

"No, they kept that a big secret. Old Griff had to tell his folks, had to tell them there was no body, that pieces showed up below mixed in with the coal, but not enough left to bury."

Dylan gulped again, but held down what remained inside. He later learned from Rhys that breaker accidents were frequent, usually a crushed finger or two, or a broken hand, but there had been at some breakers the loss of fingers, or hands, or feet, usually by boys playing near moving machinery. But a death, a gruesome death at that. They happen too, Rhys had said.

After less than two weeks of breaker work, Dylan's fingertips were tough. In the third week he learned to chew borrowed tobacco and smoked his first cigarette, though he dropped both habits quickly because he had no money to support either. Smoking, though, became routine years later, after he started work as a laborer. And he learned some words he had never heard before but which he quickly dropped from his vocabulary after using them in front of his father and receiving a stern lecture. All in all, being a breaker boy was an education, a form of schooling imposed on some twelve thousand boys like Dylan in northeastern Pennsylvania alone.

He also noticed girls at that time, partly due to the stories told by the older boys at the breaker. Such stories, he found, did not go over well with his father and, in fact, Dylan was told never to repeat them in front of his mother.

His daydreaming stopped suddenly. He stared at the breaker from the yard behind his home, wondering if the breaker boys of today were the same roughhousing, cursing, tobacco-chewing urchins of his own childhood, and how many of them carried mining scars as he did.

Of the girls he remembered from his three years of public schooling most were still working in the mills in center city or over on the South Side, there now eight or nine years. But several were married too, most by the age of fourteen to men six or seven or eight years older, in unions arranged by their parents. In fact, Dylan knew three girls in his neighborhood who were at seventeen mothers of several children, serving their miner husbands, caring for their infant children, cleaning and cooking and gardening and growing older by the day. In recent years, going to and from work daily, he passed the small shack outside the colliery and usually saw Annie Parsons busy at her chores, her three babies always nearby. Annie looked to be in her thirties, Dylan often thought as he waved hello. But he knew she was now just past sixteen.

Girls, girls! Could he face another girl with this hideous arm? Embrace her without a feeling of revulsion on her part? How would he ever support a wife? He glanced at the chair his father had built, turned again to look at the breaker and thrust his arms violently upward. "Why? Why?" he yelled.

"Dylan, what is it?" his mother shouted from the back door. "Are you alright?" she asked more softly, assured from seeing Dylan that he was probably just releasing his pain. She knew that would come. Doctor Lewis had told her and Glyn that the boy would have to make his feelings known, perhaps to a wide group of people, not just his family, before he could learn to live with only one hand.

He hadn't meant to startle his mother. He did not blame her for his condition. He had felt the frustration welling up inside and could no longer contain it.

"I'm fine, Mama. Just needed to expand my lungs a bit, that's all," he said, trying to force a smile.

"I understand, my boy. Would you like me to fetch one of the books your father brought from the reading room yesterday?"

"No, thank you, Mama. I think I'll just sit here for awhile and enjoy the fresh air."

"Ah, just like a min...," Gwyneth caught herself but she knew Dylan understood what she was going to say. "I'm sorry, Dylan, I was just thinking of how you and your father would walk up across the cemetery and stand in the breeze to clear the dust." The thought brought tears to her eyes.

Dylan lowered his eyes. He did not want to see her cry, nor did he want to cry. But her words brought back happy times when he and his father — and his brothers when they worked the day shift — each day took a shortcut through the Washburn Street Cemetery and his father would stop on top of the hill, take a deep breath and say: "Always a breeze here, lads, always good to get the dust out of your lungs. Someday I'll rest here eternally; there will always be fresh air but no more mining."

His father's dream was coming true for Dylan. There would be no more mining. But what truly concerned him was the recurring thought that perhaps eternity for him was not too far away. He had never entertained such ideas before and they scared him now. He looked up at his mother's face. She had wiped the tears away and was smiling at him. He saw hope in that face. He saw courage. He saw a future.

Chapter Four

The summer and fall of 1890 was a difficult period for Glyn Jones. As much as he tried to concentrate on his work his mind kept rolling back to the accident and thoughts of what else he could have done to save Dylan, in one piece. Pastor Evans, Brandon McSweeney, Otto Bremmer, the other miners who helped that mid-July day, even young Jamie, had told him over and over that he did the only thing possible to save his son's life. But he felt the resentment from Dylan, the one-sided talks they had over the last three months with him trying to encourage the boy — or apologize, he never knew which — and Dylan responding briefly, if at all. He thought bringing books from the community reading room would be a way to reach his son, for it gave Dylan something to do during the long recuperative period. And he knew the boy enjoyed reading; in fact, words they exchanged about the books seemed to be the only positive communications between them, even if it was only: "I've finished this one, Dada. Thank you." He wondered if Dylan was reading every book because he truly enjoyed the wide variety of subjects and novels his father had selected or because he was trying to be polite.

"We talk about them during the day," Gwyneth had told him. "He does read every one, Glyn. I know he appreciates them."

But Jones still wondered.

The only consideration that did swing him back to concentrating on his job was Jamie. He did not want his laborer to suffer from an accident — no matter how small — on account of his neglect as a contract miner. In fact, he sometimes felt he was being overly cautious, whether from fear or concern he did not know.

Jamie never brought the subject up, asking only each day, and politely, about Dylan's condition, not about the accident, nor Jones's actions, nothing but "How is your son today, Mr. Jones?" He wasn't angered by the question day after day. He felt that Jamie truly was interested in Dylan's welfare, having been involved in the rescue and being about the same age. And, from time to time, Jamie also inquired about Mrs. Jones, and about the other Jones sons. In a sense, Jamie Kerrigan, without a father, was an extension of Jones's family. There was a paternal connection; both felt it. And there was a professional connection of worker to worker, not miner-boss to laborer; though neither ever spoke of it. Still, Jamie maintained that proper distance between man and boy, that aura of respect he had been taught at home. There was no other way to address his boss but as "Mr. Jones," even in moments of hidden anger, lighthearted kidding or appre-hension. Always "Mr. Jones" first.

Their relationship had blossomed into a teacher-pupil status, more advanced than most mining teams where too many miners had nothing but disdain for their laborers because that's how they had been treated when they were subservient to a contract miner. Jones was not one to leave his laborer working below ground alone as many did. Some men he knew worked very quickly to cut enough coal for a day's wage, then left, leaving the laborer to load the cars and clean up the room. At forty-two he was getting too old to work that fast but, still and all, it had always been his method to work with the laborer until both were finished for the shift.

And as they worked, Jones taught the boy everything he knew about mining: how to cut the coal face; when to use a pick to bring down a loose wall and when to use explosives to do it; how to test a roof and to timber it safely; what was needed to test for gas; and, most important of all, having the foresight to see an accident developing and determining a course of action, whether staying to fight or to flee.

As a boy working in the Welsh mines, he had been told that American mines were safer, that the pay was better and that living was easier. None of it, he found as a young immigrant, was true, particularly about safety. He and Gwyneth had first lived in Plymouth, near Wilkes-Barre, arriving there on June 15, 1869, after a twelve-day voyage from Southampton on England's south coast to New York City. Unable to work as a miner—due to his recent arrival as an untested immigrant and as yet unlicensed by the state—he found employment as a company-employed assistant to the black-smith at nearby Avondale's Steuben Shaft, which meant he traveled un-derground only when repairing equipment and spent most of his working day helping the smithy above ground.

Less than three months after his arrival, Jones witnessed—from the safety of ground level—the worst mining disaster he had ever heard of. It came on September 6, just four and a half years after America had bled itself through a long civil war.

"One of the early methods of ventilating a mine was to build a furnace at the bottom of a shaft," he explained to Jamie one day as they ate their noon meal. "The hot air rose to the surface pulling bad air up and forcing fresh air down to fill the vacuum. The problem at Avondale, mind you, was that the shaft carried men in and out of the mine, it carried coal out and it contained the upcast and downcast systems for the air supply — everything in one shaft. There was no other exit, and that always bothered me. To make matters worse, the Delaware, Lackawanna and Western Railroad, which operated that colliery, had built its breaker right over the shaft, to save on the hauling distance."

Jamie chewed his bread very slowly, taking in every word from Jones.

"There were one hundred ten men underground early in the morning, down more than three hundred feet, they were. I was stoking the blacksmith's forge when shouts of 'fire, fire' began outside. Smoke was rising in a steady stream from the shaft and the boys in the breaker were running about, hurrying to escape. Before anything could be done flames were whipping through the wooden headframe, fed by grease on the wheels and pulleys above the cage. The breaker was emptied of workers before it too caught fire and soon everything above the shaft was burning."

"How did the fire start, Mr. Jones?"

"Some said it was sparks from the wood they were burning at pit bottom to light off the furnace. They claimed the sparks set off timbers in the shaft cribbing and the fire roared up to the headframe and then the breaker. It happened very quickly."

"My father told me about Avondale. He said sixty-one from Scranton were killed."

"Aye, Jamie, but there were others too, all one hundred ten who were below, including a boy ten, one age twelve and two fourteen. And no chance to get them out. By the time firemen got there from all of the surrounding towns it was out of control. Flames were jumping a hundred feet in the air and the breaker was rocking in the wind created by the updraft. Soon everything began to fall — the cage, the headframe, the winding gear, the breaker, everything aflame — falling down the shaft. Then I knew for sure there would be no hope, no way of saving them because no fresh air was going down, all they had to breathe was smoke and fire."

Jones took a gulp of tea, his body shaking as he recalled that scene more than twenty years earlier. He was silent, slowly munching on his bread and wondering whether he should be telling Jamie all of the details of that horrible event.

"My father came in to help with the rescue, ah, with the attempt to rescue, Mr. Jones."

A mule pulls a trip of loaded coal cars through a gangway to the mine shaft elevator. The boy seated in the front drives the mule while the boy in the back puts wooden sprags between the wheels to slow the cars.

MG369, Pennsylvania Historical and Museum Commission,
Bureau of Historic Sites and Museums, Anthracite Museum Complex

"Oh, your father was there too. Yes, there were many ready to help, some estimate in the thousands."

"He went down to help bring the dead out, Mr. Jones. He said the saddest sight was a man named John Burtch with his arm around his boy, John Junior, only twelve he was. They died together."

"Aye, I remember the name, but I didn't see them."

"You went down too, Mr. Jones?"

He nodded, recalling the ghastly sight of sixty-seven victims found in one area, all dead of suffocation.

"Some of the men still had wives and children in Wales, waiting for a letter from America with money for them to book passage. A very sad day indeed, Jamie."

"I don't understand how you could get down that shaft. My father never said."

"Well, it took hours of pouring water down to put out the flames. Then they lowered a dog and a lamp. When they hauled up, the dog was still alive and the lamp still lit, so it showed no gas present. It was early evening, as I recall, when they lowered one miner in a basket to take a look. They only left him down there for a few minutes but it was long enough for him to figure that about forty feet at shaft bottom was filled with debris. Then they sent a gang of us down with tools to clear the debris. Once we reached bottom, we moved about sixty yards up the main gangway. We found three dead mules in their stalls but no people. At the first ventilation door we rapped with a club and waited for a response; there was none. The foreman in charge didn't want to open the door for fear of fanning any flames beyond it and, exhausted as we were by then, he ordered us back to the surface."

Jamie had stopped chewing. He couldn't take his eyes off Jones as the story unfolded.

"That evening another gang was lowered but they detected gas and soon returned topside. That meant taking time to install a ventilating fan with canvas hose down the shaft to blow fresh air in. Another gang of miners was lowered. They found the fan had stirred the fire in the furnace and was spreading fumes; it took them all night to extinguish the flames. Several attempts were made on the second day to find survivors or bodies but gases were still accumulating and it took until midnight to clear the air sufficiently for searching. It was two o'clock on the morning of the third day before the first two bodies were located. Then it was decided to send down several gangs, split into four-man teams, so I volunteered again. Sometime after six o'clock one of the teams found most of the bodies lying behind a wall built by the men in an attempt to keep the gases out."

Jones paused and swallowed as he thought about the discovery.

"The other teams were summoned. By the time I got to that area, a search was being made to find anyone still alive. None were, poor devils. We found some boys in their father's arms; some kneeling as if in prayer; some with their mouths to the floor, as if to take in any fresh air below the gas. Some of the older men were just sitting, perhaps knowing their fate and simply waiting for the last breath. It took us until noon to bring the last body to the surface."

Jones could feel the tears welling up, even after twenty years. In his lifetime, he had carried many a dead miner or laborer or boy from the pits, but never had he lifted so many onto blankets for the last ride to the surface.

Minutes passed as Jones chewed on his bread, silent now as the horror of the past crawled through his entire being. Jamie looked down, his light shining away from his miner's face. He knew this man well enough to know when questions could not be asked and comments could not be made.

"But, lad, all such tragedies do lead to better times," Jones sputtered finally. "Some good came from Avondale."

"How so, Mr. Jones?"

"It brought about some changes in state law. Five months before Avondale, the Pennsylvania Legislature debated a mine safety law which called for adequate ventilation and for the appointment of mine inspectors. A state senator from Luzerne County did not want the law to apply to the entire hard-coal region, so when it passed on April 12 it affected only Schuylkill County. That left Avondale out. I think the owners were in the senator's pocket. The governor, John Geary, put the blame for Avondale right where it belonged, with the mine operators. The miners demanded changes and that very same senator from Luzerne County led the fight in Harrisburg for a new law. I guess his conscience bothered him."

Jamie chuckled, almost to himself, not wanting to question Jones nor to interrupt him.

"By March the third of the following year, the Legislature had passed a law which applied to the whole anthracite region. From then on, it was illegal to have a mine without at least two openings. There was a bit of outrage when the public learned that ventilation underground was often supplied by nothing more than the movement of coal cars, and mules, and men. But, you know, Jamie, it still took some companies more than a year to comply. That's politics and money for you!"

"But the accidents have continued, Mr. Jones," Jamie protested.

"Aye, and we'll always have accidents. It's the nature of the business. Working underground is unlike any other job. It's dangerous to begin with, but when you add greedy owners, uncaring operators and stupid mistakes by workers it becomes a daily struggle to stay alive. We work in almost total darkness except for a flame on our caps. Sometimes we're up to our knees in water. There's always the chance of gas and fires and roof falls and squeezes of the walls. I'm not trying to frighten you, Jamie, just laying the truth before your eyes. You be careful, lad."

The boy smiled as Jones's lamp beam touched his face. He could almost hear his father's voice weaving those words of caution.

"Work now, lad. We've already extended this meal too long."

"Yes, Mr. Jones."

As he turned to the coal face with his pick, Jones thought of the thousands of widows and orphans of miners left with nothing and the lucky few who were given perhaps two hundred dollars from the most generous of owners. He knew mining villages up and down the valley which had their "widow's row," an area of dilapidated houses which widows struggled to maintain for their children. Even injured miners, unable to work, had to scrounge a living as best they knew how, often depending on relatives or friends to keep them from starving.

He recalled how in the 1870s mine superintendents often stopped all maintenance work, claiming it was cutting into time needed to produce coal. But the few inspectors the state had hired argued that by not keeping drains open, or not driving needed airways, or taking out pillars that were still needed for support, a mine could be ruined in short order, and, in most situations, owners relented and ordered their superintendents to resume such work.

But owners still saw no need to hire competent men, that is those who understood mining from the bottom up, to be superintendents or foremen. The criteria for such jobs included toughness, an understanding of the need to make money by selling coal, and a willingness to not question the owner's orders. Still, some owners, by design or by accident, managed to hire those who were qualified, but everyone in that category whom Jones knew had been a miner first. In fact, Otto Bremmer had told him, in Germany a man could not take charge of a mine unless he first had three years of scientific and engineering education, including the study of geology, chemistry and mapping, and to get into such schools he first had to be a miner.

The only progress made in Jones's lifetime, in addition to the Pennsylvania law, that he could see was the fact that mine accidents became matters of public record through the newspapers, through miners' organizations and through common street knowledge. It had not always been that way. He knew that decades earlier, at least in Great Britain, government authorities did not have to be notified of mine accidents, fatal or not. In fact, outside questions about accidents often infuriated owners, who felt that such public knowledge only frightened other workers.

The following day, during their noon meal, Jamie resumed the conversation.

"Mr. Jones, my father said that the miners wanted to get all of the bodies out of Avondale, that they didn't want to leave any unrecovered because they didn't want to encounter ghosts. And I still hear stories about fatal accidents and the importance of finding the bodies."

"Superstitions, Jamie, but powerful. It's a blessing to the family to recover a man's body for a proper burial, although that still means being laid to rest under the ground. I don't really believe in the ghost theory, but many do and I respect that. And when any man claims he's seen a ghost most other men will leave the pit for that day."

"Why do you think some people see ghosts, Mr. Jones?"

"I'm not sure they really do. I've never met anyone who said they've actually seen a ghost. It's noises mainly, someone tapping on a wall, or wailing, or groaning. But think, lad, of your own time down here. There's always someone working nearby tapping into a vein. And wailing to me is almost like the sound of air, or worse gas, leaking through a hole. Groaning? Aye, when a mine settles, and they all do, the timbers will groan to let you know what's happening. So perhaps there are explanations for all of it."

"Which kind of accident is the worst, Mr. Jones?"

"I'd say fire. You can run from most roof falls or squeezes, as you saw with my boy's accident. If water breaks in from abandoned works you can sometimes climb to higher levels, unless the water comes so fast and furious you don't have time to outrun it. Explosions are usually limited to one area and so many can escape the blast. And it's possible, given time, to wall yourself off from gas. But fire is the worst, Jamie, for we work with combustible wood used for timbering, the danger of sparks or flame when gas is present, and the coal which will burn for a long time. Fire keeps moving, keeps consuming anything in its path, and destroys the oxygen we all need. The only way to extinguish a major fire is by flooding a mine, but owners resist that if possible because it means shutting down until it's all pumped out, repairing damaged timbers and track, replacing mules. It's a terrible expense."

"And terrible for the miners. No work and no pay."

"Aye, right you are, lad, terrible for us too."

"And is it all worth it, Mr. Jones?"

The miner was taken back by the boy's question. He wasn't just seeking information; this time he was looking for an opinion, perhaps a guide to his own future.

"Well now, ask yourself. I pay you one dollar and fifteen cents a day, if we send up at least five carloads. What is your time and your energy worth? I get two dollars for that same day. With that my wife and I can eat fairly well and we keep relatively warm in winter. We support our church to the best of our ability and we give gifts to ourselves and our sons for birthdays and Christmas. Beyond that we have little money left at the end of the year. But we manage and we are happy. The problem is that every family is not managing, many because of a death or injury in the mines, yours included. Is it worth it? Well, I must say that life could be easier, a bit better in many ways, but I am not complaining about my work. My wife, however, toils too hard as do most all wives and mothers of working men. Do I hope better for my sons, and for you, Jamie? Most certainly, yes, more education, better jobs, something above ground perhaps. But where is the boost that is needed to move from one rung of the ladder to the next? Someday, it will be there; someday there will be equality; someday there will be an understanding for the needs of those who are held in check by the whims of the wealthy."

Jamie, struck by the absence of hope in the answer, chewed on his bread for awhile. Then he said, "I don't see me ever getting out of the mines, Mr. Jones."

"Do you want to, Jamie?"

More silence, then: "I don't know, sir. I'm not afraid of the work or the dangers. I sometimes think I'd like to be a farmer. I like the sun and the fresh air and animals, all kinds of animals."

"You've never worked on a farm. How do you know you'd like it?"

"It's not the work, Mr. Jones. It's where you do the work, out under the sky and the sun, not in the dark."

"And the money? I have no idea how much farmhands earn."

"Nor I, Mr. Jones. But, ah there, just a pipe dream. No sense talking of dreams, is there? Stuck where we are, my father used to say. We're the coal king's slaves, he told me."

Jones turned his head toward the boy's face. He saw a countenance of hopelessness.

"Jamie," he called.

The boy looked up, saw a smile and felt a wave of support wash through his soul.

"Don't ever give up your dreams, Jamie. Life is ever changing and your time will come. Your dreams are your ticket to a better life. Bondage this may be, but we are slowly changing it. We are working toward freedom."

The boy smiled too, feeling deep inside that this man somehow always knew what was right and what was coming.

"Aye, and back to work then, Mr. Jones?"

"Back to work then, lad."

Chapter Five

Dylan found that the cold of a Scranton winter brought great pain to the stump of his arm. Just a "growing pain compounded by cold air," Doc Lewis had told him. "Keep your arm warm and don't worry about it. Nothing unusual."

But Gwyneth, as any mother would be, was sympathetic to her son's discomfort. She cut a sleeve from an old woolen sweater that hung on the back door, a sweater she used in freezing weather to run out to the shed for a bit of wood when the coal in the fireplace died overnight. It already had large holes in both elbows, and moths had eaten bits and pieces until it was no more than a few feet of open space surrounded by a few strands of wool.

"I can do without one sleeve," she told Glyn when he asked why she was cutting it. "Making a glove for Dylan's left arm."

"A glove?"

"Well, a sleeve really, sewn shut on one end, like a mitten over his arm," she told her husband, still avoiding the use of the word "stump." "See, like this," she said, pulling the foot-long bag over her own left arm.

"He'll jam his arm down inside his coat pocket anyway, just to hide it."

"I know, Glyn, I know. He's still quite sensitive about it, but this will give him some more protection from the cold."

"Right you are, girl, a mother's intuition, is it? You're a sweet one, you are."

"Oh go on with you," Gwyneth blushed, although she loved hearing Glyn's praise.

"Still out, is he, and getting late it is," Glyn said, pulling the watch from the small pocket in the front of his trousers. "Nine o'clock now. Is he down at the reading room again?"

"Every day and taking a bit of bread and cheese with him for supper."

"I seldom see him, except on Sundays. Sleeping he is when I go to work and down at the reading room when I get home."

"And usually asleep before he gets home," Gwyneth added. "Are you upset that he's not here?"

"Well, I get the feeling he is still trying to avoid me."

"And you're hurt by that?"

"Not hurt really, just puzzled about how I can get close to my son again. I know he blames me for his condition but..."

"Enough of that, Glyn. He's still confused by why it had to be him who was injured. Give him time."

"Then why does he avoid me?"

Gwyneth sighed and looked at the saddened face of her husband.

"Because," she stammered, "because when he sees your face he sees the mine roof coming down."

"Good gawd, woman, how do I ever get him past that?"

"Time, Glyn, time to heal, my love. He wants to talk to you, I know he does. But it's too soon, Glyn, too soon."

Jones buried his head in his hands and sobbed.

"I had no choice at all. I could not let him die. There was no other way."

"Everyone knows that, Glyn, and I think Dylan knows it too. But he's trying to get on with his life. He told me this morning that he's been reading about this area's history. Did you know that the Lackawanna and Wyoming anthracite coal basin is walled in by the low ranges of the Allegheny Mountains and that it is drained by the Lackawanna and Susquehanna Rivers?"

Jones stared at his wife. She was smiling. He could never resist that smile. It always raised his spirits.

"Oh, come now, girl. Are you going to give me a history lesson?"

"Ah, Mister Smarts, you might learn something. Dylan told me that last night. Did you know that the city of Scranton's original name was Slocum Hollow?"

Jones began to laugh, "I know what you're trying to do."

"And that Colonel George W. Scranton and his brother, Selden, came to this area from New Jersey and bought up a great deal of land in 1840?"

"I get your point, woman," Jones laughed again.

"Or that Lackawanna County was formed in 1878 when it broke away from Luzerne County?"

"Aha, yes, I did know that. We were living here when that happened. Caught you, didn't I?" Jones shouted as he grabbed his wife about the waist and pulled her close. "Enough history now, my love."

He wrapped his arms about her and she pulled his head down for a long, tender kiss.

"So, our son is making progress," Jones said softly as their lips parted.

"Aye, Glyn, he's going to be alright, I do believe."

"Then off to bed I am. An old history lover like me needs his rest," Jones murmured as he kissed his wife again and then strode toward the stairs.

"And did you know that the boroughs of Hyde Park and Providence merged with the borough of Scranton in 1866 to form the City of Scranton?" she yelled after him.

"And did you know that Hyde Park was named after Hyde Park, New York, and not after the Hyde Park in London?" he yelled back.

"Of course, I'm up on all the local history," she laughed.

"Goodnight, love," Jones shouted.

"Sleep well, my darling," she whispered sweetly.

A half hour later Dylan came home, a smile amid the red blast of winter on his face.

"Cold then, is it, my boy?"

"Aye, freezing, and not yet the middle of December, Mama."

"And why are you grinning, Dylan?"

"Mrs. Todd, the director at the reading room, asked if I knew anything about carpentry. She needed heavier shelves built but had no one to do the work. She got the boards and nails as a donation from Mr. Thomas, the carpenter, but he had no time to build the shelves."

Gwyneth was stunned, but happily so. Dylan had performed no physical labor since his accident, not even to bring a stick of firewood or a bucket of coal into the house, and she had not pressed him to do so. Nor did his father or brothers.

"So you built the shelves?" she asked with a hint of surprise in her voice.

"Well, started tonight, I did. And I can do it, Mama," Dylan exclaimed. "I went to Mr. Thomas's shop on Main Avenue today to ask the borrow of a hammer. He asked how I would hold a nail. Hadn't thought of that, I said. So he sent down to old Elias, the blacksmith on Luzerne Street, with a note telling Elias what to do. He made this," Dylan said as he unwrapped an oily old rag.

In the rag was a piece of very thin flat iron, about a half-inch wide and perhaps two feet long. One end was curled around in a circle perpendicular to the long section. The other end was split into a v-shaped wedge no more than an inch long and tapering down from a half inch. In the middle of the long section was a bit of rawhide cut very thin and at least two feet long.

Gwyneth stared at the strange contraption, held it, examined it closely and then asked, "And what does this do?"

"It holds nails, Mama. Look, I'll show you."

Dylan unbottoned his coat and slipped out of the sleeves, pulled off his scarf and dropped his cap on the floor. He took the iron piece, bent his left elbow and slipped his arm through the circle until it touched the elbow. Then he wrapped the rawhide strap around his arm near the wrist once, twice, three times and pushed the end under the wrapping. Finally, he reached into his right pants pocket and withdrew a nail, put it against the wall and held it in place with the wedge. With his right hand he pretended to hammer the nail into the wall.

"Job done!" he shouted, but not too loudly.

Gwyneth was astounded, not just at the device Elias the blacksmith had fashioned but at her son's willingness to move beyond his disability.

"And you've tried it? It works?" she asked excitedly.

Dylan put the nail back into his pocket, slipped the contraption off and responded, "Well, as long as I can get one or two taps to start the nail. Elias said he could adjust the arm a bit if it's too cumbersome."

"Adjust your arm?"

"My new arm, Mama, my iron arm. I can even use it to steady a board for sawing."

Gwyneth was flabbergasted. She stood, her mouth open, looking at the iron arm, then at Dylan, then at the arm again. It took several minutes for her to regain her composure.

"You don't mind the weight? That iron arm feels a bit heavy...," she began but then hesitated, not wanting to sound negative. "Of course, with your muscles I'm sure you don't mind it. Just heavy for me, you know."

Dylan began to wrap the arm back in the old rag but his mother stopped him.

"Here, I have just the thing," she said, rummaging under the kitchen cupboard for an old leather bag Evan had found lying on the street. "See if it fits into this."

"Close enough," Dylan answered as he placed the arm inside the bag with only the wedged end sticking out.

"Your father will be so happy for you, Dylan."

The boy's smile immediately drained from his face at his mother's words.

"Yes, I'm sure Dada will be pleased," he said as he picked up his coat, scarf and cap and placed them on the peg next to the kitchen door. "Almost ten o'clock, Mama. I think I'll go upstairs and read. By the way, did you know coal was first discovered in this valley back in 1799?"

Gwyneth smiled, took Dylan's face in her hands and kissed his fore-head, "No, my sweet boy, I did not know that, but I'm glad you told me. Good night."

By the time Gwyneth had finished her chores and climbed the stairs Glyn was fast asleep. She would not wake him to talk about Dylan's iron arm; that would have to wait until morning. Glyn, along with Evan and Rhys, would be up at half past five, ready for another day in the pit, time enough to talk then.

At five in the morning, Gwyneth was back downstairs, stoking the ashes and a few dimmed lumps of coal in the fireplace. She had thrown an old black shawl around her shoulders to ward off the morning cold, put the teapot on to boil, and was buttering thick slices of bread for the three lunch boxes when Glyn came lumbering down the steps dressed only in his long johns and wrapped in a blanket.

"Morning, love," he said as he stepped into the kitchen, kissed his wife on the back of her head and flopped down onto a chair.

"Aye, and some greeting that is," she said, cupping his head in her hands and kissing him gently on the lips. "Problem, is it?"

"Blooming arthritis again in my back. I didn't sleep well and now I can't straighten up."

"Then a day at home it will be!"

Glyn smiled weakly and said softly, "You know better than that, Gwyn. Can't lose a day's wages every time I feel a bit out of sorts."

"Yes, that's always the case. But I hear tell the superintendent and the foremen take the day off when they're not well. And I am sure Mr. Hyborne is not to be seen when he has the sniffles or a splinter in his pure white finger."

"Oh, what a naughty girl you can be!"

"Well, it's true, Glyn. Miners cannot afford to miss work but the bosses can. I don't call that fair. You've gone to work with near pneumonia, with a broken finger, with pain so bad you're doubled up. No, I don't call that fair at all."

She knew she had lost the argument before it even began, she always did. But she remembered the time more than ten years ago when Glyn broke his left arm in the mine. They paid him for the three cars he had produced that day, but no more. In fact, the inside foreman, a man before Otto Bremmer came, made him walk alone through the gangway to the cage, his broken arm in a sling made from the scarf he had worn to work that snowy day. Then he walked to Doc Lewis's office, still alone and in pain. Inhuman it was, Gwyneth had told him when he got home. He was off for five days, without any wages, until he felt strong enough to return to the colliery. Even then, his arm still bound tightly in splints, he was able to work only with his right arm and produce less than half his normal output of coal, even with assistance from his Slavic laborer, who said he would help without extra pay. Gwyneth recalled how they withdrew the little bit in savings from the bank to make up for the five lost days and the light production during Glyn's recuperation, plus the extra money he insisted on paying the laborer.

As Glyn hunched over in the chair, slowly sipping hot tea from a china cup, Gwyneth stood behind him, kneading her fingers into his arched back. He winced because it hurt but he knew it always helped him loosen up before going to work.

"Dylan had some news last night," she said.

"Oh, and what was it?"

"He said that prior to 1869 there were no laws governing coal mining in Pennsylvania," she said, then paused for a reaction.

"Oh, Gwyn, please, I'm not into the history lessons again. That's not what he said though, is it?"

Gwyneth laughed, knowing that her mood often infiltrated her husband's inner being and this was a morning in which he needed cheer as well as healing fingers.

"Couldn't resist that, my love. No, that's not what he said," she answered, launching into a full explanation of Dylan's encounter with the carpenter and the blacksmith and the resulting iron arm.

"Oh, bless them all," Glyn shouted as he stood, threw off the blanket, tried to stand up straight and moaned. "Oh, but that is wonderful news," he said, hugging Gwyneth though still a bit hunched over. "A breakthrough it is, a good turning point for our son. And he sounds happier, you say?"

"The world of difference, Glyn. I just hope there are no disappointments."

"With what?"

"Well, with anything."

"Just a mother's worrying. He's a man now. He can handle situations."

"Who's a man?" said Rhys as he came off the steps and moved into the warmth of the kitchen, followed closely by Evan, both dressed in their long johns but slapping their arms about their shoulders to shake off the cold of the upstairs.

"Yi, yi, boys, have some respect for your dear mother. Need you appear before her in your underwear?" Glyn shouted as he pulled on his work pants.

"I see you were dressed the same way, Dada," Evan countered.

"Enough of your lip, boy. You treat your father with respect too," Gwyneth scolded him, then smiled at both of her sons. "He came down with a blanket to cover him, not naked as a jay like you two. But enough. Time only for your tea and a bit of hot oatmeal before you're off."

"Who's the man you were talking of, Mama?"

"Why, your youngest brother, that's who," she said and launched into another telling of Dylan's iron arm.

Evan shook his head up and down as she spoke, and clicked his tongue. It was his way of showing happiness. Rhys, on the other hand, was more prone to shout and jump up and down. All of the head movement, and the clicking, and the shouting and the jumping always puzzled Glyn and, in a way, irritated him, but he knew what it symbolized and he accepted it. His two oldest sons were glad their little brother was finding himself again.

"All because of the Welsh Philosophical Society," Evan clicked.

"Well, mainly the community reading room the society offers," his mother corrected.

"You two should get involved in that society," Glyn suggested. "Discussions and debates on subjects of interest to us as Welshmen, as Scrantonians, as members of the human race. You can come with me on Wednesday nights."

Evan and Rhys stared at each other for a second, then both turned to Glyn and said, "No thank you, Dada."

"We're too young to get bogged down in philosophical debates," Rhys chuckled. "There are young ladies out there to meet and entertain."

"And soccer and dances. Much to be done, Dada," Evan joined in.

Glyn smiled, arched his back and moaned, and then laughed, "You two need to settle down. A wife for each of you, that's what you need."

"Aw, don't rush them, Glyn. Just boys they are."

"That's correct, Mama, just boys we are," Evan laughed loudly. "But we are proud and happy for Dylan. It's about time some cheer came into his life."

"Aye, that's for sure," Rhys added.

"Time to go, lads, another day. Help your old father up the hill to the pit, will you?"

"That we will do, Dada, but we wish we could work for you and let you rest here by the fire," said Evan.

Glyn swallowed hard. He knew his sons would work their souls out for him, if they could. But he also knew he had to pull his fair share of the load.

"Good men you are, and a good man we have in Dylan too. God bless him and both of you."

Ten minutes later, as the three walked through the Washburn Street Cemetery to the colliery, they heard a voice calling from behind. They stopped, turned and saw George Yancy hurrying to catch up.

"Glyn, boys, did you hear the news?" Yancy panted.

"What news, George?" Glyn shouted back as they waited for him.

"Jersey Number Eight down at Ashley...gas explosion during the night shift...twenty-six killed!" he yelled, almost out of breath.

"Oh my gawd," Glyn said quickly. "Where did you hear that?"

"Train just came up the valley...engineer yelled to my neighbor!"

"Twenty-six? Anymore down below?" shouted Evan.

"No, rest got out after fighting a fire. They found the bodies, hadn't brought them out yet when the train passed through."

The four stood motionless amidst the tombstones, shivering in the pre-dawn wind atop the hill, each one's mind numbed by the impact of yet another mine disaster.

Then Glyn spoke softly, "Twenty-six! The same number killed at Nanticoke Number One back in the mid-eighties!"

"That's right, Glyn, in '85, I believe. And was it twenty-six then too? Quicksand, wasn't it?"

"Aye, George. They broke into an old shaft that was full of quicksand. It just rushed in and covered them. Aye, quicksand. A horrible death."

"Is there any good way, Dada?"

Glyn stared at Rhys and pondered the question: "Aye, son, there is no good way to die underground. The technology keeps improving, doesn't it? But the men are still dying. It was just a year ago they used an electric locomotive underground in the county for the first time. Imagine, electric underground and the men still dying!"

Glyn stood with his head down for an instant, his sons and Yancy awaiting his next move. He sensed their presence, looked up toward the still-dark sky filled with twinkling stars and turned toward the colliery.

"There is nothing we can do for those poor devils at Ashley, boys. On to work now it is," he said softly and began to walk slowly down the other side of the hill to the bustling coal yard.

Glyn knew his age was catching up to his ability to work when a sore back or a cold or any other ailment made him feel miserable all day. To stay in a warm bed when not well, that was always his wish and the wish of every miner he knew. Laborers never seemed to complain about their health, perhaps because they were usually much younger or perhaps because they knew they still had a rung to climb to become contract miners themselves, be their own boss in a sense and order their own laborer around. And the worst feeling was to step out of a warm kitchen dressed in stiff trousers and boots still a bit damp from the previous day into the bitter predawn snap of a wintry day.

With his tea bottle slung by a rope over one shoulder, lunch bucket stuck under an arm, and both gloveless hands shoved into the meager pockets of his coat, Glyn put his head down into the wind and half walked, half slid on icy patches down through the edge of the cemetery. Workers were coming from all directions, dozens of men and boys through the cemetery like the Joneses, others up from Luzerne Street and some from up and down the depression between Hyde Park and the West Mountain known as Keyser Valley. The day shift was ready to begin.

"Okay, Glyn?" shouted another miner above the roar of the wind.

"Okay then," Glyn shouted back, unable to see who had called out but knowing it had to be a Welshman. That was the greeting often used by working men back in Wales, rather than "hello" or "how are you?" or "good morning."

A lot of men spoke to Glyn because they looked up to him as a leader. He was older than most, more experienced underground than most, a steady worker, a man who dealt rationally with stress and danger, a reasonable voice in an era when reason often prevented violence. Most miners looked to someone within their ethnic family as a man to follow, but Glyn had also attracted friends among the Irish, the Scots, the Italians, the Germans, the Slavs, and yes, even the English. And Superintendent Lordman and Booth, the outside foreman, both knew he was a man to reckon with when it came to labor troubles, Otto Bremmer had told him.

"I'm not an agitator," Glyn had protested when Otto told him how he was thought of in the company office.

"No, no, not dat," Bremmer explained. "Dey know da men vill follow you. Dey vorry about da hotheads getting you on dere side."

Having a working relationship with Bremmer was another strong point for Glyn, for he often knew what was going on in the office before anyone else. But Bremmer made sure he was never seen conversing privately with Glyn and Jones made sure that he never discussed his talks with Bremmer with the other men, not even his own sons.

Hyborne Coal had built a small shanty near the shaft to keep men out of the wet or cold weather while waiting to load the cage. It was crude: a roof made of old tin sheets; sides built of slabs cut from mine timbers that would normally have been thrown away; an opening to the weather but no door; no windows to let in light; and no heat. The men had added rough benches on both sides with wood scrounged from half-rotted timbers brought up from the pit. Joseph Lordman had announced to each shift when the shanty was built that it was done to make the men more comfortable, another benefit of working for the Hyborne Coal Company. But of the two hundred workers who went below in each shift only two dozen could squeeze into the six-foot-high building. So the first ones at the colliery got inside while the others bunched together on the leeward side to escape the wind. The choices for the men outside were to get on a cage as soon as possible or move into the shanty as others moved out. Most mornings Glyn preferred to wait outside rather than squeeze into the narrow space, but this day he was willing and able to rest his aching back with a seat inside.

News of the tragedy at Ashley spread rapidly through the miners gathering in the early morning gloom. The reaction varied. Young boys were surprised and electrified by the news, but not really saddened nor worried; accidents happened to other people, not to them. And the older men accepted it as another in a long list of fatal accidents they had witnessed or knew someone involved or were familiar with the location. In a sense they shrugged it off as a sad occasion for the families but a sign that they themselves had escaped once again. That was how Glyn took it. He knew a miner could not dwell on such events and continue working underground. But the young men—the ones mature enough to understand the chances for themselves, the ones recently married, the ones with kiddies yet to raise—were visibly shaken. They were less inclined to discuss the explosion and moved away from older men and boys who were talking about it. Some were trembling. One stepped away from a crowd and vomited when he heard an older miner talking about the bloody mess an explosion could make of a man's body.

"Morning, Mr. Jones."

"Oh, good morning, Jamie," Jones said with pain as he glanced up at his laborer standing just outside the shanty.

"Did you hear about Ashley, Mr. Jones?"

"Aye, Jamie, just a bit ago from Yancy."

"I have an uncle working there," the boy murmured.

"Oh, I'm sorry, lad," Jones said rising from his seat, hiding the pain which streaked through his back as he moved outside. He put his hand on Jamie's shoulder.

"No, no, he's okay. His brother-in-law works for the railroad. He came up on the train this morning to tell my mother that Uncle John was fine. He got out with just a few scratches."

"Praise God, Jamie. I'm relieved to hear that," Jones said, patting the boy's shoulder. He knew that losing an uncle so soon after his father's death would be traumatic for the teenager. "And you? Are you ready for work today? Will you be alright underground?"

"Yes, Mr. Jones, I will be fine, knowing that my uncle is safe."

"Then let's get moving. The line for the cage is shorter now," said Jones, his hand still on Jamie's shoulder. Temporarily he dismissed the ache in his back as they walked toward the shaft. It was this young Irish boy he was worried about, this boy who had taken Dylan's place as Jones's main concern in the pit. Rhys and Evan were men now, experienced workers, and he knew they could handle themselves in the black bowels of Mother Earth. He had always worried about Dylan, his youngest, still a boy, but never imagined he could be the victim of a horrendous accident, an accident which brought in the father as the main player in the son's rescue, or, as Dylan seemed to view it, the person who had crippled him for life.

Twenty men crowded onto the platform, the gate was closed, a bell sounded and the bottom seemed to drop out as the cage plummeted into the pit. The cold air compressed by the drop rushed up through the miners, causing them to shiver and to pull worn coat collars up tighter to their necks. Most had gotten used to the rapid descent over the years although the younger men, particularly the boys, always felt a moment of shock as the cage fell through the black hole. But it didn't take them long to learn how to cope: don't look up at the disappearing daylight or stars; don't watch the sides of the shaft as they whiz past the timbers and the rock; and never, never imagine that the wire cable will snap.

"Ah, Mr. Jones, you asked if I would be alright today underground," Jamie said as they stepped off the cage at pit bottom.

"Aye, and you said you would be," the miner responded as they turned with the others up the gangway.

"Yes, yes sir, I am, but my mother wanted me to stay home today. I told her I couldn't do that. She was shaken by my uncle's close call and she still isn't over my father's death. She was afraid for me to go to work."

"I can see how she would be afraid, Jamie. Pity we can't always do what our women want," Jones said, feeling once again the pain in his back as he trudged through the watery gangway, his head bent to one side to avoid striking the overhead timbers. "Don't be too concerned about her getting over your father's death. There are some challenges in life that we never get over."

"Challenges, Mr. Jones?"

"Aye, lad, the challenge of coping with the loss of a parent or of a son or daughter. Not moping, you understand, but remembering the good times, the comfort of someone close. You never want to forget your father, how he looked and how he worked for you and your family. That's the challenge, to remember but still be able to get on with life. That's what he would want you to do, isn't it?"

Jamie pondered the question as they walked in silence for a few moments, each enveloped in their own thoughts.

"Yes sir, that's what my father would have wanted, Mr. Jones."

"Aye, and take heart that you're a credit to him and to your mother. You're doing a man's job, Jamie. And like every other man in the pit, there are times when you'd rather be resting in front of a warm fire with a hot cup of tea but you know that to earn a wage you must give something first, is it?"

"Yes, Mr. Jones, that's what I told my mother this morning. Work first, comfort later."

"Cheers, Glyn. See you in a bit," a voice called out from behind as Jones and his laborer turned from the gangway into their room.

"Right you are, George. See you at the end of the day," Jones called back, recognizing Yancy's English accent. He stopped, peered around the corner and watched as Yancy and his laborer disappeared into the darkness. He could almost see Dylan in the swaying strides this new helper took as he lumbered along behind his miner. But it wasn't Dylan, never would be again, not down here. Dylan had lived but Jones found that he was still faced with the challenge every day of how to cope with his son's coldness and with his own questions of what else he could have done to save the boy's life, and save it wholly, the way Dylan had entered this world, with two good hands.

He found as he worked that morning that he could not follow his advice to Jamie to remember but not mope about the past. He worried about his son's future and Dylan's happiness constantly. But today, with the shooting pain in his back, he felt sorry for himself too and wished that he was home in front of that fire with a hot cup of tea in his hands. A dark, damp, dirty mine was not where he wanted to be today. The problem was that he was beginning to have more days like this one, more days with physical pain and mental anguish.

The two worked for more than a half hour with no words passing between them. Jamie could hear his boss coughing and spitting out the black phlegm that clogged his throat. It was a sound he heard often from men who had spent a few years in the pit, and a sound he was making more and more himself.

"Ah, bugger."

"Pardon, Mr. Jones."

"Sorry, Jamie, just hurting I am with this back of mine and lying in wet muck doesn't help. Excuse my language."

"I've never heard that word before."

"Ah yes, well, the Welsh use it in several ways. Instead of damn, as I just did. Or bugger off, meaning to go away. Don't repeat that to your good mother. I wouldn't want her thinking that I'm teaching you to curse."

"I've heard worse than that, Mr. Jones. More among the boys in the breaker than the men here in the pit though."

Jones chuckled: "Yes, I guess you have. But leave the language there. It's not for women or girls."

"I do that, sir."

Lying on his side in the wet dirt and dust, Jones swung his pick again and again to undercut the seam. With each swing his back muscles pulled and strained, almost going into spasms. He paused, caught his breath and swung again. It was taking him almost twice the normal time to cut in just six inches. He knew that their output this day would be low even if he worked the full shift and he wondered how he could give Jamie his full day's wage if he only cut enough coal for two or three cars. But somehow, he always managed to give the boy his due, even when Jamie protested that he hadn't earned it.

"We didn't fill enough cars this week for the amount you've paid me, Mr. Jones," he would say.

"Not your fault, lad. You had to wait on me to cut. Here now, take it. Your mother needs the money even if you don't," Jones would insist. And, later to Gwyneth: "I couldn't cut the boy's wage, Gwyn. It's basic food money for the Kerrigans." And his wife, smiling, would touch his face softly and say, "You're just an old softy, my Glyn. But we can make do with a few less coins this week."

When lunchtime came, Jones propped his pick against the wall, sat on a flat piece of coal and leaned against the handle. It felt good to push and stretch. Jamie was half through his meal of bread and cheese before Jones even opened the metal box containing his food and container of cold tea.

"Not feeling well again, Mr. Jones? Arthritis acting up?"

"A bit, boy, a bit, old age, you know."

"The company ought to take that into consideration and give their longtime miners a day to get over problems of health," Jamie suggested.

The statement startled Jones. He had never heard his laborer offer radical thoughts, radical at least to the mine owners and their assistants.

"Longtime miners? And what about laborers and boys at the doors or in the breakers? You wouldn't ask time for them to heal?"

"I don't think Mr. Hyborne would go that far and offer pay, sir."

Jones was even more surprised.

"And what makes you think he would even give 'longtime' miners a day or even an hour off with pay to get well?"

"I don't know, Mr. Jones. I was walking past a beer garden on my way home last night and passed a group of miners standing outside. They were arguing back and forth. They stopped me and several others and asked how we felt about a working man's rights. I wasn't sure what that meant, Mr. Jones, so I kept still, but others spoke out. One miner said there should be assistance for sick men. Another said the tonnage rate should be higher. They seemed to have many opinions on subjects I know little about. And one man said the new union should get busy on those things."

"The United Mine Workers?"

"Yes sir, the new union, Mr. Jones, the United Mine Workers. They said there'd be trouble if some matters weren't settled."

Jones shook his head from side to side, knowing from past experience that any gains made for working men could be endangered by hotheads who demanded immediate change but also knowing that a strong union led by reasonable men was still needed to keep peace in the coalfields.

"Best for now that you avoid such gatherings, Jamie. Let the union leaders make the right steps."

"Yes sir. I don't want to do anything to put my job in danger, Mr. Jones."

"Your job is not in danger, lad. I'll see to that. But you're too young to get mixed up in such affairs. Let the older men do that."

Jamie smiled. He felt the fatherly touch of wisdom coming from this man who was his boss and knew that Jones would guide him and protect him.

"Yes, Mr. Jones, I will."

Jones reached into his bucket, lowered his head so that the light from his hat shone into the food, fished out a bit of ham wrapped in paper, tore the meat in two, and handed Jamie a share. Then he leaned back against the pick handle, arched his back and put his share of the ham into his mouth. Just the taste seemed to melt the pain. It was always good to stop work for twenty minutes to enjoy his food. It was a working man's right.

Chapter Six

Glyn sat in the small wooden tub in the kitchen longer that night, his back covered with a towel Gwyneth had soaked in hot water.

"Feel better?"

"Pure heaven, my love. I could have sold my soul for a hot towel on my back at work today."

Gwyneth smiled. She knew how badly he had felt that morning.

"And a cold blustery day to be walking home in damp clothes. Why doesn't Hyborne build a shanty where the men could leave their work clothes and wash up a bit? No, it's always step off the cage into a wintry blast and struggle to get home before you freeze."

"A shanty for wash-up! Are you daft, woman? What owner is going to spend his money to make the men more comfortable? Better that they give us more in wages," he said, staring into the anger of her eyes. Then he flicked a bit of water into her face.

"Oh you scoundrel. Into that tub after you I'll be in a second."

"Aye, come ahead, girl. Fun that would be," he laughed.

"Shush, the boys are upstairs. And a bath they'll be wanting too. They're liable to chuck you out of that tub if you don't hurry. Coming now, they are," she whispered as both heard the stairs creaking.

"Come on there, Dada, two more for a soaking yet before food," Evan shouted as he stepped through the kitchen doorway.

"Aye, mon, three workmen in this house, you know," Rhys laughed as he moved around his brother.

"A man and two lads it is," Glyn said with authority.

"Ah, listen to that, Rhys. Why don't we dump that old tub water out back into the snow?"

"With Dada still in it," Rhys laughed, moving to grab the rope handle.

"Try it and the lot of you will end up in the snow with only your towel to keep you warm," Glyn warned.

He enjoyed bantering with his sons and, when his back wasn't aching, roughhousing with them too. He was still strong enough to take on either one, but not both. What he missed were the playful times with Dylan.

"Draw the shade please, Gwyn. These boys will be the death of me if I don't get out of the tub."

Gwyneth pulled the old bedsheet across a rope Glyn had strung in a corner of the kitchen that gave a bather privacy. Glyn, arching his back, stepped onto the floor. She had stacked his clean clothes on a chair next to the tub. As he dried with a worn towel he listened to his wife give the boys instructions.

"Two minutes in the tub each and dinner will be on the table," she told them. "Then out with the water before you go anywhere."

"Your turn last tonight," Evan told his younger brother as their father stepped out from behind the sheet to put on his shirt, socks and shoes.

"Aye, dirt from both of you and I'll be worse than I am now," Rhys moaned.

"Well, if you want to dump the tub, go down the corner for more water and heat it, then you can have your own clean bath," Gwyneth told him.

"No thank you, Mama. This will do fine."

It was always that way with baths in the Jones house, one tub of water for three, and when Dylan was still in the mines it was four. Gwyneth often wondered how families who took in boarders from the mines worked it out. Someone, perhaps many, would have water so cold and so black that it was hardly worthwhile to wash. At least her sons took turns, that is after their father had bathed first.

"Privilege of age," Glyn had told all three boys one night when they asked why he always got the tub first.

Evan was dressing and Rhys was soaking when Dylan came in the back door, the wind snapping at him as he stepped into the warm kitchen.

"Shut the bloody door, mon. I'm freezing," Rhys yelled as Dylan stood for a moment surveying who was in the kitchen.

"Enough of that language in front of your mother," Glyn said harshly.

"Sorry, everyone," Rhys said sheepishly from behind the sheet.

"And how is my Dylan this evening? Cold out there, lad?"

"Yes, Dada, very cold," he answered, a hint of frost still hanging in his voice.

"Well, a good supper tonight from your mother it is. Boiled potatoes, roast left from Sunday and hot gravy," Glyn said, smiling.

Dylan put the bag carrying his iron arm in a corner, stepped toward his mother and kissed her lightly on the cheek. He said nothing but immediately took his place at the table and waited patiently.

"Ready there, Rhys?"

"Just drying off, Mama. You go ahead with the blessing. I'll be along."

Glyn sat at the head of the table in the large kitchen and Gwyneth stood at the other end, waiting to serve her family. On one side was Evan; on the other Dylan and a chair for Rhys.

"Lord God above, we thank thee for thy bountiful gifts, for a warm house to shelter my family, for food to sustain them, for love which surrounds us. For these things we give thee all adoration," Glyn said, his eyes closed and his hands folded. It was the same prayer he said every evening but for Sunday dinner he had a longer version, a grander message of appreciation.

Gwyneth filled each plate right from her old coal stove and set it in front of each member. She knew how much each needed and never asked if they did not want a particular food. They ate what they had. Since Dylan's accident she made sure that everything on his plate was cut before she placed it before him.

Rhys popped out from behind the sheet as she put his plate on the table.

"Shirt on, son. We don't eat naked," Glyn warned as Rhys crossed the room bare chested. The young man pulled the shirt on, buttoned it and tucked it into his trousers before he took another step. He knew not to cross his father's disciplinary rules. Joke with him, yes; break the rules, no.

"Union meeting tonight, Dada," Evan said to start the meal's conversation.

"Give me a report when you get home, will you? My back has been acting up again. I think I'll stay by the fireplace tonight."

"You don't go to many meetings. Why is that?"

"Well, Evan, I have joined now, haven't I? And I've been to a few meetings. Fair play for me, now, please."

"Aye, that you have. But I've learned so much from the others about what we must have..."

"Must have, is it?" Glyn interrupted. "Is that the talk now? There are changes we need, yes, to improve safety, to give the miner a better wage. But 'must have' implies a threat!"

"To whom?" Evan challenged. "To the owners?"

"Aye, to the owners but also to the men who must work, who cannot afford to go on strike."

"You're saying we should not call strikes to correct the wrongs, Dada?"

"Not at all. Strikes seem to be a good means of bringing a grievance right to the owner, but choose your battles wisely, my son. A strike is the last resort. I've been through some and this family has suffered but I've seen people starving because of strikes."

"We have people who are worth millions of dollars because they control the mines, steel making, railroads, and manufacturing plants while their employees barely exist on a pittance. Millions, Dada, I can't even fathom a figure like that. Why do they need so much when so many have so little? And, from what I've read they have no qualms about spending it freely for all the world to see."

"The Gilded Age, they're calling it," Rhys chimed in. "Mansions for the winter and mansions for the summer, they have."

"That bothers me too but in a democratic society you're always going to have rich and poor and some in between," said Glyn. "We are not communists. Lincoln came out of a poor family to become president of this country. America offers that opportunity to every man born here. There are people in this country and in many other countries who are worse off than us. You must not lose what you have gained, Evan, that's all I'm saying. Pick your battles, boy, but only fight the ones you have a chance of winning."

There was silence for several minutes as the family ate. Glyn could feel a son in addition to Dylan giving him the cold shoulder.

"Evan, I want you to attend the meeting tonight. You're right, you do learn there. But weigh the words; don't just listen and accept what you hear. You have a good head. All three of you boys do. I've learned too, mainly through experience. Thirteen years ago, when you were about nine, Evan, and Dylan the youngest at four, there were major outbreaks of violence and strikes across much of this country. A railroad strike started in Baltimore and labor protests spread through many states. President Hayes surrounded Washington with federal troops to protect the Capitol and other government buildings. In Pittsburgh, the railroads said wages would be cut by ten percent but that train crews had to double their work time. Nothing could be done, so the railroad men struck and no freight moved. I agreed with that decision. The Pennsylvania National Guard was called in to control the situation but Pittsburgh soldiers in the Guard did not want to fight with their neighbors. Guardsmen from Philadelphia were sent and they, along with the Allegheny County sheriff's deputies, made a move against a crowd of ten thousand, including strikers, their families, and sympathizers. Shouting between the two sides escalated into a bloody battle and sixteen people were killed. That led the Pittsburgh guardsmen to lay down their weapons and join the strikers. Now, the Philadelphians were greatly outnumbered. The mob went on a rampage, stealing guns and ammunition, and burning railroad property. The Philadelphia troops had to escape twelve miles to Claremont for safety but eight of their men were killed in the move."

The boys had stopped eating. Each stared intently at their father as he spoke. Gwyneth said nothing but toyed with her food to keep from being involved in the conversation.

"The riots spread across Pennsylvania, to Altoona, Meadville, Lebanon and other towns," Glyn resumed. "United States regulars were called out; the soldiers killed several people in Johnstown. In Reading, troops panicked, fired on a public meeting, killed thirteen and wounded thirty-three. The president finally had to send regular troops into Pittsburgh to stop the destruction. It was a costly time for all, the government, the capitalists and the workers. But more strikes came, up through New York state and across the country to San Francisco. Later, a study showed strikers would be peaceful if the local government officials showed restraint in their counteractions. But those officials who used deadly force were met with deadly force. It was an eye-for-an-eye response."

Glyn paused again to let that sink in. Even Gwyneth was watching him now. She recalled the events of 1877 her husband was relating because they had shared a fear of what those incidents could do to their family.

"If there was any good from that widespread disaster it was that the American public became convinced of the wrongs suffered by working men and their families," Glyn continued. "But others thought it was the beginning of a socialist country. In many cases, it was learned that the burning and the destruction of property was done by small groups of men—some of whom were union hotheads but many were common criminals or agitators. Unfortunately, the unions got all of the blame. Even labor leaders, like Terence Powderly of the Knights of Labor, who later became mayor of Scranton, were pleading for negotiations between workers and owners and an end to all violence."

Another pause. Glyn sipped the now-cold tea in his cup.

"Our worst fears—your mother and me—came true when the violence hit Scranton, first through the train workers, then the iron and steel men, and finally the miners. We were earning about a dollar fifty per day as miners; our laborers were making about a dollar and fifteen cents. But railroad workers were only making a dollar and iron workers eighty-five cents. In 1839, I was told, miners here were getting a dollar per day and by 1849 a dollar and a quarter. When the Civil War began in 1861, large numbers of men left for army service and no one was immigrating from Europe. It was difficult to find miners at a time when production increased to fuel the Union navy, army trains and munitions factories. So wages went up dramatically and some miners were making as much as fifty dollars a week. Four years later, when the war ended, wages were cut by twenty percent. Two years after that they were cut by ten percent. In 1871, another thirty percent, and it continued until we were back to 1839 rates. Yet, the price of coal had increased as had the cost of everything else we had to buy.

"In the summer 1877, the violence hit home. First, the men at Lackawanna Iron and Coal went on strike, telling the owner they couldn't live on his wages. Then the train workers, whose pay had been cut by ten percent, walked off the job. They offered to keep trains running to carry the mail without pay because they had no complaint with the federal government, but the railroad owners said no. Then the miners wanted a restoration of the wage cuts they had suffered six years earlier, so they walked off too. There were demonstrations and union meetings, often outside, going on all around the city, It made some citizens of Scranton very nervous."

"No doubt. I'd be nervous too," Rhys said cautiously.

"Exactly right, boy, but there was no violence, no destruction of property. The mayor and law enforcement agencies were watching the situation very carefully but that wasn't enough for some private citizens. Two men who had nothing to do with the law formed an independent group which they called the Scranton Citizens Corps. Before long they had one hundred sixteen men on their roll. Within three days they collected three hundred and fifty guns and got permission to hide them in a Scranton Iron and Coal Company building. Then they obtained ammunition from a state militia unit in Pittston; that went into hiding too.

"On July thirtieth, the railroad strike was settled but the iron workers and miners were still out. The very next day the miners and some iron workers gathered outside the Silk Mill in South Scranton to discuss their problems. There were an estimated five thousand of us there listening to speakers who were trying to goad us into action and some who were pleading for calm. When the meeting ended I began walking home with a few other men, but most of the crowd, several thousand at least, headed for Central City to make a showing of their disgust for owners. That was a mistake because they knew about the Citizens Corps and its supply of guns. Well, the Corps sounded a pre-arranged signal — a church bell — that brought fifty of their members to the guns."

"I'm sure they felt their businesses, their stores or other property were going to be looted and burned," said Rhys, who drew a look of anger from Evan.

"Aye, but working men have the right to march and to discuss the wrongs," Evan countered. "And I'll wager they weren't armed."

"You're both right. The Corps members were nervous but workers do have the right to assemble. And yes, Evan, the workmen were not armed. We found out later that two dozen of the Corps members had been sworn in as special policemen by the mayor but the others who now had guns were only employees of the Lackawanna Iron and Coal Company, not peace officers. In the meantime, unknown to most of the marchers and the Citizens Corps some of the iron furnaces were being destroyed. So violence had begun. This group of workers surged onto Lackawanna Avenue, confronted the mayor who tried to stop them, and pushed him out of the way.

Fights broke out as workers tried to disarm some of the Corps men. Then, very suddenly, an order was issued to 'fire.' The crowd scattered but some men began throwing stones at the riflemen. More shooting!"

"And you were in the midst of all that, Dada?" asked Rhys.

"No, along with a few other men, I was walking up the Hyde Park hill. When we heard the shouting we turned to watch. That's when we saw rifles being leveled against the crowd. It took only minutes to clear Lackawanna Avenue. Down over the hill toward South Scranton some went; some dropped over the bank toward the river; some just tried to hide behind anything in sight; and many fell wounded or dying. The only ones standing were the Corps members, their guns still leveled as if to expect a counterattack. But there was no attack; the workers were not armed."

"Four men died of gunshot wounds on the street," Glyn said quietly and slowly. "Twelve more died of wounds in the weeks to come. Thirty-eight who were shot survived."

"I've heard about the shooting over the years, Dada, but no one ever mentioned how many died," said Evan. "How many paid for those crimes?"

"None, I'm afraid. Eight days later, charges of first degree murder were filed against twenty-two Corps members."

"And?"

"And it took a jury of their peers just thirty minutes to find them not guilty."

Rhys sat back in amazement. Evan's face flushed with anger. Gwyneth bowed her head. Only Dylan showed no emotion, staring at his father constantly without uttering a sound.

"Why isn't more said of it now?" Evan demanded.

"And what good would that do? Perhaps the men were wrong to march toward the city, knowing full well about the Corps and their weapons, but they wanted to make a point: that they would not be pushed around by greedy owners. It's history now, boys. We lost our day in court. We'll be back to fight another day. Remember what I said about choosing your battles?"

"Yes sir," Rhys responded immediately.

"We'll get the bastards someday," Evan murmured.

"I'll have none of that language before your mother or in this house," Glyn shouted. "You will apologize."

Evan turned toward Gwyneth, saw the sorrow in her eyes and said, "I am very sorry, Mama. I was out of line."

Gwyneth nodded and forced a quick smile at her son.

Glyn rose from the table, sat in a rocker near the fireplace and lit his pipe.

"I'll be going to the meeting then," Evan announced, rising and taking his coat from the hook. He looked at his middle brother, "Coming, are you?"

Rhys paused, looked across the room at his father, then at his mother. He stood, paused some more, lowered his head and said in a low voice, "I guess so."

"A report of the meeting I'd like," Glyn said as his two oldest sons walked to the door.

"Aye, sir, a report it shall be," said Evan without turning to look at his father. Rhys nodded, said nothing and both disappeared into the darkness.

"Blame on both sides, is it?"

Glyn and Gwyneth both looked at Dylan, amazed he had finally offered an opinion.

"Aye, blame on both, my son, but not severe enough to take the lives of sixteen men, leaving widows and orphans to fend for themselves," Glyn answered, more anxious to speak with his youngest son than to carry forth his story.

"Then what's the solution?"

"More trust, more caring, Dylan. Both labor and management have to learn to compromise. Work will not be available for us if there is no profit for them. We must learn that too. But, all too often, it's greed that rules the company office, not any sense of giving men a wage they can live on. And it's often bitterness which carries the shovel, not a willingness to talk like reasonable men."

The two stared at each other for a minute, not knowing where to take the conversation but not wanting to end it either. Dylan had mellowed since getting the iron arm and working with wood but he still found it difficult to speak with his father. And Glyn, despite his desire, did not want to push the boy too fast or too far. He was giving Dylan space and time to heal, not the arm, but the spirit.

"I had a talk with Mr. Thomas this afternoon," Dylan said, looking at his mother but speaking loudly enough that his father could hear.

"Thomas the carpenter?" Glyn asked, the pipe clenched in his teeth.

"Yes," Dylan answered.

"About what?" Gwyneth inquired.

"Remember I told you he loaned me a hammer to work on the book shelves?"

Gwyneth nodded.

"Well, he stopped by today with a small leather bag of other tools I might need. He told me that since he was supplying the lumber he wanted to make sure a decent job was being done. He showed me how to plane the boards and how to make sure the nail heads weren't exposed. A neater job is appreciated, Mr. Thomas said."

"And he's right. A neater job is a better job," Glyn said with a smile.

There was a hint of a smile on Dylan's face too, whether to return his father's look or to think about his newfound skills with wood, Glyn didn't know. But he didn't care which; he was happy to see even the barest of smiles from his son.

"I've been reading about mining history," Dylan said, this time turning toward his father.

"Oh, before the carpenter comes the reader, is it? That is a good course to follow, my son," Glyn said with encouragement.

"A book about British mining says the earliest strike by coal miners was probably one in 1765 but that organizing by unions did not get underway until the 1820s," Dylan rattled off quickly. "The first national union in Great Britain and Ireland was formed in the 1840s and a three-year depression in that decade forced many miners to migrate to America."

Gwyneth smiled at Dylan, then turned her face away from him and winked at Glyn.

"Did you know that, Glyn?" she asked with a grin.

"As a matter of fact, no. What else have you learned, Dylan?"

Dylan's face lit up at the question. "Well, no more about British mining that I recall, but there was a book on mining here during the Civil War. One of the interesting stories told how the Fall Brook Coal Company over in Tioga County locked out its entire work force early in the winter of 1865. Then the sheriff and army troops evicted four thousand men, women and children from company houses. Threw them and their furniture into the street, they did, into the cold, mind."

"Ah, I recall hearing about that soon after we arrived in America, but I didn't know it involved so many people," Glyn said quickly, eager to show his interest in Dylan's discoveries.

"And before the United Mine Workers of America was formed last January there were other mine unions which failed, such as the Miners' and Laborers' Amalgamated Association and the American Miners' Association," Dylan continued, spilling out the details of his reading in the community room that day.

"Aye, and after them, did your book say which unions came along after them?" Glyn asked as he swung the rocking chair to face Dylan directly.

"Well, one was the Workingmen's Benevolent Association, but I had heard you talk about that to Evan a few years ago when he moved up from laborer to miner. Let's see, if I remember correctly, the book said it was formed in 1868 down in Mahanoy City and, at its peak, had thirty thousand members, eighty percent of all the anthracite miners."

"What a memory!" Gwyneth gushed.

Dylan ignored the compliment and rushed on.

"The WBA was founded by an Irishman, I think his name was Siney. Yes, John Siney. But they had problems in persuading men from the different coal fields to act together for strength and, because of that, several strikes in the late 1860s failed."

"They believed that ultimately labor and capitalists could get along but only if corporate power could be controlled," Glyn jumped in, excited that his son was talking about a trade that had been in his family for five generations.

"Some who opposed the WBA said it was made up of Molly Maguires because most of the Irish miners in the anthracite region were members," Dylan shot right back. "But the association came out publicly to call the Mollies misguided and self-destructive."

"Aye, a false claim it was," Glyn agreed. "The WBA was able to unite workers of different mine crafts and of different ethnic backgrounds—the Irish, the Scottish, Welsh and English. It was a job, mind you, to get miners, laborers, mechanics and all the others into one agreeable group. And it was just as difficult to get the Celts to agree with the English, and vice versa."

Gwyneth sensed that her son and her husband were competing for attention, Dylan aiming at his mother and Glyn at his son. But she thought it healthy so long as Glyn did not try to dominate the conversation. And he didn't. He listened patiently as the boy continued from memory to talk about what he had learned from the book.

"The WBA favored negotiations with their employers but they also believed in strikes when all else failed. However, they were opposed to violence," Dylan finished one long recitation of facts about the union.

Glyn nodded, paused, waited for more, but Dylan seemed to be giving his father a chance to comment further.

"Well, the only thing I can say about violence is this: the WBA and the churches opposed violence, but some employers and some state authorities certainly used violence to shut down strikes. Trouble it was among the WBA members that doomed the organization. There was too little coming together from the different areas to make it successful."

"And it went out of existence in 1875," Dylan snapped back in.

Glyn nodded again, amazed at the boy's ability to remember statistics from a period which ended when he was only a babe in his mother's arms.

"Then came the Knights of Labor," Dylan started just as Glyn was rising from the rocker to climb the stairs to bed. He sat down again, his back aching from the arthritis but his heart soaring to have such a long talk—albeit an extremely dry conversation—with his young son.

"Another book then, Dylan?"

"No, same book, a brief history of unions in the American coalfields up to 1888, just two years ago, written by a professor at St. Thomas College. He said the Knights of Labor expanded very quickly after 1875 when the WBA collapsed but that they were also accused of being a tool of the Molly Maguires," Dylan said, looking at his father for confirmation.

"Aye, a man named Allan Pinkerton, who started a detective agency in Chicago some forty years ago, went along with many mine operators who raised the Molly Maguire specter. A convenient scare tactic, it was, because of all the murders back then blamed on the Mollies. Wholly unjustified though."

Dylan by now had taken his glance entirely away from his mother, who sat at the table mending Glyn's work socks, and directed his eyes and his words straight at his father. It was almost if he was testing Glyn's knowledge or perhaps proving how valuable was the time he had been spending in the community reading room. He had the gleam of a true scholar, imparting his knowledge to show he had studied well but at the same time seeking any corrections or additional information or even opinion.

"The professor said that during the 1880s the Knights favored the formation of cooperative businesses owned and run by workers. But the mine operators fought that. In fact, out in Illinois, when a group of miners tried running their own mine they failed because the railroads refused to ship their coal, but he didn't say why the railroads would do that."

Glyn puffed slowly on his pipe and looked Dylan straight in the eye.

"Why do you think?"

"Well, if it's the same out there as it was here, the coal operators owned or controlled the railroads too."

"Exactly right, Dylan. Monopoly control of an entire industry, from the coalface to the furnace. Block any segment and the coal stops. The idea of worker-owned businesses angered operators; they saw that as an infringement of their right to run the capitalist ship. And they retaliated. I recall reading in the paper back in the early 80s how miners out in Clearfield County asked for a fifteen-cent rise in rates. The operators of their mines said no and then fired the lot of them."

"But how could the Knights force action? They were against strikes!"

"True, but miners for years have had the desire to stop work when they don't see any hope. What else could they do? Part of it was pride in believing no one could grind them into the ground, but part of it was more basic: they and their families needed to eat in order to survive. Did you know that in the first half of the 1880s there were more than eight hundred strikes in the coalfields?"

"It's a way of life then?"

"Aye, Dylan, unfortunately, it is, for now. Perhaps someday the men who control industry will see the human side of manual labor. Now, as some of them say, they're concerned only about 'arms and legs,' having the manpower to do the work and making large profits."

"Will it get any better with the new union?"

"I don't know, my boy, I don't know. The labor movement seems to be like a miner without a lamp, feeling its way along a pitch-black gangway, trying to avoid the dangers while seeking a way out of trouble."

Dylan paused, obviously thinking about his father's analogy and measuring it in terms of what he knew about the new United Mine Workers, now less than a year old and still searching for answers to workers' problems.

"So as I recall from last year, the UMW was formed by a joining of the Knights of Labor with another group called the National Progressive Union of Miners and Mine Laborers?"

"Actually, it was one district council of the Knights which launched that effort, but very successfully because it ended the Knights' existence elsewhere as a separate organization," Glyn explained. "But the United Mine Workers of America—the full name—has, in my opinion, a long road to travel. First, since they were set up last January they've had major problems in uniting the miners as a strong and cooperative force that can deal with the operators. And second, so far they cover a very small piece of America. But the reason for joining the Knights with the National Progressive Union was a sound one; both unions realized that the operators were the only ones benefitting from divisions in labor's ranks."

Glyn and Dylan went on talking, not disagreeing at all, just exchanging information and ideas when Evan and Rhys stepped through the kitchen door.

"Only gone an hour, boys," Glyn said, glancing up at the old clock on the mantle. "Short meeting, was it?"

"Aye, Dada, short meeting and then a quick stop for a short pint," Evan answered.

"Too cold for beer, it is," Rhys suggested.

"Ah, there's daft you are, mon, never too cold for a pint or two," Evan chided him.

"You'll both be through your allowance this week if you get a pint every night," Gwyneth, who had not spoken for an hour, chimed in.

The boys laughed as they hung their coats and hats on the kitchen hooks. Glyn looked at Gwyneth and smiled briefly so no one else would see. She frowned a bit and looked back at her mending.

"Family meeting, is it?" asked Evan, surprised to see his father still up and obviously in conversation with Dylan.

"No, nothing like that. Dylan has been filling me in on union history, very interesting too."

"Filling you in? You, the walking encyclopedia on unions and mining. Filling you in?" he laughed.

Dylan looked over at his mother, but she stuck with her mending and didn't see the hurt in his eyes.

"Think I'll go to bed now," the young boy murmured.

"No, stay just a minute," his father urged. "We'll find out just how much these two jokers know about union history."

Dylan paused. Glyn held his breath and watched. His son slowly sat down.

"Your youngest brother has this history tiger by the tail," Glyn began. "You listen to him and you'll learn things you never knew before."

Evan could see the point. The hurt in Dylan's eyes after Evan's sarcasm had not escaped the oldest brother. He pulled a chair away from the table, began to unlace his boots, and looked at Dylan: "Well, I promised to update you on the meeting and this is the time to do it. I guess we can both tell Dada something he doesn't know, huh Dylan?"

The crippled boy, his stump hidden beneath his folded right arm, looked Evan in the face and felt the sincerity of his words. He nodded.

"Well, for the benefit of some new members tonight, the leaders reviewed the resolutions passed last January, like having an eight-hour day, getting paid in real money and not that lousy company script, opposing compulsory buying in company stores, short weighing of cars, ah, ah. What else, Rhys?"

"Hiring children under fourteen, using hired gunmen to enforce company rules, better safety procedures, those things, you know."

"How many members are you talking about?" Glyn asked.

"At the meeting, couple hundred. But total membership, up to seventeen thousand now in all the fields."

"Lot of the men were asking about you, Dada, wondering why you weren't there," Rhys said quickly.

Evan stood, walked over to his father, kissed him on the forehead and strode away smiling.

"I told them old age was keeping you home," he laughed as he bent over Gwyneth and kissed the top of her head.

"Shame on you, Evan Jones, talking to your father like that!"

"Only joking I was, Mama. He knows that. Good night all."

Rhys repeated the procedure, kissing Glyn and then his mother and following his brother up the stairs.

"Well, son, up to date now on the unions, are we? We both learned well tonight."

"Yes sir," Dylan said, quiet now that his big brothers had injected themselves into the gathering. Glyn sensed that the boy was becoming more comfortable around him, especially when he could hold his father's attention with the knowledge he had gained simply through reading.

"More talk tomorrow night, is it?"

"I suppose. I'll go to bed now then," Dylan said softly, rising to his feet, shuffling to his mother's side and kissing her cheek. "Good night, Mama."

Glyn looked at his son as the boy moved toward the stairs.

"Good night, son, I enjoyed our talk," he said.

"Good night," a bare whisper came back.

Gwyneth waited until she heard Dylan's bedroom door close before she spoke.

"He is making progess. Give him time. You'll get your kiss good night too," she said softly.

Glyn, half smiling but with eyes glistening, looked at his wife, "Aye, love, it's coming along, slowly, but coming along. Best I get that sleep now too."

As Gwyneth rose, she noticed Glyn was slow in getting up from the rocker. He looked as though he had aged in only that one day. Just the arthritis taking its toll, she tried to tell herself, but she knew it was more. It wasn't only his back that hurt. Glyn looked at her and they both knew that his heart was in pain.

It was a soft and quiet embrace. Gwyneth was careful not to hold too tightly. Instead, she gently rubbed his back, feeling the powerful muscles developed from years of mining ripple just with her touch.

"Ah, you are the great soother, my love," he whispered into her ear.

"Go on with you, always sweet-talking me."

Her words made him smile. His heart felt a pang of warmth.

They kissed tenderly, Gwyneth on her tiptoes, so that her husband did not have to arch his back to meet her lips.

"Off to bed with you," she tried to scold, smiling as she said it.

"Good night, my love," he smiled back.

Chapter Seven

"Good morning, Mr. Jones," the familiar voice called out softly in the pre-dawn darkness.

"Yes, good morning, Jamie. Ready for another day, are we?"

"Aye, Mr. Jones, ready I am. And how is your back today?"

Just the asking made Glyn straighten up. He slumped because he was tired and achy, but it always felt better to straighten up, to feel the cracking of his bones.

"Well, not bad, Jamie. Many there are who are worse off."

As the cage dropped like a rock from darkness into greater darkness, both boy and mentor were silent, as were all those on board. They were all aware that the engineer in the hoisting room was carefully watching his depth gauge as the huge platform—out of his sight—dropped. But silence on the way down seemed to be the norm for miners contemplating a plan for that day's work—timbering needed perhaps, or laying more track up to the face, or right off cutting coal. And laborers were silent because they knew their bosses were thinking about the job. But once in their rooms conversation would resume, as much as it could with whatever noise was being made and as much as the miner allowed it. Some demanded silence from their laborers, allowing answers only when they asked questions. Glyn was not one of them.

"Did you ever live in a patch town, Mr. Jones?"

Glyn was checking the roof again, although he knew the fire boss had been through earlier to test for gas and for a working roof. Jamie was cleaning up the dust and chips from the previous day and piling it with the rest of the gob to one side. Except for the scrape of the boy's shovel it was quiet in the room and conducive to talk, something that Jamie had been doing more of lately.

"Yes, Mrs. Jones and I have, after we came to America, down the line, at my first job. Why do you ask?"

"They mentioned company towns last night at the meeting."

"Meeting?"

"Aye, the union, sir. I went to the United Mine Workers meeting. I saw Rhys and Evan there but I didn't see you. Were you feeling alright, Mr. Jones?"

Glyn smiled. The boy always seemed concerned with his health, sometimes more so than his own sons.

"I didn't know you had joined the union, Jamie."

"Oh, no, I haven't, Mr. Jones, at least not yet. Just hanging around the edge, trying to learn, you know."

"No harm in that, lad, but what's this about company towns? My sons said they talked about working conditions. Hyborne Coal no longer runs a company town."

"Oh, yes sir, the main topic was working conditions. But, as the men were gathering, before the meeting started, they were talking about company towns, how bad they were and still are in some places."

Glyn went on tapping the roof with a drilling bar, listening for that telltale sign of trouble, a hollow sound. And Jamie went on pitching the gob away from the working face.

"Company towns—patch towns, as you said—are horrible places," Glyn started. "The company owns the land, the houses, the stores, the school house, even the building in which church services are held, and they control whatever police force is there. Some companies show a bit of compassion but too many, from what I know or have heard, have no concern about the condition of miners' houses. They built outhouses too close to wells or creeks or rivers. Sewage was allowed to run through the dirt streets. Houses were sometimes built between culm banks, bringing heavy dust in the wind and mud in the rain. I knew of one miner who came out of the pit after a day's work to find his house torn down and his crippled wife and six children out in the street. His wife said the outside boss had brought a crew of men over and told her to remove all of her possessions because the company needed the space to extend a culm bank."

"They lost their home!"

"Aye, Jamie, out on the street they were and forced to live under a canvas until the company had another empty house for them. Over in Tioga County, near Morris Run, a coal company superintendent forced every miner he hired to sign a paper saying the company could evict him after ten days' notice."

"Well, at least they had notice."

"What good is notice if the company owns all the houses? And a complaint could put you out of a job too. No, there were no choices. Satisfy the company or look elsewhere for work, it is."

Glyn could feel the anger welling up in his chest. He didn't want to present an angry side to the boy but neither did he want the ill treatment meted out by too many companies to be underplayed.

"Company towns are slowly disappearing, thank goodness. But there's still a way to go, not just with that type of control over human lives, but also with other wrongs. The short weighing of coal, for example; we need our own man, a union man or at least the miners' man, to doublecheck the weight of what we send up in a car. Companies paying in script rather than government money was another wrong. It meant you had no cash to buy in an independent store; you were forced to use the company store where prices were always higher. That same company in Tioga County even had the gall to stop a farmer from selling produce to families whose men were mine employees. 'Buy from him,' they were told, and 'you're out of work.' There was a strike up there in the early 70s and the Business Men's League of Blossburg supported the miners' report to the federal government that the company was paying in illegal script, which of course cut those businessmen out of any dealings with mine workers."

"Perhaps the union can stop those things," Jamie suggested.

"Perhaps. Certainly, they have to try. That's the reason for having a union, to fight greedy companies."

"Someone last night was talking about a 'bobtail check', Mr. Jones. I've never heard that before."

Jones chuckled, not at any humor but at the ridiculous meaning of the term.

"It means," he began slowly, choosing the right words. "It means that the charges you've made for purchases at the company store are deducted from your pay and you're left with nothing. Your rent for a company house, the supplies you need for your job such as dynamite or squibs or a pick, and the money your wife spends for food or clothing—they're all added up. If they're more than what the company owes you for the coal you produced then on payday you get a bobtail check, which is just a slip of paper showing you have no pay coming."

Silence. In the dark Glyn could not see the boy's face but he knew his mind was working. He said no more, giving Jamie time to digest the definition he had requested.

Finally: "How can that be? If you're just buying the bare necessities how can you owe the company money?"

"Aye, that's the question, lad. If you're just barely getting by, how can it be? Part of it is that the prices charged in the company store are higher than independent merchants'. Part is the short weights for production when your car gets topside. They all add up."

"Quite unfair, Mr. Jones!"

"And quite illegal at times, Jamie." Glyn paused, catching his generality, and added: "But remember, not all companies operated that way and now, with fewer company towns, those practices are disappearing. There are honest and compassionate operators, Jamie, but unfortunately they are few and far between. And they're usually the small, independent operators, the ones running on a thin margin of profit, not the big corporations or the wealthy owners who are looking for more money any way they can get it."

No matter how much he tried to avoid condemning all for the sins of some, Glyn found himself floating without control into that flood of controversy between worker and employer. And he did not want to mislead Jamie; he did not want to put opinions into the boy's young mind, only facts vivid enough and representative of the whole situation so that Jamie, or anyone he spoke to, formed their own opinions.

"Why, for example, Mr. Jones, should a miner be expected to provide his own light underground, be they candles or whale oil or kerosene, like we use?"

"Well, candles were never used in the Pennsylvania hard coal fields, but you're right. We have to pay for kerosene to light our way and our work, yet in the company office lamps are bought and their fuel supplied by the company."

"I beg your pardon, Mr. Jones, but the little boys who tend ventilation doors sometimes have candles," Jamie said in a soft tone, obviously designed to deny that he questioned his superior's statement.

Glyn laughed, knowing his laborer never questioned his comments. Perhaps the boy is maturing, learning quicker than the master can teach.

"Exactly right, my error. Door tenders, when they can afford them, keep a lighted candle to break the monotony of long hours alone in the dark. And you've brought up a good example. Young boys from extremely poor families sometimes can't afford to burn candles for ten hours every day. Yes, a good example of why that particular item should be paid for by the employer."

"And dynamite that you need for blasting, Mr. Jones. Why should you have to pay for it?"

"Aye, or black powder that we used to use. Why indeed? But tools, well, I'm not sure there. Workmen prefer to have their own tools, a certain type, a weight, the characteristics that separate a fair workman from a good one. Maybe we should continue to supply those."

"But why couldn't the company give you an allowance to buy tools?"

Glyn was taken back a bit. This boy was thinking ahead. Why not an allowance? If a workman wanted a better tool perhaps he should stand the extra cost. Something to consider, he thought. And why should anyone working underground have to provide the lamp—which looked like a tobacco pipe fastened to his cap—or the tightly wadded cotton it held or the kerosene or whale oil or sunshine mixture it burned. Why? Because it had always been so? That's apparently what the owners and mine operators believed. He knew for a fact that the owners were paying for new equipment being used underground. He had read in a miner's journal that an electric locomotive used in a mine in Lykens Valley near Harrisburg since 1887 had cost the owner $4,700. And they couldn't afford kerosene for the miners' lamps? And now, just in the past year, the Hillside Colliery up the line near Forest City had started using an electric locomotive. Big money for machines, no help for humanity, he mused.

"Aye, lad, why not an allowance? Something to think about, it is. But work now, time to start cutting and then too much noise for talk."

"Yes, Mr. Jones."

Four hours later, with three cars loaded, they stopped for lunch. Glyn always wished the tea he brought could be hot, at least warm, but there was no way to keep it hot from kettle to tin container. Cold tea was always a disappointing drink for him and all other British miners he knew, but there were no other choices. At least it washed down whatever he had to eat.

"Strange it is, Mr. Jones," said Jamie, sitting on a rock and holding a chunk of shiny black coal in his hand.

"What is?"

"A rock which burns."

"Indeed. And you're sitting on one end of the largest anthracite field in the entire world, one hundred miles north to south, the largest anywhere. There are some small hard-coal mining operations in other states, Rhode Island and Colorado and New Mexico, but nothing of the size we have here. "

"I've never seen soft coal, Mr. Jones. Is it much different?"

"It doesn't shine like that. Bituminous coal has less carbon, so it doesn't burn as well, dirtier it is."

"Just the two kinds then?"

"No, no, I've never seen any but there's a lignite coal, softer than bituminous yet, and brown in color. It's often found under prairies. Heat and pressure make the difference. Anthracite is harder because the material from which it was formed was under more heat and more pressure in the ground."

"How do you know so much about coal, Mr. Jones?"

"Reading, Jamie. I read everything I can find. The community room has periodicals and newspapers and books, some about mining."

"I'm learning to read, Mr. Jones," Jamie said proudly.

Glyn stopped chewing and looked at the boy. He never realized that Jamie could not read, at least not at the level quite common for his age. It was a sad feeling, this thought that the boy was missing all of the wonders of the world and beyond that could be found in the printed word, but a comforting feeling too that at least he was trying.

"Keep learning, Jamie. You'll find great pleasure and education in reading."

"Yes sir," the boy replied. "Mr. Jones, you know the big culm bank behind the tipple?"

"Aye. And what about it?"

"There's still good coal there, like this," he said, looking at the shiny rock in his hand, "at least good enough for home fires. Why do companies save those piles? They never use the coal there but they won't let us have a piece or two to take home for the fireplace. Wasted, it is?"

"That it is, lad, that it is. Well, I've heard that some companies are always planning to scrape through those banks for coal they can sell, but they never do. It just lays there, year after year."

"I've seen a culm bank down at the end of Main Avenue that glows at night. And I can smell it a half mile away, like rotten eggs it is."

"Yes, they frequently catch fire. Heat, they say, builds up inside, ignites the bony and the dust and small pieces of coal. They can burn like that for years. There's no way, I'm told, to extinguish them."

"Pretty though, all red and orange and blue at night, but smelly, ew."

"And deadly too," Jones added. "I've heard of men going home at night from a pub, too drunk to walk and getting colder with each step, lying down near a burning bank and dying of suffocation from the gas."

Jamie kept staring at the diamond sparkle of the rock in his hand.

"Beautiful but deadly," he finally murmured.

"Aye, coal is a king. Obey him or suffer," Glyn murmured back.

And with that, he arose, hung his lunch bucket on a nail he had hammered into a side timber and reached for his pick. Jamie knew that the noon meal was ended and it was time to work.

It was dark again when Glyn, Jamie, Evan and Rhys stepped off the cage. The wind had picked up and snow was falling as they slipped up the western slope of the cemetery hill.

"Goodnight Mr. Jones, goodnight Evan, Rhys," Jamie shouted above the whistle of the cold December wind as he began to slide down the southern slope toward Luzerne Street and the two-mile walk home.

"Aye, Jamie, see you in the morning, lad," Glyn shouted back, followed by a quick "night, Jamie" from Evan and Rhys.

"Why does he climb up one side of the hill just to go down the other?" Rhys asked after Jamie was out of earshot. "Quicker and easier for him just to walk around the bottom."

"The boy has no adult male company after he leaves work," Glyn replied. "I think he just likes to be part of our family as long as he can."

"Makes sense," Evan suggested.

"Guess it does," Rhys agreed, shrugging his shoulders and pushing his hands into the thin pockets of his coat to escape the icy blasts.

Dozens of miners, laborers and other workers from Hyborne and nearby collieries in Keyser Valley were ahead of the Joneses in the long trek through Hyde Park and another hundred or so followed down Washburn Street, all with the same thoughts: first, the warmth of a kitchen fireplace; then, a quick bath in the kitchen tub; followed by dry clothes; and finally, a hot meal in a clean, lighted room.

"News today, my love," Gwyneth whispered as she helped Glyn out of his old, worn coat. "Our boarders will be here within two weeks. Reverend Evans stopped by today to show me a letter from back home. Their ship was scheduled to leave Southampton on December first and arrive in New York on the seventeenth. They'll be here on the following day, if all goes well."

"Why are you whispering, girl?" Glyn whispered back.

"I haven't said any more to Dylan since I told him weeks ago that they were coming. I'm not sure how he will react," she whispered. "He's upstairs."

"Well, he'll know for sure in two weeks. Best to tell him now."

After the baths and clean clothes, the family sat for dinner. Glyn noticed that Dylan had a grin on his face, something he had not seen since before the accident.

"You look like you have something to tell us, Dylan," Glyn said.

"Yes sir, after the blessing though."

"Lord, watch over this family and all of your servants throughout the world. We wait with anticipation for Dylan's words, bless him in all that he does. Be with Evan and Rhys too. We thank thee for thy bountiful meal that we might use the strength it gives for your purposes. Amen." The prayer was a bit different from the normal words spoken by Glyn at dinner each evening, but he felt it incumbent to say something special about Dylan's news before this meal.

"Yes, lad, what is it?" Glyn asked slowly as he skewered a small piece of ham for Dylan's plate and a piece for his own plate before passing the platter to Rhys.

Dylan smiled broadly at his mother, then turned to his father, looked across at his brothers and blurted out, "I'm going to be a carpenter."

No one spoke. No one knew where the conversation was headed. And no one, certainly not his parents, wanted to embarrass Dylan by asking any dumb questions.

They didn't have to.

"Mr. Thomas, you know, Gwilym Thomas, who has the carpentry shop, wants me to work for him as a carpenter. Can you imagine that?"

"Oh, Dylan, how wonderful," his mother cried, reaching to stroke her son's disabled arm. Alarmed at her move, Gwyneth slid her hand up to the boy's shoulder and then to the top of his head.

"It's alright, Mama," Dylan responded, sliding her hand back down his arm. "I can do the work even with this," he said, looking down at the empty space below his shirt sleeve.

"Oh, I know you can, my son, I know you can," she said, weeping softly. "I'm just so happy for you."

"Well, by damn, a carpenter, congratulations," Evan shouted, reaching across the table to shake his brother's right hand. Glyn frowned at Evan's language, in front of his mother, at the family table, but he knew that correcting him at the moment could detract from Dylan's euphoria.

Rhys jumped up, reached across, slapped Dylan on the right shoulder and shouted, "Good show, mon, good show."

Glyn froze momentarily, not knowing how much good cheer the boy would accept from him — yet. He smiled and looked at Dylan with great fondness. He wanted to hug his son or at least shake his hand but he still felt that wall between them. So, instead, he patted Dylan on the shoulder and said simply, "Wonderful, that's wonderful, son. Tell us about it."

Dylan, still grinning, but looking mostly at his mother, began: "Well, Mr. Thomas came to inspect the shelves I had built at the community room and said the work was very good. He asked if I liked carpentry and said he needed help at his shop to keep up with all the orders for furniture and houses and things like that. I start work for him next Monday morning at almost the same wage I was making," his smile fading, "before, ah, before the, ah, the problem at the pit."

Glyn could feel the pain in his son's words as he spit out the words alluding to the accident which cost him a hand. Dylan still could not talk about it comfortably, and all around the table felt it too.

"You'll be a wonderful carpenter, Dylan; you have a knack for creating," Gwyneth smiled, her soft, motherly voice carrying an air of confidence.

"Aye, that's a true talent, son," Glyn added.

Dylan smiled again and continued: "Mr. Thomas wants me to concentrate on furniture and on decorative pieces of woodwork for houses that people with money like to buy. He's going to teach me to use all of the tools and about different types of wood. Perhaps I can make you a chair some day, Mama."

"I know you can, Dylan," Gwyneth smiled back. "I know you can. As a matter of fact, we will need a bench to provide two more seats at our table here. Would you do that?"

"A bench, for whom?" Dylan asked and then, quickly remembering, said: "Oh, for the boarders. Are they coming soon?"

"In two weeks," Gwyneth said, getting surprised looks from all her sons.

"But now that I'll be working you won't have to take in boarders. I'll be earning my own way," Dylan protested.

"I know you will, but they'll only be here a short time, just until they can earn enough for a month's rent someplace else," Gwyneth countered. "So the money they pay us can be used to buy the wood for a bench, and for an extra bit to buy you some carpenter's tools, eh?"

Glyn smiled at his wife, a wise woman whose suggestion also brought a grin to Dylan's face.

"Yes, Mama, that will be okay too. But I only work eight hours at the shop, so I will have time to help you with the extra work of keeping boarders."

"A bargain, my lovely one."

"I will get water from the well and coal for the fire, to start," Dylan told his mother. "I will be back earning my own way."

Glyn swallowed hard and took a deep breath to avoid moisture in his eyes. He knew it was crucial for a man, even a young man or a boy, to feel responsible for himself.

"You've always pulled your own weight in this house, my son," Glyn whispered, looking deeply into Dylan's eyes. For an instant, there was a connection between the two, a connection dating back to Dylan's childhood, to one of little boy and father. Dylan began to grin, a smile spreading across his handsome face and then, just as suddenly, it dissolved. The room was deathly quiet for a moment, his older brothers and parents apparently pausing for a response from the family's youngest member. There was none. Quickly, Evan broke the suspense.

"And who will our house guests be, Mama?" he asked.

"Hopkins they are, David and his sixteen-year-old son, Haydn."

"Oh, another Dai Hopkins, is it?"

"You have a problem with that, Evan?" his father inquired.

"No, no sir, not a problem. It's just that I already know three named Dai Hopkins."

"Well, you may call this one Mr. Hopkins and the matter will be lessened."

"Or do what the old Welsh do," Rhys jumped in. "Give him a nickname. Dai Hopkins the boarder would be it."

"What do you mean, the 'old Welsh'?" Gwyneth protested. "You boys use nicknames. I've heard you. Thomas the wood, as I've heard you call Dylan's new employer."

"Aye, but we learned that from you two," Rhys laughed, nodding at his father too.

"Well, in a small country where practically everyone was a Jones or a Thomas or a Price, and Christian names didn't vary much, you needed nicknames," Glyn cut in. "Your mother's house back home was at the top end of the village hill, so her mother was called Mrs. Evans top house. And your Uncle David delivered bread, so he was called Dai the bread. Nothing wrong with that. And if you want to know who's old, you and I can step outside and see who throws who first."

Evan laughed loudly and punched his brother in the shoulder, "There you are, boy, step outside with the mon and call me if you need help."

They all laughed, but none more than Glyn, who relished the playful banter he had always had with his sons. And, for a moment, he caught a glimpse of Dylan looking at him with that link to the past, to a time when they roughhoused as father and young son. Then, he became serious.

"I think Mr. Hopkins would be appropriate, Rhys, rather than Dai the boarder."

"Only joking I was, Dada. Respect it always is, but now with the boy, Haydn, you say, there'll be no mister from me."

"Aye, Haydn do this and Haydn do that. That'll be the ticket," Evan laughed.

Glyn knew his sons were playing word games with him so he joined in, "Yes, and perhaps I should say that after dinner Evan will clear the table and Rhys will wash the dishes."

"Women's work, Dada? You must be joking too. Carrying water and coal, yes, but clearing a table and washing dishes. What would the young lasses in the neighborhood think of us then, eh?"

"That you'd be worth marrying, perhaps," Gwyneth chuckled.

"Do Mr. Hopkins and his son have work then?" Dylan asked with a deep seriousness.

"Well, Reverend Evans said the Ocean Colliery may put Mr. Hopkins on when they open that new pit back in the Valley. No promises, you know, never any promises, it seems, but the reverend said the inside foreman told him they're looking for experienced miners. They expect to open just after the new year begins."

"And the boy, Gwyneth, did the reverend have anything for him?" Glyn asked.

"Well, Ocean is hiring some former breaker boys for outside work, whatever that includes. So they think he'll get on there too."

"Sawing mine props mainly," Evan said. "Unloading lumber, loading railroad cars from the breaker, keeping the steam boilers up for all the pit machinery, repairing mine cars, all that type of work."

"A good start for the boy," Glyn suggested.

"Aye, and he'll end up like the rest of us," Evan said abruptly. "Too afraid to complain and too stupid to get out."

Glyn looked sharply at his oldest son and Gwyneth watched them both.

"Neither you nor I have ever been afraid to complain, Evan, and if we had the means to improve our lot in life we would take it."

"You and me and a few others, Dada, but most of the men here are like tin soldiers, easily knocked over and unable to get up."

Gwyneth, although she usually avoided discussions about the mines, could not resist speaking out on this one. "That's unfair to men who are trying to feed their families. When they get knocked down then their wives and little ones go down with them."

Evan knew better than to argue with his mother, particularly with his father in the room.

"All I'm saying is that if we all stick together we will win."

"Win, Evan, win! That's what I hear from the militant union members. They just want to win, to beat the operators. We need to cooperate, to get along, for all of us to prosper."

"Are you saying it's wrong to fight the company?"

"No, I'm not. The fight comes when the company absolutely refuses to be fair. That's the time to fight, to pick your battle and your battleground, not to be street brawlers."

"Street brawlers?"

"Don't raise your voice to your father," Gwyneth warned.

"No, no, he's alright, girl, just a discussion we're having and he disagreed with my point."

A look of anger evaporated from Evan's face at his father's words. Then he chuckled. Glyn chuckled too. And Rhys joined in. Gwyneth, busy carrying dishes to the wash bucket, smiled and thought to herself how cleverly her man could defuse an argument.

"And here's another point," Glyn resumed the conversation. "The men, particularly the English and the Scots and, yes, the Welsh, and, of course, those whose families have been in this country for generations — the Americans — must learn to deal with other ethnic groups. Miners blocking laborers from getting their own rooms, even though qualified, just because they're Irish, or Slavic, or Italian. That pits worker against worker, and situations like that make the owners smile because they know the men are split."

Evan nodded as his father spoke and quickly jumped in, "Absolutely right, Dada, and split is not what we need; union is what we need."

"United is what we need; union may be the way to get it," Glyn said. "Remember the difference!"

"And it doesn't stop at miners and laborers. We need mule drivers and mechanics, blacksmiths, the whole lot of company men who work for a salary. To be strong enough to fight...ah...to deal with the company we need everyone."

Glyn smiled at Evan's correction and had to agree that an effective force to deal with an owner had to include virtually everyone who labored above ground or in the pit. He recognized Evan's drive to improve the miner's lot but he knew it would take shrewdness at bargaining, not raw courage to do battle at every turn. He and all of the miners he admired worked underground to survive and perhaps save enough money to move on to a better job. None of them were completely happy with what they had to do to earn a living. They obtained happiness from seeing their families eat regularly, from sheltering them in the wind and the rain and the cold, from sharing in their triumphs and their problems. Mining was simply a means to an end, not the end itself.

Glyn had been through strikes and shutdowns. He saw very little, if anything, solved by staying off the job. There was no money for food and always the danger of losing a house. Years earlier, when he worked down the valley, a strike lingered so long that the mine operators finally brought the mules up to pasture and had company men clean out the stalls down below. When the mine rats found there was no grain to eat, no mules' legs to chew on, no miners' lunches to steal, no scraps thrown at them, they flowed out of the pit in droves, overrunning the patch town, squeezing into houses, raiding pantries and even attacking small children. They ate soap and drank lamp oil. They bit at anything that even smelled like food. They barbarously attacked small vegetable plots behind the miners' homes, chewing what they wanted and leaving the rest to rot. They ganged up on chickens and a lone pig here and there, tearing into the flesh of the terrified home stock and counterattacking any human being who dared try to stop them. It wasn't until they had had their fill that they moved into the surrounding countryside for a wider feast. And when the strike ended and the men returned underground, he was amazed to find some rats still there. Whether they had returned from their savage outside missions or were among those which had never left he didn't know. All he did know was they were still hungry for any lunch left open and any grain in the mule stalls. But he preferred them underground, away from his family and always ready to warn him if the roof was beginning to work.

"Dada, are you awake?" Evan was shaking Glyn's arm as he asked.

"Oh, yes, son, just remembering something that happened years ago."

"I was asking about gases, about whether the operators do enough about gases."

"What can they do? Gases exist in mines," Glyn answered. "Every man has to keep his wits about him in the pit. Take methane, for example. Mix it with enough oxygen and you've got firedamp."

"One spark and it's BOOM, off you go," shouted Rhys. Gwyneth jumped at the sound, dropping silverware she had been wiping.

"Oh, Rhys, please, a bit of calm for your old mom, is it?"

"Aye, sorry, Mama. It's just that when you get a blast down there it's probably the end."

Gwyneth sighed, "I know, I know, Rhys, but don't make it sound so final."

"Whitedamp is worse," Evan stepped in. "Doesn't take much smelling of that mixture to be final. And blackdamp makes you numb, kills you by choking, it does."

Gwyneth put her towel down and walked quickly into the parlor. She closed the door between the rooms and sat in the corner rocker. When the door opened and Glyn stepped through, she looked at him with tears in her eyes. He stepped across the room, pulled her head toward his waist and tenderly stroked her hair.

"They talk without fear because they face it every day," he tried to explain. "You have to forgive them."

"I know, Glyn, but that's just why I can't stand to listen. They face it, you face it, but I can't and so I fear what it can do to all of you."

"It's the bravado of youth speaking."

"Yes, and it's the love of a mother hearing."

"I'll talk to them, love, no more conversations about such matters, not in your presence."

Glyn returned to the kitchen, closing the door behind him.

"Enough for tonight, boys, upsetting your mother with talk of gas, we are. Anyway, off to the community room I am. Anyone care to join me for some quiet reading?"

"Studying a book Mr. Thomas gave me on the proper use of woodworking tools I am," replied Dylan. "I'll be here in the kitchen."

"Down to Jenkins' beer garden for a pint then for Rhys and me," Evan said, assuming his younger brother was going too.

"Quite cold for beer, Evan," said Rhys.

"Well, stay here then in your quilt, granny."

"No, no, I'll go with you, just for the company."

Glyn watched his sons as they donned coats and scarves and caps, recalling the days of his youth when he would have gone too, for a cold pint, damn the weather. But he knew that the kettle would be on at the reading room, bubbling up and steaming with the gratifying fragrance of hot tea to soothe his chilled hands and face while the words he read warmed his soul.

* * * * *

At work the next day, Jamie brought up the subject of mine gases.

"Funny, we were talking about that last night after dinner," Glyn said.

"Yes, I know, Mr. Jones, Rhys told me outside the shed while we were waiting for the cage. That's why I'm asking."

"Asking what, Jamie?"

"You're always teaching me, Mr. Jones, about the mine and its dangers and I'm confused about gases."

"Yes, and what are you confused about?"

"Well, sir, I thought that all gases underground could explode but Rhys said no, that some can kill just by breathing them in."

"That's right, Jamie, the most common down here is firedamp, or some call it marsh gas. It rises to the top or sometimes blows out of a crack in the rock. When it hits a flame or a spark it explodes, usually very violently. That's one of the things the fire boss checks before each shift. If you ever hear an explosion from another area, lie down and bury your face in the dirt. After you feel the heat pass by get up and run. You may have burns but run to the cage or to water because firedamp leads to afterdamp, a gas which stays low. And one gulp of afterdamp could knock you out and then kill you."

"And what are blackdamp and chokedamp?"

"The same really as afterdamp, just different names, that's all."

"So they don't explode?"

"They don't have to. When you start breathing afterdamp your mind wanders, you can't concentrate or think. Your body feels weak. If there's enough of the gas around or if you don't get help quickly it could kill you."

"And whitedamp is deadly too?"

"Well, whitedamp will burn a blue flame but not explode. Some say it has a faint smell of violets but the experts claim it has neither odor nor taste. A few deep sniffs and you're gone. I'm told that long ago they lowered dogs into mines thought to be gaseous. If the dogs survived they assumed it was safe for men too. Then they used caged canaries whose small lungs would probably be choked by gas before it affected the miners. But early in this century an Englishman named Humphrey Davy invented a safety lamp to check on gas, the same Davy lamp we use today."

"But why doesn't a Davy lamp ignite the gas around it?"

"Well, a wee bit of gas enters the lamp and causes the flame to rise inside the wire gauze. But the heat in the gauze does not rise enough to ignite the gas outside the lamp. So, no explosion, just a warning of danger it is."

"And why do we call them damps, Mr. Jones?"

"Mr. Bremmer says it comes from a German word, *dampf*, which means gases. I guess the German miners carried it here from the old country. Work now, Jamie, more teaching when we eat."

As soon as they broke out their lunch buckets four hours later, Jamie was ready for lessons.

"Mr. Jones, how would you know there's a firedamp explosion in another part of a pit as long as this one?"

"You would know, believe me, you would know. I've only heard one in my life but I never want to hear another. This one was down the line, where I worked before here, and the explosion, I found out later, happened almost a half mile from my room. But we heard it, a loud roar it was, killed two men in their room and then came screaming down the gangway, exploding gas and dust as it flew along. Like thunder rolling through the sky or a runaway string of cars it whistled past us at a speed I can't even imagine. My laborer and I threw ourselves under the car up in our room, into an inch of water, face down, holding our breath. The noise was deafening, partly from the exploding gas and partly from the chunks of coal and empty cars and what was left of a mule flying through the gangway, banging the walls and the roof. I never thought we'd live through it. It ignited the dust in our room which singed our hair and clothes. But when the noise ended we took off running, not wanting to breathe in any afterdamp. Everyone was flying to the cage and demanding to be the first on. We lost three more men who took too many gulps of that poisonous air."

Jamie was staring at his boss, his jaw hanging down as he took in every word.

"You got burned, Mr. Jones?" he asked excitedly.

"Well, just singed, Jamie, no permanent scars. More scared than anything. I've heard of worse explosions where timbering caught fire and then a seam and fumes which kept the pit closed for weeks."

Jamie gulped.

"I don't mean to scare you, boy, but you must be cautious, of all things, at all times when you're underground."

"Yes sir, I try to be cautious."

"Not try, Jamie, be, you must be cautious."

"Aye, sir."

Jones knew he had to make the worse case scenario when he talked to his laborer, to impress on him the real dangers, seen and unseen, in a coal mine. Too many good men and boys had suffered horrible deaths in the pits because of their lackadaisical attitudes or of those working near them. But he thought at times he was going too far, making it seem too gory. Then, the memories of what he had seen over his years as a miner told him that he could never go too far, that the more vivid the scene the more likely Jamie would remember and take greater care.

Chapter Eight

One week before Christmas, right on schedule, the boarders arrived. It was a snowy evening. Glyn, watching through the front window, saw the sleigh pull up. The Reverend Mr. Evans was driving his big black stallion, a gift from the church so that he could make rounds. In the back seat and bundled in a heavy robe were a middle-aged man and a teenage boy. Glyn slipped into his work coat and stepped out into the blowing snow.

"Glyn Jones, meet David Hopkins and his son Haydn. Mr. Hopkins, this is where you'll be living," Pastor Evans said as he grabbed the handle of a steamer trunk.

"Welcome to Scranton, Mr. Hopkins, Haydn. Well, really, welcome to America too," Glyn said, throwing out a big hand and getting one in return.

"An honor to meet you, Mr. Jones, and many thanks for providing my son and me with refuge in this new land."

"And a pleasure to have you with us," said Glyn, grabbing the other handle of the trunk.

"Here, allow us to take that," said the boy as he and his father reached for the trunk.

"No, no, perfectly fine here," the Reverend Mr. Evans replied. "Go ahead in. Mr. Jones's family has been expecting you."

They didn't have to knock. Gwyneth, hearing Glyn leave the house, had summoned her sons into the parlor and Evan opened the door just as they stepped up from the street. The icy wind and swirling snow hid the faces of strangers but she did not need to see them to say: "Welcome to our home. Please come in and get warm. We have supper for you."

There was a momentary silence as they waited for Mr. Evans and Glyn to get in with the trunk, close the door and make the proper introductions. But Gwyneth was not about to stand on the need for proper etiquette, not when hungry, cold strangers were in her house.

"Into the kitchen with you, then," she smiled. "Sit by the fire, warm yourselves, and a cup of tea it is first off, then a proper meal."

Glyn smiled at Mr. Hopkins and Haydn, "Better to do as she says, gentlemen; you too, Reverend, or trouble I'll be in."

"Oh, off with you now," Gwyneth cooed at her husband. "There's a bad impression of me you'll have them believing."

Everyone laughed. The chill of being strangers had already succumbed to the warmth of a family willing to share what little they had with two in need.

"A cup of tea then it will be for me, Mrs. Jones, and then home again," the reverend said with gusto.

"We have plenty for supper and a plate for you," Gwyneth protested.

"No, no, thank you very much. I carried a bit of bread and cheese to the station while awaiting the train. Quite full I am, really. And poor Harry out there in the weather needs to get back in his stall. So I'll drink my tea and run."

Within minutes, the Reverend Mr. Evans had sipped and swallowed, thrown his huge scarf around his neck twice, pulled his hat down over his ears, told all he would see them at service on Sunday and was out the door.

"A good man," Mr. Hopkins suggested.

"A very good man," Glyn agreed. "My sons had offered to go with him to the train but he said it was no problem, glad to do it."

"Quite nice in here, Mrs. Jones," said Haydn, his teeth still chattering, his hands wrapped around the hot tea cup. "My father and I are very appreciative of your hospitality, ma'am, and you, Mr. Jones, and your sons. And we have a gift for the family, something my mother made."

He handed a small package wrapped in thin paper to Gwyneth, who smiled, and took it with loving hands. She untied the string slowly and unwrapped the paper. Inside was a small doily made of white lace some six inches in diameter.

"Oh, how delicate," Gwyneth sighed, gently laying the doily in her open hand so that all could see. "Your mother has an exceptionable talent to make something so beautiful. This shall go in the center of our table for all to see."

Glyn knew that his wife's words were from the heart. They had never been able to afford such luxuries but Gwyneth always swooned when she saw such intricate works of hand in the shops. And Mr. Hopkins knew the words were true too as he hurriedly wiped away a tear.

"Yes, she does beautiful work," he said. "The wife of our village doctor gave her lace enough to make two doilies, one for her to keep. But she'd like you to have it for your kindness."

Young Haydn smiled, obviously pleased that his mother's gift was so well taken, even by the men of the Jones house who commented on its intricate pattern and its perfection.

Gwyneth laid the doily in the middle of the table, smoothing out the edges and making certain that it was exactly in the center.

"Now then, these men are hungry and they shall eat," she announced, returning to business. She scurried about putting platters of lamb, boiled potatoes and green beans (which she had canned last fall) on the table. Then she added a bowl of hot, dark gravy and a plate of fresh-cut bread baked just that morning.

"No dishes or food on my doily," she announced pleasantly but forcefully.

Glyn motioned Mr. Hopkins to the other end of the table and Haydn to a seat between Evan and Rhys. Gwyneth took her place next to Dylan. The prayer was offered with special thanks for the conclusion of a long ocean voyage, a half-day's train ride from New York City and a swift but windy dash up the hill to Hyde Park.

"Perhaps you should have asked the Lord to test that bench they're sitting on," Dylan said with a laugh, looking across at his brothers and the newcomer.

The Joneses chuckled while the Hopkinses stared blankly.

"He's referring to a fine wooden bench he built for our table, the one you three are sitting on," said Glyn. "I should have given thanks for your talent, Dylan. I trust the bench."

"Well maybe you should have asked anyway," laughed Evan, rising slightly.

"You made this? It is a solid piece of work," said Haydn.

"Yes, he did," Glyn answered. "And we're very proud of his talent as a carpenter."

Dylan smiled again and slowly moved his left arm, which he had been hiding from the new boarders, up to the table. With the stump pushing down on a large spoon to hold his meat in place, he deftly cut the lamb with a knife in his right hand. Silence reigned. He had never attempted this before, preferring to let his father or mother cut any meat they had for supper. When he looked up, the first eyes he caught staring were those of Haydn.

"Mine accident," said Dylan matter-of-factly, pointing with the knife to his left arm and then went on slicing through the lamb.

"Oh, sorry, I didn't mean to stare, Dylan. It's just that I never saw anyone with, I mean, I've...I've..."

"With one hand? I get along though."

"Yes, well, you made this bench, that's proof."

Dylan smiled and looked at Mr. Hopkins.

"I'll explain it later, sir, not good to talk about during a meal."

"Oh, no need, Dylan, the reverend told us while we were waiting for our trunk at the station," Mr. Hopkins said somewhat embarrassed amid a weak smile.

It took Gwyneth's quick thinking to get the table conversation back on track.

"We are proud of Dylan's accomplishments. He is doing very well and working very hard as a carpenter," she smiled. "You can tell by how much he eats."

Dylan laughed, then Mr. Hopkins, then Haydn and Evan and Rhys. Glyn smiled, looked at his son with pride and announced: "Yes, he challenges his old father every night for the last bit of food on the plate."

As Gwyneth began clearing the table, Glyn arose, lit his pipe and offered tobacco to Mr. Hopkins, who accepted and pulled a pipe from the watch pocket of his vest.

"The parlor fireplace is lit. Let's go in there to enjoy a smoke," Glyn announced, waving his arms to indicate that the four younger men were invited too. "We'll get out of my wife's way."

It was unusual to sit in the parlor, dimly illuminated by one gas lamp and the light from burning wood in the fireplace. Electric lights had been available in Scranton for almost a decade and wealthy families and many in the middle class had them installed. The banks and large company offices also had stood the cost of putting in the new means of interior lighting, but for most families and small businessmen the use of gas illumination was still prevalent. Most businesses and the very wealthy also now had telephones, a luxury which those without saw as an extreme waste of money, except perhaps for dire life-and-death emergencies. And outside, at least in decent weather, streetcars, powered through electric wires strung above the streets, carried passengers into center city on hard pavement, rather than the dirt which still covered many side streets and all of the alleys.

Normally, the Jones family only had a kitchen fire and sat there to talk. But with company Gwyneth demanded that they use the front room. There were only three wooden chairs in the parlor and a small table large enough to hold a half dozen cups of tea. The walls were bare save for a crocheted decoration Gwyneth's mother had made years ago and a foot-long wooden cross hung on small nails between the window and front door. The other walls were interrupted by the fireplace, the stairwell, and as of late a bed for Glyn and Gwyneth with a draw curtain for privacy. For Christmas, Gwyneth had put bits of fresh evergreen from West Mountain around the cross and strung green and red ribbons on the rough wooden mantle. In the window were more colored ribbons and in the center of the room, fastened to the ceiling, a sprig of mistletoe.

Glyn ushered Mr. Hopkins and Haydn to two of the chairs and he took the third. Almost on cue, Evan and Rhys carried in the new kitchen bench, knowing full well that their mother would be horrified if they sat on the bed with company in the room. Each took an end with Dylan seated in the middle.

The room was quite cramped, now that the extra bed had been put into place. But on a cold winter's evening it was cosy enough as heat from the fire and six bodies permeated the air.

"You may never know how much you have done for my family," Mr. Hopkins began. "'Tis a fine family you have, Mr. Jones."

"Ah, but we are just repaying the kindness given us when we arrived in America, Mr. Hopkins."

"Well then, I suppose it is appropriate for you and me to discuss our understanding of boarding at this time, Mr. Jones?"

"Aye, but we can wait until you're working for any payment, Mr. Hopkins. No rush, you know."

"Not a problem. The good reverend said on the ride from the train station that the inside foreman has positions for both Haydn and me starting next Monday. No mining yet but they'll use us to finish work in the yard. Underground we'll be when the new year starts so it's less than a fortnight of topside work. But a pay we'll have by month's end."

"Ocean ready to go so soon, is it? I didn't realize they'd be mining that quickly."

"Well, driving a gangway first, the reverend said. Between the rockmen and the miners they expect to have it ready for rooming by spring. So we can make payment for boarding on December thirty-first."

"Mrs. Jones estimates your food at seven dollars weekly, or fifty cents daily for each. She will give you oatmeal in hot water and tea for breakfast and a cooked dinner every day, pack your lunches for work and have three meals on Sundays. If she finds she can do it for less she will."

"I'm sure that's most generous, Mr. Jones, but can you convert that to pounds for me? We have not yet mastered your money system."

Glyn chuckled: "I'm sorry, completely forgot about that, and we went through it too. Yes, Evan, fetch a pencil and a bit of paper and ask your mother to write it out, although we'll have to estimate what the exchange rate is now."

"And for the room, Mr. Jones?"

"Oh, one dollar and a half each for the week. Evan, ask your mother to figure that too."

"That is quite generous, Mr. Jones. The reverend said rooms here in Hyde Park generally cost up to two dollars per week for each. Are you sure that will be enough?"

"Mr. Hopkins, it doesn't cost us much more to have two people than one in that room. The only additional would be an extra bit of coal or wood to heat bath water. Ah, and that brings up another matter. With six men bathing every day we would be better off with two tubs than one."

"I can buy an extra tub, Mr. Jones."

"Fine, and when you get your own house you can take it along—your first piece of furniture," Glyn chuckled.

"Aye, and an important piece at that," Mr. Hopkins laughed.

Through it all, the sons, all four, had remained quiet. This was family business and family business was conducted by the head of the household. But it was important for both fathers to have their sons present as a learning experience.

"All said and done," Glyn said, turning to the younger men. "Tea then. Dylan, see if your mother can join us with a fresh pot of tea. That's a good lad."

Within minutes, Gwyneth opened the parlor door and carried in a small tray. On it were a steaming pot covered with a tea cosy, seven cups in saucers and a plate of cookies.

"Oh, goodness, Welsh cakes!" Mr. Hopkins exclaimed, his jaw dropping as he eyed the plate.

"Mrs. Jones bakes them to perfection," Glyn said, "but in this country they call them cookies, so we've become Americanized, and Welsh cookies they've become."

"Precious they look," sighed Haydn, his lips parted as if tasting the currant-filled circles of dough.

"Then you should have one," Gwyneth said, passing the plate.

"And precious they taste," Haydn added. "Such like Mama's."

His face saddened when he realized what he had said and, as he glanced at his father, he could see a bit of sadness there too.

"We both miss Alice—his mother, my wife," Mr. Hopkins said quietly as he admired the cookie in his hand. "The voyage was long and difficult, very rough at sea. We both had a bit of sea sickness, and homesick we got as well."

"And before you know it, she will be here with you," Gwyneth said with a sparkle, adding, "Other children too, Mr. Hopkins?"

"Aye, an older boy, Thomas, young man really, twenty-one now. He stayed there to take care of his mother and our daughter, fourteen-year-old Beth. Our plan is for them to join us in the summer when the ocean crossing should be a bit easier. We have a house left by Mrs. Hopkins' parents after they passed on. A solicitor in Swansea offered a price for it when he learned we'd be emigrating and we made an arrangement, half now to pay for our passages and half next summer with the provision that they can remain in the house until then."

"Are you leaving other family then, Mr. Hopkins?"

"No, no one now. Both of our parents have passed on and Mrs. Hopkins had no siblings. My only brother was lost in an explosion at the thousand-foot level where we worked. His wife, a hussy she was, ran off with another man after my brother died. So, no, no relatives there now, just the five of us. But work was bad in our village and I'd heard so much about opportunity in America, so come we did."

"Aye, our story too. Better work here. Economic move it was, and for you too."

"Yes, new start, you know, for all of us. No freedom in Wales, it is. Headmasters are killing the language. If a student is heard speaking Welsh in the classroom he is sat in a corner with a sign hung from his neck reading 'Welsh Not!' "

"Outrageous," Gwyneth almost shouted. "Who is ordering that?"

"Coming down from the government, it is, from educational people in London. They want English only spoken."

"Why does the queen allow that?" asked Rhys in anger.

"Victoria is English. Does that answer your question?" Evan answered.

No one spoke for several seconds, but Glyn and Mr. Hopkins nodded in agreement.

"Yes, unfortunate it is that English rule extends over the Welsh, the Scots and the Irish, not by choice, mind you," Glyn said, looking at his sons. "Why, we haven't even had a true Prince of Wales for centuries, sons of the sovereign they are now. But bear in mind that mixed marriages have matched Welsh with English and English with Scots and Scots with Irish. The blood isn't as pure today as it once was, so peaceful coexistence is the watchword now, over there and over here. We must be careful not to blame the common English people for the way their government has treated conquered countries."

"Good advice, Mr. Jones, peace it should be. But overbearing the government has become when it involves our language and our culture," Mr. Hopkins said.

Gwyneth, tired of politics and looking for a new subject, asked, "You worked in the mines too then, Haydn?"

"Oh, yes, Mrs. Jones, as a butty."

"Some still use that term here, Haydn, but most now call it 'laborer.' That's what I was before this," said Dylan, raising his left arm. "And Rhys is still a laborer."

"Aye, but not for long. Mr. Bremmer is expecting one of the miners to pack it in soon, too old he is, and he told me I am first in line for that room," Rhys said proudly.

"Wonderful news, that is," said Mr. Hopkins, smiling.

Glyn smiled too, but Gwyneth wasn't happy about the coming move. She'd rather that her sons, all of them, were out of the mines, and Glyn too. But she never said as much, never brought it up except very privately to Glyn.

"And other terms, are they perhaps different too?"

"Such as, Mr. Hopkins?"

"Such as sprags."

"Sprags are still short pieces of timber to wedge into the car wheels to slow them down, just as they are in the old country. And the boys who risk life and limb doing that in the pit are called spraggers, as they were in Wales."

"Aye, there's a boy working the breaker who lost three fingers while running alongside a quick trip trying to slow it down in our pit," Evan added. "Hit a narrow wall in the gangway, he did. It knocked him down while he was trying to get a sprag in. His hand went into the wheel and came out minus the last three fingers."

Gwyneth winced and wished, after all, that she hadn't changed the subject. She stood, wiped her hands — though nothing was on them — with the apron she wore constantly and announced that she had work in the kitchen and could she be excused. Mr. Hopkins and Haydn stood briefly as she left the room.

After the kitchen door closed, Glyn resumed the conversation: "Yes, terrible accidents they've had with these boys. You know, other than explosions and roof falls, almost half of the accidents we have in the anthracite fields involve spraggers riding atop coal-filled cars down the incline. They either hit a low ceiling, which can take a head off, or they fall between the cars and are run over. We've had many a boy lose fingers, or a hand, an arm or a leg. The lucky ones lived."

Dylan looked sharply at his father. The comment struck a nerve, but he said nothing knowing, from his own reading in the community room, that the statement was true.

"I've heard about the company stores here. We don't have them," Hopkins said, looking at Glyn.

"Well, none here in Scranton now but they still exist in some places. My former job a few miles south of here was for a company which always raised prices at their store whenever they needed extra money to replace a dead mule in the pit."

"Imagine that!"

"Aye, God's truth it is, raised prices to buy a new mule. One of the wives overheard the store manager telling a clerk."

"And do your pits have a fire man?"

"Fire boss here. But same as Wales, he checks each work area for gas, loose roof, proper ventilation before the shift starts. Chalks the slate for every miner to check as he goes in. If the air is bad we wait for the brattice men to adjust the ventilation flow through the works."

"You use brass checks on a pegboard to know who's underground?"

"Aye, same as you did there."

"Then being a miner in America is not much different from being a miner anywhere else?" Hopkins asked.

"I don't know about all countries but it's pretty much the same as Wales or England, Scotland and Ireland too I suppose."

"Boys operating ventilation doors?"

"Yes, mostly boys—and we've lost many of them too—fall asleep they do and let a trip come crashing through the door. A boy was killed down near Wilkes-Barre just last year. He woke up too late, jumped to open the door just as the cars came crashing through. Only son of a widow woman. Pity! But there have been some men relegated to being nippers too—some too old or too badly injured in an accident for any other work. Lonesome job it is for any age, just sitting there behind a door for ten or twelve hours listening for the sound of a trip coming, no one to talk to except the rats and some little nippers too poor to afford a candle to open up the darkness."

"Important job though, Dada," said Evan.

"Aye, important it is. Without them we wouldn't breathe very long. Without proper ventilation we'd be plagued by dust, by gas, by explosions. Breathless it would be without the nippers. Quite a science it is to know how to move air in, through and out of a mine. Without it we would all suffocate."

"Without it, we wouldn't go down," Evan laughed.

"Yes indeed. Topside we'd be, boy," his father chuckled.

"You use brattice boards then to direct air?" Hopkins asked.

"Yes, or brattice cloth and also piles of gob if it's available and plentiful, which it usually is," Glyn answered. "But the dangers still exist, whether in Wales or Pennsylvania, don't they?" he added wistfully.

"What is the worst danger here?"

"According to the experts, Mr. Hopkins, roof falls cause most of the accidents in the hard coal mines. The black powder we used took a heavy toll, bad fuses mainly which caused men to go back to check why there was no blast, at least none until they were too close. And working in darkness, unable to see an approaching trip if other noises drowned out the sound of wheels coming. But most of the lives lost are due to explosions and fires. Some have been killed by water breaking through and sweeping the gangway with a terrible rush. About five years ago a miner down near Nanticoke cut into what the engineers called a geological depression full of quicksand

and water. Twenty-six men and boys either drowned or were suffocated. They searched for weeks but the amount of water and torn remnants of the mine were so tremendous that they had to quit the search."

"You and I have been down there a good many years, Mr. Jones, and like me, I imagine you've had a few scratches."

"Exactly right, Mr. Hopkins, but care it is that saves us; not watching the danger signs could soon put us in our graves. Gray hair we both have and turning white rapidly, but we are still here. From my reading I know that an average of three miners or laborers are killed every other day in these anthracite mines. I have no idea how many are injured, but it has to be a frightful figure."

"And the mines here, I understand, are generally not as deep as those back home."

"Quite right, at least in the hard coal fields. And here in the Lackawanna Valley the Dunmore Number Four vein is the lowest at some six hundred and fifty feet. They call it the China Vein," Glyn said with a snicker. "They don't know how close to China mines in other parts of the world really are."

"But one of the problems here, Mr. Hopkins, is the steepness of some coal seams," Evan said with authority. "Down in Schuylkill County they get very pitched, almost like working uphill. In the mines it pays to be Welsh, probably all under five foot eight we are here in this room, like most of the other Welsh. Easier to stand up straight underground."

"Quite right," said Glyn. "Quite right."

"And tough too," Evan continued. "Lean and ready, we are. And you too, Mr. Hopkins, and Haydn."

"Still under thirteen stone I am at forty-one," Mr. Hopkins said proudly, throwing out his chest.

"Pounds here, not stones, Mr. Hopkins. Let's see, thirteen stone would put you at one hundred eighty-two pounds, about my weight too. These boys are a bit lighter but someday they'll grow up into men like us," Glyn laughed.

"Aye, and rid of the silly superstitions when we are full-grown we'll be," Evan snapped back.

"Superstitions?" Haydn asked.

"Eat in the same spot each day and with the same people. Ride in the same seat of a man-trip car at a slope mine. Don't begin a new job on a Friday. Once you put your tools away don't go back to your room. Never take a woman underground," Evan answered.

"I think miners everywhere have superstitions. And you're right, a bit silly most are," said Mr. Hopkins.

Glyn yawned, apologized and announced: "Another day of work to-morrow, so I shall say goodnight. Mrs. Jones will have bricks from the fire wrapped in thick cloth for the bottom of your bed, Mr. Hopkins. You'll need them on a winter's night like this."

"Ah, sounds quite pleasant indeed. Haydn and I appreciate that, Mr. Jones. And once again we thank you and your sons and your wife for such wonderful hospitality."

They all stood simultaneously, shook hands around and stepped into the kitchen, each to pick up a bed-warming brick.

"A wonderful meal and a delightful evening, Mrs. Jones. Thank you so much."

"You are most welcome. Good night, Mr. Hopkins. Good night, Haydn. I trust you will sleep well."

"Here, we'll take that," said Evan, motioning Rhys to grab the other handle of the Hopkinses' steamer trunk. "Into your room it will be."

Left alone in the kitchen, Gwyneth put her arms around Glyn's waist and looked into his sleepy eyes, "A long day for you, my love. Did you have a good chat with Mr. Hopkins?"

"That we did. Talked mostly about your beautiful gray hair," he said, running his fingers across her head.

"Off with you, a pack of lies you tell. Sleep you need."

They kissed tenderly in the silence of the room. Then Glyn turned and walked into the parlor. The warmth of the dying fireplace—a far cry from the deep cold of the second floor—was a pleasure on this, their first night to sleep downstairs.

"No bricks needed here, Gwyn," he said, poking his head around the corner. "I'll keep you warm."

"Hush, they'll all hear," she replied, pushing him back into the parlor and following him in.

* * * * *

As the week wore on into Christmas, Glyn noticed the melancholy look of both boarders when all was quiet. But smiles returned when conversation began, a break for both so far from family at this time of year.

As was the custom of the Jones family and many others in their situation, Christmas gift money was pooled so that each member received one gift from the rest of the family. But this year, they included the Hopkinses in their sharing. For the men it was a pouch of pipe tobacco, for the sons scarves Gwyneth had knitted—including one hastily assembled late at night for Haydn—and for her a dark blue glass butterfly pin for her Sunday dress. The Hopkinses made a special effort too, buying the Jones family a fine chicken for Christmas dinner.

The mines were closed on Christmas day, which meant a day of rest but a day without pay for the miners and their laborers. Glyn took it gladly.

"Time with family is more important than money," he told the other six at dinner when the subject of a lost day of wages came up. He wished momentarily that he had not phrased it that way, for he could see a look of homesickness in both Mr. Hopkins and his son.

"I'm sure that Mrs. Hopkins and the other children are looking at this Christmas as the first step toward reuniting your family, Mr. Hopkins," Glyn added. "And that indeed will be a blessing."

There was an awkward second of silence as the two men looked each other in the eye, a look—Glyn thought—not of strangers but of brothers.

Then: "Aye, Mr. Jones, a blessing it will be and another day closer we are. Jesus will deliver them to us. Merry Christmas, sir, and to you madam, and young gentlemen," Mr. Hopkins beamed. Each raised a wee glass of whisky saved for the occasion, thrust it forth, and shouted the cheer: "Merry Christmas."

Chapter Nine

By late January, the Hopkins family had found a suitable house for rent at a price they could afford on Lincoln Avenue, just around the corner and a block up the street from the Jones home. Mr. Hopkins and Haydn moved in on February first, a wash tub and steamer trunk their only possessions. From Glyn they purchased the bed with the straw-filled mattress which they had used as boarders and, for the price of the lumber, Dylan built them a plain, sturdy table and two stools.

"By June, when my family arrives, we shall have enough furniture to make us all comfortable," Mr. Hopkins told Glyn the day they picked up the table and stools. "And we shall pay you, Dylan, for your labor."

"No need, Mr. Hopkins. That is my gift to you."

Picking up used furniture in Hyde Park was not a problem. When the last member of an old family died, or a family moved, or someone found they had enough to buy new furniture, pieces were always placed outside the house with a "for sale" sign attached. And what was broken, and the Hopkinses bought for a pittance, Dylan would stop by in the evening and repair, never wanting to take a cent for his work. By May the Hopkins home could boast three beds, three bedroom storage boxes, the kitchen table and stools, three more kitchen chairs, and two fine old wooden chairs and tea stand for the parlor.

"We'll wait for Mrs. Hopkins to buy what she needs for the kitchen. She is selling what we own back home and will use those funds to get what she needs here," Mr. Hopkins told Gwyneth one day after church services.

Both father and son had worked steadily since their arrival, he now as a full-fledged miner in the new Ocean Colliery and Haydn as a laborer for another miner. They learned to cook too; well, as much as they needed to learn to survive, but on Sundays they always found themselves invited after church to dinner at the Jones house. And, knowing full well what it cost to feed a family, they always brought something for the meal — a freshly killed chicken or a sack of potatoes or a bag of vegetables. They lived a simple existence in their rented house, spending time a woman of the house would have normally spent to put easy meals on the table or wash clothes. They found that whatever needed mending was always spotted by Gwyneth who then insisted that she repair it and, in return, there was always a bag of salt or peppermint candies for her. They paid little attention to keeping the house spotless, having neither the time nor the inclination to fuss like Mrs. Hopkins or any other woman would to keep her home in top condition. But it was liveable and they survived as the months from winter to summer dragged on.

On the fifteenth of June, Mr. Hopkins, Haydn and Glyn borrowed the Reverend Mr. Evans's horse and buggy for the drive down into central city to the railroad station. Following with a wagon borrowed from the carpentry shop were Dylan, Evan and Rhys. The rest of the Hopkins family was arriving, fresh from the ship in New York harbor. It was a joyous though tearful reunion at which Glyn and his sons stood back while the hugging and kissing went on.

Finally, embarrassed that his friends were awaiting an invitation, Mr. Hopkins — now known as "Dai" to his benefactor — turned to him and then to Mrs. Hopkins, saying: "And this is the gentleman I've mentioned in my letters, my very good friend, Glyn. Mr. Jones, this is my wife, Alice Hopkins, my son, Thomas, and my daughter, Beth."

The introductions continued around the circle until everyone had been included. Dylan was particularly taken by the girl, who proudly told everyone that she was now fifteen, having had her birthday aboard ship. But still young she is, he told himself and dismissed any further thoughts.

Gwyneth was waiting in the Hopkins house when they all arrived, having days earlier told Dai she would cook a meal for the family in their house, take her own brood home and let the Hopkinses settle in and get reacquainted. It was a wondrous time, for the new arrivals, for those who had waited so long to see them again, and for those who had provided so much for this new group in a new world. Glyn was pleased with what his family had accomplished.

* * * * *

Just days after the Hopkinses were reunited, Dylan was asked by Mr. Thomas if he could supervise a group of three carpenters being sent to a lake ten miles north of Scranton to build a boathouse for the Winola Social Club. Dylan snapped at the chance to show that he could direct as well as build.

"I'll give you a list of the materials," Mr. Thomas told him. "Take enough tools in the wagon so that you're not running back and forth, and two tents you can set up on the club's grounds. No sense driving back to town just to sleep at night. The club's cook will keep whatever food you need on ice but you'll have to cook your own on an open fire. Ever been on a camping trip, Dylan?"

"No sir."

"Well, you're going on one now."

The plan was to build the boathouse on the shore of Lake Winola for a group of extremely wealthy Scranton families who owned a lodge and a dozen cottages where the women and children spent their summers. The boathouse, Mr. Thomas explained, would provide cover for ten rowboats and six canoes. It would be connected to a stone dock already in place and built on stone pilings, also in place, to avoid damage from winter's ice. The lake side would have a solid wall to keep wind from rocking the boats while club members were trying to embark. The other three sides would have partial walls on top.

Two of the carpenters were a year younger than Dylan and had more experience but showed no visible sign to Mr. Thomas that they could manage other workers. But they appeared perfectly willing to follow orders. Dylan knew from his time in the shop that both Jeb and Sam could do good work as long as someone was there to push them along. His third helper was a steady worker but a bit slow in comprehending instructions. However, Dylan found that the man, whom everyone called "Old Pete," though he was only in his forties, was a perfectionist who, once he knew what to do, would work until the project was finished. All three found in Dylan a boss who, though young, had a way with tools and with people and an amazing ability to use his iron arm in all types of carpentry work. He was eighteen now, having just passed that birthday in May, probably — he thought after the Hopkins family arrived — about the same time "the little girl" (as he called her) Beth turned fifteen.

"The cook's name is Pierre LaPlume, French obviously," Mr. Thomas told Dylan as they packed the freight wagon on Monday morning with lumber, tools, food, tents, some pots and pans and a lantern. "During the winter he cooks over in central city at one of the fancy restaurants but in the summer they steal him away to run the lodge. He knows you'll arrive today and he has agreed to make a small space in his ice box for some of your food. Old Pete knows how to cook; he did it on cattle drives from Texas to the rail heads in Kansas back when he was young. LaPlume will show you where the club will allow you to pitch your tents down by the water and next to the woods, far enough away from the lodge and cottages so that they won't see you, except when you're working. That's the way they want it, Dylan. Snobbish bastards they are, but it's a job and they're paying good money for the work."

"I figure a week for this, with a separate slip for each boat and canoe," Dylan said as he studied the drawing Mr. Thomas had prepared for his crew.

"Yes, you'll get a half day's work in after the ride up there this morning. Take advantage of daylight and get some work done in the evening. You could be finished by Friday or Saturday. But get it under roof first to keep the sun and rain off your backs. I'll take a ride up in the buggy Wednesday to bring fresh food."

Dylan, knowing Mr. Thomas to be a shrewd businessman as well as a skilled carpenter, took that to mean that he would be up to check on the work. He could afford to send anyone up with food. Dylan was not one to slack off on a job but this was, after all, his first chance to supervise on a project far from the carpentry shop and out of the owner's sight. He figured it was Mr. Thomas's right to check on his employees and work he had guaranteed to do.

It was a slow ride to Lake Winola with two mammoth draft horses pulling the loaded freight wagon over dusty roads, north up the Keyser Valley, then a left turn through the Notch up into the Abingtons. Old Pete, wordless as he drove the team at a slow walk, kept his eyes on the reins, and on the horses and on the road, and, every once in a while — as if he had no one else aboard to watch the load — turned in his seat to check the contents of the wagon.

"Watch where you're goin', Pete," Jeb laughed. "We'll watch we don't lose nothin'."

"Just checkin'," replied Old Pete.

Dylan, sitting next to Pete, glanced back at Jeb and Sam stretched out in the morning sun on top of ten-foot timbers and smiled, "Aye, just checking we are. Don't let any of that food bounce out."

Jeb laughed again, "No fear, Dylan, long as Sam here doesn't eat it all afore we arrive."

"Ain't touched a crumb, boss," Sam yelled without even lifting the cap which protected his eyes from the brightness of a June day.

It took four hours to reach the lake, one more to unload the lumber near the dock, one to set up camp and take food which would spoil to the lodge ice box, and one to waste just looking at the lake and the huge expanse of open lawn between the cottages — six on each side of the lodge — and the lakefront while pretending to be actively involved in moving lumber from this pile to that pile. There were children and young people in the lake, decked out in the latest bathing fashions, and others sitting on the dock and in wooden chairs on the lawn. Women with parasols had disappeared into the cottages or moved to their cottage porches, apparently to read, when the carpenters rode in with their wagon. But the children stopped their play to stare and young ladies, without parasols, furtively glanced at these young men from the city who were glancing back at them. Nearby, young men in knickers and white shirts and straw hats who had had the full attention of the ladies stood, hands on hips, scowls on faces, staring too at these sweaty workmen who had invaded their territory.

"Boys," Dylan said softly, even referring to Old Pete, "Mr. LaPlume has suggested to me that we avoid talking to the women or anyone else while we're here. The older men—the fathers—left by train this morning for their offices in the city but their wives and children will be here all week, as they normally are through the summer. And he says that staff and workers here speak only when spoken to."

"Yes, Dylan, only when spoke to," Old Pete responded.

"I wouldn't give them my time even if I had some," Jeb snorted. "Look at those dandies. Why aren't they somewheres workin'?"

"Mr. LaPlume said the young men are college students home for the summer. Some of the young ladies live at home, some are in what he called finishing schools and here for summer."

"College students, huh! Does that mean they can't work in the summer?"

"It means, Jeb, that they can't get those white shirts dirty," Sam snickered. "They need 'em when they go back to college."

Dylan smiled, agreeing with what they were saying but knowing that one word misdirected could cost Mr. Thomas the entire job.

"I'd suggest only that we do our work unless, of course, you want Mr. Thomas to replace you," Dylan cautioned.

"Yes, Dylan, do our work," Old Pete said softly.

"Pete, a clock in the lodge says it's going on three. Why don't you go finish setting up camp, put some rocks up for a fireplace, get in a pile of wood, and start cooking supper. We'll move lumber out on the dock, quit about five to eat and then put in an hour or two this evening."

"What do you want to eat, Dylan?"

"Oh, I don't know, Pete, surprise us."

"Potatoes and some salt pork, Dylan, and biscuits too?"

"That's fine, Pete, fine. We'll be along in a few hours."

The children out swimming in the lake stayed where they were, on the far side of the dock, out of the way but still close enough to watch everything that happened. It was almost like they had never seen men doing physical labor, Dylan thought, catching their stares out of the corner of his eye. At times he heard matronly calls for this child or that to "come in" as women at their cottages noticed their offspring observing the workmen. Some of the calls were for the young ladies, who continued to prance along the shore line until the call was repeated in a huskier, stronger and louder voice. And when the young ladies reluctantly marched across the lawn the young men followed like sheep being collected by a trained dog.

All that was fine with Dylan, who had noticed Jeb and Sam were spending a bit too much time peering around four-by-four-inch posts to catch the eye of some smiling lass. But when the water and the lawn were cleared of distractions the work went smoothly, Dylan giving directions, the other two obeying almost before the orders left his lips. It was a good working relationship, this, between three young men who respected each other's abilities, performed with expertise and steadily moved the project along. By five o'clock, when they could smell pork cooking from just down around a bend of the water, they had posts laid between the stone pilings, spiked together and fastened into pins jutting up from the stone.

After supper, with Old Pete helping, work continued on tying the posts into pins on the dock. And with that solid foundation completed, Dylan announced, a full half hour before sundown that they were done for the day.

It was while they were putting their tools away at dockside that Dylan noticed one young woman, among many strolling in the cool evening breeze, watching him. He glanced back, but then remembered what Pierre LaPlume had said about talking to people who lived there and turned away. It seemed to him that in the ten minutes it took for the carpenters to store everything under canvas the woman — a girl really, he reasoned — never stopped watching him. He said nothing to the others about this particular girl because they were glancing too at more than a dozen girls watching the workmen clean up for the night. Only Old Pete kept his mind on the job of shutting down the work site.

Back at their tents, the carpenters sat around a camp fire enjoying cigarettes and a few nips from a bottle of whisky which Jeb had smuggled aboard the wagon

"Quite a sight, weren't it?"

"What was?"

"All them girls agigglin' and watchin' us," said Jeb.

Sam snickered and Dylan smiled. Old Pete watched with no reaction.

"Sure are a pretty lot," Jeb added.

"And stuck up, I bet," said Sam.

"Well, I'll take stuck up if'n I could have one of them gals right here, right now."

"Member what Dylan said. We ain't s'posed to talk to 'em," Old Pete warned.

"That's right. Best be careful of that. We don't want the Winola Social Club to cancel Mr. Thomas's contract for the boathouse. If that happens we'll all be out of a job," Dylan said with authority. "It's been a long day, boys, and I'm going to bed. Up at daybreak we'll be and on the job right after breakfast."

Dylan crawled into one of the small tents and Old Pete followed. Jeb and Sam, who were staying in the other tent, remained at the fire, still chewing about the girls they had seen.

"Up at daybreak, boys, remember," Dylan shouted.

"Right, Dylan, we'll be up."

On Tuesday, Old Pete was awake before dawn, had a fire built, coffee boiling and bacon on a frying pan. The smell of food had the others out in minutes, rubbing their arms in the chill of a lakeside morning and enjoying a smoke as the sun rose from across the water.

"Damn, bacon sure looks good," said Jeb as he forked three pieces onto a metal plate. "And tastes great too. You really learn to cook like this out West, Pete?"

"Yup. In the seventies we was driving cattle from Abilene up to Dodge City. Did all the cookin' for twenty hands. Stews, soups, cakes, pies, biscuits, anything the trail boss wanted."

"What brought ya back East?"

"Got pretty wild out there. Too much shootin' and fightin'. Yearned for some quiet."

"So ya traded the Wild West for quiet Scranton?"

"Yup."

"I'da stayed out West."

They had been sawing and hammering for at least an hour before any of the Winola Social Club's summer residents made an appearance, and then it was a few young men in their knickers and white shirts.

"Quite a racket for such an early hour, don't you think?" said one who had walked down to the dock.

"I'm very sorry, but we've got to begin early to get done on time," replied Dylan, looking up from the wooden horses where he was cutting boards.

"How do you cut wood with only one hand?"

"I've learned to get along," said Dylan, pushing the saw again.

"I'm speaking to you. Do not ignore me," said the young man.

"I'm not ignoring you; I'm just busy."

"See here, do you know who I am?" the young man demanded.

"No, I don't."

"I am J. Wellington Hyborne the Second and my father, as president of this club, is the person who hired your firm to build this boathouse. So, when I speak to you, you listen. Do you understand?"

Dylan's saw had stopped as soon as the name Hyborne was announced, not because he was shaken by the young man's demands but because the name alone welled up inside him like a growing volcano. This was the arrogant son of the arrogant man who owned the mine where he had lost his hand. He wanted to tell this starched white excuse for a man what he thought of his father, and now of him too. But the words of Mr. Thomas and of the club's cook stood like a wall between him and this pompous ass with arms crossed on his chest who wanted to know why carpenters made noise in the morning. For awhile Dylan just stared.

Then, laying down the saw and straightening up, he rolled up his left sleeve to expose the rest of his iron arm, and with arrogance in his voice, he explained, "I use this to hold whatever I'm cutting or hitting in place," his voice rising and slowing as he emphasized the hitting part.

Hyborne, though taken back a bit, stood his ground, "And how did you lose that hand?"

"In your father's coal mine," Dylan said defiantly. "I was a laborer who got caught in a roof fall. That's how I lost my hand. Now excuse me, I have work to do."

Hyborne threw his head up, sniffed and strode away toward the lodge. He stopped, wheeled about and shouted back, "We arise here at eight o'clock but your infernal noise this morning has disturbed the sleep of everyone." Then off he strode again.

The helpers had watched from the dock but had said nothing. As Hyborne disappeared into the lodge, Jeb snickered, "I hope LaPlume burns the bastard's eggs."

"Careful, boys. Can't get into trouble with the employer," Dylan warned, wondering then if he himself had stepped beyond the limit. He really didn't care personally and, in fact, would have perfectly loved to tell Hyborne to get lost, but he knew from a business standpoint that the job was a lucrative one for Mr. Thomas and, indeed, for him and his crew.

By nine o'clock, the younger children were out from breakfast, ready for a swim or boating, followed shortly by a half dozen young women—teenage girls really—in their flowery summer dresses, some with cascading straw hats and others with parasols that kept the sun at bay. It was obvious that the young women were prancing in a long-distance attempt to flirt with the carpenters. But Dylan soon noticed that one, a small girl with long auburn hair and dreamy eyes, just sat on a bench without a hat or parasol and watched them work, never smiling nor moving closer nor seeking the carpenters' attention. She seemed, he thought, to be in a dream world, obviously not interested in prancing around the lawn with the others. And she was the same girl who had watched him the night before.

By late morning all of the rowboats and canoes which had been moored on the open side of the dock were being used, some just a hundred feet or so off shore, some further out. The girl who had been sitting alone was gone. Dylan scanned the lake and saw, in one of the nearer canoes, a flash of that auburn hatless head seated in the middle, a young man paddling from the bow and another from the stern. They seemed to be in a sort of jousting contest with two other young men in another canoe, aiming for each other and then pushing away just before either craft was rammed. The girl was sitting on the floor, rather than on a seat, and holding on to the sides with both hands as the contest continued amid great splashes of water and loud squeals of laughter. It appeared to Dylan that she was afraid and — although he could not hear her voice — urging the boisterous paddlers to stop.

As he watched, the contest became more ferocious with paddles used to gush huge amounts of water into the other canoe. The girl now was plainly screaming and those in other boats turned to see what was going on. Suddenly, the canoe in which she was riding was hit a glancing blow and over it went, dumping all three occupants into the lake. The two young men in the attacking canoe paddled away furiously toward deeper water, pulling the other canoe behind them and cheering their victory. The two young men in the water began swimming toward shore but the girl, obviously not a swimmer, shouted "Help!" and then disappeared. In a flash, Dylan tore off his shirt, pulled off the iron arm, kicked off his boots and dove off the dock. When he came up he could see the girl more than fifty feet away, screaming for help and splashing her arms as she went under again. The two men in the water, oblivious to the unfolding tragedy, kept stroking toward the dock. As they passed him, Dylan screamed, "She's drowning! Help her!" Both, intent on saving their own lives, ignored him. In the distance, he could see young people in the other club boats further out in the lake watching but not moving an oar or paddle to save one of their own. With powerful strokes he had learned every summer swimming in the Lackawanna River and before that in the Susquehanna, Dylan soon reached the spot where he had last seen her. Suddenly, she popped up again — possibly for the last time, he thought — not ten feet away. Within seconds he had his right hand locked on the back of her dress. She was motionless now as he turned and began a backstroke toward the dock. The weight of her soaked clothing was slowing him down and tiring him out. Surely, surely someone will row up and pull them into a boat. But the hands he felt immediately under his shoulders were not from any boat; they were from someone behind him in the water.

"We got ya, Dylan, we got ya," he heard Jeb shouting in his ear.

"I got the girl, Dylan," another voice rang out. It was Sam on his other side.

Dylan rolled his head toward them. Near the dock he could see Old Pete in the water up to his neck and behind him, standing on the beach, the two young men who had abandoned the girl. As he rolled back he saw a rowboat moving swiftly toward them from the middle of the lake. But before the boat could reach him and with help from Jeb and Sam, and, when they got into shallower water, from Old Pete, he was lifting her limp body up onto the dock. By then, the two men on the beach had run out on the stone walk and the rowboat carrying two more had pulled into a slip. The ones from the boat rolled the girl over on her stomach and began pumping her back. A trace of water spilled from her lips, then a deluge and spasmodic coughing, then choking and more water, followed by a cry. The girl's eyes flew open and her arms flailed as she fought the fear of choking. One of the young men rolled her over again and lifted her into a sitting position, calming her with soft talk and a gentle patting with his hand on her back. It took several minutes for her to calm down and, by this time, other boats had come in and women from the cottages had gathered on the dock to see what all the commotion was about.

The crying continued. Dylan and the carpenters climbed out of the water and stood on the dock watching the girl. As she settled down, she looked into the eyes of the young man kneeling and holding her. "You," she sputtered, "you, whew, you pulled, whew, me out, Chester?" she asked him.

"No, it was him, Lily," he replied, pointing to Dylan.

The girl looked up to see a young man, stripped to the waist, dripping wet, his muscular chest still heaving with each labored breath, his right hand rubbing his stomach, his left arm—minus a hand—hanging limp.

"You?" she asked, a faint smile spreading across her lips.

"Well, with help from my friends here, ma'am."

"It was him who went in after ya, ma'am," Jeb said.

By this time, an hysterical woman was standing above the girl, shouting, "What happened here? What happened?"

"Lily almost drowned," shouted another girl who had just arrived in a canoe.

"Oh, God save us," the woman shouted, putting a hand to her forehead and then collapsing in a dead weight into the arms of one of the men who had abandoned the girl in the water.

"Mother, she is alright now," the man shouted to the woman whose weight was pulling him to his knees. It was only then that Dylan realized the man was J. Wellington Hyborne the Second. "Here, Chester, help me get my mother up. I'm afraid she has fainted."

"I'm still trying to help your sister, Wellington. She had a close go of it out there," Chester replied.

Dylan was flabbergasted. In one morning, he had come into contact with the son, daughter and wife of the man in whose mine he was injured, the man for whom he and his brothers and their father had slaved for years but never saw. As Wellington dealt with Mrs. Hyborne, Dylan turned his attention to the girl, Lily. She was still looking directly at him, the thin smile now extended over her radiant face, still wet with tears and water running from her auburn hair. It was evident to all around that she was smiling at this young carpenter with one hand and he, without really thinking about it, was smiling back.

"And your name is?" she asked, her chest still heaving in an attempt to equalize the air pressure in her lungs.

"Me?"

She nodded.

"Dylan Jones, ma'am."

"I'm Lily Hyborne, not ma'am," she said softly amidst her struggle to breathe properly.

It was the prettiest voice Dylan had ever heard.

"Yes ma'am, Miss Hyborne," he stammered.

"No, just Lily."

"Oh, damn, Lily," her brother interjected, still fanning his mother. "He's just a common laborer. She's Miss Hyborne to you, Jones."

"Wellington, who saved you when the canoe went over?" Lily asked, still sitting and resting her head against Chester.

"You were on the dock when we pulled in," Chester said, looking over at Wellington. "Had you been in Lily's canoe?"

"Yes, you were," Lily answered. "You and Charles. How did you get ashore, Wellington?"

"They swum in," Old Pete spoke up. "I was standin' in the water close as I could get to you, Dylan. Never did learn swimmin'. These two young gentlemen come hustlin' in," he said, pointing to Wellington and the young man beside him.

"You left me out there, Wellington?"

"I thought you could swim, Lily."

"You know perfectly well that I cannot swim. My own brother and you left me out there to drown."

"I'll get Mother up to the cottage for a rest," Wellington said to no one in particular. "She's had a shock."

"So has your sister, Wellington," said Chester with a hint of anger. "You mean to tell me you did not try to rescue her? By the time we heard the shouting and rowed over, Mr. Jones and his boys were out to Lily and dragging her back."

"Don't accuse me, sir, of abandoning my own baby sister. I thought another boat had picked her up," Wellington, obviously flustered, shouted.

"Come, Mother," he said, half dragging a confused Mrs. Hyborne up. "We'll get you a bit of brandy. Give me a hand here, Charles."

"Lily?" Mrs. Hyborne called out.

"I'm alright, Mother, you go along," the girl said sweetly. She made no attempt to escape the comfort of Chester's embrace but she was shaking and apparently still weak. "Well, I certainly do owe you for saving my life, Mr. Jones," she said, taking her eyes off her mother and transferring a steady glance to Dylan. "You are a very brave man."

A coat of crimson was rapidly spreading across the young carpenter's face as he grabbed his shirt to cover the nakedness of his upper body in front of the young lady. He even kept his left arm beneath the shirt.

"Just Dylan, Miss Hyborne. My dada is Mr. Jones."

"Yes, just Dylan then," she laughed, the first audible notice that she was back in control.

Dylan thought her a very brave girl to have almost drowned and now, though still seated, able to laugh. He also thought even less than he had earlier in the day of her brother.

"I can't believe Wellington and Charles would swim in without helping me," Lily said to Chester.

"Well, the excitement of the moment, terror and all that, you know," Chester responded. "Don't judge them too harshly."

Dylan knew Chester and the other man in his boat were the only ones from the club who even tried to help. He respected him for that and felt Chester was trying to calm both brother and sister by asking her not to judge Wellington too harshly. For his part, Dylan felt that, were it not for Mr. Thomas's business, he would have taken Wellington and Charles back out to the middle of the lake and thrown both back in.

Lily lingered on the dock until she felt strong enough to stand and walk.

"Thank you, Dylan, you're a hero," she said softly, holding out her hand. He took the soft white fingers in his calloused grip and held them gently for a moment. Then he shook her hand, lowered his head as if acknowledging a queen and let his hand drop away. She turned, steadied by the arms of two other girls, and slowly paced up the dock and across the lawn.

"Wonderful girl you have there," he said to Chester.

"Oh, she's not mine. I'm engaged to another. But you're right, she is a wonderful person," Chester said with a wink. "Sorry, old man, that we didn't get there faster to help you. That was an heroic effort on the part of you all."

When the dock had cleared, Dylan smiled at his friends, pulled his shirt on, strapped on his iron arm and announced: "We still have a boat house to build."

* * * * *

Each day thereafter, both morning and afternoon, Lily stopped to speak with Dylan for a few minutes—nothing personal, just common talk overheard by anyone close by, including the other three carpenters. Chester would stop by too to exchange words about the weather or how the project was coming. But no one else, other than LaPlume the cook when one of them had to get food from the kitchen, spoke to them. Mrs. Hyborne never stopped to thank Dylan for saving her daughter's life, although he could not imagine that Lily had not discussed it with her mother. Jeb had brought that point up a day after the incident, but had his own reason for the lack of any such admission of appreciation: "The whole lot think they're so much better than us, mate. It's not in their bloody nature to thank someone below their level."

"Lily and Chester did," Dylan protested.

"Exceptions to every crowd," Jeb replied.

In fact, neither Mrs. Hyborne nor Wellington the Second even came near the dock for the rest of the week and by Friday afternoon, when the crew put a coat of paint on the finished boathouse, Dylan announced that rather than spending another night they would load their wagon, tear down camp and return home that evening. He had told Lily when she stopped that afternoon that they'd be leaving within the hour and he detected, he thought, a hint of sorrow in her voice.

"Oh, I shan't see you again, Dylan," she had said, holding out her soft hand for him to hold and to shake. The grip, tighter than the first time, lingered while they exchanged goodbyes. Then, she was gone, back over the lawn toward her cottage. Dylan thought he could hear sniffling as she turned away. He felt a longing in his chest but said nothing more and, sensing that his work mates were watching, turned to the wagon to hide his eyes from all.

Mr. Thomas was still at the shop, working late on a Friday night, when the wagon and four carpenters pulled in.

"Oh, thought you'd wait until morning to start back," he said to Dylan. "But anyway, welcome home and a job well done. One of the club members stopped over this morning and said you boys did a superb job. Told me about rescuing the young lady too, he did. How'd you like to go back up there on Monday? They want us to build another cottage."

Dylan beamed, "I'm all ready, Mr. Thomas, but I've never built a house."

"Aye, I know but you did a swell job heading up this crew. I'm sending Ronny Davies along to boss the house crew. He knows about building houses. But no reflection on you four. You all want to go along? It'll be about six weeks of work at the lake."

"I'm game, Mr. Thomas," Jeb said with glee. Sam, smiling, nodded several times. Old Pete nodded his head just once; he never wasted any words or motions.

"Fine, boys, we'll load up the heavy stuff Monday morning and you can go camping again."

Dylan grinned from ear to ear. Six weeks at Lake Winola, camping out, building a house, seeing Lily. Life couldn't get any better.

Chapter Ten

Glyn much preferred summer to winter. From November through at least March he went to work in the pre-dawn freeze and returned home in the windy chill and dark of late afternoon. For most of the remainder, the sun was up — or almost so — as he walked to the pit, but the heat of a Scranton day was not yet upon his back, and when he staggered home it was in the often pleasantness of declining degrees. Underground it made little difference, the mine being a constant fifty-six degrees Fahrenheit summer or winter. For the most part, he — and other underground workers — saw little of the hot sun. Unlike farmers, whose skin darkened about the face and neck, and on their arms from hands to where their rolled-up sleeves covered the bareness, miners were only exposed when they were working in the family garden, or painting a house, or repairing it, or playing soccer, or lying drunk on a day when — for whatever reason — the mine was shut down. Even on Sundays, there was only a limited time outside: to church for sure all morning; in the house to visit or read all afternoon, except when there was a special social event outside, and those were quite infrequent.

"Do you mind the sun, lad?" he had asked Dylan after his week building the boathouse.

"Sometimes," was the short answer.

"You always enjoyed swimming in the river," Gwyneth suggested.

"Aye, Mama, but then you're really out of the sun," came the longer, conversational response. "Working under it all day can be draining, but at the lake there always seems to be a breeze."

"I assume, given that females were about, you were not allowed to chuck your shirt," Glyn tried again.

"Right."

"This girl you saved from drowning, Mr. Hyborne's daughter, does she know you worked for him?" Gwyneth asked.

"Aye, Mama, she knows, as does her brother and, I presume, her mother."

"And she still stopped each day to see you?"

"No, she didn't stop to see me," Dylan fibbed. "It's just that she came to the dock along with all the others and she was more apt to offer normal conversation than them. That's all, nothing special. Just talk about the weather and the boathouse. That was all."

Glyn took it in and believed. Gwyneth felt there was more to the whole affair, after all the girl was the offspring of a man hated throughout Hyde Park for the way he treated miners and their laborers. Not that Hyborne was alone in that distinction. Most—but not all—mine owners and their superintendents were despised by the men and boys who went into the pits each day.

They felt superior, these owners and their lackeys, Evan was fond of saying. They stare down from their lofty and grand houses upon the rest of humanity, interested only in how life benefitted them and caring not one iota for the welfare of other human beings, he said frequently.

Glyn usually agreed with Evan on the generalization, although he cautioned his oldest son against putting all people from one social or economic class into one basket. There are exceptions, he had said on many an occasion when Evan's heated attacks rose above rational thought.

But not one of the Joneses or their friends had ever met an owner or his wife or their children. The owner and his family were seldom seen by common folk because they did not walk the streets, nor did they shop, nor attend social functions designed for the masses. They even attended other churches, mainly Episcopalian or Presbyterian. They were always white and Protestant and usually descended from English roots. In some areas, of course, a few ambitious and successful Catholics were making inroads, but mostly they were in the political realm, not the closed atmosphere of a Lake Winola Social Club.

* * * * *

On this Monday morning, just as the sun was breaking over East Mountain, Dylan was rolling his clothes up in a rubber poncho and answering questions, mostly from his mother, about the mysterious Miss Hyborne. He had gulped down a cup of tea and stuck a piece of burnt toast in his mouth which conveniently prevented him from saying more than he felt was proper.

"I have to go, Mama. They'll be waiting at Mr. Thomas's. We have to load the wagon."

And with that he was gone. It was strange for the whole family to not see Dylan for five days. Last week was the first time in his life that he had been away from his family for such a long period. And now, this Monday morning, it was happening again. He was anxious to get to the lake, anxious to learn the art of building a whole house, anxious to spend nights under canvas, anxious to renew conversations.

"In a hurry he is," said Evan, who was still dawdling over his tea.

"Aye, probably got too much sun at the lake last week, and now asking for more," Rhys chimed in.

"I don't think it's the sun," Gwyneth said slowly.

"Ah, then what, my love?" Glyn inquired.

Realizing she was treading on unstable ground as to Dylan's connection with Miss Hyborne, she switched gears quickly: "Well, I, ah, I think it's this challenge of learning to build a house. Dylan always has looked to a challenge, hasn't he?"

"Challenge he'll have too with that lot," said Evan. "Hobnobbing with the gentry. Ah, not for me. No, thank you, not that snobbish bit of rubbish."

"Hush your tongue, Evan Jones. That's no way to talk about people you don't know and basing it all on how one owner treats his workers. His wife and children may be very delightful people," said Gwyneth, like Glyn trying to balance the scale but knowing deep down that the high and mighty, generally, were, well, high and mighty.

"Sorry, Mama, just thinking out loud I was. But you must admit there's little concern among the owners and their supers for the working man. Caution is thrown to the winds by those who man the office. Look at that accident in Jeansville, the patch near Hazleton, last February. Two miners firing near a section abandoned due to flooding years earlier. The company says it was safe because the map shows they're working sixty feet from the old section. Well, they were only five feet away and their shot not only brought down the coal but the wall as well. The two were lucky; when the waters flooded in it washed them through the gangway to safety. But seventeen other men drowned that day. They pumped two thousand gallons every minute for days before the rescue team could even get into the pit. Then it took them twenty days to find the survivors, five men still alive by the skin of their teeth because they ate their clothes and bark from the timbers. They found six bodies, besides the poor buggers who drowned, but could barely recognize them after the rats had finished chewing on them."

"Oh goodness, Evan, do I have to hear that at breakfast?"

"Hey, boy, enough now! Your mother doesn't have to know all that," Glyn shouted.

"Aye, Papa, enough, but where does it end? Answer me that, please," Evan said slowly and quietly. "No more now, Mama, I promise. Time for work it is."

* * * * *

It was a gorgeous morning as Glyn, Evan and Rhys stepped out the kitchen door—the huge, golden sun just peeping over the valley, bringing a touch of warmth to dry the dew. Up and down Washburn Street the day shift for three pits in Keyser Valley was heading to work—hundreds of men and dozens of boys with lunch tins strung by rope over their shoulders soaking up the brightness of a summer day before descending into darkness where the daytime temperature would be thirty degrees cooler.

Evan could not let the matter of a miner's rights drop, and as he walked he talked: "You've said yourself, Dada, that in the past thirty years more violence has come from the top than the bottom. Owners hiring their own police force, their thugs, secret agents, even the state militia, to keep the miners in line. Is it any wonder that labor finds it necessary to retaliate to protect ourselves, our homes, our families?"

"You're right, Evan. It's just that your mother does not have to hear about it so bluntly. Talk to me about it, not her," said Glyn as they walked around transit workmen laying brick for the trolley from Hyde Park to Center City.

"And where do we get with it all? We spin in circles, we do. How long ago was it—more than twenty years now—that the Workingmen's Benevolent Association was formed at Mahanoy City? You told me last year that you recall the newspaper saying well over twelve thousand miners attended that meeting, and some papers said twenty thousand. Twelve or twenty thousand, it makes little difference! All those Welsh, Scottish, Irish and English voices crying for fairness, but the owners fought and killed that union. I don't think they're going to have such an easy time killing the United Mine Workers."

Glyn listened intently as his son expounded. He could not disagree; it was all true.

"Cheap labor they have, and plenty of it, so why should the owners spend a bit of their profit to improve efficiency or safety or common decency?" Evan's voice rose with anger.

"They accuse miners of destroying equipment and burning buildings, and I must admit that has happened, but they think nothing of arming their supervisors and telling them to shoot, and harassing union men and running mine families into the ground," added Rhys, who usually left the union talk to his brother but when aroused could voice his feelings too. "Hell, they control everything: the mines, the railroads, most of the stores, politics."

Glyn nodded. His sons knew their history, but they also knew feelings, their own and those of other men who labored in the pits. And while he often encouraged them to look for the good in all situations, he realized that at this point in their lives they faced mostly bad.

"There was another disaster much closer and just a few years ago than the one you mentioned at the patch town near Hazleton," Glyn said, looking at Evan. "The engineers say there is a hidden valley under the Wyoming Valley down near Wilkes-Barre. It was cut by a glacier long, long ago and then covered over with dirt and stone, the Buried Valley of Wyoming, they call it."

"Ah yes, I almost forgot, the flooded mine at Nanticoke. Cut into that underground valley, didn't they?"

"I remember that too, Dada," said Rhys. "Couple dozen miners missing, wasn't it? And they never found the bodies."

"It's not how I want to go," Glyn whispered. "Get my body out and put it in a proper grave, if possible."

Rhys reacted with alarm, "Not you, Dada, you'll die in bed, peaceful and warm, a very old man. You'll not die in a pit."

"And how will you prevent that happening to any of us, Rhys?" asked Evan.

"You could get a job as a top man, Dada."

"Unloading cars from the cage? Not likely the company would give me a position like that," Glyn responded to Rhys's suggestion. "Nor a bottom man, loading cars on the cage. No, no, if I'm to be underground it's at a face I want to be, my own boss, not working for the likes of J. Wellington Hyborne. No, I see little change for my generation. It's what I've grown accustomed to, boys. But for you two, now there's something worthwhile to bargain for."

"Fight for, Dada, fight for," Evan shouted.

"Just a difference in the wording, son, and in the approach to management."

Glyn was quite aware of the problems one union after another encountered in trying to infiltrate the anthracite fields. He knew that owners, most of them, could be very cruel and very greedy, and they spread that conception of business down through their top lieutenants — the colliery superintendent, the outside and inside foremen and the breaker boss. But there were exceptions, as he had always told his sons. And one within their little world was the inside boss at the Hyborne pit, the big German Otto Bremmer, who had the magic to make the mine hum with production without trampling on the rights of the miners, the laborers or the company's underground employees. Glyn knew Otto was treading a fine line and probably only held on to his job because he was an expert at getting the work done. If someone came along who could get the job done as well but who also was cruel and greedy, then Otto would be gone.

The problems with some of the earlier union efforts, Glyn knew from experience, were many. Some, obviously, were too violent, turning off any support they may have garnered from nonmining interests in their community. Others, like the owners, were too greedy, making demands on businessmen who controlled the available labor force, commerce, the money supply and politics. Some union enthusiasts were of a completely different stripe, suggesting that labor and management share problems and solutions because, they reasoned, both sides had a mutual interest in earning money from coal. That idea was laughed away in the words of one company president who, after the strike of 1869, said: "We are not prepared to take in new partners."

Glyn realized there had to be a way to convince owners that such matters as adequate pay and safety were beneficial to the industry as a whole. But as long as major capital investors controlled the railroads — and decades earlier the canal system — that moved coal from the pit to the customer's fire, Glyn knew the union's chances of survival, let alone success, were minimal. The nation's largest canal system had been built to transport coal and its success made it the first big inland system of moving goods to market. But it, like the railroads which followed, was controlled from the top with no regard whatsoever to what happened at the bottom. The railroad expansion came during the Civil War out of necessity, but after 1865 the rail companies expanded their routes and began buying up thousands of acres of coal fields. Such action was allowed under a law passed by the Pennsylvania Legislature in 1868 and the railroad controllers took full advantage of it to cut competition and to guarantee that their product — coal — always had a means of transport — rail. The result was that most of the small, independent coal producers — who could not guarantee their product would be transported — were forced out of business.

The war had brought another problem to the coal fields, though at the time it seemed more like a blessing. Wages increased by sixty percent between 1860, a year before fighting broke out, and 1866, a year after the South capitulated. But, during the same period, the cost of living rose by ninety percent. Glyn, through his reading of that period, learned the meaning of a new word: inflation. Then, in the decade of the 1870s, the greed of a handful of capitalists in America and their speculation in vast areas of the business world led to economic panic, failed businesses and national depression. Greed now had personal names such as Gould and Vanderbilt.

The power of such men and the empires they controlled seemed unstoppable in Glyn's early experience as an American worker and he wondered, as did many others, whether unions or the law or reason could ever prevail. The United Mine Workers of America, now a struggling infant of eighteen months, was the latest David to take on Goliath, but miners, almost to a man, wondered and questioned and prayed if this might be the Moses who would lead them to a promised land. One place where they simply had to wield some power was in the state Legislature, until then awash in influence and friendship and money from the mighty railroad-coal conglomerate.

In Pennsylvania, the Reading Railroad had become the largest of the anthracite roads, indeed a company whose power extended across America. Down in the Schuylkill field, the Reading was king, driven by the ambition of lawyer-businessman Franklin B. Gowen, the man credited with putting the knife to the so-called Molly Maguires, a shadowy—some said nebulous—group of Irish miners which Gowen claimed polluted the coal industry. The Reading had competed against and beaten the canals, giving the railroad a strangle hold on the transport of coal. Some said it was out to strangle the people it needed most—the miners.

Despite conditions for those on the bottom rung of the coal empire—the workers—the industry flourished, growing Scranton from a village of a thousand in 1850 to a city of well over fifty thousand in 1891, and its own moniker, "Anthracite Capital of the World." The four anthracite railroads had terminals and repair facilities that were the talk of the entire industry. But the city wasn't just resting on coal; its leap forward was powered by a wide variety of industries including prepared foods, stoves and other iron products, materials for building construction, carriages for transportation, and clothing. It was, as the nineteenth century was coming to a close, the biggest industrial center in northeastern Pennsylvania.

Glyn saw many of those other businesses led by prosperous and ambitious men but he also saw a different level of treatment for their employees. It wasn't the best that could be hoped for but it was several steps above where the miner stood with his employer.

And it wasn't just Scranton where money and social standing ruled. Twenty miles southwest, the city of Wilkes-Barre had its share of class distinction. Two dozen coal corporations ruled the roost from the Wyoming Valley more than fifty miles south past the Hazleton area. They were powerful enough to keep out competition and lock the region into economic dependency on the back of one industry—coal.

The Joneses had walked along in silence for several blocks, enjoying the morning sun which began to spread its warmth through their shirts and coats. It would be pleasant, Glyn often thought, to have this temperature constantly underground but at four hundred feet below the surface he knew it would be down in the fifties. At the end of a summer's day shift, as all of the miners trudged home, sleeves were rolled up past elbows, and the coats needed underground while eating lunch were slung over weary shoulders.

As they slipped down the cemetery hill toward the colliery yard they were greeted by gangs of other workers coming around the hill from Luzerne Street and the area south of Hyde Park with shouts of "how's it, Glyn?" and "top a' the day, gents" and "morning, boys." The crowds from ethnic neighborhoods—scads of Welsh and Scots, some English, a few Germans, a mixture from the Slavic countries whose ability to communicate was severely restricted by language, and hordes of Irish—lost their allegiance to a foreign homeland when they entered the colliery yard and became miners. It was necessary to work together to survive underground. But, for most, that necessity ended when they left the yard at day's end.

Evan was prone to begin a tirade against mine owners when he got into the company of other miners and this morning was no different. It almost seemed that he wanted to be within earshot of someone from the management side to give them a fresh view of labor complaints. It was his way of "fighting back."

There had been an incident the previous week where coal company police roughed up a man accused of stealing coal from the culm piles which surrounded the Hyborne colliery. Those who witnessed the event said the man, a crippled ex-miner, was putting pieces of discarded coal into a cloth sack for his home fire. The man hobbled away and dropped his bag when two policemen appeared but they went after him, slapping him about the back and shoulders with billy clubs as he sought to escape.

Evan was talking about the incident to a group of young miners as they crossed into the yard, "He dropped the damn coal, so why did they have to beat him? Bloody awful that was."

"They could have given him a lecture or a warning," said one of the miners. "No reason to beat the poor chap."

"If we ever get a voice in the Legislature in Harrisburg the first thing we need outlawed are the bastard Pennsylvania Coal and Iron Police," Evan responded. He knew from his own reading and from talks with his father that the C and I Police were established by the Legislature in 1866, just a year after the Civil War ended, but were controlled and paid by the companies which owned the mines and iron works. For the first two years, the C and I had jurisdiction only in Schuylkill and Luzerne Counties and many believed they were created to control the Molly Maguires. Evan never understood how the governor could commission such a force and give it the full powers of public police.

"They are a total abuse of power," Evan raged. "They protect strike-breakers, they intimidate strikers and they start riots, then blame the miners and iron workers. I am ashamed that some men on the force are Welshmen."

"Aye, but there are English and Germans too," yelled someone.

"And a few Irish," yelled another.

"It only shows how desperate some men are to get out of the mines, to wear clean clothes every day and to exercise a bit of power," Glyn suggested as if excusing those who had joined the force. "In the old company towns and the patches yet today the owners use them to control the miners' private lives, to prevent what they call immorality from gaining a foothold, to evict families from company houses and to collect debts. That leaves very little freedom for families."

"Well, like the incident last week, those jackals too often turn to the gun and the club when...," Evan began.

"When they should use reason and patience," Glyn finished the thought, smiling at his son and getting a nod in return. "You know, our saving grace at times is the fact that local courts and local government police don't always get along with the C and I Police."

"But the C and I have power on their side—the owners—and they control local politics," said Evan.

"Quite true, quite true," sighed his father.

"Some who hold local office are just figureheads, put in office through the power of the industrial giants," Evan continued, shouting now to whomever would listen, and most all did. "And who controls our Legislature? The Reading Railroad, a coal owner."

There were shouts of support across the yard from miners and laborers. Company men kept quiet because they knew one wrong word caught by a member of management would bring instant dismissal. Then, like a blast from a heavenly trumpet which drowns out all other sounds, the breaker whistle shrilled through the ears of the yard crowd to announce the day shift was ready to dig coal.

Crammed together on the cage with men speaking several languages, Glyn thought of the conversation just minutes earlier when Evan and others pointed out that a common enemy—the Coal and Iron Police—was made up of men from a mixture of ethnic groups not uncommon to the mix that was plunging hundreds of feet to another day of hard and dangerous work. The men in the yard had come from neighborhoods all over West Scranton like Welsh Hill, Scotch Road, Murphy's Patch, Hun Town, Little Italy and a full ration of uncomplimentary names for Slavic areas. They all worked together underground but—except for a nationalistic joining of Welsh, Scots and some English—they seldom mixed above. They had their own churches and forms of recreation; they went to separate taverns or beer gardens; their children married within their own ethnic group. Those whose native language was English found pleasure in attending readings and debates and discovered that what books were available in community rooms were in their language. For those who spoke little or no English the chances for similar opportunities were slim or none.

And now, trying to raise a fledgling union to a competitive level with corporate giants when miners could not even agree to live together raised serious doubts in Glyn's mind. The giants, he reasoned, even had their wives and children summer together at the lake. It was, he knew, a class struggle between those on the highest level and those on a multitude of lowest levels. What had become near equality at the top was still far from equal at the bottom and that, at least in Glyn's mind, spelled disaster for a union seeking a common denominator for power. There were too many factions: miners holding sway over their laborers; laborers who fought with company employees in the pit; company pit workers who relished a job topside. To begin with, the company employees for the most part wanted no part of a union although many knew full well they worked under conditions they considered quite unfavorable.

It was a dreadful situation for the new United Mine Workers of America, as it had been for the unions which came earlier. The owners, on the other hand, delighted in the hodgepodge of ethnic masses, encouraged it and added to the mix by advertising in foreign lands for workers. And in this, the last decade of the nineteenth century, the mix was changing rapidly. Glyn had read that in just the last five or six years the number of miners in the Scranton area had flopped from a majority of men born in America to a figure of ninety percent Hungarians, Italians and Slavs. The newcomers were willing to work for less to keep themselves and their families from starving and, in the process, they were driving the native-born and British miners out of the pits.

One scholar Glyn had read said mine owners could control their pits by keeping a large labor supply available, thus driving wages down through competition, and by keeping those they employed near the starvation level. The English-speaking miners, while being shoved out, also found they could be shoved up, to work in the still-developing western states where a smaller work force meant higher wages or to become mine foremen or superintendents and even, in a few cases, mine owners in the East. The Americanized British, one mine official said, had been better workers because they had a long history of mining techniques and therefore became better bosses.

Over time, Glyn had seen a pattern of ethnic control used by the owners to keep the lower classes at each other's throats. They would fire a large number of men from one ethnic group and replace them with an equal number from another group. It served the owners well, keeping the miners at loggerheads with each other rather than with management.

He didn't know the numbers of other groups in the Scranton and Wilkes-Barre area but Glyn had been told by those who recorded such figures that there were seventy thousand Welsh just in the Lackawanna and Wyoming valleys by 1890, a huge number considering that the whole of Wales was only the size of the state of New Jersey.

Ethnic considerations also affected the mining industry's work schedules. On Saint Patrick's Day, the Irish miners skipped work for the local parade. On Saint David's Day, the Welsh stayed home to celebrate their patron saint. Some celebrated Christmas on December 25, others in January. It became a superintendent's nightmare to try and figure which group would not show up on any given day. But common to all groups for missing work was a factor not associated with any nationality or religion — alcohol. Miners who were still too drunk the morning after avoided the mines like a plague on any day.

Part of a miner's work day was to stop at a neighborhood beer garden at the end of his shift, still filthy with coal dust and mud, black face and hands, lunch tin slung over his shoulder. In Scranton, the normal one drink before trudging on home was really two drinks, a shot of whiskey and a beer chaser. Some dumped the shot of whiskey into the glass of beer for a boilermaker. The consensus was that the combination washed coal dust from the top of the body to the bottom where it would be flushed out with the urine. When medical science finally determined that that was not true it made no difference. A shot and a beer became traditional and on payday when the miner presented the envelope to his wife she knew that the small bit of missing cash had been used as her husband's "traveling money." The stop had also become a social event where miners who normally did not see each other in the pit could exchange family news, gossip, and jokes, and, when the occasion demanded, serious debates on issues of the day.

Most of what was consumed was beer or ale because it was cheap and not as debilitating as hard liquor. Besides, one never knew where the whiskey came from. The shot with his beer was easily handled but more could be devastating, particularly if it was rotgut whiskey.

Glyn had read extensively about mining history. He knew that the industrial revolution, powered by coal, had risen rapidly in Great Britain a century earlier and had moved across the Atlantic to some extent in the person of British coal miners. Their expertise in the developing American mines brought a dramatic increase in the speed of that revolution in his new country. The English had the money to get the mines up and running, And along with the Welsh, the Irish and the Scots they had the experience. In the decade before the American Civil War more than thirty-seven thousand miners from Great Britain had immigrated. In fact, every family Glyn knew back home in Wales had at least one member in America, en route to the States, or seriously considering the relocation.

And that movement of British miners had continued. But, after a major strike across the coal regions in 1877, the owners began looking abroad — this time past the British Isles to the continent — for a new supply of labor. They found them in Eastern Europe, in the decade-old Hapsburg Empire. Miners came from the dual monarchy of Austria-Hungary and from neighboring Russian provinces. It was the first real crack the owners found against the growing power of early unions and the revolt of English-speaking miners. The newcomers were from more than a dozen ethnic groups in that part of Eastern Europe where serfdom still flourished, each with their own language and customs. They were mostly Roman Catholic or Greek Orthodox. The only common thread seemed to be they were all dirt poor.

In America, they lost one strand of their ethnic character. When English-speaking Americans could not decipher all of these strange languages they lumped the new arrivals into one catch-all category — "Slavs." In reality, not all were from Slavic sections, including Lithuanians, Hungarians and Italians. But they were covered by the title nonetheless. This flood of humanity, pouring into a developing nation mostly as low-skill agriculture laborers who had been bound to aristocratic farm owners, found themselves, for economic reasons, swept below the soil they had once tilled, swept into the mines, at first as laborers or in menial helpers' jobs. Some came, not for money, but to escape persecution for practicing their religious or political beliefs or to avoid becoming cannon fodder for a dictator's army or to escape the near-slavery conditions imposed by strong landowners.

Glyn had been there when the flood began. He understood their need to earn a living and he understood the owners' desire to hire cheap labor. The Slavs were willing to work longer and harder; they were agreeable to probing dangerous areas below ground and hazardous situations in order to prove their worth as workers; they were willing to take less for doing more. It was a period of change in the American coal industry which everyone had to pass through before conditions improved for all miners. And for those improvements, Glyn knew that eventually the Slavs and the British, the Italians, the Germans, the French and every other nationality represented in the pits had to come together in agreement and, if necessary, as friends to deal with company greed. That had been part of the test for unions of the past and was continuing to be the test for the United Mine Workers.

Glyn's natural curiosity had led him to greater contact with Slavs than most miners had. He asked about their homelands and their families. It was part, he reasoned, of the great transition from seeing a man to really knowing him and a step in the long journey toward union solidarity. He knew that their wives, partly from lack of money and partly from the language barrier, had great difficulty in obtaining medical help, particularly with the birth and rearing of their children. Poor diets and unsanitary living conditions contributed to the problem. As a result, infant mortality ran exceptionally high, sometimes as high as forty percent, and three-quarters of those who died were under the age of five. Diseases such as measles and typhoid took a frightful toll of young lives.

He also knew — from personal experience, not books or newspapers — that social activities which brought different ethnic groups together were another step toward agreement and friendship. The Irish miners, he had observed, enjoyed sporting contests. They loved to run, to lift heavy objects, to jump over anything, or to box anyone, particularly if there was a prize and recognition for the winner or the chance to gamble a few coins on the outcome. The boxing matches were usually in or behind a tavern, bare knuckles, punch til you're knocked out or exhausted or losing too much blood, and then a beer and a handshake and cheers all around.

Soccer or rugby — the favorites of all the British — were reserved for Sunday afternoons when the mines were shut. Often they matched rival ethnic groups where the betting ran high for an Irish team to trounce a group of Welshmen or Scots or English.

In the secretness of night, cockfights in yards behind saloons or in distant barns were the rage of working men, their money on the table as the birds splashed blood in their front.

There was also, Glyn noticed, a growing tendency for ethnic differences to diminish in moments of patriotic fever. Becoming an American citizen was important to all immigrants because it meant the family, through its male voters, had a voice, however small, in the government. For the masses it was a privilege they had never enjoyed before. On the Fourth of July, or any government-sponsored patriotic holiday, miners of all nationalities made visible at least one small American flag on their house. They gladly participated in or stood watching every patriotic parade in their community. It was a coming together, Glyn saw, like nothing else in their daily experience.

But when would it all be enough? When would the miners all come together as brothers with a common interest to match the power of the owners? In his lifetime? He often doubted that but hoped and prayed with fervor that it would come to pass while his sons yet had time to rise from the dust.

Jamie was moving an empty car up to their breast when Glyn arrived.

"Good morning, Mr. Jones."

"Ah, good morning, Jamie, early start, is it?"

"No sir, only just came down on the drop before you. I saw you talking with your sons and some other men but I didn't want to interrupt to tell you the cage was up. I knew you'd be on the next trip. Evan was saying something about the Coal and Iron Police."

"Aye, lad, some bad doings from those boys at times."

"My father had spoken to me once about the Molly Maguires and the Coal and Iron Police down in Schuylkill County back before I was born. Do you know about the troubles there, Mr. Jones?"

"I dare say any man in this pit over the age of twenty-five can tell you something about that situation, Jamie. Why do you ask?"

"I only learn by talking, Mr. Jones, no school lessons like the rich boys. And I want to learn."

"Too much to talk about now and little time during lunch. Tell you what, can you come to my house Sunday afternoon, after you go to Mass and I to services? We'll have a sit in the yard with lemonade and some of Mrs Jones's Welsh cookies. We'll have time to talk then with no interruptions."

"I don't know where you live, Mr. Jones."

"Fourteen twelve Washburn Street, between Lincoln and Sumner Avenues. Two o'clock Sunday, is it?

"Aye, Mr. Jones, two o'clock Sunday, and pleased I'll be, sir."

Chapter Eleven

It was almost midnight Friday when Dylan got home from Lake Winola. Except for his mother everyone was asleep, a night's rest necessary before the pit on Saturday.

"You needn't have waited up, Mama," he said as she gave him a hug and a kiss on the cheek. "Up early you'll be to pack lunches tomorrow."

"Ah, but you're my boy. I needed to know everything is alright."

"Everything is fine. We didn't leave the lake until almost seven and then we had to unpack the wagon at Mr. Thomas's shop and stable the horses," he said, feeling he had to account for all of his time.

"Not checking up on you, Dylan. Just want to make sure you get some supper. Work tomorrow, is it?"

"No, Mama. Mr. Thomas gives us Saturdays off because we put in extra long days at the lake. But tired I am and yes, I've had something to eat. Off to bed now for me," he said, moving toward the door into the parlor and the stairs.

"Anything interesting this week?"

"Just working on the foundation and frame of a cottage, that's all," Dylan said, pausing in his movement.

"Was Miss Hyborne there to talk with you?" she persisted.

Dylan, his head turned away from the kitchen and in the semi-darkness of the parlor, shot his eyes upward and sighed. Do we have to go into that tonight? he thought. But he knew some answer was required.

"She stopped by, as did many others, to watch the work. Seeing a building go up is something those people have probably never watched close up before. Well, good night, Mama."

And with that he moved quickly up the stairs and carefully closed his bedroom door, not wanting to disturb his father or brothers.

Hours later, at breakfast, Glyn asked first, "Dylan was late coming in then, love?"

"Yes," Gwyneth responded, repeating her son's explanation of the late start and unloading the wagon. "He's off work today so I'll let him sleep."

"A good week at the lake, was it?" Evan asked.

"Aye, they did the foundation and framing of a cottage."

There were no more questions, so Gwyneth said no more either. Within minutes, she was alone in the kitchen, ready for another full day of housework. Some Welsh cookies for tomorrow, she decided, remembering that Glyn said Jamie Kerrigan and Brandon McSweeney were coming in the afternoon. She began to mix dough and checked to make sure she had enough currants and sugar.

* * * * *

On Sunday, after church school and the sermon — always in English in the morning but in Welsh at evening service — the Joneses hurried down Main Avenue and then up Washburn Street to get dinner over before company arrived in the afternoon. The Welsh cookies were stacked on a plate on the sideboard and lemonade was on ice in the box, all in plain view, so Gwyneth warned her men the treats were for afternoon company and not as dessert.

Brandon McSweeney arrived shortly before two o'clock, knocking only once out front before Rhys opened the door.

"Looking splendid you are, Mr. McSweeney," said Rhys, holding the door wide and motioning him in. McSweeney went to a Presbyterian church in Hyde Park so Rhys had never seen him dressed up before in black suit, white shirt, starched collar, black tie and bowler hat. The Jones boys had already removed their ties and collars but, following their father's rule, remained in their suit trousers and white shirts for company. Glyn was still fully clothed in his church attire, stiff collar and all. Gwyneth stepped into the parlor — an apron over her Sunday dress — exchanged greetings and returned to the kitchen to wash the dinner dishes.

"Good of you to come, Brandon," Glyn said, smiling. "It's important to young Jamie and an honor for me to have you as a guest."

The two miners had become fast friends since the day, a year before, when the Scotsman helped Glyn get Dylan out of the mine.

"You say he wants to learn about the Mollies, Glyn?"

"Aye, the boy craves learning but, without formal schooling and no father to tell him about mining history, he has little chance. I see you've brought some notes."

There was a knock at the back door. Glyn pulled out his pocket watch; it was precisely two o'clock. Gwyneth was at the door before he got into the kitchen, opening it to a boy with hat in hand and a serious look on his face.

"Yes, can I help you?" she said.

"Ah, it's Jamie," said Glyn, looking over his wife's shoulder. "Gwyneth, this is Jamie Kerrigan, my laborer."

The boy bowed his head and bent at the waist, looking for all the world like he was meeting the Queen of England. "I am very pleased to meet you, ma'am. My mother sends these," he said, holding a half dozen field daisies out to her.

Gwyneth smiled, accepted the flowers and stepped back.

"And Jamie, this is Mrs. Jones," Glyn continued the greeting, stepping back too. "Come in, lad, come in. But why not the front door?"

"Respect for Mr. and Mrs. Jones, my mother said, back door you go."

"Front door for you next time it shall be," Gwyneth told him.

Jamie moved through the doorway cautiously, eying the wife of his boss — a woman he had never seen before — and looking about the kitchen as he stepped inside.

"This is a grand house, Mrs. Jones," the boy said.

"Thank you, Jamie, and thank your mother for the flowers. I shall put them in some water."

"Yes, ma'am."

"I have a surprise for you, Jamie. Mr. McSweeney has come too," Glyn said just as Brandon and Rhys stepped into the kitchen. "Here, let's sit outside."

As each offered, Jamie shook hands with McSweeney and the three Jones boys, all of whom he knew from the mine, although he had not seen Dylan since the accident. Evan, Rhys and Dylan had been told by their father about Jamie's desire to learn more about local history and Brandon's willingness to share from his personal experiences. They decided they'd stay home this afternoon and listen too. Besides, there were Welsh cookies and lemonade. How often do you get treats like that? They brought chairs from the house for themselves, their father and Jamie. Brandon was directed to the large outdoor chair Glyn had made for Dylan after the accident.

"Jamie, I asked Mr. McSweeney to come over because he was working down in Schuylkill County during the troubles with the so-called Molly Maguires," Glyn said as they all settled in.

"Aye, Jamie, if you have the time and the inclination, I should explain a bit of what led up to the hanging of twenty men more than a decade ago."

"I have the time, Mr. McSweeney, but I don't know what inclination means."

"Ah, neither do I, Jamie, neither do I," Evan laughed.

"Well, just the desire to know something," Brandon answered.

"Oh, plenty of that, Mr. McSweeney," Jamie smiled.

"I worked some in Ireland afore coming to the States. My brothers and I would cross the sea from Scotland at harvest time when the mines were slack back home. Worked on estate farms, we did. There was a history of problems in the rural areas of Ireland, dating back to the 1700s, when landowners treated Irish laborers, and us too, as—how should I put it?—no better than the remains of a meal. There were secret groups among the Irish laborers, or so they said, that were mixed up with violence toward landowners. From these groups emerged one known as the Molly Maguires. It was such a shadowy presence and difficult for outsiders to really know the truth of what was happening."

"Not a union then, was it, Mr. McSweeney?" said Rhys.

"No, no, never that, just a secret organization and sometimes, I thought, more ghostly than human. Played on the minds of men outside the group, you know. No public meetings or parades or signs, that sort of thing, very hush it was. I ran into it again when I immigrated to the States and went to Schuylkill County because they were hiring for the pits. There had been a great deal of trouble, not just in that county but throughout the North over conscription for the army during the Civil War."

"Conscription, Mr. McSweeney?"

"Forcing men to join the army, Jamie. Part of the problem was the rich could buy their way out by paying three hundred dollars for a poor man to take their place as a soldier. And when you and your family are on the verge of starving three hundred dollars is quite appealing. The other part was that some men, a great deal, in fact, just felt the war was not of their making and they wanted no part of it. At one point, I read much later, there were riots in New York City that left many dead. At any rate, between bitter feelings over the war and the way Irish miners were being treated in the 1860s and 1870s violence became a way of life in the lower coal fields. There had been talk before the war that the Molly Maguires were behind the earlier troubles and, of course, that talk continued. But, as it had been in Ireland, there was no proof that such an organization existed here."

"But the Irish did have the Ancient Order of Hibernians," Evan suggested.

"Aye, they did, and that was aboveboard with meetings and public notices. And many of the Irish miners belonged to one of the early unions, the Workingmen's Benevolent Association. However, it did not take long for the leaders of industry, particularly in mining and railroads, to begin blaming troubles on both of those groups and, what was even worse, associating them with that nebulous group called the Molly Maguires."

Brandon paused as Gwyneth came through the back door carrying a tray with cups of lemonade and a large dish of Welsh cookies. She offered a cup to each and put the dish on the ground.

"Now eat before the ants get to them," she scolded, but with a smile, before going back inside.

"There's one man who is prominent in this story," he continued, biting down first on a doughy cookie and then taking a sip from his cup. "His name was Franklin Gowen, the son of Irish Episcopalian immigrants. Before the Civil War broke out he read law one winter and was admitted to the Schuylkill County bar. In 1862, when he was twenty-six, he was elected district attorney. In 1864 he was appointed to head the legal department of the Philadelphia and Reading Railroad. At the age of thirty-two he became acting president of the Philadelphia and Reading Railroad and a year later was named president."

"Quite a rise for a young man," said Evan.

"Quite indeed," Brandon agreed. "And with Gowen in charge, the railroad controlled most of the transportation in the lower anthracite field. But he wanted more. He wanted to control the mines and the sale of coal too."

"Greedy bast...," Evan caught himself, remembering it was Sunday and he was in his father's presence. "Greedy, wasn't he?"

"Very," said Brandon. "He gained control of coal production by raising rates the railroad charged to transport it. Later, he was able to get around a restriction against the railroad owning land and thus was able to purchase coal fields. One of the continuing problems he faced was the existence of the union and he attacked it by claiming the union and Ancient Order of Hibernians and the Molly Maguires were all part of one organization. It struck home with the public because of the unresolved acts of violence that had been occurring for years."

"Finally, someone to blame, though falsely," said Glyn.

"Exactly, make up the stories, blame your enemies. Mr. Gowen was a talented man and he had a plan. It included buying sixty thousand acres of coal land in 1871 and 1872 for the railroad. Two years later, the company bought another forty thousand acres. There had been a miners' strike in 1871 and that infuriated Gowen. They say he made up his mind then and there to kill unions forever in the coalfields. He first strengthened the Coal and Iron Police—you all know about them. Then he hired a private detective named Allan Pinkerton and told him to get a spy into the Hibernians' organization. The talk in later years was that the Pinkerton men were to gather incriminating information and to quietly encourage more violence, killings and beatings of mine officials."

"Fan the flames!" shouted Evan.

"Right, more flames, more smoke, more confusion, more blame on the Irish," said Brandon. "But it didn't succeed overnight. There was a big strike in 1875, brought on by a twenty percent wage cut for contract miners. They referred to it as the Long Strike because it went on for more than five months. It soon turned violent. The Coal and Iron Police, Pinkerton men and thugs hired by the coal owners attacked strikers and ran rampant through the patch towns. A mine boss shot and killed Edward Coyle, who was a union leader and an official of the Hibernians, and another striker."

"And did he pay for his crimes?" Evan demanded.

"He was acquitted," Brandon said quietly.

"Damn," Evan muttered but got no reaction from his father.

"By the time the strike ended, Gowen's railroad owned forty mines and had nine thousand employees. Without a doubt, they controlled the lifeblood of Schuylkill County. But the fight kept on, from both sides — trains derailed, mine buildings burned, that type of destruction. And it extended beyond Schuylkill County, into Northumberland, lower Luzerne and down into Carbon. The union tried to stop the violence, knowing full well it was exactly what Gowen wanted as part of his effort to foist on it the label of Molly Maguires. It was a desperate time for everyone, particularly the miners' families, living on bread and water and roots and wild plants. By mid-June the union gave up, beaten. Many of its members were blackballed from mining jobs. Publicly, the union conceded. Privately, some men refused to quit. People were murdered or beaten, on both sides. Vigilante groups hunted down whomever they thought was to blame. In the town of Wiggins Patch just before Christmas of 1875 they killed a man and a woman in their homes in front of their families, but no one was ever convicted of those murders. The crackdown had actually begun three months earlier when dozens of men accused of being Molly Maguires were arrested. It was learned years later that the arrests were planned during a meeting in the Philadelphia offices of Gowen's railroad."

"What happened to the men who had been arrested, Mr. McSweeney?" asked Jamie.

"It didn't take long for Gowen's plan to move to its next step. In January 1876 the first trial opened in Mauch Chunk in Carbon County. Five men were accused of murder, mainly on the evidence presented by one prosecution witness, James McParlan, a Pinkerton agent who had infiltrated the Hibernians and, he claimed, the Molly Maguires."

"McParlan was later accused of being an agent provocateur, isn't that right, Brandon?" Glyn suggested.

"That he was, but only by public opinion, not legally by the police."

"An agent what?" Rhys interrupted.

"It means a person who is hired to incite someone else to break the law," his father explained.

"McParlan was a native of northern Ireland and a Roman Catholic, and he was intelligent, so it was no problem for him to join the Ancient Order of Hibernians," Brandon said.

"And the Molly Maguires too," said Jamie.

"Well, he said he infiltrated such a group, if it ever did in fact exist."

"Are you saying the Irish were falsely accused?" Evan demanded.

"No, some were probably guilty as charged," Brandon answered. "But you have to remember that it was not only the Irish who were violent. In 1874, a group of Irish miners was attacked by a big group of Welsh and German miners; the Irish fought back and killed one of their attackers. Two weeks later, two Irishmen were attacked by Welsh and German miners again and one of the two was killed. There were even horrendous fights between Irish and Welsh fire companies in Schuylkill County."

"Over what?"

"Over ethnic differences mainly, sometimes just drunken brawls and often job discrimination against the Irish. Remember, this was a violent period in our history, still is to some extent. But I am not convinced there was a conspiracy by so-called Molly Maguires to assassinate those they did not like. Did some Irishmen commit murder? Yes. But so did those from other ethnic groups. Did some use the Hibernian organization as a means of keeping in touch with others in order to wreak havoc? Perhaps. Was there a structured Molly Maguire group? Maybe, but I see little evidence of it."

"Mr. McSweeney, how do you know so much about all of this?" Jamie asked.

"Well, as we said earlier, I was working in the mines there, and since then I've read everything I could put my hands on about that period," Brandon answered, waving a stack of papers in his hand.

"You were talking about troubles caused by other groups, Brandon, and that there had been murders even during the Civil War," Glyn said. "That was long before McParlan was brought in. Why hadn't there been arrests earlier?"

"Indeed, why hadn't there been? Pinkerton began sending agents, including McParlan, into the area in 1873. Eight unsolved murders had occurred in an eleven-year period before 1873, four of them in Schuylkill County, but no one had been arrested, no one charged. Eight more murders occurred during the two and a half years that McParlan was involved, thus the claim by some that he was an agent provocateur. The question arises whether McParlan, if he was as close to the assassins as he claims, could have prevented some of those murders. These sixteen crimes were the ones for which twenty men were hung and twenty more were sent to prison for years, at least in one case for life. In addition, a woman and a sixteen-year-old girl were convicted by Gowen juries of perjury after they testified in two of the cases; each of those females served more than two years in prison."

"And you say some of the men who were hung or imprisoned were guilty?" Evan inquired.

"Oh, no doubt, some confessed. But I'm also convinced that some were not. The crime rate did not change much during the so-called Molly Maguire era nor after it. Crime was and is a part of the mining community, for many reasons. And it's not just the miners who commit violence! There are mine owners and managers who instigate trouble, not personally but through the troublemakers they hire as guards and police."

"Aye, unfortunately," Glyn sighed.

"One of the few things my father told me about was how the church treated the Molly Maguires, Mr. McSweeney," Jamie said in a soft voice, sounding like it was a subject he should not even broach.

Brandon glanced around the circle and wondered for a moment how he should answer.

"You're a Roman Catholic, Jamie, and the rest of us are Protestants," he began slowly, picking his words carefully. "And what I have to say does not reflect my view but only what happened and what was said at the time. Your church opposed any secret groups and particularly violent groups, as it rightly should. It stood with the owners and the capitalists, indeed with anyone who opposed what many believed to be a very active Molly Maguire conspiracy. A man by the name of Woods, who was archbishop of Philadelphia, publicly condemned the Ancient Order of Hibernians and the Molly Maguires. Strangely, the archbishop, a native of England, had been a Protestant who converted to the Roman Catholic faith many years earlier. Later, it was reported that he was a close friend of Franklin Gowen. He had issued a pastoral letter in 1863 against secret societies including the Molly Maguires, and in 1875 he reissued the letter and added the words 'otherwise the Ancient Order of Hibernians.'"

Jamie gasped and the others wondered what the boy might say. Glyn knew he would be respectful despite his thoughts. "I don't know what that all means, Mr. McSweeney," the boy said.

"It means the archbishop excommunicated members of the Hibernians and the Mollies."

Another gasp!

"But some local priests had a much different version of the troubles. After the trials, they allowed condemned men the church sacraments, something they should not have done in view of the archbishop's action," Brandon explained.

"You said twenty men were hung and twenty went to prison, so forty had been arrested for those sixteen murders?" Rhys asked.

"No, no, more than that," Brandon responded. "Nine were acquitted and two others were not even tried but some of those had agreed to testify against other men. And at least five men fled the area and were never tried. So well over fifty were arrested initially."

"How could they testify against others unless they knew who committed the murders?" Rhys said.

"Well, the two who weren't even tried had confessed to taking part in two murders but Gowen let them go after they agreed to testify for the prosecution."

Rhys shook his head in disbelief, "Someone who confesses to murder should pay a penalty."

"Aye, but in this situation they didn't."

"Brandon, I've never understood how the state of Pennsylvania rammed these cases through, at least the ones where there was a great question of guilt," Glyn commented.

"The state remained out of the whole affair," Brandon said. "Private detectives hired by the Reading Railroad investigated and provided the main witness, McParlan. The Coal and Iron Police, paid and controlled by the railroad, made the arrests. The railroad president was the main prosecutor and his company lawyers assisted. All the state provided was the courtroom and the hangman's noose."

"They stood back and let it happen?" Evan shouted.

"Aye, lad, aye."

"But how, how do you get a jury to go along like that?"

"Well, in one case they picked jurors who did not like the Irish. And they took some who, for a variety of reasons, would normally have been discarded. One potential juror told the court he understood little English and would not be able to understand the proceedings; he was seated anyway by the judge. Another admitted that he had been in a vigilante group that had harassed the Irish; he was seated too. Every Irish Catholic whose name was on the list of jurors was blacklisted by the prosecutors and the court went along. Of the twelve finally selected in this case, at least three were recent immigrants who barely spoke English."

"And Gowen got away with that?"

"Not just in this one case! All of the trials were handled that way."

"Going back to the murders themselves," Evan began. "I understand not all involved mine officials?"

"Three were public officials—a burgess, a justice of the peace and a policeman."

"So they did not involve complaints by miners?"

"That's right, Evan."

"And some of the victims were Irish?"

"Just one. But he was a mine superintendent."

"And there were more than just one or two trials?" Rhys asked.

"Oh my, yes, they went on well over two years, from January of 1876 until August of 1878, in four separate counties—Schuylkill, Carbon, Columbia and Northumberland."

In the sun—which miners rarely faced—the heat was too much for men in coats and ties. Both came off and sleeves were rolled up. Another pitcher of lemonade was brought out by Gwyneth, along with a second dish filled with Welsh cookies.

"Of those who were hung, were any innocent in your opinion?" Evan asked.

"Many may have been. I just don't know about most. However, I'm convinced that two were sent to the gallows as innocent men. There's too much background to get into but trust me when I say I've read and listened and talked and I am thoroughly convinced these two were executed by the state of Pennsylvania without proof they had done anything wrong," Brandon said, waving his sheaf of papers again. "One was Alexander Campbell who had been a miner for less than two years after emigrating from Ireland in 1868. He was a treasurer of the Hibernians and a hotel owner, first in Tamaqua and then in Summit Hill. Gowen had obtained a conviction against Campbell in the 1875 murder of John Jones, a mine superintendent. But it was a flimsy case and Gowen was afraid the state Supreme Court would overturn the decision in an appeal demanded by Campbell's wife. So Gowen and his allies had Campbell indicted for another murder, that of Morgan Powell in 1871, also a mine superintendent."

"So one of those murders was several years old before a trial took place," Glyn noted.

"Yes. And the strange thing about the 1871 murder was that two men had been arrested and tried, but acquitted for lack of evidence, without Campbell ever being mentioned as a suspect. In fact, people in Powell's neighborhood said they thought he had been killed by another Welshman because he had been living with the man's wife. But the jury convicted Campbell of that murder too. Two other men were also indicted for Powell's murder but a police captain admitted to a defense attorney's questions that he had offered both their freedom for testifying against Campbell. He said he told them they could be executed if they went to trial. He even said he gave money to the families of both men while they were in prison awaiting trial."

"My gawd," Evan whistled. "Where is the justice?"

"The other," Jamie asked excitedly. "Who was the other innocent man?"

"In my opinion, mind you," Brandon answered quickly, "and, I dare say, in the opinion of many others, John Kehoe was innocent. He was also born in Ireland, worked in the mines and then bought a tavern in Shenandoah. Later, he moved to Girardville and purchased another tavern, called the Hibernia House. He had also been elected high constable, or police chief, in Girardville. He was charged with the 1862 murder of Frank Langdon, a mine foreman."

Again, Glyn picked up on the dates, "So this was a murder which took place at least fourteen years before a suspect was tried?"

"Exactly. Kehoe was well known. As a tavern owner he was fairly well off financially. As a politician he was successful in his community. But he was also an official of the Ancient Order of Hibernians and that may have been his downfall in the eyes of Franklin Gowen. McParlan had been testifying in these trials that the AOL and the Molly Maguires were one and the same, so the connection was made all along that being an AOL official meant you were a Molly Maguire official and the Molly Maguires were murderers. The local press, which was pretty much for the prosecutors, labeled Kehoe 'king' of the Mollies. I'm sure it was a conviction which Gowen relished but I'm also sure he had the wrong man."

"Bloody hell," Evan fumed, this time catching a stern look from his father for such language on the Sabbath. "Didn't the families or friends of the accused testify?"

"In some cases, yes," said Brandon. "But most men who were employed by the mines or the railroads were afraid for their jobs, so they stayed away. The ones initially charged with some of the murders who testified for the prosecution were, for the most part, let go. It was an atmosphere of fear controlled by Gowen and his associates—the mine owners, the railroads, the politicians. Few miners—even fellow Irishmen—were willing to let their families starve in exchange for possibly, and just possibly that's all, helping one of the accused. A few miners testified for the prosecution, possibly because they thought they would lose their jobs if they didn't."

"Couldn't they appeal?" asked Rhys.

"Yes, and in at least one instance which I recall, someone did. Alexander Campbell's wife travelled to Harrisburg to see Governor John Hartranft. It was reported she made an emotional appeal for her husband's life, telling Hartranft that her husband was set up by Gowen because he had supported the union and worked against Gowen in supporting people for public office. Hartranft said he was sorry but there was nothing he could do. It was rumored the governor privately told some assistants his political career would be ruined if he pardoned any of the Mollies. As she left his office, Mrs. Campbell told Hartranft they were murdering her husband.

"The strange thing about that case," Brandon continued, "was that the governor took a long time to sign death warrants for the men sentenced to hang, almost as though he realized there was something amiss about the whole affair. In fact, the Carbon County district attorney—some say under pressure from the Gowen camp—wrote a letter to Hartranft on May 21, 1877, urging that he sign the warrants and schedule some of the executions for a month hence, June 21."

"And?" Evan asked.

"And he did. There was no further delay after he received the letter. The newspapers were alive with outrage against the Irish, particularly the Mollies. On May 22, the governor signed the warrants. The following week, one of Campbell's attorneys appealed to the state Board of Pardons, saying those who testified against his client were only trying to save their own necks. But he knew there would be no pardon, so he asked instead that the death sentence be commuted to life in prison."

"And?" Evan asked again, more irritated than before.

"Nothing changed. All appeals were turned down by June 16. The stage was set for ten hangings on June 21, six at the Schuylkill County Jail in Pottsville and four at the Carbon County Jail in Mauch Chunk. It came to be known as Black Thursday. Over the next five days those towns began to fill up with hundreds of vigilante volunteers, Coal and Iron Police, local police, state soldiers, newspaper reporters, and people from, they say, at least a dozen other states, all coming to watch the show. It was in all the papers."

"How true," said Glyn. "I remember the newspapers here were filled with the news. They said the Mollies had lied, that they were monsters. They said the Irish in general were violent and criminal. It was a terrible time, Jamie, for your people. It almost seemed that the Gowen forces arranged to schedule half of the executions for the same day so the news would spread far and wide that the people who controlled industry had won and that unions and miners and the Irish could not and would not have any voice."

"Where were you that day, Mr. McSweeney?" Jamie asked softly.

"I was in Pottsville. I couldn't believe that it was going to happen. This was going to be the largest mass execution in Pennsylvania history. Most miners stayed away from work that day and so did thousands of other people. I was standing on the hill leading up to the county jail early in the morning. The place looked like a castle, a dark foreboding stone wall probably forty feet high surrounding the courtyard where six men would be hung. I could see into the yard through an iron gate. The whole scene reminded me of tales of medieval torture and death behind towering stone walls, of peasants and others who had crossed the line of conduct with the lord of the manor. It had been cool and cloudy that morning, raining from time to time, most unlike a late June day in that area when the sun would have risen warm and bright. The crowd grew larger as the morning rolled on; it became unruly, extemely noisy, almost like a party; I was pressed against the iron gate. Far down to the right in the yard, in a narrow corner where outer wall met inner building stood a huge wooden scaffold. There was very little activity there, just a few men who seemed to be checking the platform and the hangman's ropes. I couldn't stay; I had had enough; I walked away."

Silence. Jamie was staring at Brandon as he spoke, tears rolling down his face. Glyn's head was bowed, not moving. Rhys was shaking his head from side to side, almost disbelieving this story but knowing full well it was true. Evan was raging, his jaw set solid, his face pointed at the sky, his fists clenched. In fact, they all knew it was true, all but Jamie that is, because they had read about the troubles and the trials and the hangings for years.

"A few years later I met a miner who had, at that time, been a guard at the jail in Mauch Chunk. He said he had the same emotions that day but he couldn't walk away. He had to watch them hang four men inside the jail, at the end of the cellblock," Brandon paused, swallowing hard. "He said that before they led Campbell out of his cell, Alex pushed his palm against the dust of the cell wall and said something to the effect that the impression would remain there to show his innocence. I'm told that even today, fourteen years later, the mark is still there, despite efforts to wash it off."

Jamie gasped, "He was innocent!"

"Well, I think he was, but a mark on a wall, I don't know, Jamie. I'm not a great believer in the supernatural. Just strange it is, that's all."

"Ghostly," suggested Rhys.

"Aye, I'll give you that," Brandon agreed. "This guard reminded me that Archbishop Woods of Philadelphia and Bishop O'Hara of Scranton had excommunicated everyone who belonged to the Hibernians and that put the local parish priests in a difficult position. The priests knew they had to give comfort to the men preparing for death by the rope or they would risk condemnation from the families and friends. He said they did give comfort and each of the four went to the gallows with courage, ready to meet their maker. The same happened at Pottsville, the priests celebrating mass, conducting last rites and giving absolution. There were no screams or pleas, just condemned men accepting their fate. But a priest there named Daniel McDermott did create a bit of excitement after the executions when he called a press conference and said — publicly, mind you — that he was convinced Thomas Duffy and James Carroll, two of the men just hung, were innocent. He said no more, just walked back into the prison and that was that. It was widely thought in town that he was try-ing to clear his conscience."

More shaking of heads. Then Jamie asked, "Mr. McSweeney, why did they hang the men at Mauch Chunk inside the jail?"

"I guess because of its location. Remember I said about a hill where the Schuylkill County Jail sits, almost like a fortress it is. You can't see over the courtyard wall, never mind climbing it. But the Carbon County Jail sits on West Broadway Avenue, just up the street from the business area. Mauch Chunk is a small town, squeezed between the hills. The jail has a little exer-cise yard, visible from the street through an iron fence. And the building sits back against a towering hill which looms above the yard and the cell block. It is very exposed. The jail is a narrow building, with cells on two tiers in the lone cellblock. In the basement are sixteen dungeon cells. But it is a stone building as well, so well secure inside. In the three days before the executions, Pinkerton detectives were spreading stories that the Mollies were going to attack both jails to free the condemned. They claimed there were thousands of armed Mollies in the hills outside both towns. They even had the sheriffs believing that because both of them told reporters who wanted to witness the hangings that they would have to be armed and deputized in case they had to help fight off an attack."

"Quite hard to understand, really," Glyn said. "From what I've read both jails were so strong and well fortified that it would have been almost impossible for a trained army to break in."

"My thoughts exactly," said Brandon. "Pure poppycock. I believe those Pinkerton claims were part of the arrangement to gain more widespread publicity about the threat posed by so-called Molly Maguires. But it worked. It attracted more attention, to the point that people who lived in both areas were in the streets, armed to the teeth, ready to fight off a rescue attempt."

"And nothing happened?"

"Nothing, Rhys. There were no attacks, no threats, no proof of any plan of rescue. But I think the Mauch Chunk hangings were done inside because the yard was too public," said Brandon. "The guard said they brought the four out of their cells on the upper level of the cellblock. The gallows were constructed so that they stepped onto the platform from that level. He said they were placed facing each other and dropped to their deaths to the lower level, in front of dozens of witnesses."

"They hung all four together?"

"Aye, Jamie, all at once. Brutal it was."

"And at Pottsville too?"

"No, there they hung in pairs, three hangings for six men, out in the yard."

"Not more civil though," said Glyn. "In fact, it seems the horror was spread over more time."

"Yes, and it may have been planned that way."

A pitcher of lemonade sat heating in the sun, untouched. More Welsh cookies had been brought out too but attracted only an occasional fly.

"And what of the others, Mr. McSweeney, the other ten men?"

"Their executions were spread over the next two years, three on the same cold day of March in 1878 in Bloomsburg, Columbia County, another a few days later in Mauch Chunk, and two more that year in Pottsville. There were two in January 1879 in Mauch Chunk, one in Pottsville that same month and the last one in October in Sunbury, Northumberland County."

"When did Kehoe die, the man you said the press tagged as king of the Mollies?" Rhys asked.

"By himself, in Pottsville, exactly one week before Christmas of 1878."

"And you thought him innocent?"

"As did many others. Kehoe had been active in politics but he greatly angered Franklin Gowen when he convinced Irish voters, who were expected to vote Democratic, to support Hartranft, a Republican, for governor in 1873. Gowen had chosen Cyrus Pershing, a Democrat and a judge, to win the governor's race. In 1876, Gowen and Pershing got even. Gowen had Kehoe arrested for the murder of Frank Langdon, a mine foreman, who was killed during a drunken brawl at a picnic in 1862. At the time, two men had been arrested for manslaughter, tried and acquitted. Fourteen years later, when Gowen went after the so-called king of the Mollies, he discovered that Kehoe, while still working in the mines, once had an argument with Langdon. Presto: instant murder charge! The news was that Gowen stacked the jury with Irish haters and directed the prosecution himself. The two men who had been acquitted of the crime years earlier — who had admitted they'd been involved in the fight — said Kehoe was not even involved. And the judge who sentenced Kehoe to be hung...."

"Was Cyrus Pershing?" Evan guessed loudly. "Lying bastards!"

Brandon nodded affirmatively. Glyn said nothing, too shocked by this story he had never heard before.

"Where was the government in all of this, the police, the Legislature? You were correct when you said they provided only the courtroom and the gallows. The shame of it all," Evan shouted.

"Politics and power ruled," replied Brandon. "Kehoe might have been spared, even the governor hinted at that, except that he had also been indicted for three other murders, though never tried for those alleged crimes. The governor, this man whom Kehoe had helped win the office, waited until after the November election of 1878 to sign the death warrant. Less than a month later Kehoe was hanging from a noose in front of one hundred and fifty witnesses in the Pottsville yard with hundreds more, mostly miners, staring at that mammoth dark stone wall from the outside. He was buried at Tamaqua next to his sister-in-law, Ellen McAllister, who had been murdered by vigilantes two years earlier."

"Did the Molly Maguires really exist, Mr. McSweeney?"

"There were no membership lists, no reports of meetings, nor letters. Even the courts, in trying all these people, never really proved such existence. All we know for sure is that all of the men who were hanged were Irish-born or Irish-bred, were Roman Catholics, were miners or minor businessmen in mining towns and were members of the Ancient Order of Hibernians. You tell me, did the Mollies really exist?"

Jamie stared blankly at the Scotsman.

"So Gowen won," Rhys said with sorrow.

"Well, for the time being he did. But before the hangings even began he was having trouble with the Brotherhood of Locomotive Engineers, and most of these men were not Irish. There were riots in Philadelphia which killed thirty people. Then came strikes by the Welsh, the Germans and Swedes in the mines. A number of people on both sides were shot dead, but Gowen couldn't blame this on the Hibernians because he had decimated their leadership. As a result of the problems, his company went into receivership and the English board of directors fired Gowen as president. He moved to Baltimore and began a private law practice, seemed to be doing well at it too although he had neither the power nor the money he had enjoyed as a company president. In December 1889, less than two years ago, as Glyn knows, his body was found in a locked room in a Washington hotel, half of his head and face blown away, a gun lying nearby. Suicide, the police ruled. But even then, there were those who said the Mollies had gotten their revenge. Some said he was done in by guilt over sending twenty men to the gallows but others say that's nonsense, that he didn't give a hoot for those men or their families. One explanation that does make sense is he was depressed because his plans for glory had failed and he couldn't face the world as just another lawyer. Sad, isn't it, for all?"

"I have no mercy for the man," said Evan bitterly. "He got what he routinely handed out to others, a violent end."

Chapter Twelve

"Did you ever hear the story of the Molly Maguire trials?" Dylan asked the crew as they bounced along in the big supply wagon on the road to Lake Winola Monday morning. And before anyone could give him a decent answer he launched into a recitation of the facts — as many as he could remember — that had flowed from Brandon McSweeney.

"You believe all that, boss?" Jeb shouted with a laugh up to Ronny Davies after listening for more than ten minutes.

Davies turned from his seat next to Old Pete, who was skillfully maneuvering the horses along the rutted road, and replied: "Aye, from what I've heard, Jones is pretty accurate. Don't know that anyone was innocent, but who knows for sure? It was a long time ago."

"I think those damn Irish were guilty as hell," Jeb shouted again.

Davies looked at Old Pete and just shook his head: "What does he know about it, Pete? He was just a baby when the trials took place."

"Was still out on the plains when all that happened. Reckon I can't say nothin' 'bout it," Old Pete drawled. "C'mon, boys, get amovin' now," he clicked at the horses. "We's gonna have to make a trip back to town in 'bout two days, Mr. Ron."

"For what?"

"More lumber."

"No, Pete, not this week. Mr. Thomas is making arrangements with the railroad. On Wednesday we'll take the wagon down to the siding east of the lake. Railroad is bringing lumber on the flatcar every Wednesday from now on and they'll just dump it there. We have to meet the train about four o'clock to load up the wagon. Can't let that wood lay there. Somebody will snatch it away. You and Dylan will go for it."

"Yes sir, every Wednesday. Dylan and me."

157

Both Jeb and Sam were fast asleep on top of the wagon as they pulled up to the lake. Old Pete was, as usual, concentrating on the task at hand — guiding two huge black horses pulling a heavy load along the dirt road. Ronny Davies was studying a diagram of the cottage they were building, making plans in his head for what they would do that day. Dylan was watching the road ahead as they approached the Winola Social Club, looking for whomever might be standing along the road to welcome them back. And she was there, watching cautiously from the steps of the lodge, smiling as the wagon lumbered past but not getting up. Dylan was glad for that. No embarrassing scenes, he thought. But oh how he longed for her.

"Whoa, boys, whoa," Old Pete called out as the wagon moved into what would be the front yard of the new cottage. It was at the end of the line of cottages, a good hundred yards from the lodge but closer to the lake because the cottages arched out in a semi-circle from the lodge. She was walking toward the boathouse now, Dylan noticed as he climbed down.

"Dylan, take that box of perishables up to LaPlume's icebox. Pete, get some coffee boiled and some bread and cheese out for lunch. We'll eat as soon as we get the wagon unloaded," Ronny barked. "Then we'll get working on this one."

The box on his shoulder, Dylan walked briskly toward the lodge, alive again in the fresh breeze off the lake and fresh green of the lawn. He loved the place. It was so clean, unlike Hyde Park where coal dust settled on everything, inside and out. It was a different world, a reason for being young, an answer to the question miners always asked: Will it ever be better than this?

From the corner of his right eye, Dylan could see the form turning from the boathouse and moving toward the lodge. They were on a collision course and he wondered if prying eyes were watching from windows in cottages. He could not change his route; to his right was the lake, to his left the private cottages, ahead the lodge. His heart pounded like an oar on a racing boat. Dare he look, or stop and wait, or offer a greeting? He could sense a face at every window but when he glanced to his left there were none. It was almost as if the premises were empty of all save one young lady and himself. Couldn't be, Dylan reasoned. Others must be around; she would not be here by herself.

Suddenly, the voice caught up to him: "Hello, Dylan. It's nice to see you again." It was almost a whisper, barely loud enough for him to hear, designed perhaps so that no one else could hear.

He turned his head slightly. She was now just twenty feet away, closing rapidly on his path.

"Oh, good morning, Miss Hyborne," he whispered nervously, more afraid of saying the wrong thing than having someone overhear.

"It's good to see you again," she repeated in a lilting voice, now ten feet off.

"Yes, ma'am, good to see you too."

"Are you going to the lodge, Dylan?"

"Yes ma'am, to the kitchen, food for the icebox," he stammered, his eyes fixed on the box.

"Do you mind if I accompany you?"

"Well, ma'am..."

"Just Lily please, Dylan."

"Yes, well, Miss Lily, I have to go to the back door, you know."

"And I shall go in the front. Lunch is being served. But I'm sure I will see you again, soon."

"Ah, yes ma'am," he said, feeling the sweat beneath his shirt and beads of perspiration trickling down through his curly brown hair and behind his ears. He moved toward the side of the lodge quickly as Lily stepped briskly onto the front porch and disappeared behind the double screen doors. He was sure someone, anyone, had seen him talking to the daughter of the man who owned the mine his family depended on for a living. But no one was at the windows; no one was walking across the grass. He jumped up the two steps leading to the kitchen, pushed the screen door and stepped in.

LaPlume was seated at a small table, nibbling on bits and pieces of what he had just prepared for lunch and sipping on a glass of red wine.

"*Bonjour, mon ami,*" the cook said with a grin. "Dylan Jones, so you return again, my friend."

Dylan thought perhaps the man had had too much wine.

"I see you're busy with lunch, Mr. LaPlume. I just have some things for your icebox."

"No, no, not at all," the cook assured him. "My job, the cooking, is finished—another masterpiece for the dining table. The steward and his people are serving. They are working now. I am enjoying a respite from my labors, eating lunch as you Americans say. So, another week. Do you enjoy it here, Dylan?"

"Yes, it's a beautiful place."

"With beautiful people, well, some beautiful people, *oui?*"

"Yes," Dylan stammered, not knowing what LaPlume was getting to.

"Come, sit for a moment," the cook said. Then, in a low voice, "She is a beautiful young lady, *tres belle, n'est-ce pas?* She was here, in my kitchen, just yesterday, asking what time your wagon would arrive today."

Dylan froze. He knew the orders. Do not bother the people of the club. Keep your distance. Was this a warning passed by a mother or a brother through the cook for him?

"You are a young man, my friend. She is a young lady. True, you are from different worlds but that has happened before, many times, many times. Caution, my friend, caution."

"I really only spoke to her after she almost drowned in the lake," Dylan said apologetically. "I didn't bother her."

"Tsk, tsk, I find no fault with you, Dylan. I offer just a caution. I hear them talking about the young carpenter with one hand."

"Who? Talking? What about?"

"Calm yourself. There is nothing to worry about. It's talk about how you rescued her. But these people—at least most of them—add meanings to events, meanings they conjure up in their minds. They're afraid, afraid of being soiled by the world. They protect their own. They stay within their walls."

Dylan was frightened. He realized LaPlume was trying to tell him something and he thought he knew the message. But he wasn't sure. And he couldn't ask without letting his own feelings filter out.

"Yes, well, thank you sir. I have to get back. We'll be starting soon," he said, backing out of the kitchen and away from the cook, to the door, to the safety of the empty lawns, back to the comfort of his own walls.

He was glad the wagon still had plenty of lumber to unload. Physical labor always soothed his mind and calmed his nerves. He could shut out the problems and questions and concentrate on the boards. A half hour later, when they stopped to eat lunch, Dylan wanted to talk, to keep his mind on other matters. The talk he got, but not on other matters.

"Saw ya walkin' with Missy Hyborne there, Dylan," Jeb chuckled.

"You saw nothing of the kind," came the angry reply.

"Wasn't that Missy Hyborne, Sam?"

"Sure looked like her from here."

"See, Dylan, Sam saw her too."

"Look, what you saw was Miss Hyborne walking to the lodge for lunch. Our paths just crossed, that's all. So forget it."

"Mind lads, enough," Ronny said with a ring of authority. "We all know the orders, no socializing with the folks here. I sent Dylan up to the kitchen with food. If someone crossed his path that's not socializing. So we'll hear no more about that."

"'Nough coffee for all to have 'nother cup," Old Pete offered, pot in hand.

"I'm ready to work," Dylan announced, rising from the grass and shaking the grinds out of his tin cup.

It was a hot afternoon for setting joists atop the walls to tie all of the first floor together. Dylan had never had to wear a hat in the summer, except down the pit to hold his light. But he had learned since becoming a carpenter that a hat was a blessing in the heat of a summer afternoon. Except for Old Pete, they all wore caps — dai caps, the Welsh called them; to the English they were pitchlies. Pete had learned in the West that the best protection came from a wide-brimmed Mexican sombrero made from straw. His was torn in spots, caked in sweat and dirt, with a splash of red near a hole on one side. "Blood, I reckon," he had said when Jeb asked him about it one day. "Fella I got it from was stone-dead on a trail outside Dodge City. Had a hole in his head 'bout right here," he said, poking a finger into the hat.

Hats helped but Jeb the previous week had wanted to shed his shirt. Ronny put a stop to that idea. "Not with those ladies around here," he told Jeb.

The hammering attracted a crowd of children and a few of the young adults, as it always did. Lunch had finally ended in the lodge and everyone, except for the mothers, was looking for some exciting way to spend the afternoon. It didn't bother Ronny; he was old enough to go on with the job at hand without being distracted. Jeb and Sam loved it; they could legitimately ogle every young lass within sight without drawing a rebuke from the boss. Old Pete would look up when someone approached, tip his sombrero, maintain a poker face and immediately return to his task. But it bothered Dylan; he found himself scanning the crowd, looking for one special face.

Most of the lumber, at least the large pieces, had been pre-cut at the sawmill by Mr. Thomas's son, whose first name was Thomas too. He was almost a partner in his father's growing company — the biggest in Hyde Park, indeed one of the largest in the entire city — and, like his father, commanded a certain amount of respect from employees. But, out of earshot, some workers referred to him as Tom Twice. For the Welsh it was natural to hang a nickname on anyone whose names were so common in Wales that it was difficult differentiating between two or more people from the same village. And the habit had crossed the ocean with the immigrants. But among the non-Welsh it seemed so childish, almost of a mocking nature. Tom Twice, indeed! But Thomas Thomas had made it no easier on himself with his work custom — a good idea nonetheless — of reminding carpenters to measure twice, cut once. One day, Jeb almost found himself in the kettle with Thomas Thomas when the call went out: "Remember, Jeb, before you put a saw to that board measure twice so that you only have to cut once." "Yes, Tom Twice," Jeb replied in a whisper which he did not think would be overheard. "How's that again?" asked Thomas. "I said, yes, Tom, measure twice," Jeb whistled.

Jeb was whistling this day too, more out of attracting attention and smiles than carrying a tune really. But, under review by a pretty crowd, he was a good worker, fast and accurate, so Ronny never tried to shut him up. No harm, he thought, but annoying at times!

Ronny and Old Pete stood on the floor roping both ends of each large timber, while Jeb and Sam and Dylan—seated atop the joists already in place—hauled the pieces up, set them in place and nailed them down. The three young men had become quite adept at walking across the joists, hands free, without a hint of losing their balance, although at times Dylan came close and Jeb almost walked off into space while eying a particularly fetching young lady.

By the end of the workday—really only a half day after the morning trip—they had all of the joists fastened down so that not even a giant blast of wind could knock over the skeleton building. They had framed openings for a front door and a rear door, for three large windows in the parlor, two in the dining room, two more in a second sitting room and one small window for the kitchen, a room which would probably never be used unless a family's personal cook was brought along.

"Good job, lads," Ronny told them, checking his watch for the time. "Almost six-thirty it is. Time for supper then."

Dylan stood atop what would become the second floor of the cottage, stretched his arms and felt the breeze coming off the lake cool his sweaty brow. It would be a glorious place to live. This building, which the club called simply a cottage for summer living, will be double the size of his parents' house with four large rooms downstairs and four bedrooms, plus a room they called a bath, up. The bath, Ronny had said, would actually contain a large tub for bathing, several basins for a washup, and the necessary chamber pots for nighttime use.

"And who will fill the tub?" Jeb had asked.

"Mr. Thomas said they have some common maids who go from cottage to cottage, boil water and haul it upstairs," Ronny replied. "Posh it is, lads."

"I've seen those maids scurrying about," said Jeb. "They keep their eyes to themselves, looking at the ground as they move. Some smart-looking lasses among them too. Wonder where they spend the night?"

"Rooms on the second floor of the lodge," Sam had answered, much to Jeb's surprise.

"Oh, watching them, eh? You are a sly devil, Sam," Jeb said.

"And you keep away from that lodge, both of you," Ronny warned.

Dylan recalled the conversation as he stood on the joists and wondered, looking around, where that so-called bath room would be located. He could see, in the near distance, dozens of children and women and young people like himself moving toward the lodge. Dinner time, he remembered, for them too. One form lingered, near the boathouse, with the early evening

sun glistening and the lake breeze lifting long auburn hair. She was looking toward the new cottage, toward the second floor, toward him. There
was only a hint of an arm raising and, it seems, waving slowly, just once
and done. Then the head turned toward the lodge and the body floated
across the lawn. Dylan just stared. He had been within his walls and now,
almost by choice, he had been forced out of their protection again.

After supper, the five men lounged around an open fire, drinking hot,
black coffee, smoking hand-rolled cigarettes, finishing off slabs of apple
pie Old Pete made from an apple tree he found at the edge of the woods,
and watching the golden sun slip below the wooded hills across the lake.

"Boozers and fighters is what they are," Jeb said, breaking the spell of
sun watching.

"Who are?"

"Damn Irish, that's who."

"What brought that up?" asked Ronny.

"Aw, just thinkin' about all that talk this mornin' 'bout the Molly
Maguires. They got trouble 'cause they were lookin' for trouble. Drink and
fight, that's it for them."

"And no one else drinks or fights, is it?"

"Ah, but that's all they do, drink and fight, drink and fight. They bring
their troubles on."

Ronny laughed. "And Welshmen? They neither drink nor fight?"

"Well, you and Dylan are the only Welshmen in this here camp, and I
don't see neither of you drinkin' and fightin'."

"Oh, I've seen some dandy drinking and fighting, by Welsh, by Scots,
by English. We all do it," Ronny said. "What sets you against the Irish so?"

"Me old man," Jeb replied softly. "He was Irish. When I was seven, he
run out on my mother and sister and me. Just damn took off. Some who
drank with him every night said he told them he was headin' west to pan
for gold."

"So you're Irish yourself!"

"No, no way. Me mother was full-blooded Cherokee who was brought
east as a girl. "

"So half Irish then?"

"No, that's the half I threw away. He's gone and good riddance."

"And your mother and sister?"

"Gone. Try raising two kids as an Indian woman with no means of
support. She slaved at the lowest levels to feed us. I went to the breaker at
eight. Me sister died of the measles. Short story, ain't it?"

"What happened to your mother?" Dylan asked.

"Worked herself to death," said Jeb, his head down, his eyes staring at
the fire. "No-good bastard just left us and for what? A few flakes of gold.
Well, I hope he found it. I hope he's chokin' on it."

Jeb flattened himself on the ground, pushed a log under his head and rolled another cigarette. No one else spoke. No one wanted to ask any more questions. Dylan disagreed with him about the Irish, not that they didn't drink or fight, but he thought them no better nor no worse than any other ethnic group. Beyond that and what he had seen or heard of Irishmen in the mines he knew little about them, or their habits or their customs. They stuck to their mostly Roman Catholic churches while the great majority of other immigrants from the British Isles — the English, the Scots and the Welsh — were the backbone of the Protestant movement in Scranton.

During the time Dylan had spent in the reading room, recuperating from the accident, he had read about this own people mostly. He knew that some Welsh and Scots — men who had immigrated years ago — had moved up the economic ladder in mining to become foremen, even superintendents of some collieries. The English had moved up too, but socially as well as economically. He knew from census material provided by the government just in the past year that a third of the Welsh in America were located in Pennsylvania and almost half of that number in Lackawanna and Luzerne Counties alone. In Scranton itself, two-thirds of the Welsh lived in Hyde Park. Even the language was alive in the churches, on the streets, in the mines, in the heart. There was still a Welsh newspaper there, Welsh cultural organizations, Welsh choirs galore. They still reveled in the Gyfanfu Ganu — the beloved Welsh singing of hymns by an entire audience — and competed in the Eisteddfod for prizes given to the most accomplished musicians and poets. And on March 1 of each year the Welsh worldwide joined in honoring their patron saint, David, much as the Irish annually praised their beloved Patrick. Dylan knew that St. David was a Welshman, a fifth-century cleric who lived on the west coast of that small country and he knew that St. Patrick was not Irish but rather came from somewhere near the border between modern England and Wales and so was either Anglo-Saxon or Welsh. And he knew that all three Celtic groups — the Welsh, the Scots and the Irish — had for centuries battled Anglo-Saxon, then Norman and finally English attempts to conquer them. So why, Dylan often wondered, did the Welsh and the Irish, in particular, battle each other so often? One day, when he asked the question out loud, Evan had answered, "Because it's no fun fighting with the English. They feel they're above all that."

Dylan was surprised, during one of his reading sessions, to discover that the great percentage of foreign-born residents of Scranton in 1890 were not Welsh, as he had assumed from what he saw in Hyde Park, but rather were Irish. More than 8,000 Irish, a report said. The Germans were next with some 5,500 and the Welsh third with almost 5,000. Next came the English with 3,000, the Scots with less than 600, the Russians with almost 500 and Italians pushing 400. No one had bothered to separate the generic Slavs into Polish or Hungarian or any other nationality, but the Slavs, and any others not listed, did total more than 2,000.

His father thought the Irish more bitter because it had only been forty-five years since the potato famine devastated the emerald isle, killing three quarters of a million through starvation and forcing hundreds of thousands to flee to distant shores, many to America. There were still old men and women in Scranton who had survived what his father had called "a horrendous crime of greed against the poor Irish." And the children of those survivors knew full well the story. Glyn had explained to his sons that poor tenant famers and their families in Ireland subsisted mainly on a diet of potatoes, but between 1845 and 1847 a blight destroyed the potato crop. Wealthy Irish and English landlords could have fed the starving masses to some extent but they choose instead to ship their grain and meat to other countries for greater profit. No wonder the Irish are still angry, Dylan had responded. But he knew now that it went beyond that. He had seen, in the mines and throughout his immediate world, how Irish laborers were mistreated, blamed for every fracas, ostracized for believing in a pope and the teachings of Roman Catholicism, taken advantage of by other ethnic group, except now for the Slavs, who were even below the Irish in the eyes of many Americans.

As Dylan thought about the Irish and their problems he wanted to avoid any further conversation with Jeb, at least right now, so he arose, stretched, and told the others he was going to walk along the lake. He was happy that none offered to go along.

It was an overcast night, not a single star showing and a shadowy moon barely visible across the lake in the dark sky. Electric lines had not yet been strung from the city out to rural locations and only the faint flickering of gas and oil lamps and candles could be seen in the cottages. Some were completely dark, indicating the residents were already asleep or not home. But there was plenty of light and lots of noise coming from the lodge. Music from several instruments — dance music it seemed like — flowed into the warm summer air. Pierre LaPlume had told Dylan that the younger people at the club had dances or parties or games several times each week to give them something to do besides read or talk or listen to their mothers lecture them on proper etiquette.

He knew he shouldn't be walking up toward the boathouse but he felt safe that no one would spot him, that everyone would be enjoying themselves in the lodge. He walked out on the dock, the sound of his boots on wood muffled by the creaking of the structure as slight waves, spawned by the evening breeze, slapped against the metal drums floating underneath. He'd had enough of Irish talk and thoughts for one day, time now to clear his head, to think good and happy thoughts. He sat cross-legged at the end of the dock, swaying gently with the rhythm of the water's movement. He put one hand and a handless arm straight up, stretching his shoulders and back. It always felt good to stretch after a day's work and a fulfilling meal.

He heard the slight sound behind him and froze. Someone was walking out on the dock, someone with soft, slow steps. Just came out to check on the boathouse, he was ready to explain. Wanted to make sure the nails were holding properly and couldn't do it in the daytime when the dock was in use, would be the line. Maybe the approaching form wouldn't see him in the dark. He drew himself in, trying to make as small a silhouette as possible. The footsteps continued. Then, a voice, whispering, questioning, "Dylan, is that you?"

A woman. "Yes," he answered, "just checking on the boathouse I was." He got to his knees and slowly swung his torso and head around. She had called him by name, in the dark. Only one woman at the club really knew who he was, or so he thought. "Finished here now, going back to camp I am," he said, quickly standing. "Sorry I disturbed you, ma'am."

"Dylan," the whispering voice cooed. "It's Lily. No need for you to leave."

"Miss Lily," he shivered. "Oh my goodness, Miss Lily. I can't be here, ma'am."

She was only three feet away now and blocking any escape he had from dock to land. He pinched his eyes to look beyond the dark form closing in on him. There seemed to be no one with her or behind her. She was alone, on the dock, with him, in the dark.

"Oh silly, of course you can be here. You're checking the boathouse and I'm just out for a walk to get some fresh air. Please sit, Dylan, and stay a minute. I didn't realize it was so dark out. I'd be afraid to sit here by myself," she said as she melted down onto the wood.

Despite the evening breeze, Dylan began perspiring, not out of fear that he would be caught—he could easily slip into the water and float away—but because he felt the warmth of her presence and the odor of her perfume. Her head was framed in the scant light escaping from the lodge and he could see wisps of long auburn hair being lifted by air moving across the lake. He crumpled slowly and found, as his knees met the dock, that the edge of her soft dress was touching the coarse material of his trousers. He shuddered. Visions of her drowning and of him pulling her safely to shore skimmed across his brain. He could barely see her face but he knew she was smiling. His hand was resting on his right knee, the left arm hanging limp at his side. His mouth was dry, his lips quivering, no more words came. Then he felt a touch, a small finger sliding over his hand, massaging his large, rough fingers gently, and then withdrawing. He could hear Lily sigh, ever so softly, and he knew, he really knew that the pain in his chest would not go away.

"I missed you, Dylan," she murmured, her fingers crawling over his flattened hand.

"Please, Miss Lily, I'll get in trouble," he pleaded but not really wanting to let go of the moment.

"Shhh, no one knows we're here," she whispered. "I owe you so much, Dylan. You saved my life."

"Anyone would have done the same," he stammered.

"But no one did, except you. You offered your life for mine."

"But I, ah, I, it was what I had to do. My life was not in danger. I'm a good swimmer. I'm..."

"Shhh, you are my hero, Dylan Jones."

They both heard the noise, the unmistakable slamming of the screen door at the lodge, and both looked instantly. Someone was standing on the front porch, outlined by the lights from inside. A flash from a match, a cigarette being lit. They froze, waiting for the figure to move but it didn't. Then a voice from the figure, calling, "Lily, oh Lily, are you there?"

"It's my brother," she whispered. "You stay here. Don't move. I'll go back to the lodge and take him back inside. Then you can get back to camp safely."

"Yes, yes, of course," Dylan whispered. "I hope you're not in any trouble though."

"No problem, Dylan," she said. She began to rise but then paused, leaned over and kissed him on the cheek. It came so quickly that he was shocked. He almost drew back but didn't. It was not a passionate kiss, just a peck on the cheek like that from a friend, or a mother, or sister, or, or someone special. "Until tomorrow night then," she whispered.

"Yes, just here walking," Lily shouted, now on her feet and moving off the dock. "I'm coming in now. I needed some fresh air after all of that wonderful dancing." And with that she moved quickly across the lawn and up to the lodge. Dylan watched, not moving, not rising, apparently not seen by Lily's brother. Lily skipped up the steps, took Wellington's arm and disappeared into the lodge.

Dylan was still perspiring, from what he could not imagine. He rose slowly, tiptoed across the dock to the lawn, turned quickly to the left and hurriedly walked along the shore back to camp, wondering just what she meant by her last few words.

Ronny was smoking his pipe as Dylan wandered into the camp site, which was hidden from the lodge by a grove of trees and a thousand or so yards.

"Need a little private time, eh boy?"

"Well, ah, yes, Ron," Dylan said nervously, wondering what the boss had heard or seen. "Just walking along the shore, that's all."

"Heard some shouting from up that way, someone calling for a Lily, and a female answering."

"Oh, yeah, Ron, I heard that too. I think there was a dance or something going on in the lodge."

"Right you are, something going on. Well, early start in the morning, Dylan. All the boys are sacked out. I'm going too. You?"

"Yes, in a minute. I'll just douse the fire here."

"Aye, the fire needs dousing."

It was a troublesome sleep for Dylan. He was physically attracted to Lily Hyborne but he knew he had to avoid her at all costs. He could not avoid seeing her during his workday because, like many others, she had access to the entire property, including the new cottage, and on Monday he noticed she had sauntered by after lunch. But what concerned him the most was her statement about tomorrow night.

* * * * *

It was still dark when Old Pete shook him, "Dylan, time to get up, coffee's boilin'."

Ronny was up and dressed, sipping from a tin cup. Jeb and Sam were still in their pup tent but arguing over whether it was time to rise. "Hey, gents, it's up for both. Dawn it will be before you've got your trousers buttoned," Ronny said loudly.

Old Pete had a dish of hot oatmeal for each man as they crawled out, pulled on their pants and shirt, and stretched. There was also a half loaf of bread and some homemade strawberry jam.

By the time they had eaten and drunk two cups of steaming coffee, the first shafts of sunlight were sliding through the forest to the east. Time for work.

"Boys, Mr. Hyborne told the boss he wants no hammering up here until at least eight in the morning," Ronny announced as they gathered their tools.

"Good, so we got more than an hour til we go to work," smiled Jeb.

"No, that's not it. Seems Mrs. Hyborne complained that the early morning noise was disturbing their sleep. So from now until eight we'll do measuring, sawing, gathering the things we'll need for the day, anything but pounding. And no loud talking either, lads."

"Their sleep? Lazy bastards don't do nothin' all day. Do 'em good to get up early," Jeb complained, the smile gone.

"Jeb, I'll tell you once. You keep that kind of talk down here at camp. Anyone who steps out of line or says the wrong thing is going back to town and taking it up with Mr. Thomas."

"Only jokin', Ronny," Jeb smiled again.

The scheduling worked out to Ronny's satisfaction and by eight o'clock they had cut and hauled most of the lumber they would need for that day. When the pounding began it brought children out of the cottages, followed by the young men and women and finally the mothers. The children came to the new cottage first to gawk at the workers until their mothers had Pierre ring the loud bell on the lodge porch announcing breakfast.

Dylan was helping Old Pete lift boards to Jeb and Sam working on the second floor when he first noticed her standing less than a hundred feet away. She looked so radiant, he thought, the bright morning rays glancing off her long auburn hair. There were two other young ladies — girls really — with Lily but they came nowhere close to her in figure, or beauty of face, or radiant smile. Dylan took a quick peek, then another, pretending to scan a broad area from the boathouse to the lodge. She smiled broadly when their eyes met and he blushed, then quickly looked back at his job.

"Aye, careful there, Dylan, almost tripped over that keg of nails you did," Ronny called out.

Dylan had been moving while he glanced in Lily's direction and he did stub his boot on the keg.

"Right, bit of dust in my eye here, Ronny," he fibbed.

Dylan wasn't sure how many times Lily happened by during the day but it seemed that each time he glanced up toward the lawn in front of the lodge she was either standing, or sitting in a large outdoor chair, or walking between the lodge and the dock. He didn't know if the other men had noticed, but of course there were a lot of people strolling back and forth throughout the day. For lunch, Old Pete had packed some cold meat and bread and cheese and brewed tea over a small fire he built at the job site. There would be no walking back to the camp just to eat. But those who ate quickly were allowed to stretch out on the warm grass behind the new cottage for a short rest and, except for Old Pete, they all took advantage of those few minutes in the shade.

After supper and some talk by Ronny about what he hoped to accomplish the next day they all stretched out before a fire to smoke and talk and sip warmed-up coffee still in the pot from breakfast. When the sun began to set, Dylan glanced out toward the lake, his mind racing as to what that night would bring and what he would do. It seemed like a magnet drawing him to his feet and moving him toward the lake.

"Another walk to clear your mind, Dylan?" Ronny inquired.

"Yes sir, just going to enjoy some quiet by the water."

The trees next to the camp blocked sight of the lake but Ronny watched as Dylan wandered somewhat aimlessly to the west, toward the water. No one else seemed to pay any mind. Old Pete busied himself with cleaning up the supper dishes. Jeb and Sam commenced a game of poker near the fire. And soon Ronny lost sight of him as Dylan's outline in the fading sunset meshed with the trees and brush to the southwest.

Dylan glanced back several times to make sure he was out of sight from the camp before he turned south along the shore toward the dock. He wasn't sure why he was heading toward the dock, he tried to convince himself. That's stupid, his conscience weighed in; you know where you're going and you know why. Twice he stopped, faced the lake and stared and once he turned completely around and headed north along the shore. He was half angry with himself when he turned again and moved on toward the dock. He could see lights in the lodge again this evening, but no music, just the sounds of people laughing and shouting. A party, that was it, a party tonight in the lodge. He would just walk to the dock and then head back to camp. No stopping, just to the dock and return.

In the moonlight he could tell there was no one on the dock as he approached. This is silly, he told himself again; I must go back. But he paused, then stepped up on the wooden planks, his weight causing the dock to shudder and squeak. He walked slowly out to the end, glanced across the lake, turned and started back for shore. From his right, behind the wall which protected the boathouse from lake wind he heard a sound — just the lake breeze blowing around the boards, he thought. He started again and a soft voice whispered, "Dylan."

He froze, his brain hoping it wasn't her, his heart praying it was.

"Dylan, over here," the voice whispered.

There was no mistaking that soft murmur. Dylan stepped from the dock to the boat slip and cautiously moved into the shadow of the wall.

"Lily?"

"I'm so happy you came, Dylan," the voice answered. A hand reached out to his arm and drew him into the darkness.

It was almost an hour before Dylan reappeared in camp. Old Pete and the boys had turned in but Ronny was still slouched by the fire, puffing on his pipe and still sipping from the tin cup.

"Good walk, was it, boy?"

"Aye, fine walk, Ronny. Best I get some sleep. Good night now."

"Yes, need your sleep, Dylan, busy days ahead, so we must save the nights for rest. Can't be too cautious, you know."

Dylan stopped and looked at his boss. Ronny stared back, a sharp look in his eyes.

"Doings at the lodge again tonight?"

Dylan wondered at the question and answered, "I could hear some noise from the lake, just shouting and laughing. I don't know what they were up to."

"The whole club there?"

"I don't know. I assume so," Dylan said nervously.

"Ah, well, good night then, lad."

* * * * *

On Wednesday, after dark, Dylan left camp again with Ronny watching. This time there was no hesitation. He moved quickly toward the dock after losing sight of camp but he was ever so cautious in making sure that neither Ronny nor any of the other workmen followed him out toward the lake. Lily was there waiting in the dark. There were no words between them, only a tight embrace and passionate kiss. Dylan was perspiring, knowing not where his behavior would lead them but caring not for anything other than the moments with her.

An hour later he reappeared in camp and found Ronny again lounging by the fire and smoking his pipe.

"Everything okay then, lad?"

"Yes sir, but why do you ask? Am I not doing my work satisfactorily?" Dylan asked with a tone of annoyance.

"No problem with your work, Dylan. In fact, you're the best worker I have on this job. No, no, not your work. Just want to make sure that, well, personally, that you're okay."

The hinting was obvious now. What did Ronny know? Had he followed to the dock? Did he know anything about Lily?

"I'm fine, Ronny. It's just that I need time alone, to unwind, to think."

"How long since your mine accident, Dylan?"

"Almost a year now. Why do you ask?"

"I've never worked underground, just topside a few years as a carpenter, but I know a lot of miners and I've heard about a lot of bad accidents. I guess it takes a long time to get over what happened to you."

Dylan relaxed. Ronny knew nothing about Lily. It was the loss of his hand that mattered. They both smiled as Dylan began shaking his head up and down.

"Aye, you're right, Ronny, the hand," he said, extending his left arm. "I'm still getting used to not having it. Takes a while, it does, and time alone, you know. But I can do the job. I'm not afraid of work."

"Oh, no quarrel, Dylan. You've become a good carpenter and, as I said, you're an excellent worker. No, just worried about your mental state, I guess. But I can see you're okay so I won't be a mother hen," Ronny chuckled.

"Thank you, I appreciate your concern. But I am fine, really I am."

"Well, in that case I'll say good night, Dylan."

"Yes, good night now."

* * * * *

Thursday dawned with a light shower but as the sun rose over the trees its heat soon dried everything in the open around the lodge. Dylan was working on the second floor with Jeb and Sam after enough lumber was hauled up to keep them busy framing out the walls and adding the ceiling joists. All that morning a young lady sat on the dock, probably unrecognizable to the others at that distance, but Dylan knew from the long hair waving in the breeze that Lily was staring at him. At frequent intervals he removed his hat and pretended to be fanning himself. And when he did, she changed position and raised her hands. He smiled and knew that she was smiling too. He felt like he was in heaven.

She disappeared into the lodge when the dinner bell rang but was sitting in the shade of the boathouse wall when Dylan climbed back up to the second floor after his lunch was ended.

That night's rendezvous came on schedule in the deepening darkness but it was short-lived. The mothers had brought in a biology professor to give a lecture on nature and Lily told Dylan that she had excused herself from the lodge under the pretense of having a headache and was returning to her family's cottage.

"I noticed on leaving that a number of the younger children were missing. They have a habit of skipping out on boring events and so we never know where they might be. I wouldn't want them to find you here, my Dylan, but I also realize that this is the last night we'll see each other until you return on Monday. I shall miss you terribly," Lily said, almost tearfully, holding him tightly. They stood against the wall to avoid silhouettes in the moon behind the lake, talking little but touching and kissing until the sounds of children laughing swept across the lawn.

"Oh my, they're outside running around," Lily whispered. "See, you can see them just in front of the lodge."

Just then the screen door opened and someone stepped out onto the lodge porch. A woman's voice shouted, "You children, get in here now or go back to your cottages. Be quick about it."

Dylan could see small forms on the lawn scattering, some one way and some another. "They could be coming down here," he warned. "You best go now."

Lily held him tightly and pressed her lips against his. "Oh, Dylan, I love you. I want you forever."

"Go quickly, Lily. On Monday I'll return. Go now, my sweet one."

Her hands slowly slid down his arms. She grabbed his right hand and gently held the stump of his left arm. Then she pulled herself to him again and kissed him with such force that his back was rushed against the wall.

"Lily, I, I love you too. But go, go now."

Seemingly satisfied by his declaration, she eased away and then hurried across the dock toward her cottage. Dylan, sensing that the children could be anywhere on the lawn, removed his boots, lowered himself quietly into the waist-deep water and slipped away in the dark. Ten minutes later, dripping wet, he cautiously approached camp. There was no sign of Ronny or the others, only the sounds of several men snoring. Dylan removed his shirt and trousers and hung them on a clothesline near the fire to dry. Then he hunkered down near the flames to dry his body. He wondered as he gazed back in the direction of the cottages whether Lily had gotten home without being discovered and assured himself she had. Then his mind wandered off into the future and he agonized over what might lie ahead.

Chapter Thirteen

There was an eerie silence Friday morning as the crew finished break-fast and hiked to the work site. All of the cottages were normally quiet awaiting the lodge bell to announce breakfast but there were usually a half dozen young children who somehow managed to sneak out early to watch the men start their relatively quiet preparations for the day's noisy opera-tions. Today, there were none.

"Odd," said Dylan, who noticed immediately.

"What is?" asked Ronny.

"No children about. First time that's happened since we've worked here."

"Aye, hadn't really noticed, usually are a few running about. Perhaps their mothers gave orders to sleep in."

"Yes, perhaps."

For the hour they spent sawing boards and moving supplies and tools in place to await the required eight o'clock hammering time no one showed up. And at eight, when the bell rang, everyone seemed to empty out of the cottages together, stream toward the lodge and disappear inside. There was none of the usual flow, a few here, some more there, a process which took at least ten minutes until all had sauntered into the building for the morn-ing meal. Today, within a minute or two, all had appeared from their cot-tages and disappeared into the lodge. Dylan noticed too that no one, particularly the girls, turned to observe the workmen. It was if they did not exist. And in particular, he noticed that from Lily's cottage only two people emerged, a woman and a man—her mother and her brother perhaps, or so it seemed from a distance. Had he missed her leaving earlier? Was it even the right cottage? Perhaps she had stayed at a friend's for the night, one of the cottages at the far end of the lodge, too far removed from the work site to clearly determine any specific person. There had to be a simple explana-tion, he knew. But, what if she was ill, confined to bed this morning? Would he find out? With whom could she trust a message? Dylan's brain began to churn with the uncertainty of where Lily was at that moment.

Finally, he fell back on the process which always gave him some peace of mind: logic. Yes, he reasoned, she had stayed at another cottage—she had told him once before that the girls often slept over at each other's cottages. Yes, it was a cottage at the far end, one from which he would not be able to pick out individuals in a crowd, even one with long auburn hair, particularly if she had it covered with a straw hat. Yes, she was fine and he shouldn't worry; she would appear later.

By mid-morning, with breakfast in the lodge long over, no one came to watch the workers. No one was at the dock or in the boats. Everyone had come out of the lodge before nine o'clock and immediately returned to their cottages. Strange indeed, Dylan thought.

"Is this some kinda religious day?" Jeb wondered aloud as he pounded nails on the second floor to tie the plates atop the walls to the beams which would make up the ceiling.

"Whadda ya talkin' about?"

"Well, just look here, Sam, we ain't seen a livin' soul 'cept when they went to breakfast and then back home."

"No religious day I know of, but I'm not an expert on Presbyterians and Episcopalians, which I think most of these folks are," said Ronny. "Maybe they're all taking a trip somewhere today and are packing up. Don't worry about it. We have enough to do getting those beams secure before we leave, and we need to be out of here by three o'clock. Still have to tend to the horses when we get back tonight."

At noon, Ronny ordered Old Pete to get the remainder of their food out of the cook's icebox and throw something together for lunch. "Can't take any food that needs icing back with us. Might as well eat it up now."

As Old Pete came trudging back carrying a box of food, Dylan asked quietly, "Did the cook say where everybody is, what's going on with all the quiet, Pete?"

"Nope, said he never seen these folks so tied up inside 'emselves. Didn't hear no word from no body 'bout what's goin' on. Kinda queer, ain't it, Dylan?"

As the afternoon wore on and the men hurried to get the second floor beams fastened down and the whole structure braced in case of winds over the weekend, nothing changed. No one appeared. And no sounds escaped from the cottages. The warm morning sun had disappeared and storm clouds hovered over the lake as they loaded their tools, tents, clothing and supplies into the wagon and rode slowly across the lawn to the dirt road leading home. Dylan, sitting atop his bedroll in the back, kept watching for a sign that someone had come out to watch them leave, perhaps to smile or faintly wave. There was nothing.

Rain began falling gently as they moved away from the lake. Jeb and Sam dragged an oilcloth over themselves and soon fell asleep. Old Pete had donned a western-style greatcoat to keep himself dry while Ronny pulled on a homemade hooded poncho. But Dylan just sat, watching the lake and the cottages disappear from sight. It was as if the place had been deserted.

"Getting wet, Dylan?"

"What, oh aye, Ronny, hadn't noticed. I've got a bit of canvas here. All right I'll be."

"I hope so, Dylan, I certainly hope so," he said as he rolled a cigarette amid the drops.

The rain increased in intensity under a black sky throughout the long afternoon and by the time they pulled into the carpentry shop stable early that evening they were thoroughly drenched, despite their coverings.

"After we unload everything, dry off all the tools and oil them down," Ronny commanded. "I don't want to see any rusty equipment come Monday."

"Ronny, there's a note pinned to the work board for you from Mr. Thomas," Dylan shouted above the din of thick raindrops pounding on the tin roof.

Wiping his hands dry, Ronny opened the envelope addressed to him and read quickly. "Dylan, boss wants you and me to wait for him. Says he should be back by seven, half hour from now," he said privately.

"No problem. You can send the others home; I'll oil the tools since we have some time," Dylan offered.

Shortly after seven, Mr. Thomas came in with the buggy and handed the reins to the stable boy. "Take care of the rig and old Zeke," he said, patting the horse on the head and holding out a handful of straw for the dripping animal. "You fellows come in the office with me."

Thomas filled a kettle with water from a barrel and put it atop a bucket-a-day coal stove, which was always kept lit to just boil water for tea in the summer and to heat the small room in winter. He hung his soaked raincoat on a hook, shook the water off his hat and motioned them both to sit. "Tea first, boys, then talk, is it? How is the job going, Ronny?"

"Right on schedule, Mr. Thomas. Ready to start on the roof next week."

"Fine, fine," Thomas mumbled. "I knew I could trust you boys to do a good job on the cottage. Ever smoke a cigar, Dylan? I know Ronny has."

Dylan shook his head "no."

"Here, a cigar for each of you for being good workers. Light up. I'll get the cups ready. I have no sugar nor cream here. Is black alright?"

Both nodded affirmatively and glanced at each other as Thomas turned to reach three old, cracked china cups. Dylan could see his own thoughts reflected in Ronny's eyes: Why was Mr. Thomas treating them like business associates rather than employees? It had been a strange day and the strangeness was continuing into the night.

Thomas poured each a cup of tea, settled into a big chair behind his battered and dusty desk, and looked at both men with what seemed to Dylan to be a hint of sadness in his eyes.

"I was summoned to Mr. Hyborne's office downtown late this afternoon," he began. Dylan winced. Ronny leaned forward. "We have a serious problem. But I am not placing any blame because all I know is what Hyborne told me in the company of his attorney and Mr. Lordman, the mine superintendent."

"I can explain, Mr. Thomas," Dylan said, his chest pounding.

"Wait, my boy, wait, let me finish. As you both know we were ordered by the Winola Club to have no social contact with the members, in fact no contact at all unless it was part of our work responsibility. The exception, of course, was Dylan's rescue of a young lady from drowning."

"Miss Lily Hyborne, sir," Dylan whispered.

"Yes, Miss Hyborne. And that is the problem. Her father claims that last night, after she had returned from a solo walk to the lake, she confided to another young lady, one of her close friends, that she had fallen..." Thomas stammered, taking a sip of tea, and then continuing in a soft voice, "that she had fallen in love with a young man, one of the carpenters."

"Yes sir," Dylan said, his head lowered. Ronny stared at Thomas and then at Dylan and lowered his head too.

"I was afraid there was something going on, Mr. Thomas," Ronny said apologetically.

"You knew about this, Ronny? You knew they were meeting secretly every night?"

"Not exactly, sir, but I had suspicions. However, let me assure you, sir, Dylan is a good man, an excellent worker. I'm sure he did nothing wrong."

"Yes, he did do something wrong, Ronny. He disobeyed the order to avoid contact."

"I mean if he was meeting the young lady I'm sure he was a gentleman, sir."

"Well, I see what you're getting at, Ronny. I believe that too, but it's not the point, is it? There was no contact then in the daytime, during working hours?"

"No sir," Ronny responded. "Of course, we always had a crowd of spectators, mainly the young children and some of the young ladies and young men."

"Including Miss Hyborne?"

"I really don't know who she is, sir. I wasn't at the lake when Dylan rescued her and no one ever pointed her out. But I can assure you there was no talking with the members while we were working or at any other time."

"Except after dark!" Thomas said, a hint of anger in his voice.

"Not by Ronny, not by the others, Mr. Thomas, just me," Dylan said strongly.

"You arranged a rendezvous with the young lady every night, Dylan?"

"The first night—Monday—I was sitting on the dock alone when she came. It was not arranged. The other nights, well yes, I guess we had a common understanding that we would meet on the dock."

"And I pray, my boy, that you were a gentleman?"

"Yes sir, we did nothing to shame ourselves or our families."

"What did happen? Just talk, then? No touching?"

"We held hands, sir."

"And?"

"We kissed."

"Oh, dear God," Thomas moaned. "But you had no relations with her? You understand what I mean, son?"

"Yes, Mr. Thomas, we had no encounters of that sort."

"Hyborne thinks you did."

"I swear, sir, we didn't. Doesn't he believe his own daughter?"

"Apparently not. Do you know how old Miss Hyborne is, Dylan?"

"Seventeen, sir, a year younger than me."

"And how do you feel about her, son?"

Dylan paused, swallowed, looked at Ronny, swallowed again, looked at the floor, and said, "I love her too."

"Oh, dear God!"

The silence dragged on until Dylan said, "I am sorry, sir. I know I disobeyed the order. I will take whatever punishment I deserve but I will not deny that I love Lily."

"The punishment has been decreed by Mr. Hyborne. If I do not release you from employment he will cancel all current and future contracts with this company."

Dylan swallowed hard but did not argue.

"I have almost twenty men working in good steady jobs," Thomas began, obviously pained by what had happened and anxious to explain his dilemma. "They and their families depend on our trade for a living. I cannot make them suffer for your error."

"Yes sir," Dylan murmured.

"I should have asked if something was going on," Ronny said quietly. "I let you down too, Mr. Thomas."

"Aye, you did, Ronny, and Hyborne asked about that, although he apparently didn't know you had suspicions. But Hyborne wants a new foreman on the site Monday, and I have to bend to that wish too. However, there was no demand that you be released. I will move you to a house we're building on Swetland Street and send Jim Lane, who's overseeing that job, to the lake. That will satisfy everyone, I believe."

"That's very kind of you, Mr. Thomas," Ronny said. "But I wish that Dylan could be kept on too. He is a good worker."

Dylan said: "I appreciate that, Ronny. But, Mr. Thomas, I can't understand why a good friend of Lily's would repeat what she was told."

"She didn't, Dylan. Hyborne said the two girls were talking in the lodge after they thought everyone had left for the night. It seems that Miss Hyborne's brother was in the kitchen looking for a late night dessert and overheard the conversation. He told his mother, and others apparently. Then he came into town this morning and told his father."

"Mr. Thomas, I thank you sincerely for all you've done on my behalf. I'm only sorry that I let you down. If there's nothing else I'd best get home now. I have a lot of thinking to do."

"Yes, I imagine you do, son. But I'm not finished. I am not giving up on a good carpenter, an artist with wood. I have a plan which we must keep to ourselves. Hyborne insisted that I remove you from my company or face a severe loss of business, but that's as far as he went. You have a knack of carving and shaping wood, talent that's hard to find but needed to satisfy the people with money who want those refinements built into decorative work outside and inside."

Dylan, and Ronny, were puzzled. Where was this leading? They were eager to learn.

Thomas continued: "Up on Price Street, back near the valley, I own a small building that I've used for storage of cut lumber, pieces mainly that are too good to be thrown out, but a great deal of it. I propose to sell you that building for a nominal sum so that you can set up your own business, mainly that of fine woodwork. I will also sell you sufficient tools to start. I, in turn, will buy finished work from you for installation into buildings I am constructing."

Ronny was smiling but Dylan had questions.

"This is a generous offer, Mr. Thomas, and I certainly appreciate it, but how could I earn enough to feed myself and pay you for a building and tools and wood?"

"We shall delay any payment until you are earning sufficient amounts, Dylan. But it won't be easy. This could mean a great deal of work; the demand is there. Long hours, boy. I will order work from you but you are also free to do work for others. I make no demands upon your loyalty.

However, and I warn both of you, this arrangement remains with us. No one else must know."

"My parents! I cannot keep that from my parents," Dylan protested.

"Ah, yes, I agree. Tomorrow evening, after your father returns from the pit and has had his meal, I shall stop by their house and we will all discuss our plan. Agreed?"

Dylan broke into a wide grin, "Agreed, sir, and bless you."

"Ronny, I do not want you to think that moving to a new job is a lateral step or a step backward."

"No, Mr. Thomas, I do not think that."

"In fact, Ronny, if you stay with my company I can guarantee you a higher level of compensation in the near future."

"That's very generous of you, Mr. Thomas."

"No, not generous, good business is all. I do not intend to have Hyborne force me into losing the two best men I have, although for you, Dylan, it will be under a new and, I trust, satisfactory arrangement. Now, that concludes our business and I'm happy that it has worked out to everyone's satisfaction. So, Dylan, off you go to do some thinking. And I pray that whatever your future holds you may find happiness even without Miss Hyborne."

"Without, sir?" Dylan asked. "I'm not sure I understand."

"There was something else," Thomas began, unsure whether he should proceed but knowing that Dylan had a right to know. "As I was leaving Hyborne's office his lawyer told me privately, and with a smirk on his face, I might add, that Hyborne was sending his daughter to a very private school someplace in New England."

"New England?" Dylan shouted. "Where in New England?"

"He would not say, though I did ask. Her train leaves tomorrow."

"I must see her," Dylan pleaded, fighting back tears. "I'll go to the station."

"Think, boy, think of how hard that would be for her. And I imagine her brother, who knows you on sight, will be there along with some of Hyborne's paid thugs to keep you apart. It would be an ugly scene. And remember, your father and your brothers still work for the man. What would it solve? If you love her, Dylan, you will do what is best for her."

Tears flowed as Dylan buried his head in his arms. He could feel Ronny's arm across his shoulders and Thomas's hands on his arms.

"I may never see her again," he sobbed.

"In a few years, both of you will be old enough to do what you please. Give it time, boy, give it time," Thomas encouraged. "Don't destroy it now."

Dylan could hear the voice of his father in Thomas's words and knew it was a voice of reason, a rational approach to what seemed to an eighteen-year-old an impossible situation. Yes, he would wait. He would find out where Lily went; he would write of his love to her. And in time, as Thomas had said, it would work out.

He rose slowly, his face streaked. He was embarrassed to have cried in front of other men, but he could see a token of understanding in the eyes that looked warmly back at him.

"I'd best go home now," he said, taking a deep breath. "I have a lot to tell my parents."

"Aye, lad, a great deal. And tomorrow, after dinner, I will come and we will talk some more."

Thomas put his hand out and Dylan shook it, feeling the squeeze of enduring friendship. Ronny patted his back and whispered, "Good luck, mate."

Dylan walked home slowly through the rain, now coming in sheets to slash his face and thoroughly soak his clothes. His mind churned with how he would explain the story to his parents and his heart ached to know that Lily would be leaving Scranton. But he knew Mr. Thomas was right; trying to see Lily at the station would not stop her from leaving but could cause her — and him — untold pain.

He approached the kitchen door, his mind decided on how to tell his mother and father — from the beginning, without interruption, without tears, like a man. He opened the door and stepped into the fire-warmed room. He hadn't thought about Evan and Rhys being there, but on such a wind-swept rainy night there wasn't much else for them to do. And there they sat, all four members of his family, looking up at once as he stepped dripping onto the bare kitchen floor. They all smiled. Gwyneth rushed to kiss him on the cheek. And Dylan stared, his jaw hanging loose, his hands atop his sodden head, the tears flowing.

Two hours passed before the talking ended, the explanations given, the reasoning offered, the solace rendered. His mother had tried to have him change into dry clothes but there were more important considerations. He sat before the open fire, the rain drying in his trousers and shirt, talking his heart out and finding a willing audience. Gwyneth was in tears and Glyn near so. Evan and Rhys, hardened by life and more accustomed to the joys of youthful living, listened respectfully to their younger brother. They all agreed that the offer by Mr. Thomas was a blessing, that his suggestion to avoid the train station was sound and that Dylan, at eighteen, still had a great deal of time to pursue any future plans. No one suggested that he had overstepped the bounds of social standing, though Dylan felt strongly that at least his parents probably felt that way. It was how they had been brought up, he reasoned.

Buoyed spiritually by the strength of his family's love, Dylan, now physically and mentally drained, excused himself for bed. "Tomorrow will be another test," he told them sadly. "I pray I hear no train whistles."

"Buck up, mon. You'll be fine," smiled Evan, slapping Dylan's shoulder.

"Aye, Dylan, all will be mended," added Rhys.

Gwyneth could say nothing as she hugged her son tightly. But Glyn's words stuck with Dylan as he struggled up the stairs. "Keep yourself occupied tomorrow, son. T'will be easier."

Chapter Fourteen

On Saturday morning, Dylan was up with his father and brothers as they prepared for work and when they left he helped his mother clear the breakfast table. Then he fetched two buckets of water and a load of coal for her cooking fire. By the time the sun had cleared the horizon he was off to Price Street to examine the building Thomas had made available. It was a gorgeous morning, with a slight breeze, the kind of day he normally relished, but on this morning his thoughts were elsewhere. He knew the train to New York City would leave at eight and he assumed that if Lily was going to New England she would be on that train. As he walked up Lincoln Avenue and past St. Patrick's Orphanage at the top of the hill he could see Central City off to the east and knew that just beyond the tall four-story buildings was the station. He paused to stare and, as he felt tears coming, pressed on across Jackson Street until the view of Central City was blocked by houses. At the next corner he turned left on Price, headed west down the hill toward Keyser Valley and left his dreams — at least romantic dreams — behind. Just before the tracks that carried coal trains through the yards of a dozen mines he found the building, a small sign over the door identifying it as "Thomas Lumber; Gwilym Thomas, proprietor; Office at 1506 Luzerne Street."

He tried to peer through a window but dirt prevented that. So with the key Mr. Thomas had given him Dylan unlocked the door and stepped into his future. Even in the daylight the inside was so dark that he was forced to leave the door open. The front room was small, no more than ten feet square, and covered with broken furniture — mostly chairs — that had been cannibalized of spindles and slats, backs and seats, apparently so that new furniture could be made. The dirt and the mess of wood really didn't bother Dylan but the solitude did. There were no sounds from outside as he rummaged around and then opened another door. In back was a larger room, dirtier than the front room, but five times the size. He had heard that Thomas started his business in this building, so he imagined this was a workshop and the front room an office. The workshop had five large windows along each side which, despite the grime, let in sufficient light to see what was there. A dozen or so panes of glass were smashed although Dylan could see no earthly reason why anyone would try to burglarize the place. Just young boys throwing rocks, he guessed, with no plan to get inside. The room was filled with old lumber, scraps mainly, stacked in no particular order as to width or length. Two old work benches were in the center, and back in the southwest corner was a waist-high fireplace, chimney and bellows—still with coal at the ready for a blacksmith to step right up to work. On the eastern wall were two huge doors, like those in a barn, which led to an alley running the length of the building.

He wondered how much Mr. Thomas would charge him for the building and whether he would get to keep the scrap lumber and the work benches. First though he would have to give the place a thorough cleaning; it was not a coal mine. As he rummaged through the big room Dylan suddenly heard the whistle of a train running empty cars down the valley to the coal yards. He knew there were no passenger trains on these tracks but just the sound, and the solitude of the building, were too much. He sat, he wept and he thought about Lily.

* * * * *

"Ohh!"

"What's the matter, Jamie?"

"Ohh, it's my belly and a pain in my chest, Mr. Jones. I must have eaten too quickly."

"Aye, sounds that way. Get a piece of coal, about the size of a walnut. Just pop it in your mouth like a ball of hard candy. It's a bit of heartburn you have."

"Chew on coal, Mr. Jones?"

"No, just suck on it."

"How does that help?"

"No one seems to know. It just does, like an old mother's remedy," Jones chuckled. "You'll be fine. Just rest there a bit."

"There seem to be many miners' remedies. Like your moustache, Mr. Jones. It seems a good many miners have a bushy moustache that drops below their mouth. My father used to say it filtered out the dust."

"Well, mostly for show this one is. I seem to spit out as much dust as I did before I grew it. But the hair gets caked too, so perhaps it does some good."

"And chewing tobacco, Mr. Jones, does that help too?"

"Well, I smoke my pipe and sometimes roll a cigarette but I never took to chewing. Same thing there, lad, some say the chew absorbs some dust and it makes you spit more. The spitting is good; you can see that blackness coming out. Though caution it is, never spit in the presence of a female, Jamie; bad manners, you know."

"Yes sir. And about beer, Mr. Jones."

"And what about beer?"

"Some of my friends say to spit out the first pint, to get rid of the dust, but to pee—excuse my language, Mr. Jones—to pee out every pint after to eliminate the dust already in your body."

"You can swill your mouth out with water. No need to waste money on beer for that."

"You are opposed to drinking beer then, Mr. Jones?"

"No, no, I enjoy a pint or two. I am opposed to drunkenness, Jamie. There's no good comes from a drunken fool."

"Sliver says many miners believe that spitting tobacco juice on an open wound can slow the bleeding and keep the dust out."

"Yes, I know of that. It seems to work somehow. Some men even urinate on an open wound; they say it cleans the wound and hastens healing."

"Saints preserve us! Who would think of peeing on themselves to clean a cut?"

"Anyone desperate enough when they're in the pit and far from a doctor."

"Would you do..., ah, someone's calling, Mr. Jones."

The voice rang out like thunder, "Jones, you dere, Jones. I need you to take a look at this timbering."

"Sounds like Mr. Bremmer," said Jamie.

"Aye, I'll go see what he wants," Jones agreed and shouted, "Coming out then."

Jones ducked his head as he moved from the face out through the tunnel to the gangway. Otto Bremmer was leaning against the wall, looking first to the left and then to the right.

"How are you, Glyn?" he said quietly, sticking a huge hand out.

"I'm fine, Otto, and you?" Jones said as he took the inside foreman's handshake.

"Goot, goot. I don't think da boy can hear us."

"No, no, can't hear anything from out here unless you shout. What's wrong with the timbering?"

"Oh, nothing. I just didn't vant da boy to hear us talking. I hear about Dylan's problem with da Hyborne girl. Dot's too bad. Da boy has had his share of problems."

"Yes, he's pretty badly shaken. But there's not much anyone can do. How did you hear about it so fast? We didn't even know until Dylan got home last night."

"Da outside foreman and I vere called into da superintendent's office after da shift ended last night," Bremmer whispered, looking again to both sides of the tunnel to make sure that no one overheard. "He had message dat Mr. Hyborne vanted entire Jones family out."

"Let go from this pit?" Jones asked incredulously.

"Yah, you and both sons. But I tell him dat's no good. I say union would shut da pit and yard down 'cause da men look up to you. Lordman say he don't believe any man vorking here has dat much pover. He ask Booth and Booth surprise me, he agree dat you are respected by all da men here and dat it could mean big strike. So Lordman tell Hyborne last night and Hyborne talk vith three, four udder owners in da valley. Dey don't vant strike over some little family problem and dey tell Hyborne to back off. Lordman tell me dis morning dat Hyborne's very upset but doesn't vant to anger udder owners."

"So no one loses their job?"

"Dat's right, Glyn, no one."

"I thank you, my friend, for the good word, although I think you overestimate me. I have no such power over this union."

"Dey look up to you, Glyn. I hear it in my rounds. They respect your opinion."

"But they wouldn't strike just because I lost my job."

"It vas my opinion. I don't vant this pit closed by a strike," Otto smiled.

"You are a decent man, Otto."

"Yah, and you too, Glyn. You don't deserve to lose your job."

"Well, a third of Mr. Hyborne's wish will come true."

"How's dat?"

"Rhys will be quitting next week. He's got the promise of his own room with Newton Coal Company down in Pittston a week from Monday."

"Yah, I hear dey vere looking for men down at Twin Shaft Colliery. Vell, Rhys vill finally become a full-fledged miner and hire his own laborer. Goot for him. He going to come home at night?"

"No, no, ten miles each way. Too far to travel. He's going to board with a family my wife and I knew when we lived in the section. He's twenty-one now, old enough to be on his own."

"So you lose some money?"

"A bit, but we're okay. We won't have to take in boarders this time. Dylan and Evan are still at home and Dylan earns more than he did here as a laborer."

"I got to keep moving," Otto said. "I just vanted you to know vhat happened. But not a vord, right? This is just between friends."

"Not a word, Otto," Jones vowed as Bremmer slipped away into the darkness.

* * * * *

Glyn was angered that Hyborne wanted to take out his revenge on the whole family. And why did Hyborne assume that Dylan alone was to blame? Was that the reaction of a girl's father or the lashing out of a man with power, money and high station in life? Glyn could sympathize with a father's reaction and he knew full well from his own station how power corrupted opinion. His anger was kept under wraps as he walked home with Evan and Rhys. He would not repeat Bremmer's comments, even to them. There was no need to, particularly with Evan, whose own anger could very well reopen the wound. No, best it be left unsaid. What happened happened and there was no rectifying the situation. The power to act was now only in the hands of J. Wellington Hyborne, not Glyn Jones.

"You notified the company today that you're leaving then, Rhys?"

"Aye, Dada, told Mr. Bremmer, I did, just before coming up. He didn't seem a bit surprised. There's little emotion from those Germans, you know."

"Ah, but they are very good people," Glyn told his son. "Bremmer is an honest man."

"A company man too," Evan chimed in. "And you can't trust a company man."

"Maybe some, lad, but Bremmer is different," said Glyn.

"Oh, come on, Dada, his first concern is the company."

"No, I think you're wrong, Evan. His first concern, it seems to me, is safety, and that's how it should be."

"Well, perhaps Bremmer is safer and a bit easier to talk to than that empty-headed cuckoo outside."

"The outside foreman, Charlie Booth?" Rhys inquired.

"Ah, don't let that bastard hear you calling him Charlie," cautioned Evan. "Curtains it will be."

"No, no, I called him Mr. Booth. Only spoke to him once since I've been in the pit."

"Aye, respect it is, son. That is always the best approach," said Glyn.

"Yes, respect you've always taught us, Dada, and I'd call him Mr. Booth too, but I'd have my fist doubled up behind my back because he'd have no respect for me."

"Evan, you're a good man and a good son, but you have a bit of the fight in you. You're like my father was."

"And proud I am of that, and of you too, Dada. But I think the owners and the supers would as soon kick us into the gob as give us a decent living.

I was too young to know much of him but the men at the pub look back lovingly at the three terms served by Terrence Powderly as mayor of this city. He took the power away from the snobs who control anything and everything in their path. A laboring man he was and a laboring man he remained, they say."

"Aye, a good man was Powderly. I guess you were about ten when he was first elected but you were underground as a laborer before he left office. Don't you recall the problems he had railing at the oppressive action taken against working men?"

"A boy sixteen has girls to look at, not politicians, eh, Rhys?"

Rhys smiled, not wishing to get in the middle of a discussion between his father and big brother.

"Well, I guess Powderly was a lone star in our empty sky," Evan continued. "But the owners still treat us worse than animals. When there's a strike they hoist the mules up, put them into a green pasture and let them romp and eat until it's time to go back to the pit. They hoist us up and keep us scrambling in the mud, searching for enough food so that we're not too weak to go back."

"The mules don't strike, Evan," the annoyed father responded. "But do you think a mine mule has a better life? Have you ever gone down after the Sabbath's day of rest and seen the hundreds of dead rats lying in the stalls, trampled to death by frantic mules whose legs were being eaten away by those rodents? Is that a better life?"

"Well, at least the rats and mules battle each other for rights. We seldom do. They trample us under the feet of power, they do, and we are like timid mice, not fighting rats."

"Oh, Evan, Evan, you have such a power of speech. Use it to advantage, to better conditions in the pits, not to anger the people who create those conditions."

"Are you saying, Dada, that we should not challenge the owners and the managers and their lackeys?"

"Aye, challenge, but pick your battles, son, don't fight for the sake of fighting. We have a life outside the mine. We are not stupid people."

"They think we are."

"Well, some might, but they are wrong, Evan. We read newspapers, as they do; we read monthly magazines, as they do. We have organizations for political reasoning, for music appreciation, for dancing, for the culture of the Welsh and every other ethnic group in this town, and they do too."

"But never together, Dada, always separate."

"Aye, always separate. But would you be comfortable with Mr. Hyborne standing next to you in a pub?"

Evan laughed, "I certainly wouldn't buy him a drink, and I wouldn't accept one from him, I wouldn't."

"Then separate is comfortable?"

"Yes, Dada, but where is the fairness in that?"

Glyn realized he had no answer.

"We can glory in what we do have," he said. "We have the right to vote—that's how Powderly became mayor. Miners and other working men are inspired when they have the right to elect those who represent them in the government."

Evan nodded his head in agreement.

"We can take pride in the fact that we are working people; we earn every penny," Glyn said earnestly to both of his sons. "We can be proud that we live in America where we can fly the flag every day or never, as we choose. We struggle, no doubt, and perhaps it is not fair but this is not a dictatorship, Evan; this is a democratic government which someday will learn to dispense fairness as well as justice."

Evan accepted the advice, knowing his father had always believed that hard work and fair play would eventually bring order out of chaos. It was enough of a lesson for him for one day.

As they walked through the kitchen door, the three miners forgot their strained discussion to linger in the blessed fragrance of Gwyneth's evening meal still cooking over the fire.

"Hurry, the lot of you," she said. "Quick baths it is. When Dylan got home an hour ago he was so black I thought he was back in the pit. Spent the whole day he did at his new shop, cleaning it, he said. I sent him down to invite Mr. Thomas to supper since he was coming here later to talk with us."

* * * * *

Gwilym Thomas was a huge man, standing well over six feet and weighing, Glyn estimated, about fifteen stone—or about two hundred ten pounds in American figures. Glyn stood five foot eight and was stocky at one hundred eighty pounds, a normal size for most Welshmen. Thomas and Jones had known each other for some ten years as members of the same Congregational church but had never had a long personal discussion. Glyn knew only that the carpenter had emigrated from North Wales where he had worked in the slate quarries.

"More room then in slate, Gwil, was it?" Glyn asked as they worked through the large supper.

"Oh, aye, Glyn, bumping my noggin I'd be in coal," Thomas chuckled.

"How did you move to carpentry then?"

"When our smithy died back home, the foreman said I had the size to do the job, so he switched me from the shovel to the hammer. But when I came here I'd had enough of cooking over that heat so I became a carpenter. Always preferred wood over iron anyway, easier to work with, you know. It's been a good life, and lately a prosperous one too, thanks to the good work and devotion of men like Dylan."

"Well, and your support of our son has been a blessing, Mr. Thomas," Gwyneth said as she poured him a fresh cup of tea.

"He has earned it, I assure you, Mrs. Jones."

Dylan blushed, feeling the praise even though he knew his actions at the lake had put the Thomas company in jeopardy.

Supper was followed by a dessert of freshly baked Welsh cookies, a shot of whiskey for everyone, except Dylan and his mother, and a fresh pot of tea — and then adjournment to the parlor. "I'll get these dishes cleaned up. You go ahead," Gwyneth motioned to the men.

"I thought you might want to know of our arrangements, Mrs. Jones," Thomas said.

"Aye, Gwyneth, the dishes can wait," Glyn suggested.

"Rhys and I will clean up, Mama. You go in the parlor and sit," Evan commanded. "The details we can get later."

They began with Dylan apologizing to all for his actions.

"Water over the dam, Dylan," Thomas said. "The future is where we begin anew."

No one asked about how the affair began or to where it had progressed. Neither Glyn nor Gwyneth wished to embarrass their son further and both knew that the truth — as Dylan would surely give them — could change nothing. But the night before, in the privacy of their bed, they shared the hope that whatever had transpired was over, hopefully just an outbreak of youthful exuberance and freedom, a passing fancy that could never come to fruition in the social climate of their day. And for Thomas, the matter was a personal affair between the girl and Dylan. His only concerns were that a company rule had been broken, or at least bent, and the threat that his other employees and he himself could be financially damaged. No, the heart of the matter was the future and how best it could be planned to benefit all.

Thomas went through the plan he had revealed to Dylan the night before and which Dylan had explained to his parents. "I just want to make sure we are in agreement on the details," he told them. "But this morning, as I put more thought into it, I decided to make a revision, as it were."

"You've been more than generous in this matter, Mr. Thomas. I'm sure any revision would be welcome," Gwyneth said.

"Well, let's hear it out, girl, so that we all understand," Glyn suggested.

"Yes, well then, I've mentioned how valuable Dylan has been to my company, growing as it is by leaps and bounds with all the people moving into Scranton. I can no longer do small projects, houses only, it seems, but not complaining I am. I've had to learn how to become a businessman as well as a carpenter and one of the lessons has been that faithful, talented employees are what leads to new business. So what I'm about to say might be seen as friendship—and in a sense it is—but more than that it is good business."

Dylan sat with his elbows on his legs, his hand folded under his chin, engrossed in anticipation of what Thomas was going to revise. His parents sat back, arms folded, quite convinced that Dylan was still coming out of his experiment with love more winner than loser.

"I got to thinking, and I know this has been on Dylan's mind since last night; anyway, I got to thinking about how he could pay for the building I offered. Here is my proposal: he can have the building free of charge on two conditions..."

Dylan let out a sigh of disbelief. His mother put one hand to her mouth in amazement. Glyn continued to sit and stare at Thomas, awaiting the conditions.

"The conditions are these: that for the next five years he not go into the housing construction business in competition against me, and that for the same period he not sell fancy woodwork for houses in Scranton to anyone but me. He can sell furniture or any other wooden objects to anyone else, but not fancy woodwork for houses."

"For five years?" Glyn asked for confirmation. "No competition and no fancy house work to other builders?"

"Exactly."

"And I pay no rent for the building?" asked Dylan.

"No rent, and at the end of five years I sign the deed over to you. But during those five years I continue to pay tax on the property and will make major repairs. Keeping the building in minor repair will be your responsibility," Thomas explained.

"I was up there this morning, Mr. Thomas. There is a lot of old lumber in the building that is still useful and..."

"Yours to keep and use as you see fit, Dylan; a beginning, shall we say, on your stockpile of supplies. I shall also provide a basic set of woodworking tools which will go with the building. And, in five years, you will own the tools."

"That is a very generous offer, Gwil. But why do you give so much to someone who broke your rules?"

"Glyn, there is nothing I can do about that now and, in fact, I was thinking about this arrangment before the affair at the lake brought Hyborne down upon us all. The offer may sound generous but it is a business offer which benefits both Dylan and my company. He is a talented young man. I've known that for quite some time. My company can use his talents in sculpting this fancy work the upper class demands today."

"And after five years...?" Glyn began.

"After five years he can begin his own house construction company or sell to other builders or do anything else he wants. He will be free of his obligation to me and will be the owner of a fine workshop and tools. Believe me, he will work hard and prosper. I have no fear of that."

"What if I need help, another carpenter perhaps for busy times?"

"You have the power to hire whomever you choose, Dylan. The profit you make can be divided as you see fit."

"I have no knowledge of business, Mr. Thomas, although I am willing to learn."

"In the reading room where you built the shelves are books which explain all of the business terms you need to know," Thomas said, a broad smile spreading under his bushy whiskers.

"I don't know what to say, sir. I am indebted to you for a second chance."

"Dylan, your debt will be paid by your skill."

Glyn patted his son on the back and Gwyneth reached out to hold his hand, both smiling and both thanking Thomas for his offer.

"Well?" asked Thomas.

"Sir?"

"I haven't heard whether you intend to accept my proposal."

"Oh, my, yes sir, Mr. Thomas, yes sir," Dylan shouted, rising and extending his hand.

"My boy is not old enough to sign an agreement but I will gladly do it for him," Glyn said with enthusiasm.

"Sign? There's nothing to sign, Glyn. I know you and your family. There is great trust here. Dylan's handshake is all the assurance I need. But, if you think it best, I can have papers drawn up."

Glyn extended his hand. "No, not on our part, Gwil, a gentlemen's agreement we have. Aye, Dylan?"

"Aye, Dada."

Gwyneth rushed to the kitchen on the pretense of getting hot tea but Glyn knew her well enough to accept that she was rushing to share the news with Evan and Rhys. In minutes all three were crowding back into the small parlor. Evan also brought a tray with four shot glasses of whiskey from a bottle they saved for very special occasions.

Gwyneth went back to the kitchen to tidy up, as was her custom, even though the boys had professed to finishing the chore. It was the men's time for talk, and a smoke and perhaps one more shot.

"Mr. Thomas, it's a shame that all business owners don't have your sense of fair play then," Evan said, lifting his glass in toast.

"Well, I find a great deal of fair play in the men I deal with," Thomas replied, his face showing a bit of question over the statement.

"Well, I was really referring to the pit owners, sir, not the retail businessmen."

"Oh, well, different circumstances, aren't there? And I agree, Evan. The vast majority of pit owners have never played fairly with workers."

"Not really good businessmen either," Glyn chimed in. "Pit owners like Hyborne run very inefficient operations, and the miners pay for it."

"How's that, Glyn?"

"Well now, we get paid by the ton, not by the hour. The company keeps us waiting for empties to load, for timbers, for any supplies they provide. Waiting with nothing else to do. If we do nothing we don't get paid but neither do the owners get any coal to sell. Inefficient it is. But the owners don't care. If they want more coal they hire more miners rather than making better use of the men they already have."

"I fail to understand fully how owners would benefit from having more miners," said Thomas.

"Well, companies sell miners tools and the powder for blasting. If it's a company town they sell them groceries and rent them a house. It's a lucrative business, Gwil."

"So whether the miner is working fulltime or not he still has to buy groceries and pay the rent?"

"Exactly right, Gwil."

Glyn paused and Evan took up the cause: "The owners complain they have no control over the miners but they do; they control the price we get for the coal. And they say miners can earn a great deal more by loading more cars but, great ghosts, a man can only work so fast down there. And they've been cheating us for years by giving short weight on the cars sent up; that's why we need our own man to check the weights."

Evan's words were being spit out rapidly and loudly, an easy indication he was becoming agitated. It always happened when he talked about the mine owners and Glyn knew how to slow him down.

The father put a hand on the son's head and again commanded the conversation: "Quite right, and they have other techniques, Gwil. Send up a load with too much rock or gob and they dock you but it's them who decide how much is good coal and how much is impure. Now then, I'll give you that some miners try to load the bottoms with a bit of weight that's not good anthracite but they're few and far between because a good miner knows it's being checked. Hyborne's men have been known to chalk off a whole car against a miner because there's some bony in it."

"No credit for the good coal on board?" asked Thomas.

"That's correct, sir, no credit at all," Evan jumped back in. "And no credit for coal that gets knocked off the car after it leaves the miner's room."

"If that coal is picked up who gets credit for it?"

"The company, sir, the company, and the miner will never know what happened to those lumps."

"At pits where the miner is paid by the carload rather than by weight some companies changed the shape of the car by tapering out from the bottom to the top. So the miner loaded more coal but got paid the same," said Glyn. "And in the breakers, most companies will not pay the miner for pieces too small to sell. The problem is that some have increased the size of the holes in the screens so they can claim more small pieces. Grossly unfair!"

Thomas sipped his tea, listening intently to these miners' stories of exploitation.

"I knew there were problems. I did not know the details. So the need for unions, eh?"

"Aye, and growing is the need to organize and fight," said Evan. "The United Mine Workers got moving last year with 17,000 members in the coal fields, a good many of them in the anthracite pits, mostly Protestants and Irish Catholics. The cry went out this year from the union for an eight-hour day and some blasted company in western Pennsylvania's soft coal area responded by cutting the pay of 9,000 men, mostly Slavs, Hungarians and Poles. The miners were not unionists but the UMW supported a strike, its first by the way. That brought most of those men in as new members."

"So the union won that skirmish?" Thomas asked.

"Well, it made a point, winning a battle but not the war," said Glyn. "The company retaliated by getting rid of some experienced men and bringing in some greenies at lower wages."

"But it's battles like those which make us stronger," Evan said defiantly. "If we had bosses like you, Mr. Thomas, there'd be no need, but the stingy coal barons are pure carbon blocks of greed."

The talk about the treatment of miners went on for another hour and Thomas noticed a pattern of behavior from the four Joneses. Glyn was rational. Evan was argumentative and opinionated. Rhys was agreeable, murmuring "aye" or "that's right" to everything his father and older brother said. Dylan was silent, whether it was because he was out of the mines or because of his new business relation Thomas did not know.

At eight-thirty, as Gwyneth entered the room with the offer of more tea, Thomas said he had to be going, thanked her for supper, shook hands with all in the room, and told Dylan he would visit the new workshop Monday morning with an order for fancy wood trim on a house under construction.

That evening, as he lay in bed and stared out at the stars, Dylan's thoughts of Lily were interspersed with the new life ahead. He separated the two, mindful he could do nothing about her but do much about the offer Gwilym Thomas had spelled out.

In the days and weeks and months which followed, Dylan became involved more and more in his work at the shop. He could have labored five days each week; he chose six and would have made it seven but for the wrath of those whose beliefs taught that the Sabbath was reserved for God. With the work provided by the Thomas Company and the few pieces of furniture he was making on special order his days were amply filled and he found that, at night, as he drifted off to sleep he always wondered about Lily, where she was, what she was doing and, most importantly, if she was thinking about him too. He got his answer just after Thanksgiving.

It was a story in the *Scranton Times'* society section, announcing "the engagement of Miss Lily Hyborne, daughter of Mr. and Mrs. J. Wellington Hyborne, this city, to Mr. Jackson A. Dumont of Boston, a recent graduate of Yale University." Dylan read on to discover only that Lily was described as "a student at a private school for young ladies in New England." The wedding was scheduled for the following year. Dylan listened quietly as his mother read the item on a Monday morning. Then he walked to his shop where, alone with his dreams, the tears flowed for hours.

Chapter Fifteen

After Lily's wedding in 1892—held in New York City rather than Scranton—Dylan wondered if she had played him for a fool. But he resigned himself to the belief that she had had only a young girl's crush on him for saving her life, not a true love. Still, he could not put her out of his mind. At nineteen, he had become independent through his carpentry shop and was more inclined to labor at his workbench than to pursue any interest in women. In fact, his work for the Thomas Company had been so superior to any fancy woodwork produced by others in Scranton that he found it beyond his capacity to keep up. So, early that fall, he offered a position to young Haydn Hopkins as an apprentice carpenter.

"My Haydn admires Dylan so much, Glyn," Mr. Hopkins had said one Sunday morning in June as the men stood smoking and conversing outside after church. "Ever since he and I boarded with you he has talked about Dylan's skill with wood and I know he would prefer that to the pit. He's seventeen but will probably remain a laborer for at least three or four years before he gets his mining papers. Perhaps something will come along at Gwil Thomas's shop one of these days."

That evening, as the Joneses were walking to the Sunday night service, Glyn told Dylan about the conversation and Haydn's interest.

"Well, perhaps Mr. Thomas will have an opening," Dylan agreed.

Nothing came of it as June and then July passed. But in the heat of August the building trade in the city seemed to suddenly plunge forward. Thomas and all of the other home builders were swamped with contracts to finish homes before winter set in and Dylan, in turn, was loaded with orders for mantels and fancy work for inside and out, for decorative fences, and for furniture. Recalling his father's conversation with Mr. Hopkins, Dylan stopped on his way home from the shop one evening in September and asked Haydn if he would like to come to work for him, at pay comparable to what

196

he earned in the mine. There was no hesitation and, one week later, after giving notice to the Ocean Colliery, Haydn became Dylan's assistant.

"We may have some slow time this winter and the money may not be too good," Dylan had warned, "but I'm trying to put off the furniture work until after the housing season."

Haydn was not discouraged. He was out of the pit, a job he found wanting because the miner who employed him was one of those colliers who pushed as much work as possible on his laborer. And he never enjoyed the darkness nor the dampness nor the dust, although he had no fear of toiling beneath thousands of tons of earth and rock.

For Dylan it was companionship in the large shop where the workday often stretched into twelve hours, particularly during the housing season, and a full day on Saturdays. He had spent the previous year alone at work, alone with his thoughts, which often included Lily. The dreary winter days — when housing work slowed and he had time to clean out the shop and spend careful hours on furniture — had been the worst. Other than visits twice a week from Mr. Thomas and deliveries of lumber or pickups of finished work, Dylan wrestled alone with his thoughts as he worked. No one had asked him about Lily, knowing full well that her wedding day was approaching.

Haydn's presence changed much of that. There was talk about projects and planning, discussions about woodworking versus mining, forays into politics and religion, and comparisons of favorite beer gardens, as most bars in Scranton were called — a tag applied, it seems, by German immigrants. There was laughter too, an ingredient which had been missing from Dylan's life for more than a full year. The relationship soon developed into one of two young friends carving out a niche for themselves in the business world rather than that of boss and employee.

Dylan also became closer to the Hopkins family, often stopping there for dinner after he and Haydn had left the shop late. "No sense in two mothers warming up the supper," Mrs. Hopkins had said the first time she invited him to stay. Mr. Hopkins and Haydn's brother, Tom, now twenty-two, would join them at the table for a cup of tea as the two young men ate. And always hovering in the kitchen, busy it seems with cleaning up after the meal, was Beth who, Dylan was told one evening, had turned sixteen.

* * * * *

It was an eventful year for another of the Jones boys too. Evan, ever faithful to the union cause, was approached by the fledgling United Mine Workers of America leaders to become a full-time, paid employee, charged with traveling throughout the northern anthracite field to bring new members into the fold. The salary, as they called it, would be the same as the wage he was earning as a miner, plus a bonus as the membership grew. The Hyborne Coal Company's owner, so adamant a year earlier that the Jones family be booted out of his mine, was now rid of the second son. But the smiles of owner, superintendent and outside foreman soon dissolved into anger when the energetic Evan Jones began his new career as a union organizer.

A year later, its membership rolls growing, the United Mine Workers suffered a setback they had never anticipated—collapse of the stock market. The 1893 crash not only took its toll of the wealthy but filtered down through the levels of all types of companies to the point where workers lost their jobs, including miners. The union lost members and its finances were eroded as the depression worked its deadly fingers into every aspect of American business. Evan hung on, earning less and working more, and knowing that it was all the UMW could do to hang on to a pared-down staff. He thought they could survive. But he hadn't figured that the union's leaders—greedy as some owners, he thought—would take a step in 1894 which almost sealed the organization in its tomb: a national strike.

He argued against the decision, recalling his father's frequent advice to carefully choose one's battles, but no one listened. The call went out across the country, to every mining area and every pit with UMW members: We will reduce coal stockpiles to force owners into increasing the tonnage rate. Glyn told Evan it reminded him of the disastrous strike in 1875 which failed so miserably that thousands of miners and their families were saved from starvation only through the charity of their neighbors.

Evan persevered, believing so strongly in the union that he was forced to take on temporary laboring jobs to pay his fair share of household expenses while retaining his position as an organizer. As economic times began to improve so did the union's finances and successes.

* * * * *

In 1895, the Lackawanna and Wyoming valleys were shaken when a roof fall at the Dorrance Mine near Wilkes-Barre killed fifty-eight men and boys in one afternoon. It was the worst mining tragedy in the northeast in more than a quarter century.

It shook Gwyneth more than it did Glyn, which was so often the case among mining families and particularly those in which the woman had both husband and sons working underground.

But it was nowhere near the personal tragedy for them which came the following year.

In the early part of the decade it had become common for owners to keep crews working seven days a week, disregarding Sunday as a day of rest for those who worked at a colliery—except the office staff. Most miners did not object because they needed steady work to support growing families.

Word came to Scranton early on the morning of Sunday, June 28, 1896, that there had been an accident at Newton Coal Company's Twin Shaft. The crew on a work train came up the valley sounding the alarm that something had roared and shaken the ground at about three o'clock that morning in Pittston. Rescue workers were needed.

"Three shakings there were," one of crewmen shouted as the alarm was spread from Keyser Valley down through the streets of Hyde Park. "A cave-in at Twin Shaft they think. They've sent in a rescue team but are looking for more help."

Gwyneth and Glyn were at the siding just six blocks from their house within minutes as men and tools were loaded onto a flat car.

"No women, ma'am," a trainman yelled as Glyn hoisted his wife onto the car.

"Our son works at that mine. She's going," Glyn shouted back. "Stand aside."

"I've got orders," the trainman protested as he tried to push Gwyneth off.

Within seconds, the trainman was flat on his back with Glyn hovering over him, still holding the front of his coat in two clenched hands. "I don't give a damn about your orders. Our son could be down there," Glyn shouted again.

As the trainman climbed back onto his feet, he shouted, "You'll be in trouble over this, son or no. I've got orders." And with that he felt himself falling off the car, a quick right punch from Glyn catching him off guard. There were no more complaints as the trainman got up and rushed off down the track toward the engine.

"Bloody hell," Glyn yelled, more upset than Gwyneth had ever seen him before. She began to cry, upset not by the quick fight but by the prospect of what they would find at Twin Shaft.

It took a half hour for the train, its two flat cars loaded with miners, carrying shovels and picks, and one woman, to reach Pittston. The pit yard was awash in people, men scurrying to and fro, women and children crying. A state mine inspector, whom Glyn knew, was near the cage, supervising the lowering of rescue teams.

"Joe, I'm here to help," Glyn shouted above the noise.

The inspector put a hand on his chest, holding him back.

"Glyn, I don't want you to go down."

"My boy, Rhys, he works here," Glyn yelled in a panicky voice.

"Yes, I know, I've talked to him."

"You talked to him, today? Since this morning?"

"No, no, over the past couple years. He came to me once and told me who he was," Joe stammered, moving his hand from Glyn's chest to hold his arm.

"Is he below?"

"His name is on the list, Glyn."

"Oh my gawd," Glyn whispered, his knees buckling and a cold sweat breaking out on his brow. "Are you sure, Joe?"

"Rhys Jones, yes, right here," the inspector said, pulling a sheet of paper from an inner pocket. "Stands out, one of the few Welshmen in this pit. Mostly Irish here. But we don't know his situation yet, Glyn. In fact, we don't know how bad any of it is. Mrs. Jones here too?"

"Aye, she could not stay at home."

"Take her over to the shanty. I'll keep you informed," said the inspector.

Other women had crowded into the small shanty where miners normally waited in wet or freezing weather for the cage to load. The wailing of so many people was too much for Gwyneth and she pushed Glyn back out into the bright sunlight.

"I can't be close to that, Glyn," Gwyneth cried, nodding toward the shanty. "Best wait out here, alright?"

"Yes, my love, we'll wait here."

Two hours passed before the first rescue team surfaced to find hundreds of men, women and children in the coal yard. Fresh teams were waiting to take their place, anxious to descend to help find friends or just fellow miners.

"That team was down since the breaker whistle blew more than six hours ago," the inspector explained to Glyn and a knot of miners around him.

"Is it bad, Joe?"

"They dug into the fall but didn't break through to any openings," came the solemn answer.

By noon, after another train was dispatched from Scranton, Evan, Dylan and the entire Hopkins family had joined the Joneses. Mrs. Hopkins had brought a basket of buttered bread and containers of tea, now cold, and shared it not only with her friends but with strangers too.

As the day wore on into early evening and the second and third rescue teams emerged from the pit with neither survivors nor bodies Glyn feared the worst but said nothing to Gwyneth. The inspector gathered only men near the cage after the third team came up and told them: "It appears the roof fall covered a very large area, probably where most if not all of the men were working. We've hit no gas pockets, no smoke or fire, nothing to indicate an explosion. Neither have we heard any tapping or other signs of life. We will continue digging through but I'm afraid it looks hopeless."

Glyn's shoulders sagged. Others in the group cursed. A few openly shed tears. All turned and walked away, seeking family members with the news.

Glyn walked slowly back to his loved ones and friends. He reached out for Gwyneth, held her tightly and sensed that she knew the answer to any question about Rhys. He felt her slipping out of his grip, obviously on the verge of fainting, and motioned for Evan and Dylan to sit and hold her as he fanned her blank face with his cap.

Gwyneth looked into her husband's eyes, tears streaming from her own, and murmured, "My boy, my little boy."

Glyn held her tightly again, the sorrow from his eyes running down over her cheeks, and whispered, "We must not lose hope, my love."

Late into the night, an announcement was made by the inspector standing atop a coal car: "We will continue digging but I must tell you that the team now in the pit has not found any remains."

A great cry arose from the masses filling the yard, most of them Irish. Names were screamed; protests were made to God to spare a husband, a grandfather, a father, a son, a brother. Most were on their knees, some with arms stretched skyward.

"There's nothing we can do here," Glyn announced sadly to his family and to the Hopkinses. "If men are found we will be notified."

He knew it sounded like a cruel move, but he also knew that there was, as he had said, nothing at all they could do.

On Monday morning, the Jones family returned to Pittston, prepared to wait until some final outcome was determined.

Shortly after noon, a mine inspector gathered the families in the yard and announced, "Our rescue efforts have been in vain."

Gasps of breath and sobbing permeated the crowd, but the reaction was muted. Everyone in the mining community knew that after twenty-four hours without a sound from the missing there was scant hope that anyone would be found alive. Glyn and other miners clung to the knowledge that men could survive underground for a week or longer without food, subsisting only on natural water seeping into the works, particularly in a roof fall situation. Explosions caused by gas and the fires they spread were different because fire consumed the oxygen trapped men need to survive. But a roof fall meant one of two things: being caught underneath and crushed or being cut off from escape but alive. However, being cut off also meant that the oxygen supply could be depleted in short order or that trapped men could starve. The key to survival in a roof fall was to dig, from both sides. And digging from one side was what the rescue teams had been doing for more than thirty hours. But they reported no tapping, no sounds of life from beyond the fall.

The inspector, who waited patiently for his announcement to sink in, continued: "The fall area is extensive and we're now sure that all of the men working were in that area. We are proceeding quite slowly, timbering as we go to prevent further falls."

Gwyneth sagged in Glyn's arms and sobbed uncontrollably. Every family huddled, men holding women and women with their arms around little children, as if to hold them back from becoming miners later in their lives.

Glyn asked again to be allowed to go below as a rescuer but was turned down, as were other close relatives of the trapped men. "Your families have been through too much; we don't want you to get injured here," they were told.

By the following day, the families were informed that other rescue teams had gotten into the mine from an airshaft and had worked their way through the gangway to the blocked area.

"We are now on both sides of the fall," an inspector told the crowd still filling the coal yard. "It's much larger than we anticipated, covering perhaps two hundred acres, twenty times what we originally had thought. The danger of digging into an area that immense poses tremendous danger to rescue crews. We are dispensing with further rescue work because it is obvious that no one could have survived."

And with that shouts of anguish, and screams, and wailing broke out. There were those who demanded that the digging continue while others — particularly miners — tried to reason with their families that the situation was hopeless, that all were dead.

Gwyneth accepted the fact, knowing full well that Glyn had already accepted it. But she found it difficult to believe that her son's body would not be recovered for a proper burial.

At the memorial service in their church the following Saturday Pastor Evans placed a bit of solace in Gwyneth's heart when he said that the true Rhys in spirit was now resting at the hand of God while the earthly Rhys was at rest with his work mates in a grave guarded by the Holy Spirit. Both she and Glyn, and their sons, were the sole beneficiaries of a massive outpouring of grief and support from their own congregation since Rhys was the only one from Hyde Park who had died. They knew that in churches throughout the Pittston area, mainly Roman Catholic, there were congregations who had to share with many families.

Fifty-eight were lost at Twin Shaft, the same number killed just a year earlier at nearby Dorrance. They were the two worst tragedies in the northern anthracite region since fire killed one hundred seventy-nine men and boys at the Avondale pit near Plymouth, just a few miles from Pittston, in 1869.

The governor ordered an investigation of Twin Shaft after hearing reports from some employees that the mine was unsafe. The Joneses followed the proceedings religiously in the *Scranton Times*. One miner, among a group of four who had left the pit before the roof caved, testified that the mine had been a dangerous place for six months because the gangways were too wide and the supporting coal pillars were too weak. He said the four miners left because the roof was cracking but the others, facing disciplinary action if they abandoned their jobs, stayed. One crack was so wide, the miner told a hearing board, that he was able to stick his arm in it.

A week of hearings brought support for the miner's testimony, but it also brought claims of lawful and safe mining by company officials and inspectors. Glyn read intently, siding generally with the miners' versions. Evan, perusing the same material, held that the owner and the company managers were guilty of gross negligence and should go to prison.

"Dirty bastards killed my brother," he shouted out one evening as he and Glyn walked home from a union meeting.

"I'll not hear those words in the presence of your mother," Glyn fumed.

"No, I'll not repeat them in front of her, Dada," Evan said, his voice toned down.

It was three months before the governor's board announced the results of its hearings. They said the mine superintendent—one of those killed in the fall—had made a terrible decision. Finally convinced of the danger by the miners, including the four who refused to work any longer that night, the superintendent moved his crew to the middle of the area where the roof seemed to be the weakest. The board agreed that he should have started to shore up the roof from the edges where it was strongest and then worked toward the middle.

"It's the old story," Evan complained alone to his father after the board announced its conclusion. "Improper or missing maps of the workings, robbing pillars still needed for support, an inadequate number of inspectors to make more frequent checks and a company official without proper experience directing the work. Greed it is, Dada. Make money by whatever means, forget about the men."

"Aye, boy, that's the heart of it now. Pity it is," said Glyn, knowing he had to agree with Evan's evaluation. "We lose Rhys; your poor mother's heart is broken, and mine too, and nothing changes."

"I looked at the union records on Twin Shaft yesterday," Evan said quietly. "Nine men killed from 1889 to 1895, and almost two million tons mined in that time. I would never admit it to a company man, Dada, but that is a decent record. There are many pits with less production and greater numbers of accidents."

Glyn was shocked to hear his usually fiery son say that the deaths of nine miners was a decent record, so callous it seemed. But then he realized that Evan was right, that too many mines had worse records. Still, to Glyn, one death was one too many. And his son's death was one that he would never commit to the record books and forget.

Christmas that year became a very solemn occasion for the Jones family. Glyn was surprised to see that instead of a gay ribbon in the front window Gwyneth had hung a black cloth. He could not fault her. The joy of the Christ Child's birth was too much for her to bear.

It became a project of the entire Hopkins family to see the Joneses through the holidays and, in particular, it was when Dylan first noticed that Beth suddenly appeared to be a young lady rather than a girl.

There were exchanges of gifts and invitations to dinner and many activities at church for both families to share. And Dylan found that Beth, who had been like a sister to him ever since he had hired Haydn to work in the shop, was not really a sister anymore. The death of Rhys brought her more to Dylan's side as a comfort and in her he saw the first warmth to his soul since the announcement that Lily was to be married.

"Everything seems to have changed, Mama," he said the night before New Year's Eve as he spoke to Gwyneth about Beth.

"I've noticed. For the past few years it's been tease and tickle, like brother and sister. It changed when Rhys was taken," Gwyneth sighed. "One blessing taken, one received."

"How so, Mama?"

"Rhys, my quiet one, gone to be with the Lord," she began to sob.

Dylan reached out for her hand and squeezed tightly and nodded, tears glistening in his eyes.

"But you seem to have found yourself in the wood shop these past few years and I noticed how Beth, ever since the funeral, has taken it upon herself to comfort you. No more tease and tickle, is it? No more children at play."

"Long time since I was a child, Mama. Twenty-three now it is."

"Aye, a man you are. And Beth? At twenty a woman she is. Are there feelings, my boy?"

"I don't know, Mama. Fear it is, I think."

"That one woman — girl really — treated you badly. Fear of that happening again?"

"Aye, perhaps, Mama, perhaps that's what it is."

"Then give it time, Dylan."

"Yes, Mama."

Chapter Sixteen

Evan agreed with union leaders late in the spring of 1897 that it was time to call a national strike of coal miners, this time over wages. It would begin, they decided, as an act of independence on the Fourth of July. And on that date, as America celebrated its birth, the strike spread across the country from northern Illinois. More than one hundred and fifty thousand miners — most of them actually not yet UMW members — walked out of the pits. The economy had moved back up the scale since the crash of '93 and business was booming. But the mine owners had not anticipated a strike and had no time to build up a huge reserve of coal for their markets.

In mid-August, Evan told his father that organizing in the northern anthracite field still fell far behind that of other mining areas. "We Welsh, and Scots, and English, yes even the Irish, we've had the best of it all these years. It's difficult to recruit members when the men feel they're doing just fine. But the Slavs, those poor devils, they're still feeling the pinch, and they're the ones who should be joining us. When they learn English they begin to realize how they're being cheated. I read just yesterday, Dada, about a costume ball in New York's Waldorf Hotel this summer. One wealthy man came wearing a gold-plated suit of armor; the newspaper said it cost him ten thousand dollars. Decadence, pure decadence!"

"Aye, a waste, boy."

"Yes sir, a great waste! But a crime too."

"And would you have communism take the place of a democracy, Evan?"

"No, a bit of socialism perhaps, or just a bit of social conscience would do."

Glyn liked what he was hearing from his oldest son. Evan, at twenty-nine, was sounding more like his father — angry but rational over treatment of the working class.

"I'll be away for part of the summer working on just that problem, Dada."

"Oh, how's that?"

"The union has assigned me to help down in the Hazleton area. There's more cooperation now than there had been between the English speakers and the Slavs. Strength in numbers, as you always said. And the owners fear that. They've always tried to drive a wedge between those groups to keep them at each other's throats."

"How well I know that," said Glyn. "But why down in Hazleton?"

"There's been a problem at the Honeybrook Colliery in McAdoo. The company ordered its mule drivers to feed and groom their animals after the shift ends, so they get no pay for that time. Twenty of them refused, were discharged this week and have set up a picket line. We've been told that two thousand men are going to walk out too. With all of that unrest the union felt it was a good time to sign up new members in a number of small towns, including some patches."

"Such as?"

"Places I've never heard of, in addition to McAdoo—Audenreid, Harleigh, Cranberry, Jeansville, Ebervale, Harwood, Beaver Brook, Lattimer."

Evan left Scranton two days later, assigned to a small hotel room in Hazleton and to an organizing team led by an Irishman named John Fahy. He was disturbed by what he saw: company dominance over mostly Slavic miners, although Italian workers were involved too, and a growing number of marches and rallies held by the miners to gain community support. There were two schools of thought, both in the towns and in the two regional newspapers. One called the marches and rallies "patriotic"; the other termed them a "reign of terror."

Hundreds of miners were making an all-out effort to extend the strike into the lower half of Luzerne County and over into Carbon County, a move Evan favored to gain power for the union's position.

The *Wilkes-Barre Times* condemned the effort as an attack against community security and the private property of mine owners. The *Hazleton Daily Standard* suggested the owners negotiate and compromise to end the unrest. But the power of mine ownership held sway when Luzerne County Sheriff James Martin was convinced by the owners to post public notices warning that "unlawful assembly" and "lawlessness" would be punished.

Martin had deputized eighty-seven men and armed them with rifles to enforce his warning. Evan was told that some of the deputies were also members of the Coal and Iron Police, the organization authorized by the Legislature but paid and controlled by the coal companies. His immediate thought was of the Molly Maguire stories he had heard years earlier and the role played by the C and I Police in the arrest and execution of so-called Mollies.

In the first week of September, Evan followed huge crowds of miners from pit to pit as they convinced others to join their walkout. One pit still operating was at Lattimer, a company town owned by the Pardee Coal Company and located two miles north of what then was the strike zone. Pardee also owned a mine to the south at Harwood and those men had joined the strike.

Evan, John Fahy and other UMW organizers were in Harwood on September 9 when a miner from Lattimer walked into town and announced that the Lattimer men would join the strike if the men from Harwood called them out. At noon the next day the march began with an estimated three to five hundred men following two miners carrying American flags. Most spoke little if any English but they reasoned that by marching unarmed and remaining nonviolent they would be protected by the laws and flag of their adopted land. Even John Fahy urged them to be cautious.

In the short time he had been in the area, Evan learned that a half dozen wealthy families controlled the coal lands in this area some thirty miles southwest of Scranton. They owned the mines, the railroads, banks, lumber companies, mills, the iron industry, retail stores and the dreaded company towns with their company stores. He had also learned that Sheriff Martin had once been a miner and wondered if his allegiance was to those from the pits or to those who controlled commerce and elections. Evan also knew that the region's coal operators had imported labor from eastern Europe to weaken the English-speaking miners who constantly demanded improvements in their working conditions. Now, much to the owners' surprise, these newcomers — these Slavs and some Italians — were turning against the masters. Their paternalistic attitudes challenged, the owners fought back.

Moving through the group of marchers, Evan tried to converse with as many as could understand him. His words were of UMW support and the need for miners to band together for the common good. Some of the men answered him in sufficient English so that he knew they understood; others smiled or grunted or held up their hands to let him know they did not comprehend.

The afternoon sun beat down on the dusty road as the marchers reached the Hazleton city line. Sheriff Martin and his deputies were waiting, along with the city police chief. Evan hurried to the front of the line.

"These men are demonstrating peaceably," Evan shouted at a nearby deputy, a middle-aged man with sweat pouring over his face.

"They're rabble-rousers. They need to be taught a lesson," the deputy responded.

Up ahead, Evan could hear an argument between the leaders of the march and the sheriff, then saw some pushing and shoving. A deputy near the sheriff grabbed one of the American flags and tore it to shreds, shouting, "You Hunkies ain't got no respect for our flag and you don't have the right to carry it."

As Evan neared the fracas, he could see the police chief stepping between the sheriff and the miners. He overheard the chief telling the sheriff that the men had the right to march peaceably and could continue if they agreed to follow him on a bypass around the city. As they marched off under the chief's direction, Evan noticed the sheriff and his deputies boarding trolleys moving north. On the other side of the city, the trolleys, delayed by passenger stops, came in sight of the marchers again and then sped off to their next stop: Lattimer.

An hour passed before the miners reached the outskirts of Lattimer, a dusty little village of two streets and two coal breakers. On one street, Quality Row, were the modest homes of skilled miners and bosses; on the other, Main Street, were the tarpaper shacks of the laborers, mostly Italian immigrants. The streets forked at the edge of town, merging under a huge tree

Unarmed Slavic miners march through Luzerne County to seek support for a work stoppage from miners at Lattimer, Pennsylvania, on September 10, 1897. Within hours, the county sheriff and eighty-seven men deputized for the march and equipped with rifles opened fire on this group, killing nineteen miners and wounding at least thirty-nine.

Charles H. Burg Collection, MG273, Pennsylvania State Archives into the road leading from Hazleton. As the marchers crossed a small rise to the fork they were confronted again by Sheriff Martin, standing in the shade of the tree, and his deputies, lined up parallel to the road and across it.

Something had changed, Evan thought as he surveyed the line of rifle-toting men blocking their path. The size of the armed group had doubled, it seemed. He was bothered too by the lay of the land. Across the road from the deputies was an embankment, topped with the trolley tracks. The marchers were trapped between the rifles and the raised ground.

Evan sensed an immediate danger as the miners walked slowly past the raised rifles and toward Sheriff Martin standing in the road, pistol in hand. Martin shouted: "You must stop marching and disperse. This is contrary to the law and you are creating a disturbance. You must go back."

Those in front of the procession stopped at the warning, but the men following who had obviously neither seen nor heard the sheriff kept moving. Martin grabbed one man and pulled him to the side of the road. As Evan hurried forward to restore calm, several marchers began to scuffle with Martin to free their comrade and the column moved ahead. Martin grabbed another miner, put the pistol to his head and pulled the trigger. Evan froze. Then he realized the pistol had jammed and the miner broke away. He glanced quickly to his right and then to the front and saw the entire line of rifles raised in firing positions.

"Down, down," he screamed, dropping to the road, covering his head with his hands and wondering momentarily how many would understand his English words. He heard the command "fire" and then a deafening roar as dozens of rifles spit out into the crowd. He saw the flag bearer, a Slovakian named Steve Jurich, thrown off his feet by a bullet which smashed into his head. More riflemen joined in the slaughter as terrified marchers ran toward the embankment, climbing in an effort to reach safety on the far side. Shot in the back, some tumbled down into the bloody road. A voice screamed, "Shoot the sons of bitches." The shots kept coming and Evan felt he was in the final moments of his own life. He lay there quietly for seconds, then rolled over as the firing stopped and glanced around. There were bodies all around him, either motionless or twitching in pain. Some deputies came runing to offer aid to the wounded while a few strolled through the killing field and kicked the living and the dead. One man, agonizing with a bullet wound, pleaded with a deputy for water and a got a reply, "We'll give you hell, not water, hunkies." Some just walked away, laughing, to reboard the trolleys.

Word spread quickly, even back to Hazleton. As Evan and others tended to the wounded and tried to console the dying, wagons began rolling in to carry the living off to hospitals. Someone counted the dead and wounded as they were removed and Evan heard the numbers: nineteen killed and at least thirty-nine wounded. The casualties, he learned later, were Poles, Slovaks and Lithuanians.

The Reverend J. V. Moylan of St. Gabriel's Roman Catholic Church in Hazleton would later call it a "brutal and unjustifiable massacre."

Some of the deputies, shaken by what they had done, went into hiding. Sheriff Martin went quickly to Wilkes-Barre where his attorney sealed him in a hotel room. A few coal owners fled to Atlantic City, New Jersey, and registered at the Traymore Hotel under false names. The non-Slavic residents of the region, fearful of attacks by immigrant families, stayed indoors and awaited the arrival of a state militia unit ordered to Lattimer by the governor. But there were no reprisals. Evan found that relatives of the victims were dealing with grief, not revenge.

He attended the trial in Luzerne County after the sheriff and his deputies were arrested and charged with murder in what by then had been titled "the Lattimer Massacre."

"It was a joke," he told Glyn later at home. "The district attorney was forced to present a case which named the sheriff and all of the deputies as a single defendant in the death of one man, Mike Cheslak. Of course, it was impossible to determine which man had shot Cheslak. And a lawyer for the defense—the son of a wealthy family in the region—labeled the marchers 'a barbarian horde' who had threatened the country and said the deputies had stopped a bloody war from breaking out. Can you believe that? A bloody war from men who were not armed, shot down in cold blood by a bunch of hotheads! My gawd, what gall! What absolute bastards, shooting down men who were simply trying to improve life for their loved ones! Not guilty, the jury said, the whole blooming bunch, not guilty!"

Evan shook with anger as he recalled the day. Then, after calming down, he said quietly: "But you know, Dada, the memory of those men lives on. Throughout the anthracite fields we have been signing new members by the hundreds, perhaps the thousands. The courage of those marchers is bringing them in by droves. 'We are united behind our brothers,' they're telling us. 'They died for us and we'll not forget them.'"

"And you won the strike. From what I've read almost all of the companies gave in," said Glyn.

"Aye, but just a battle, Dada, and a costly one at that. Just a battle, not the war."

Evan would not repeat the tale to his mother. What she knew she read in the paper, and that was bad enough, she told her son. What worried her most was that her oldest son had been in the line of fire. Gwyneth almost wished her entire family, like Dylan, could be free of the mines and union activity.

"I doubt we'll ever again see the likes of Lattimer," Evan told her months after the incident when Dylan brought the subject up at dinner. "The horror of it affected too many people—the local authorities, state officials, even the mine owners. No, Lattimer put an end to wholesale slaughter."

"You are probably quite right about that. Just yesterday I heard the Hazle Brewery story," said Glyn.

"And what was that?" Dylan asked.

"Oh, I thought I had told you all," Evan apologized. "Interesting story it was. After the jury found them not guilty the deputies went back to Hazleton, straight to the Hazle Brewery, to drink to their victory in court. Well, somebody bragged about the party, and the people in Hazleton began calling it Deputies Beer rather than Hazle Beer. The brewery went bust."

"Put it out of business?" exclaimed Gwyneth.

"Aye, one of our organizers there said it left a bad taste in everyone's mouth, as a figure of speech, of course. No one wanted to be associated with a beer those murdering deputies had celebrated with."

"Not the brewery's fault," suggested Dylan.

"Well, you could argue that. But evil is what the public perceives evil to be, isn't it?" Evan responded. "Public pressure can do in any business."

"I avoid that in my business," said Dylan.

"Well, mon, you're dealing with one customer at a time, not thousands. But if your house carving isn't what it should be public pressure would come down on you too, just through neighbor talking to neighbor."

Dylan thought about that for a minute, nodded his head in agreement with his brother, and moved the subject in a completely new direction, "We're talking about a change at the shop."

"Who's we?" Glyn asked.

"Haydn and me," said Dylan. "It's been five years since he's been working there and a full year since Mr. Thomas signed over the building and equipment to me."

"And a prosperous time it's been too," said Gwyneth, smiling.

"Aye, you've been quite successful, son," Glyn added. "But what's the change?"

"I asked Haydn if he'd like to be a partner rather than an employee. He accepted. It will be Jones and Hopkins Woodworking Company now."

Evan frowned and asked, "Why? You had no obligation to give away part of a business you've worked hard to build."

"Neither did I have to pay for the business. It was given to me by Mr. Thomas, remember. I felt it time to give something to another man," said

Dylan. "Besides, we'll share in the work as well as the profit. There's enough of both for two."

"Now, Evan, you've always said the working man deserves more, perhaps a share of the power and the profit," Glyn mused.

"Aye, I was thinking only of my brother," Evan smiled. "That surely is a magnificent gesture, Dylan."

"No, as Mr. Thomas told me, it's just good business. Haydn is skilled enough to work for anyone, even start his own business. But if we stay together, we both prosper."

"Well put, little one," Evan laughed. "And since you have dramatic news, I'll announce mine too. While I was in Wilkes-Barre for the deputies' trial I met someone in a tearoom."

"Tearoom?" roared Dylan. "You mean barroom, don't you?"

"No, no, respectable I am now with the union. Eating lunch I was when a young lady at the next table dropped her napkin. Being the gentleman that I am..."

Dylan laughed and Glyn smiled a loud "oh my," but Gwyneth hushed them both and asked, "What then, Evan?"

"Well, I was eating alone and she was without company too, so a conversation we started. School teacher, she is, in Wilkes-Barre. Teaching little ones for five years now. Very pretty girl. Father is a baker and her mother runs the bake shop. He's Irish, she's Welsh."

"Ah, Saturday trips to Wilkes-Barre the past three weeks! Union business you said," Gwyneth squealed. "A woman it is!"

"And what's wrong with that?" demanded Glyn.

"Nothing at all. At twenty-nine it's time he was looking toward the future."

"Oh, Mama, just a friend she is."

"And getting older every day!"

"She's twenty-three and looking better every time I see her," Evan said, winking at his father.

"Does she have a name?" Dylan asked.

"Norah...Norah Murphy it is."

"And should I tell Norah Murphy what a cad she's been seeing?" Dylan laughed.

"Shame on you, Dylan, a prize your brother is," Gwyneth scolded.

"Aye, a booby prize," Dylan laughed again and then ducked as Evan swung at his head.

Glyn sat back in his chair and smiled. It was the first time since the death of Rhys fifteen months earlier that joy had permeated his entire family, and one of the few times since before Dylan's accident in 1890 that his youngest son showed such a jovial attitude.

"I'm sure she's a nice young lady," Glyn said softly.

"Aye, brother, sure I am too," said Dylan, patting Evan's knee. "It seems like there's much news today and as long as we're talking about women I have another announcement."

Glyn and Evan looked puzzled but Gwyneth surmised what was coming: "Beth?" she asked.

"Aye, Mama. I know now and Beth says she does too."

"Know what?" asked Glyn.

Dylan blushed.

"Something between you and Beth Hopkins?" asked Evan.

"Something like that."

"Well, I'll be. That took a few years then, didn't it? Love is it, boy?"

Another blush and, "I guess so, Evan."

Gwyneth began to cry and Glyn arose from his chair to comfort her. Then Evan got up, pulled Dylan from his seat and hugged him tightly, "A good choice, little brother, a good choice."

"No tears, Mama, happy I am," said Dylan.

"Oh, you two, tears of joy they are, for the both of you, and for Beth and Norah too."

Chapter Seventeen

In April of 1898 Evan and Norah were married and, a month later, Dylan and Beth. Evan at thirty was a half dozen years past the average age for men to marry in that region, but Dylan, just turned twenty-five, fit the pattern. Beth at twenty-three and Norah at twenty-four were a year or two past the normal marrying age. Gwyneth and Glyn were anxious for grandchildren but such thoughts were never expressed to their children. However, Gwyneth was also worried about health problems babies and young children faced. Among Welsh families, the average number of children had been eight but statistics showed that four would die as children, mostly in the summer when unsanitary living conditions and childhood diseases were at their worst. She and Glyn had decided, soon after their own wedding, to limit their offspring, determined to not subject a brood to the harsh realities of a miner's life. They stopped after the third, more due to the advice of a physician than their planning, though Gwyneth privately wished that she could have had one more and that it would have been a girl. Within the year, Evan and Norah presented Glyn and Gwyneth with their first grandchild, a boy named David. And in June 1899, Dylan and Beth joined the parade with a son, Jonathan. The first two granddaughters came in 1900 when Norah gave birth to Mary, while Beth, whose Christian name was really Elizabeth, presented the family with baby Barbara.

Glyn and Gwyneth were alone now in the house on Washburn Street but the mortgage had been satisfied and they could afford the luxury of their five-room dwelling without taking in boarders. One of the three bedrooms was used for storage and a second was assigned as the nursery whenever the babies were brought for a visit.

The woodworking business of Dylan and Haydn, now his brother-in-law, provided a profitable living for both. After their wedding, Dylan and Beth moved into a house just a block east from his shop on Price Street.

Haydn married in 1900 and located his bride in a small house on Lincoln Avenue, just three doors from his parents' home.

Evan bought a house in the village of Old Forge, five miles south of Hyde Park and ten miles north of where Norah's parents lived. But, unlike his brother, he was often away from home two or three days a week, traveling on union business into the anthracite fields south of Wilkes-Barre.

It had been a busy period for the United Mine Workers since the partially successful strike of 1897 and Evan was part of the team which signed up eight thousand new members — mostly Slavs — in the hard coal region. He had been told that people of Slavic origin now made up fifty percent of mine workers; twenty years earlier it had been about five percent. In fact, a union letter reported there were more than 100,000 Slavs living in the Scranton and Wilkes-Barre areas, a third of them Polish. The huge immigration in the last two decades of the nineteenth century had also brought in 16,000 Welsh to Lackawanna and Luzerne Counties. By 1900, a third of the 93,000 first-generation Welsh living in the whole United States were in Pennsylvania, and most of them in Lackawanna and Luzerne Counties.

The growth in population also brought more churches, saloons, banks and fraternal organizations to the anthracite region of eastern Pennsylvania. As the twentieth century approached, the region boasted 143 Roman Catholic churches plus 46 missionary stations and chapels; the priests were serving more than a quarter million members. Protestant churches numbered 307 but with only 62,000 members.

In Lackawanna County alone there were 591 saloons and the number was growing. Evan had asked during his travels how many there were in other counties but the answer he received was that no one had time to count them all. He found them quite the same in all counties, selling lager, ale and porter beers, sometimes liquors, a great deal of whiskey and often wine.

The UMW was keeping close tabs on the area. They knew that personal deposits in Scranton banks in 1900 averaged $178.45 but that among miners it was only $152.85, and some union officials felt that was an argument in favor of higher wages. To those who argued against that position, saying perhaps miners were not as thrifty as other people, Evan countered that miners represented more than half of the shareholders in Lackawanna County's building and loan associations. In addition, seventy-five percent of miners had helped set up fraternal organizations which provided insurance for sickness or death. Evan knew of a few mining companies which did help by providing a job for the widow or a small pension or a place to live. A few firms even got involved in the maintenance and management of insurance programs. Evan had explained to his father how one company charged men twenty-five cents per month and boys under sixteen half that. When a member of the insurance program died all other members made a one-time twenty-five-cent payment. The family got seventy-five dollars for the funeral. In injury cases, victims who could not work got five dollars weekly but only for six months. However, most companies — as everyone knew — did not even inquire about a family's welfare after the man of the house had died in the mines.

And insurance was necessary in an industry where the chances of being killed in an accident were almost triple those of railroad workers, a dangerous industry in itself. Since 1870, when Evan was just two years old, 10,318 men and boys had been killed in the anthracite fields and more than 27,000 had been injured. One company in the northern region, during 1900 alone, reported 149 men killed and 4,181 injured on the job. No one even knew how many children were left fatherless.

Public hospitals, including several operated by the state, were using tax funds and contributions from coal companies and churches to help cover indigent care. Workers who were unable to pay at times got free treatment. Some mine owners, Evan found to his surprise, freely gave to needy causes such as the hospitals, although they would not agree to pay the miners what he considered to be a fair living wage.

* * * * *

In August 1900, at a district convention, union delegates voted for several demands, including the first wage increase in twenty years. The owners said no and a strike was called.

"We walk out today," Evan told Norah in mid-September. "And we know that 80,000 non-union miners are going to join us tomorrow."

Within a week the total on strike exceeded even the union's expectations. "They estimate 127,000 are out," Evan beamed at his wife. "If the number is accurate that's ninety-seven percent of the miners."

Glyn, out of touch with Evan for weeks at a time, kept up with his son's travels and successes through newspaper coverage of the strike and information posted by the union. He was supporting the strike at Hyborne coal just like every other below-ground worker there, supporting the needs of younger miners who were still trying to raise children and handle unyielding mortgage or rent payments.

"It may be difficult for us with no new wages since 1880, but think of the effect on these young men," he told Gwyneth one evening at dinner. "Aye, greed has gripped the fields far too long. This is a fight we picked and one we have to win."

"I read in the paper today about a woman who goes about promoting the strike," said Gwyneth. "And a Jones she is. What do you know of her?"

"Oh, Mother Jones, as they call her. Yes, yes, a sight to see, I'm told, though I haven't seen her. Mary Harris Jones, Evan told me last time he stopped. She's a miner's widow. Evan said she was involved in the Pittsburgh riots back in the late '70s, that tragic fight which took some lives in Chicago in the '80s and the railroad union strike a half dozen years ago. A fighter she is, though she just looks like a kindly old grandmother, according to Evan."

"Does she work for the union?"

"Not that I know of. She just shows up, leads marches, talks quite vigorously, I'm told, to bands of strikers. Evan saw her a few times. Wears a flowered hat and carries a black umbrella all the time, he told me. Quite a sight, I take it. She gets everybody marching—the men, the wives, even the children. Evan said the union had to calm her down a bit when some company owners threatened to have the police arrest her."

"Were they afraid of a revolution?"

"I don't know, love. But strikers do not revolt against the government. They're not anarchists or revolutionaries, even when there's violence. They're just men trying to scratch out a living for their families, asking for a fair share of the profit in their pay."

"Don't I know that, with you and the boys!"

"Aye, you know miners as well as anyone."

"Some hotheads there are, Glyn, but I've never known a group of miners to march on owners with drawn weapons or threaten their children with starvation or homelessness."

"Sounding like your oldest son, you are, my love. Another Mother Jones in the making?"

"Oh, off with you, just saying what I know, that's all."

"Mother Jones is doing a job, Gwyn. I give her credit for that. But Evan says there are other factors—the Lattimer Massacre, which turned many people against the brute force of owners and politicians who backed them, and a push by the man elected last year as president of the UMW, John Mitchell."

"A young man, I understand."

"Aye, love, just thirty. He makes sure everyone knows what wages are in the anthracite fields, from two hundred ten dollars to six hundred sixteen dollars a year, the *Times* reported, with an average of three hundred seventy five dollars, hardly enough to keep a small family alive. Many thousands still live in company houses where they can be evicted on a day's notice and deal as best they can with company stores. A tragedy it is that could continue into the new century in just a few months."

"And you still have men outside the union! Why is that, Glyn?"

"Well, fear of owners for some, I imagine; distrust of unions in general by others; English-speaking miners still opposed to the Slavs and others whose language they don't understand. Many reasons, Gwyn. In the .

Scranton and Wilkes-Barre areas almost a third of the workers are non-union, so they are a minority, but a powerful minority nonetheless."

"Will there be a settlement for wages?" she asked.

"Pushing they are to match what the bituminous miners got—a forty percent increase and a cut to eight hours in the day's work. Who can tell the outcome? But try we must. Did you see the public letter the union sent to the newspapers?"

Gwyneth shook a no.

"It said the railroads which carry coal are the hard coal miners' real enemies. They who own the collieries and the railroads take small profit from the coal, thus keeping the miners' wages low, but charge tremendously to transport coal to market, three hundred percent higher than railroads in the soft coal fields."

"Not surprising is it with the way the railroads have bought out so many coal fields?"

"No, love, not surprising."

* * * * *

The UMW won a ten percent pay raise in the strike. It forced owners to recognize grievance committees set up by miners. And it got reduced charges for the cost of blasting powder.

But it did not win recognition for itself as a bargaining agent. Anthracite miners still had a nine-hour workday. And they still had no agreement on checking the fairness of a company's weighing system.

"However," Evan told his father on a visit home with Norah and the babies, "it was still the most successful strike hard coal has ever seen. We did get a foot in the door. No longer will the owners ignore us."

* * * * *

Early in 1901, the union noticed that coal owners had begun erecting substantial fencing around their property. They increased production and stockpiled the extra output. They hired more guards. But the UMW was growing too, adding members throughout the anthracite region day by day.

That year, the Jones family grew by two more granddaughters, Joy to Norah and Evan, Johanna to Beth and Dylan.

Glyn was more satisfied with the 1900 settlement than Evan, seeing a bit more money in the pockets of the young family men in the Hyborne pit, and a bit more for him and Gwyneth to spoil their half-dozen grandchildren. Evan's song, despite his proclamation of the strike's success, chanted that more—much more—was needed. He saw a bad sign in the deterioration of ownership by small independent company owners, men more likely to treat labor fairly, although there were even exceptions to that—

J. Wellington Hyborne, for example. As ownership moved upward it also spread out from the mine fields to the corporate offices in distant cities, chiefly New York and Philadelphia, where the plight of mining families meant very little. A man he only knew by name, one J. P. Morgan, seemed one of the chief roadblocks to even an inkling toward parity for the mine worker.

* * * * *

In January 1902, Beth produced another son, whom she named James after her maternal grandfather, with Dylan's blessing. Two months later, Norah gave birth to a girl, Elizabeth, who immediately became a favorite of her namesake, Auntie Beth.

Glyn, now fifty-six, had pure white hair but was still trim enough to put in a full day underground. Gwyneth, two years younger, had what Glyn called "a head of gorgeous gray." She did not mention it to her husband, but to her children and their spouses she often talked of the marked increase in his coughing and the black phlegm he spit up every day, always outside the house.

Evan, ever mindful of the power of the railroads, told Glyn that the roads now controlled almost ninety-seven percent of the total anthracite fields in Pennsylvania.

"Power like we've never seen, Dada. And dangerous too."

On May 12, UMW President Mitchell agreed to "a temporary suspension of work" after he was backed into a corner by the railroad presidents, some of whom said they would go bankrupt before they recognized the UMW or any union. The United Mine Workers had asked for a twenty percent wage increase; Mitchell said he would lower the demand to five percent. To the railroad presidents that was a show of weakness. No deal, they told him.

On June 2, demanding at least a ten percent increase, more than 147,000 hard coal miners walked off the job.

"We're still behind the wages of the bituminous men," Evan complained to his father. "The owners are turning their backs on even the basic need for safety in the pits. Last year, one hundred eleven men were killed in the anthracite region. We still have eight-year-old boys working in breakers when state law says you must be at least fourteen. And we estimate there are ten thousand boys under fourteen in the mines. When does it all end?"

"The fact that some boys disobey the law is the fault of their families as well as mine managers," said Glyn. "Bear in mind that there can be fault on both sides. Evan, is this a fight you can win?"

"I know, I know, Dada, pick your fights, you always said. Well, this is a fight we need and a fight we can...no, no, not can, *must* win."

Months went by with no letup by either the union or the owners. Mining families spent what little savings they had for food after late-spring, home-grown vegetables were gone.

"We estimate that anthracite miners and laborers and other men in the pits, their wives and children total well over seven hundred thousand people," Evan told his mother one Sunday when he brought his family for a visit. "We've gotten relief funds from the bituminous miners and money from other supporters — well over one million dollars — but it won't be near enough if this goes on much longer."

"Aye, your father has been giving money to Jamie Kerrigan, a bit anyway."

"Jamie Kerrigan? Is he still your laborer then, Dada?"

"No, no, twenty-five years old Jamie is now. He's had his own room these past two years. Married he is but he still takes care of his poor old mother."

"And how can you, on strike too, afford to help Jamie?"

"Oh, we didn't tell you? Your father has been working during the strike for Dylan and Haydn," Gwyneth answered.

"Driving a team, I am, making deliveries for the boys. They're always looking for help in the summer when houses are going up. Jamie will only take a dollar a week, for food only, and he marks down every dollar and the date. He said he'd take it only with the understanding he'd pay it back. And he will. You know Jamie."

"Aye, I know Jamie and he will pay you back. But can't Dylan put him on part-time if the woodworking business is so busy?"

"Oh, Jamie is working. Planting crops he is at farms up the mountain. The pay is not very good but the farmer says he'll make it up in vegetables when the harvest comes."

"Quite a boy he is," said Gwyneth.

"Man now, love, not a boy any longer," Glyn corrected. "Mama and I are fine, Evan. Enough to eat. I suspect Dylan and Haydn are paying me more than they normally pay a wagon driver, but they say no."

"Pitiful it is, Evan, to see women picking through the culm for bits of coal for cooking," Gwyneth sighed. "And guards running them off. Can't feed raw food to little ones, you know. And it's good that it's not winter or we'd all be freezing."

"The companies complain about the picking," said Evan. "They say that coal is worth a good deal of money, but they leave it in those piles like so much garbage. Ah, the greed, it spreads even to the dumps. At least it's quieter up here. Down in Shenandoah, the governor sent in the National Guard after some strikers beat a man to death. Hotheads on both sides, there are."

"Soldiers! I imagine the union boys are upset with that," said Gwyneth.

"Well, initially, but the Guardsmen have been very reasonable and tolerant. The miners don't like that soldiers were called but they don't hate them like they do the Coal and Iron Police and a thousand private detectives the companies brought in. Those are the mean bastards."

"Evan! Your language!" Glyn said sternly.

"Oh, beg pardon, Mama. Forgot where I am for a moment. But some mean actions have been taken. An owner down in the middle fields evicted thirteen mining families from his company houses. One man said the only reason he could think of for having his family thrown out was that his son had assisted a relief group that was collecting food for families who were really in dire straits."

"No other reason?" asked Gwyneth, astonished.

"None that he knew of," said Evan. "Another miner working for the same owner was evicted from a house occupied by his family of eleven, including seven children and the wife's parents. The older couple was sick, in fact the grandfather was ill in bed, when the sheriff came and ordered them out."

"Right away?"

"Aye, Mama, and the sheriff had men pile all of their furniture out on the street."

By August, when the miners were scraping the bottom of the relief barrel, a letter written by a coal company executive to a minister who supported the strikers was made public. It spread not just across the coal regions but across the country as well. The letter writer, one George Baer, arrogantly claimed that the welfare of miners would be handled not by the union but by the coal owners because, he wrote, God had given control of the property rights of the country to Christian men of property.

The *New York Times* editorialized that "a good many people think they superintend the earth, but not many have the egregious vanity to describe themselves as its managing directors." And in Chicago, the *Tribune* wrote: "It is imprudent, it is insulting, it is audacious, of the coal presidents to speak of 'lawlessness' in the coal regions when they themselves are the greatest offenders of the law."

Glyn was amazed when Evan showed him reprints of the Baer letter and of newspaper reaction. He had never, in his long career as a miner, seen such public support for those who toiled in pits across the country.

"The best part," Evan smiled, "is how this one incident has turned the public in our favor."

But the strike continued and in late summer fear began to grow by those who used anthracite to heat their homes and power their factories that stockpiles would not last once cold weather approached. That fear spread even to the White House when President Theodore Roosevelt told his attorney general to examine the need for the government to become involved. The examination would include whether the coal companies had restrained trade and therefore broke federal antitrust laws. It was not just Pennsylvania that worried. From New York came word to the president that coal prices there had jumped from six dollars to twenty-six dollars a ton. The president predicted fuel riots if action was not taken.

"What of soft coal?" asked Glyn in early September. "Why can't the East Coast get soft coal? They're not on strike."

"Oh, they can, to be sure," Evan explained. "And at five dollars a ton. It's politics and money that's driving the demands for action. Republicans blame Democrats and vice versa. The companies that sell only hard coal don't want to lose their markets. All made up, it is. Even Roosevelt is being pushed to take over the hard coal fields. A senator from Massachusetts wrote to him, saying that the attitude of the mine owners 'is a menace to all property in the country and is breeding socialism at a rate which is hard to contemplate.'"

"Strong words," said Glyn. "Something has to bend soon."

And by early October something did bend. President Roosevelt summoned coal company presidents and United Mine Workers' officials to Washington. The president asked both sides to come together for the good of the nation.

UMW President John Mitchell agreed, but asked Roosevelt to appoint a commission to examine the problems and come up with solutions. Mitchell said his union would abide by the commission's decisions.

George Baer, the man who had written the August letter which moved public opinion to the miners' side, spoke for the railroad companies which controlled most of the mines. He told Roosevelt that the companies' miners were abused and maltreated by the UMW and accused the union and Mitchell of violence and crimes.

John Markle, one of the independent mine owners, asked the president if the companies he represented had to bargain with a "set of outlaws." Markle then told Roosevelt: "I now ask you to perform the duties invested in you as President of the United States, to at once squelch the anarchistic conditions of affairs existing in the anthracite coal regions by the strong arm of the military at your command."

Roosevelt was notably disturbed by the comments of Baer and Markle. Later, it was reported that he said, referring to Markle, "If it wasn't for the high office I hold, I would have taken him by the breeches and the nape of the neck and chucked him out of the window."

Roosevelt wanted the miners to go back to work and await a federal commission investigation. But the owners would neither agree to abide by the commission's decisions nor to arbitration, and they made no promise to recognize the UMW as a bargaining agent. On October 8, the strikers held meetings across the region and voted to remain on the picket lines. Mitchell, his back against the wall, told Roosevelt he could not accept the president's suggestion. The strike continued.

Roosevelt made the next move, letting it be known that he was studying a plan to send in federal troops to take control of the mines. That shook the coal companies and by October 11 the government and the owners had an agreement in which the president would appoint an investigating commission. Based on that promise, the miners voted to return to work on October 23.

Evan attended most of the hearings, held over three months in Scranton, Wilkes-Barre, Hazleton and Philadelphia with more than five hundred fifty people testifying, most of them for the union men and non-union workers. Heading the legal team for the miners was Attorney Clarence Darrow, who had gained fame in 1895 while representing labor in the Pullman railroad strike.

"Darrow was fantastic," Evan told his parents. "He said the coal companies are fighting for slavery while the miners are fighting for freedom. He proved that half of the anthracite miners earn less than two hundred dollars a year and that only five percent make more than eight hundred. And he summed up by saying that those who run industry should step aside if they can only be successful by imposing starving wages and relying on little boys. He was marvelous."

"The *Times* carried a story about a boy named Chappie," said Glyn.

"Ah, yes, Andrew Chappie," said Evan. "Chappie's story told at the hearing was electric. This twelve-year-old boy was being paid forty cents a day to work in a breaker, but the company never gave him the money. They used it to pay off debts owed by the boy's father. And the father, listen to this now, the father had been killed in a mine accident four years earlier. Outrageous, isn't it?"

It was March 20, 1903, before the commission made its report. With it the miners got a ten percent wage increase, an eight-hour workday and the right to have their own man—at their expense—double-check the weight of coal cars. But the commission did not insist the companies had to recognize the UMW as the miners' official representative.

"A great number of men feel we lost the strike because we did not gain recognition," Evan told his father. "But this was just one battle in the war. Next time we'll get that."

Glyn smiled.

"This was a major victory in my estimation," Evan smiled back. "A decade ago, the UMW represented fewer than ten thousand. Now we speak for more than one hundred thousand."

"And there have been smaller victories along the way," said Glyn.

"Such as what, Dada?"

"Governor Stone signed a law two years ago saying that all mining companies with more than ten employees have to provide first aid supplies and a clean place where injured workers could be treated."

"Yes, a good and necessary move, but not one I consider of great importance to the men."

"I prayed for such a move when we brought Dylan out on a board," Glyn said firmly, a touch of irritation in his voice.

"No disrespect meant, Dada. I'm talking about improving the financial lot of miners."

"And I'm talking about keeping them alive!"

"They're digging fifteen million tons a year, just in Lackawanna County. The men need a bigger share of that profit."

"I don't disagree, Evan, but you have to recognize that money is not everything. In fact, it's nothing if injury keeps you out of the pit. What are the numbers now?"

"Men?"

"Men and boys, mines, tonnage. What are the numbers?"

"In the whole of the anthracite region in Pennsylvania, about one hundred fifty thousand workers, more than three hundred sixty collieries, somewhere around fifty-seven million tons annually."

"And I read that the fatality rate is now about seven workers for every million tons. Is that correct?" Glyn asked.

"Aye, about that."

"That's a lot of good men, and boys too, Evan. Not too good at math am I but that looks like about four hundred dying every year. And how many thousands injured?"

"Don't know off hand, Dada, thousands though, as you say."

"Tell the union to pay attention to men too, not just money. They're not arms and legs, you know. They're human beings—fathers and husbands, brothers and sons."

"Aye, Dada."

* * * * *

In 1903, the Jones boys and their wives brought forth what would be the last of their offspring. For Norah and Evan, it was their second son, Ian. But the big surprise came when Beth delivered twins, Hannah and Christine.

On Sunday afternoons, when the grandchildren came to visit, Glyn and his sons would take the older ones on a wagon ride to downtown Scranton where they could climb down the banks to the Lackawanna River and strive, with pinched eyes, to see if any fish swam by. Glyn could remember the rivers and creeks when he first came to Pennsylvania. Fish were plentiful. The water was decent enough for wading, and usually quite clear. Now, with mine water leaking or being pumped in, the waterways ran black, wading was even frowned upon by children, and fish — if there were any — were never caught.

Around the mine yards which dotted the valley from Scranton to Wilkes-Barre and the hills around those cities, culm banks and the dust which blew from them had long since choked out or buried whatever grass, shrubs, wild flowers or trees had existed. The valley, Glyn noticed, had in thirty years become a dreary place to the eye. Gray and black, dusty and dirty, it was a dismal sight. The industry which had kept Glyn and his family housed and clothed and fed had also destroyed much of their world.

Glyn had seen a Census Bureau report at the community reading room which suggested that the coal industry between 1880 and 1900 had a major impact on the country's ability to advance swiftly as an industrial power, indeed as an emerging world power among the industrial nations. He recalled some of the language: "...the country's progress has been due largely to the abundance and cheapness of its mineral fuels, chief among which is coal."

The America he knew had moved from a nation of farmers to a nation of heavy industry. He himself had gone from using candles for light underground as a boy in Wales to whale oil and, since the turn of the century in 1901, to a carbide lamp, which produced light from the reaction of a chemical compound with water. He had used black powder for blasting and was now using dynamite. Changes were coming faster and faster with each passing year.

The railroads now owned or controlled almost all of the anthracite coal deposits in America, which was really eastern Pennsylvania. But he knew their power would eventually wane. The signs were there. The role of the Coal and Iron Police had diminished significantly in the past year as the United Mine Workers gained strength. Now, the union could shut down mines in a large area and the C and I Police were powerless to prevent it. There was too much territory to cover, too many mines, too many miners. Besides, no one tried to replace striking workers, so picketing and disorder were minimized and a police presence was not needed. It was rapidly becoming a different world. The coal companies were learning that it was more productive to deal with the UMW, which was reluctant to call strikes or walkouts, and instead focused its ammunition on safety, and working hours, and, of course, pay.

"It's not how much you earn that matters," Glyn had told Evan one day as they discussed the changes. "It's what your money can buy. A thousand dollars is of no use to a man if it costs him twice that to live. It's the price we pay you must focus on, not the jingle in our pockets."

The coal owners also found their world changing dramatically. The strike which brought the president of the United States into the national limelight left the public unsettled over what many referred to as the "robber barons" of industry. The owners even found themselves at times to be the objects of antitrust suits, something quite new and unsettling for those who had enjoyed decades of unbridled growth in wealth and power. The industry in both the anthracite and bituminous regions had gained the attention of Americans across the land in the last thirty years of the nineteenth century, producing ten times what it did in 1870 for a national total of 350 million tons in 1900. And it provided a living for miners and laborers, whose numbers rose from 186,000 to 677,000 in those three decades.

"We can't deny that we owe much to the pits, and, fair play, to the men who own them," Glyn said, much to Evan's consternation. "They have provided us with the means to have a home, food and clothing for our families."

"Owe? You must be joking, Dada. Do we owe anything to the gods of greed?"

"Now, now, boy, I know many have been unfair, greedy, uncaring. But some have been decent men. Where would we be if they just closed all the pits and moved on with their money to other pursuits? I ask you that: Where would we be?"

"You have a way with words, sir," Evan smiled. "But I can't use your arguments to convince men to join the union."

"No, I realize you can't, son. But be fair, be fair to all with whom you deal. The changes we see will have to be dealt with as they arise. And some, mind you, will put men out of work, permanently."

Twentieth-century miner Jim Line crouches to move coal in a South Wales pit in the early 1990s.

Author's photograph

"We're already feeling that with the undercutting machine. One miner with a machine is worth an extra arm to the company and that means another man with only a pick loses half his pay. And it's the skilled worker who loses, those most likely to join the union. This machine hasn't helped anyone but the owners. It makes for more explosive dust, it brings the gas out faster, it makes breathing harder, it deafens and therefore destroys the ability to hear a roof cracking, and the vibration is enough to keep a man's insides jumping for days. No, no, Dada, we gained nothing from this machine."

"But, Evan, the machines will keep coming and the jobs will become fewer. Perhaps it's time for miners to look elsewhere, as Dylan has, to shape a life."

"We're still a strong industry, Dada. Everyone needs coal, for power, for heat, for cooking. We have a long road to travel before it comes to an end and we must make that journey as safe and as profitable as possible for the men who go below."

"Aye, I totally agree, son, but there will be roadblocks and storms and changes perhaps neither of us can imagine in this twentieth century. Be wary of too many wars, concentrate on winning the battles."

Chapter Eighteen

It was the middle of May in 1904, on an unusually warm day for that time of year. For almost a year now, Glyn had abandoned his walk up the Washburn Street Cemetery hill.

"Haven't...the wind...for it," he gasped to Brandon McSweeney as they walked home from their shift, around the hill to the street rather than over the top.

The Scotsman McSweeney had been having the same problem, constant coughing and black phlegm jumping from his throat with every spit. The cough was common among miners, particularly those who had spent a lifetime underground breathing in dust by the hour. It was a sound heard every day, in the coal yard, on the cage going down or coming up, on the streets, during church, in the stores, at the dinner table, in bed.

"Damn dust," Glyn, fifty-eight this year, would mutter under his breath—not really wanting to be heard—whenever a coughing spell began. And then he'd spit black, thick mucus, but only underground or in the yard. At home or in public he would disappear and, when finally alone, hack until he thought his lungs would tear. It was not something miners went to a doctor for; there was nothing they could do. "Miner's asthma," they would call it when asked. "Spit it out," was the only advice.

But there was still a climb, though not as steep, up Washburn Street, and Glyn—Brandon too, but not as often—would stop, catch his breath, move on, stop, gasp, move on. Walking was difficult, worse than working underground, although that had become a chore too.

The heat of this May afternoon struck as soon as he stepped off the cage. From the fifty-eight degrees below to a hellish eighty-five in the coal yard. First came a chill which surprised him, but a chill it was. He shivered as the hot sun soaked into his damp, coal-blackened work clothes. Then he began to sweat as he moved with Brandon toward the gate. His

228

jaw ached and the pain spread down through his left arm. He said nothing as they walked up the very slight incline to Washburn, then turned right and started up the street.

They had gone a block — Brandon slowing his own steps so as not to hurry his friend — when Glyn stopped for the fourth time to catch his breath. Brandon took a step forward but Glyn did not move. A hammer was thumping on his chest and his head was spinning. Brandon stopped and turned. He looked at Glyn's vacant eyes and a whiteness spreading across his face. A hand went out to help and as Glyn reached for it he went down, slowly to one knee, then both. He put his other hand on the ground to steady himself. Then he felt a crash and blackness overcame his every sense.

A crowd gathered, miners mostly on their way home. Glyn, on his back, opened his eyes and tried to breathe. It hurt too badly to suck in much air. Brandon was pouring the last of his cold tea over Glyn's heated face and holding his hand tightly.

"Top...of...hill," Glyn pleaded. "Fresh...breeze...there."

"We'll get you to the top and to home," Brandon responded excitedly.

Glyn could feel hands and strong arms reaching under his back and his legs. He knew he was off the ground, floating, it seemed, up the street. His head raced in and out of the darkness. He couldn't understand what was being said or even what was happening. The next time he awoke he recognized Gwyneth's voice and felt quite still, the moving having stopped.

"Where?..." he asked, unable to say more. He knew that Gwyneth was holding his hand and moving an arm across his face. A cool wetness crossed his brow with each sweep. And he could hear other voices but recognized none.

"Doc Lewis is on his way," a deep voice announced.

"You're home, my love," Gwyneth said softly, her hand holding his. She was careful that the tears rolling from her eyes did not drop on his face. "Are you still in pain?"

"Chest...hurts," he struggled. The room, he felt, was spinning though he could see nothing but a dim light in front of his half-closed eyes. Then the blackness came again.

When the light reappeared, he could feel someone's hands moving over his chest and a very low voice saying, "It's his heart, Gwyneth. I'm afraid he's very weak."

The night passed though Glyn was barely aware of the passage of any time. In the morning, as he opened his eyes, he could see that he was in his bed. He struggled to move.

"Easy, Dada, no need to get up."

"Dylan?"

"Aye, Dada, Dylan and Mama too. And Evan will be here shortly. Down in Shenandoah he was when they located him."

"Gwyn?"

"I'm right here, my love."

Glyn turned his head toward the other side of the bed and could faintly make out blurry figures in the room. "Who?..."

"It's David Hopkins, Glyn," he heard Gwyneth respond.

"Easy does it, mate," Hopkins said cheerily. "My Beth—your Beth too really—is here."

Glyn could barely see Dylan's wife as she knelt beside his bed.

"Beth," he whispered.

"Here, Dada," she said, choking back her tears. Glyn smiled. He loved hearing his daughters-in-law call him Dada, and both had ever since their weddings.

The procession continued all day but never disturbed his deep and frequent lapses into sleep. The Reverend Mr. Evans sat quietly in the corner, comforting all who came into the room. By midafternoon the six children of Beth and Dylan had spent a few minutes with their grandfather. The younger ones knew not what was happening and wanted to hug him but were gently told that kisses on the cheek would be fine because Grandpa was quite sick.

By late afternoon, Evan—rushing home from Shenandoah by train—had picked up Norah and their five little ones and gotten to Scranton.

That evening, after their shift ended, Jamie Kerrigan and Brandon McSweeney came to pay their respects. And later, Otto Bremmer, the big German inside foreman, and the English miner Andrew Yancy came in just to touch Glyn's outstretched hand. There were Italian miners and Poles, Lithuanians and Irish, young men who barely knew him and old men who told Gwyneth they knew no one better. It was a steady procession which greatly worried her but one which she did not want to stop.

"They're just looking and moving on," Doc Lewis reassured her away from Glyn's hearing. "I see no great harm and Glyn is recognizing many by name. He may not last much longer, Gwyneth."

By early evening the house was empty of visitors. Dylan's children were taken to the David Hopkins home and Evan's to Haydn Hopkins's house to be bedded down for the night. In the gathering dark, Gwyneth sat on the bed, holding Glyn's hand and stroking his brow with a damp cloth. Evan and Dylan sat on chairs on either side, watching their father's pale face and listening to his labored breathing. Doc Lewis and Pastor Evans stood at the foot of the bed, ready to give whatever assistance was necessary to Glyn and his family.

At precisely ten o'clock, Glyn opened his eyes wide, looked at Dylan and whispered, "I'm sorry about your hand, boy." It was the strongest his voice had sounded in two days.

Dylan's eyes filled as he stood, bent over the bed, kissed his father's forehead and whispered back, "You saved my life and gave me a blessed existence, Dada. I love you for all of that."

Glyn smiled and turned his face toward Evan, saying, "You're the man of this family now."

Evan dropped to his knees, held his father's hand and kissed it gently. As the tears rolled and his head shook from side to side all that escaped his lips was, "Dada, Dada."

Then Glyn looked up at Gwyneth and tears came to his eyes as he watched the pain in hers.

"My love," he whispered very slowly. "Rhys is here...with my pick...and my lunch bucket. It's time...to start...the new shift."

Then Glyn Jones reached up with both hands, clasped them together, brought them down to his chest, sighed, closed his eyes and died.

Epilogue

Although Glyn Jones, his family, his friends and his employer are fictional representations of life in the anthracite coal region of northeastern Pennsylvania, the world of "hard coal" was very real. Like Glyn Jones, thousands of miners have died from the breath-starving disease of anthracosis, better known as black lung.

And they died in real-life disasters as portrayed in this story: in 1869 at Avondale's Steuben Shaft where a fire killed one hundred ten men and boys; in 1890 at Ashley's Jersey Number Eight mine where quicksand poured in and took twenty-six lives; in 1895 at the Dorrance Mine near Wilkes-Barre in which a roof fall buried fifty-eight miners, followed a year later by a roof fall at the Newton Coal Company's Twin Shaft Mine which also killed fifty-eight.

They perished before the rifles of excited and nervous civilians who sought to stop them from demonstrating for better working conditions and higher pay. In two instances, unarmed miners marching for their rights were shot down in cold blood. First was the shooting on the streets of Scranton when a group of private citizens killed sixteen and wounded thirty-eight coal miners and iron workers in the summer of 1877. Then, twenty years later, eighty-seven hastily deputized men lined up against an unarmed group of marching Slavic miners and opened fire in Luzerne County, killing nineteen and wounding thirty-nine in the infamous Lattimer Massacre. No one was ever convicted of either crime.

At least two of the men who died on the gallows in the ongoing battle against a group of Irish coal miners—known as the mysterious Molly Maguires—are now believed to have been innocent.

For about thirty years, from the late 1800s through World War I, this anthracite region produced an estimated ninety-five percent of anthracite coal used around the world. The mines then employed some two hundred thousand men and boys and were part of the reason why Pennsylvania was considered one of the greatest industrialized areas on earth.

Hard and dangerous times continued well into the twentieth century although some safety precautions were still being shunted. For example, in 1908 the federal government recommended that coal dust be sprinkled with water to make it nonexplosive. That knowledge had been around for years but was frequently ignored by mine managers. A year earlier, the U.S. Geological Survey had completed the first national study on deaths in coal mines, which said the rate was 3.39 per thousand employees. The study pointed out that the American rate was double that of Prussia, triple the rates in Belgium and Great Britain, and four times those of France. And it wasn't that American mines were more dangerous; in fact, mines in Belgium were deeper and more hazardous. The difference, the study noted, was that European countries had passed strict safety laws and were vigorously enforcing them.

More than sixty-one thousand employees died in all United States coal mines from 1839 through 1914, a study reported. The number one cause was crushing or suffocation from roof or wall falls, followed by crushing between underground coal cars or between such cars and the tunnel walls, and third was explosions.

But there were positive gains. Open flames on miners' hats to illuminate their work area gave way to lamps powered by a battery pack and helmets before World War I. By 1920 the lamps were in common usage. Before World War II erupted, the use of dynamite underground had been replaced by safer explosives. In 1933, President Franklin D. Roosevelt's National Industrial Recovery Act finally gave miners rights they had been seeking for decades. They got an eight-hour workday and a minimum daily wage. The act said they could live where they wanted and buy in retail establishments of their choosing and not be forced into company-owned houses and stores. And it gave them the right to be represented by the United Mine Workers of America. Four years later, a new law gave them the right to organize nonunion mines.

In 1913, one of their own made it to one of the highest posts in the land. W. B. Wilson, a Scotsman who immigrated to the United States with his parents and began working in the mines at the age of nine, was appointed as the first secretary of labor by President Woodrow Wilson. He was one of the founders of the United Mine Workers of America and had served as its secretary treasurer for eight years beginning in 1900.

However, not all climbed so high. It wasn't until after World War I that mining families began to literally emerge from the dirt of their existence. Most mining communities, particularly small towns, still had dirt streets and no place to dump garbage. And in wet weather the dirt turned to mud. But they survived on dreams, scrimping and saving to buy a home, or a business, or a small farm, determined to do everything possible to keep their children from descending into the deadly pits.

In 1935, there was another bright spot, at least for miners who were vocal and active in seeking better working conditions. The Pennsylvania Coal and Iron Police was disbanded as an organization, thus ending a strange chapter in the attempt to control labor. The force had been created by the Legislature in 1866 but it was controlled and paid for by the coal and iron-producing companies. And the governor had given those companies a commission granting the C&IP the full powers of a public police force.

There are about five hundred square miles of territory in the half dozen counties comprising most of the anthracite region and about one-fourth of that area was or is affected by mining operations. Today, culm banks still dot the landscape and crumbling breakers can be seen. In places, stripping operations have replaced the underground method of removing coal. All have had a tremendous effect on the land—in terms of polluted streams and rivers, surface subsidence which can swallow whole buildings, and unquenchable underground fires in old workings. One of the most famous incidents of an old mine continuing to exact a toll in modern times is in the small town of Centralia in southern Columbia County. Fumes from a fire burning out of control since 1962 in old passageways beneath the community created such a poisonous atmosphere that the federal government, in 1983, paid to move everyone to a new location; practically all of Centralia's citizens took advantage of the offer.

If mining did one thing for the region, it provided a new industry: tourism. Underground tours are available in several locations as are above-ground visits to old mining towns and historic sites. One of the strangest sights is in the old Carbon County Jail in the county seat of Jim Thorpe, formerly called Mauch Chunk. Alexander Campbell, one of those accused and convicted of murder in the infamous Molly Maguire trials, pressed his hand against the wall of his cell just before he went to the hangman's rope. Campbell reportedly told his jailers: "That mark of mine will never be wiped out. There it will remain forever to shame the county that is hanging an innocent man." Visitors to the jail—now a museum—can still see a mark which resembles a handprint on that wall, despite efforts to erase it.

Campbell was hung along with three other so-called Mollies inside the jail, filled with spectators, on June 21, 1877. On the very same day in neighboring Schuylkill County, six more men accused of being murderers and members of the Molly Maguire organization, were hung in the jail's yard as two thousand people looked on. The two events in separate counties were the largest one-day mass execution in Pennsylvania history.

Hangings of men identified as Molly Maguires went on for eighteen months as ten more went to the gallows convicted of murder. They included John Kehoe, the alleged Mollies leader. Kehoe was a former miner, a tavern owner and a constable. In the 1970s a movement was started to get a posthumous pardon for Kehoe on the belief that he was railroaded into a death sentence on scant evidence. On January 11, 1979, the Pennsylvania Board of Pardons recommended that the action be granted and Governor Milton J. Shapp signed the pardon the next day, terming the conviction a miscarriage of justice. The effort had been led by Kehoe's granddaughter, the late Alice Wayne, and his great-grandson, Joseph Wayne, who continues to operate a small tavern in Girardville where Kehoe's Hiburnia House tavern was located.

On a plaque outside the Schuylkill County Jail, the pardon is recorded with the notation that it reflects "the judgment of many historians that the trials and executions were part of a repression directed against the fledgling mineworkers' union of that historic period."

And in 1993, at a mock trial held in the Carbon County Courthouse using evidence from the original trial, Alexander Campbell, an alleged Molly, was acquitted of murder.

The huge influx of experienced miners and those willing to learn from Europe was stopped by the Great Depression, both here and abroad. In Scranton and Wilkes-Barre, many of the Welsh and their English, Scottish, Irish and Slavic neighbors were forced to move in order to find work (although the heaviest concentration of Welsh in the United States still lies between those two cities). A great many went east to the industrial area of New Jersey or south to the Philadelphia region.

The decline in the 1940s of King Coal — as the industry came to be known — has been attributed to several causes. First oil and then gas and electricity took ever-increasing shares of the home heating market and the fuel of choice for industry. The cost of bringing coal up rose tremendously as the mines went deeper. The price for new technology and machinery and safety became more than the product could bear. And it grew exceedingly difficult to recruit young men for jobs underground when their parents were pressuring them to attend college or at least work in a different arena.

The message was finally hammered home in 1959 along the Susquehanna River in Luzerne County. The Knox Coal Company had been mining close to the river bottom, too close in fact, and on an icy day in January the surging, flooded and ice-choked Susquehanna broke through. Three miners drowned immediately. Thirty others were trapped underground, desperately seeking a way out. Eventually, nine more drowned. Nearby railroad tracks were relocated toward the swirling whirlpool pouring into the tunnels so that thirty railroad gondola cars and four hundred mine cars could be pushed in to plug the hole. Utility poles, huge rocks and other debris were poured in. It was estimated that water flowed into the mine at the rate of twelve million gallons a minute for forty-eight hours. By the time it was stopped days later, some ten billion gallons had flooded underground mines a half mile wide and more than three miles long. It eventually stopped work in some two dozen mines and spelled the doom of mining in the Wyoming Valley.

King Coal never came back from that last major blow.

Acknowledgments

For an understanding of life among mining families and the significant historical events of the late 1800s and early 1900s in the anthracite mining industry, I depended on the assistance and advice of several people. A great deal of credit goes to all of them.

Robert Prosperi, the knowledgeable educator for the impressive Pennsylvania Anthracite Heritage Museum in Scranton, provided valuable assistance in recommending historical source material. And Chester J. Kulesa, the museum's curator, provided a large choice of period photographs. The museum is administered by the Pennsylvania Historical and Museum Commission.

Technical information on mining practices, material and equipment was willingly offered by two mining engineers, Fred Spott of Scranton and Alex Chamberlain of Bloomsburg, Pennsylvania, and by John Podgurski, a mine inspector for the U.S. Mine Safety and Health Administration in Wilkes-Barre.

A practical knowledge of mine work was offered by Roger Beatty of Exeter, a miner who later became a high school history teacher but who still guides tourists underground on weekends and in summer months at the Lackawanna Coal Mine in Scranton. An old friend, James Line, a former coal miner in Abertillery, South Wales, Great Britain, provided information over a long period of time and an underground tour.

Tom McBride, curator of The Old Jail in Jim Thorpe, the county seat of Carbon County, took time to sit and talk with us in the cell block where some of the Molly Maguires were hung. The old county jail is now a museum. The town of Jim Thorpe was formerly known as Mauch Chunk.

Numerous underground tours conducted by retired miners at the Lackawanna Coal Mine gave a personal look at mining techniques and a feel for "working underground."

Assistance on trips to check out sources and sites and continuing encouragement in the writing of this story was given by my wife, Mary Jane.

For further reading on this subject I recommend:

- *Hard Coal, Hard Times*, by David L. Salay
- *The Kingdon of Coal*, by Donald L. Miller and Richard E. Sharpless
- *Where the Sun Never Shines*, by Priscilla Long
- *The Fed: A History of South Wales Miners*, by Hywel Francis and David Smith
- *Flames and Embers of Coal*, by Ellis W. Roberts
- *The Breaker Whistle Blows*, by Ellis W. Roberts
- *A Molly Maguire Story*, by Patrick Campbell
- *Making Sense of the Molly Maguires*, by Kevin Kenny
- *How Green Was My Valley*, by Richard Llewellyn
- *The Knox Mine Disaster*, by Robert Wolensky, Kenneth Wolensky and Nicole Wolensky
- *Wales in America: Scranton and the Welsh 1860–1920*, by William D. Jones
- *One Sunset a Week*, by George Vecsey
- *Anthracite Coal Communities*, by Peter Roberts
- *Growing Up in Coal Country*, by Susan Campbell Bartoletti
- *History of the Lackawanna Valley*, by H. Hollister